"The blind doctor, Zinaida Lintvaryova, stays in my heart long after I close Alison Anderson's beautifully written book. The young Chekhov himself cannot outshine Zinaida as she urgently explores life, science, art, family, and love, her passion defying death."　　　　—Helen Simonson, *New York Times* bestselling author of *Major Pettigrew's Last Stand*

"A beautifully crafted and richly evocative homage to Chekhov, wrapped in a compelling modern mystery."
　　　　—Cathy Marie Buchanan, *New York Times* bestselling author of *The Painted Girls*

"*The Summer Guest* gives us all of the pleasures of a superb mystery novel, but most of all it is a profound meditation on the power, and necessity, of the imagination. What a deeply moving novel."　　　　—Ron Rash, *New York Times* bestselling author of *Serena* and *Above the Waterfall*

"*The Summer Guest*, with its ineffable Russian atmosphere, has the savor of a text that is deeply rooted in the author's experience— Alison is a translator as well as a novelist—yet leaves ample room for the delights of the imagination, with that little extra touch of soul, so very Russian, that is elegantly known as melancholy."
　　　　—Muriel Barbery, *New York Times* bestselling author of *The Elegance of the Hedgehog*

"A richly researched and subtly nuanced mystery that explores the intimate relationships of one of Russia's best loved writers and poses intriguing questions about the fine line between art and deception."　　　　—Kathleen Tessaro, *New York Times* bestselling author of *The Perfume Collector*

"With lush prose and a painter's eye, Alison Anderson explores the delicate beauty of melancholy in the lives of three spiritual 'sisters' connected across time and space by the words of a blind woman's diary. Chekhovian in its precision, *The Summer Guest* finds rays of hope in the deepest loss and reminds us that our unfinished stories may be the most meaningful."

—Charlie Lovett, *New York Times* bestselling author of *The Bookman's Tale*

"Subtle and haunting. . . . The most piercing story belongs to the diary's author, Zinaida Lintvaryova, or Zina, trapped by blindness and a deepening illness at her family home of Luka, on the river Pysol, in the year 1888, who finds reprieve in her notable guest, also a doctor, on the cusp of literary stardom. Mournful and meditative, the diary's bittersweet passages on Zina's illness and darkened life are punctuated by lively exchanges with the charming and ambitious Chekhov. The novel is deeply literary in its attention to the work of writing and translation, but also political in its awareness of how Russian-Ukrainian relations have impact on the lives of Anderson's heroines (both the historical and present ones). Ardent Chekhov fans will appreciate a brief immersion in the world he must have known for two summers, while readers of any stamp can enjoy the melancholy beauty of a vanished world and the surprise twist that, at the end, offers what all three characters have been searching for—'something completely unexpected and equally precious: another way of seeing the world.'"

—*Publishers Weekly*

"A leisurely story of everyday life's minor dramas in which what isn't said and what doesn't happen are more important than dialogue and action—that sounds Chekhovian, and, in fact, Anderson's elegant historical novel, narrated from multiple perspectives, features the Russian writer as a character. . . . This alluring and deceptively ingenuous novel demands close consideration from its readers, contains an internal mystery, and packs a heartbreakingly lovely emotional punch."

—*Booklist* (starred review)

"Multi-layered. . . . Captures a classic Russian theme—the beauty of sadness—with a portrait of friendship between a relatively lighthearted Anton Chekhov and a young woman doctor. . . . A metafictional paean to literature's capacity to seduce us and make us see the world differently." —Heller McAlpin, *LitHub*

"The interplay between past and present . . . draws readers into the novel and enables them to believe they have actually met the great playwright. . . . Illuminating. . . . Anderson, a noted translator . . . has a sure touch in dealing with her material. An impressive work, highly recommended to lovers of literary fiction." —*Library Journal*

"Inspired by a real friendship between Chekhov and a Ukrainian family, you will fall in love with this gorgeously written historical fiction novel." —*Serendipity* magazine

THE
SUMMER
GUEST

A Novel

ALISON

ANDERSON

HARPER PERENNIAL

NEW YORK • LONDON • TORONTO • SYDNEY • NEW DELHI • AUCKLAND

A hardcover edition of this book was published in 2016 by Harper Collins Publishers.

P.S.™ is a trademark of HarperCollins Publishers.

FIRST HARPER PERENNIAL EDITION PUBLISHED IN 2017.

Designed by Fritz Metsch

Library of Congress Cataloging-in-Publication Data
has been applied for.

ISBN 978-0-06-242338-2

17 18 19 20 21   OV/LSC   10 9 8 7 6 5 4 3 2 1

For Amelia,
and in fond memory of
Gina Berriault,
who loved Chekhov

Note to the Reader

Zinaida Mikhailovna Lintvaryova's journal is based on a true story, on the little that is known about her from Anton Chekhov's letters and the obituary that he wrote when she died.

The town of Sumy is located in eastern Ukraine. Both Ukrainian and Russian are spoken there, as they were in Chekhov's time. For the sake of consistency, I have generally used the Russian versions of Ukrainian proper nouns (Kiev for Kyiv, Elena for Olena, etc.) throughout the book, except when referring to certain contemporary events, where the Ukrainian is more appropriate.

The tyranny of the visible makes us blind.
The brilliance of the word pierces the night of the world.

—CHRISTIAN BOBIN

Cast of Characters

The Lintvaryovs

Aleksandra Vassilyevna, landlady, owner of the Luka Estate
Zinaida Mikhailovna (Zina), her eldest child, a doctor
Elena Mikhailovna (Lena), a doctor
Pavel Mikhailovich (Pasha), manager of the estate, a
    revolutionary
Natalya Mikhailovna (Natasha), a schoolteacher
Georgi Mikhailovich (Georges), the youngest, a musician
Antonida Fyodorovna (Tonya), Pasha's wife

The Chekhovs

Pavel Yegorovich, the father
Evgenia Yakovlevna, the mother
Aleksandr Pavlovich (Sasha), the eldest son, a writer and
    journalist
Nikolay Pavlovich (Kolya), an artist
Anton Pavlovich (Antosha), a doctor and writer
Ivan Pavlovich (Vanya), a schoolteacher
Maria Pavlovna (Masha), the only daughter, a schoolteacher
Mikhail Pavlovich (Misha), a student

Their Guests

Aleksandr Ignatyevich Ivanenko (Sasha), a flautist and cousin to
    the Lintvaryovs

Valentina (Vata), another cousin

Aleksey Nikolayevich Pleshcheyev, a poet

Kazimir Stanislavovich Barantsevich, a writer

Marian Romualdovich Semashko, a cellist

Aleksey Sergeyevich Suvorin, a wealthy Petersburg publisher

Pavel Matveyevich Svobodin, an actor

Grigory Petrovich, a loyal servant

Anya, a cook

Ulyasha, a maid

Roman, a coachman

Artyomenko, Panas, and Mishka, Anton Pavlovich's fishing
    companions

THE
SUMMER
GUEST

SHE WROTE:

The road is leading into the distance, the distance where we are going and which we cannot see; there's a slight rise toward the horizon of tall grass and a long line of poplar trees. It's deserted, we have the whole world to ourselves; the tall grass is bending to the breeze. The air is the color of candlelight on an icon. The sun has almost reached the horizon. There's not much time, and yet you feel, with so much space around you, that nothing could ever change: not the sun, or the tall grass, or the road into the distance.

She was pleased with her words.

Well, not exactly her words; they were meant to be his words, and only as she reported them. Perhaps he had said something quite different. They had been for a ride in the carriage, and these words were a gift of vision, a way of helping her see the world. The difficulty lay in capturing a moment: his voice, its warmth and depth, was lost already. What could a short paragraph do to convey so much—the road, the trees, the sky, the light, a whole vista no one could see now, except through words? And his presence there, with her, a brief respite in her darkness, his breath, his low laughter.

You take the words, she thought; by themselves, individually, they are almost meaningless. You take them one by one and you build not only a description, a vision, but also a memory, where you are present, and he is present, too, though neither of you is described by those words. What sort of magic was this?

If she were sentimental, or mystical, she might invoke love, or faith; but for now she must be satisfied with craft. Yes, craft. They were someone else's words, after all; she was not the author. Just the scribe, the interpreter, the diarist, the translator.

THE
FIRST
SUMMER

A journal. That is what I need to fill these dull long hours when I used to be working, helping others and forgetting myself. Now it seems I must remember. A journal will occupy me, although there won't be much to say.

Or will there? If my life were as it had always been until this untimely rebellion of my flesh, I would indeed have little of interest to relate. A catalogue of peasants' woes: Grigory Petrovich has the gripes again, Anyusha is suffering from sciatica and about to give birth, Kostya's toes were crushed beneath the cart wheel. My own provincial life: visits to neighboring estates, conversations when we all find a moment to be together, Pasha's problems, as usual, with the authorities. His politics, of some concern to the tsar's representatives in our remote province. There would not be much to say about me. But that bit of flesh in my brain is forcing me to withdraw from the life I knew, and I become the subject of my life. This embarrasses me and seems wrong, but Mama and Elena have encouraged me, and now they bring me tea and ink and a bound notebook and sit quietly by me while I scribble as clearly as I can. Mama says, rather too wisely, I am certain you will discover the territory of the soul, as once you discovered the human body.

I laugh and say, You mean I am to dissect myself?

You may dissect us all, in a manner of speaking. You must do what you can, whatever is necessary, to live with your diagnosis.

I'm a doctor, still, and I know what awaits me. Professor Chudnovsky himself was clear about that. I am living, as the

English say, on borrowed time. To whom am I to repay this time, and when?

I am young, only thirty, and in our family we live long lives. We are not consumptive, nor are we drinkers of alcohol; we eat well and go for long walks, summer and winter alike. What have I done to deserve this? It's nothing I caught at the practice, no, no contagious disease like typhus or diphtheria; I am simply a victim of chance misfortune. Yet I have been a useful person: If I had believed in God, I would now lose whatever tattered faith remained. Why has He chosen to take me away when I am useful to Him? Or am I, precisely, too useful, interfering with His ways?

I recall our friends in Kiev, the Zemlinskys, their youngest son was stricken in this way. They asked me about his headaches. There is so little one can do to relieve the pressure. I prescribed laudanum, then morphine. Now the headaches have come to me, though not yet so terrible. Elena will bring me what I need when the time comes . . . I try to accept my fate, if one can speak of fate.

Still I cannot believe what has befallen me, if belief is to the mind as faith is to the heart: My emotions rebel. They were trained for the useful life of a country doctor and its attendant satisfactions and disappointments. I was not meant to be taken so early from my family, and from this task that has given me a sense of honor and accomplishment, and pleasure, too.

Elena has promised that I may continue to work with her now and again. She will be my eyes; I still have my hands and my mind and my experience.

Pasha is a fine brother. He has made me a special device, a box to hold my ledger, with a ruler that I can move down the page after each line, measuring two fingers' width—there are little notches. It will keep your letters and lines straight, he says, so that what you write will be clear.

For whom am I writing? I won't be here, some old crone by the fire, to reread my youth. It must be a sort of testament to my family when I am gone. I have nothing else to leave them.

KATYA SAT AT her computer, drumming her fingers next to the keyboard. Peter had told her it was time to find a translator for the Sumy diary.

He called it the Sumy diary. *Zinaida Mikhailovna* was too much of a mouthful, he said. They had been married for over twenty years, and he still couldn't get his tongue around some of *your long Russian names.*

Over the years she had learned to be indulgent. His passive Russian was excellent, as were his endearments. Katyusha, Katyenka, Katyushka—those names he could handle. Although sometimes it was simply, most affectionately, Kate.

What would they call it: *The Diaries of Zinaida Mikhailovna Lintvaryova?* He was right, it was a mouthful, no mainstream publisher would ever bring out a book with such a title, even for a work of nonfiction. She wanted to find something that would convey the Russianness, and the fact that it was a diary. Perhaps *Something Something colon,* then *The Diaries of . . .*

Perhaps the translator would have an idea. A translator would have more distance, obviously, might be able to find those few words that would draw the reader's interest. At the end of her message, Katya would write, *We don't have a title yet. If you have any ideas as you work on the text, please let us know.*

Now for the translator.

There was that American woman in France who'd done the Crimea guidebook. Anastasia something. Harding, that was it. Or Vassily Yuryevich. But Vassily Yuryevich was a man. It might be better to have a woman for this project, a female sensibility. She would have done it herself, but she did not want to act as a translator; her English was good enough for most things, had been good enough for those other projects, with the help of an editor, but this was different.

She typed *Anastasia Harding* to take a closer look at the woman's background. Many novels translated from French; the most recent one had a very favorable review. Good. The guidebook had been a one-off, and it had been excellent. Not a great deal of work from Russian otherwise, but what mattered was her English, after all. And her female sensibility.

She must care for Zinaida Mikhailovna as much as I have, thought Katya. Together we must bring her back to life, along with her famous guest.

That night, in bed, Peter turned to her. I have a good feeling about this project, he said. It will get us back on our feet, I'm sure of it.

Katya was not so sure. They were governed by something larger than themselves, bearing down on them and their small publishing house. Banks, credit crunch, bailouts, crisis, recession; e-books, online booksellers, the disappearance of bookshops, the closure of libraries, the decline of reading. The monolith of market censorship, too. Oh, the irony, thought Katya, to have left the Soviet Union only to find another form of censorship. All the poetry she had been unable to publish as a student, when she was being watched; she had left her homeland as a young wife, in love not so much with her young husband as with the idea of becoming a poet in the free West. *The Free West.* Hah.

Well, none of that mattered anymore.

She reached for her husband. She loved him more now than she had in the early years; her present misgivings about the future sharpened her love, brought an almost physical ache of impending loss. It was not something she could say to him, not yet; she had to try, with him, for his sake, to focus her energies.

Polyana Press had been their life together, after all; the child they did not have, the novels and poems they did not write, the journeys they did not take. Perhaps that was why, now, it was failing. They should have loved it for its own sake; it should not have been in lieu of something.

They had been distant with each other lately: He had his worries, and she had hers. They couldn't share those worries, or it might have brought them closer.

Perhaps you're right, she whispered. It could be a great success: We have to believe in it, make it happen.

Trust me, Katya, please, I know what I'm doing. He touched her cheek, then left his finger there, while he looked at her in that way she had almost forgotten.

They made love that night for the first time in many months. For so long, their separate worries had deadened desire, even tenderness, but they understood that this silent reproach was not personal, that it came from anger at the injustice of their life at that time, the casual, random cruelty of what had befallen them. Katya had found her private way to accept, to overcome; Peter was still searching, dreaming again like a boy. But perhaps. This wild idea of his.

In the dark they smiled at each other. He stroked her cheek again. She reached out and touched his: warm stubble. This tenderness felt new.

And have you found a translator? he asked.

I think so. Anastasia Harding. If she agrees.

And how long will it take?

Not long. A few months.

A year, then, until publication, give or take. Can we hold on until then? Give it everything we've got?

Of course, she whispered.

He sighed, content. She turned her head away. There was a mutinous tear. She told herself it was a tear of emotion—this unexpected closeness. And the release, the letting go. All good reasons for a tear.

ZINAIDA MIKHAILOVNA'S DIARY arrived in her inbox one day. Like a misdirected parcel intended for someone else, as if it had been forgotten in a dusty provincial post office and finally found its way to her, a century late, and only because its intended recipient was long departed from this earth. There was a message from the publisher, Katya Kendall at Polyana Press in London. Ana had worked for them in the past, translating a guidebook to Crimea.

She had hesitated to take on the guidebook at the time, as she would now with Zinaida Mikhailovna. Russian was difficult, its beauty idiosyncratic and complex, and it intimidated her. Ana's Russian was perfectly adequate, but she didn't go looking for translations from Russian; they found her. As Katya Kendall had found her that first time, and for a few weeks Ana's mental space had been all Crimea. She had found herself dreaming of tsars' palaces and Chekhov's dachas, of craggy slopes dropping into the Black Sea, and exotic resorts with names like Feodosia and Koktebel and Gurzuf. There were the markers of history, like the Livadia Palace, where the last Romanovs had lived briefly and the Yalta Conference was held, and the villa where Gorbachev was staying at the time of the coup.

Now this new message, just there in her email. *Dear Anastasia (if I may), We are terribly excited about this project,* Katya Kendall enthused. Would she have a look at the enclosed text and let them know at her earliest convenience whether it was something she would like to take on?

Ana stopped and looked out the window at the lake and the mountains. The sun was setting, leaving a wild streak of light among the clouds; it had rained earlier. She had no reason to refuse; the text, or the ten pages that she had scrolled through, seemed fairly straightforward, even if the language was dated. Four months, she figured, all told. She wasn't busy, she needed the money. She decided to sleep on it and give Katya Kendall her answer in the morning. Just a formality, sleeping on it; she knew she would say yes.

The publisher had attached a second document, an obituary. Ana skimmed it.

Much later, after she had finished all the rest, its poignant relevance would leave her unable to translate it for three days.

In a postscript, Katya Kendall had written: *I thought we could use the obituary as an introduction or an afterword. It's a remarkable document. Like everything he ever wrote. A story in itself.*

At the time Ana didn't realize who *he* was. She missed the author's name in small letters at the bottom of the obituary. Would it have made any difference if she had seen it at once? It was odd, too, that Katya Kendall did not mention him in the body of her message, but then perhaps she was like that, discreet to the point of evasiveness.

The shadow of Zinaida Mikhailovna's soon-to-be-famous summer guest fell later onto the page, and by then Ana had befriended the diarist in that odd way translators sometimes have, if they are lucky, of knowing their authors through a text, of inhabiting their identity and seeing through their eyes.

The next morning she wrote back to Polyana Press, told them she was interested, and requested a slightly higher rate, citing the antiquated language.

It was Peter Kendall who answered, tersely. *Unfortunately, given the economic situation, we cannot offer a better rate.* The contract was enclosed. If she was still willing to go ahead, would she print out two copies, sign them, and return them to him?

In the contract, there was a special clause stipulating that the subject of the translation was to be kept confidential.

First false warmth of spring. I am sitting in the conservatory in a thick coat. I close my eyes, listen to the birds, and wish I knew the notation for birdsong, so that in dark silent times, winter times, I might ask Georges to play their song to me.

I beg Mamochka to find me something to do, some vegetable to peel, some simple sewing I could do blindly, so to speak. She pushes me away with words of comfort: I must rest, preserve my strength.

I have not had a seizure for some days, but I fear one might be coming. A strange light-headedness, a giddy centrifugal pull on my senses. I think of Elena and everything she has to do, how busy she is these days on calls or with the patients who come to the house. Our peasants are a worrisome lot, and I fear she spoils them; they come to her for a hangnail. Because she is kind, and does not talk down to them, but listens and tries to prescribe a better life with the small means at her disposal. Sometimes a smile suffices, especially with children. It is like religion for them; they place their faith in her and are healed. We speak of it sometimes at dinner; Pasha and Georges scoff; Mamochka nods wisely; Natasha laughs and ridicules us all.

Yesterday Mamochka told us that this summer she will let out the guesthouse. It will go some way toward helping with the household expenses. I fear the arrival of some noisy, vulgar family from Moscow, newly wealthy and full of crass disregard for our provincial ways. Natasha laughs and says that such people go to Yalta, where they can be seen. Who can see them here?

April 25, 1888

Great excitement on the estate. Through our cousin Sasha
Ivanenko, Mama has found a family to rent the guesthouse for
the summer. A family from Moscow. One of the sons, Mikhail
Pavlovich, came to have a look; he told Mama that one of his
brothers is a gifted artist, and another a promising writer, and
his sister is a teacher; both his parents are still alive, and all
the family will be coming at various times over the summer.
So Mamochka is brimming with enthusiasm and delight: She
can already imagine the wealth of conversation they will bring,
the entire outside world—news of Petersburg and Moscow and
perhaps even Vienna and Paris—to our humble Luka.

There is a great flurry of cleaning and preparing and I am
often on my own, feeling useless and frustrated. Mama gave me
some silver to polish—that I could do—but then Ulyasha grew
impatient with me, as she wanted to put everything away again
as quickly as possible, so she tended to snatch things from me,
kindly but firmly.

They arrive next week. I hope they will be sociable, amenable
to sharing conversation. I hope they won't get into political
quarrels with Pasha and Georges. I mustn't get too excited—
what if they turn out to be the self-regarding, pretentious sort?
But knowing Mama, and knowing Pasha, who must have shown
this Mikhail Pavlovich around, they would not agree to come
to us if they were not curious, open-minded people—artists,
teachers, precisely. The guesthouse is rather run-down as well—
Grigory Petrovich had to spend the morning repairing the steps
to the porch! The young man didn't seem to mind; according to
Pasha, he just laughed and said, This will be the perfect antidote
to Moscow, we are coming for the tranquillity and the river and
the garden—and there is so much space! he exclaimed over and
over. We live in a chest of drawers in Moscow, he said.

Imagine. A chest of drawers!

It's true, we cannot imagine how people must live, cramped in flats in Moscow and Petersburg. Here we have so much land and sky . . . I feel it even now that the light has gone—I venture to say I feel it more strongly, this space, when I stand out in the garden and breathe in the fresh air, and the odors come to me from near and far—the linden trees, the river, the stables, incense from the village church, the dog who's been swimming, the earth after rain, the lovely aroma of burnt caramel from Kharitonenko's factory, and Pasha stopping by in the evening, smelling of good hard work. That's how the world comes to me these days.

Sometimes I like to think I can smell the clouds, a faint crisp dampness, full of blue.

May 6, 1888

They have arrived! Mama and Pasha greeted them and helped them settle in. They are not all here yet, just the mother, daughter, and middle son. The father and other brothers will arrive over the course of the summer. The daughter is a teacher, like Natasha: such good company to look forward to! Mama says we are to let them get settled and tomorrow they'll come for tea. They are tired after thirty hours of train from Moscow.

Pasha says the young man was very gallant and polite but also joking quite easily with Mama and teasing his own mother.

I am infinitely relieved. I was so afraid that they would be like that family who took the summer villa on the neighboring estate all those years ago. Andryusha—Andrey Kirillovich; I've never forgotten.

In the meantime, Natasha reads to me. What a luxury. Sometimes she reads too quickly, her voice tripping over the words—that's her personality, forever in a hurry. We've had *Anna Karenina* again, but she gets impatient with it, impatient with Anna, and with Levin, and with Tolstoy, and our reading degenerates into arguments about the place of women in literature. So, lately she has been reading *lighter* things, as she calls them—articles from the major papers or short stories; but there, too, we find reasons to argue, or to conclude that life is unfair, and what shall we do about it?

Yes, I say, our lot as women is unfair—but look at our peasants and their children—isn't their lot even worse? Are we not, in fact, incredibly fortunate?

She tells me that it is relative. She says if I remove the peasantry from the equation, we women become the peasantry. Even if our good fortune, as the Lintvaryova sisters, has been to be educated and enjoy a degree of freedom, that does not reflect the situation in general, and we should use our good fortune to help others, etc.

But we do, I protest, we are helping—

—those less fortunate, she interrupts. But what have we done to change the status of women as a whole?

By example, I insist. If other women see that they can receive an education, become doctors and teachers, find equal positions in work—

She laughs and says, But most women don't want what we have. They don't see the situation as it truly is. And authors like Tolstoy do not help, writing of fallen women and ingenues . . .

Natasha, surely you're exaggerating or simplifying, I counter. One spoiled aristocrat from Petersburg with a broken heart does not represent Russian woman.

But you have heard how Tolstoy exploits his own wife—he

could not write if he did not have her there. Although perhaps that is where she wants to be.

Natasha is eager, almost angry, tapping her foot on the floor.

I wish I could see her: her pink cheeks, her eyes burning dark with anger, her eyebrows never still, lively with irony or astonishment. But I cannot, so I say, We would have to ask Sofia Tolstoy herself if that is where—who—she wants to be. We don't know if she is oppressed or willing.

How could she be willing? Running his household and copying out his dreadful handwriting and keeping all the children and visitors at bay, always in his shadow—

Perhaps she reckons his shadow is better than no shadow. Is it such a bad thing to be in the shadow? Have you thought of the power she might have, agreeing to the shadow?

I smile, and though I cannot see her expression, there is a sudden calm in the room, an end to foot-tapping and exasperated sighs. I have humbled my little sister, but I do not know if it is my shadow—the one in which I live now, permanently—or that of the great man himself that gives her pause for thought.

GOD, IT WAS COLD.

What weather deity had invented that terrible wind they called *la bise*? He must have been a friend of Monsieur Guillotin of infamous revolutionary fame, thought Ana as she stepped out into the street: Her hair tore at her cheeks, her scarf streamed behind her, and her coat flapped against her legs as if to keep her from walking.

The village was deserted; a last copper sheen caught the roof tiles, and beyond, the russet plaid of fields, the jagged parade of mountains. She walked quickly, pulling her shapka down tighter over her ears, holding her scarf to her nose, her eyes tingling, strained from a day's work. Not what she had expected, two proto-feminist sisters discussing Tolstoy; but what a restful change from the frivolous or self-absorbed contemporary French novels that were her usual source of income. So what if it wasn't going to pay much—there were times when work must be about more than income.

But it wasn't easy to make ends meet, even with the better-paid commissions from bigger publishers—the crime novels and thrillers and bestsellers—that she'd been taking on since her divorce. Her colleagues who did commercial translation made twice as much. When they raised their eyebrows at her, half in commiseration, half in consternation, she pleaded job satisfaction. And she'd made it this far, living on her own in this village for the last three years; she squared her shoulders and raised her chin as her thoughts compelled her onward, into the wind.

Did she miss the easy days, back in Paris, with a husband?

Easy only to a point, easier financially; as his business grew, Mathieu had taken on more and more of the burden of expenses. But ultimately, the financial inequality (among other things, not least of which was his infidelity) became a source of strife between them, and they parted. Not amicably, but knowing it was for the best. While Ana's lawyer had urged her to claim a *prestation compensatoire*, she wanted total independence. There were no children; she wanted nothing more to do with that part of her life. She was still trying to understand why her reaction had been so violent: Was it the knowledge of having spent twenty years with someone only to end up complete strangers? Or the realization she had nothing to show—not really, most of the books she'd translated were out of print—for all those years? Mathieu had gotten the flat in the Marais (it had been in his family since the Revolution, after all), and Ana had accepted a small moving allowance that enabled her to resettle.

She did not like to think about Mathieu. Once the divorce and the move were behind her, she tried to pick up her life where she had left off before him, as if she were still in her early thirties, but she soon realized that society had changed (as had she, simply by aging physically, if nothing else—the eloquent streaks of gray in her long hair, which she refused to color) and the world was not about to let her get on as she would have liked. So her initial relief at being on her own soured into resentment toward Mathieu, and because she did not want him to poison her life, she forbade herself from thinking about him—a proscription that was often unsuccessful, given precisely such moments when her mind was allowed to wander. She had tried to rescue the good memories of their early years but thus far had been unable. Perhaps it was too soon; perhaps the weight of more recent incompatibility had buried their early happiness for good. How much was her own fault, too? Hadn't she married him for the wrong reasons—the stability, the companionship, the passport? Which was also why, out of a distorted sense of pride, she had wanted no *prestation compensatoire*.

For three years now she had been starting over, starting from scratch—relatively late in life, according to some, but you couldn't dwell on that fact or you would founder in useless projection and disappointment. That was how she saw it.

And her newly regained freedom meant she could organize her days as she saw fit. On a fine day, she could jump in the car and head off exploring the back roads of Haute-Savoie and neighboring Switzerland. The expanse of nature was new to her. She had not known until now how vital it was to her well-being, how comforting and sustaining the presence of clouds and mountains and a glimpse of lake could be. Or something as banal and universal as a bird or a tree! Not that there weren't parks in Paris, and lovely ones—but so much land and sky to oneself, even in a bitter wind like this, was a luxury that no city, however spacious and elegant, could provide. Sometimes she missed the near-village life of her Parisian neighborhood—the cafés and boulangeries and small shops where everyone knew her—but this village, even with its dearth of shops and cafés, had opened other doors through which she began, tentatively at first, to explore her solitude, and through solitude—as if she found herself in a hall of mirrors—her very sense of who she was, who she wanted to be.

Not that she didn't miss or need people from time to time; they were not far from Geneva, and in half an hour or less, she could be there for her required dose of crowds and people-watching. She had one close friend in Geneva, Yves: They had been together on a summer language course to Moscow back in the early 1980s and had kept in touch. When she missed other friends, she called them on Skype or took the TGV up to Paris for the weekend. But more and more, she found that people were *all so busy*. She settled ever deeper into her isolation: At least it offered the consolations of beauty.

And now this real, bone-chilling winter of the kind you rarely felt in a city, with its climatic fug of traffic and people and the proximity of warm interiors. She pulled her scarf tighter, thumped her arms around herself, half-hug, half-encouragement. She must find a fake fur in a thrift shop somewhere.

Her Ukrainian heroines would not have feared the cold. Any more than those brave protesters on the Maidan in Kiev did; some of them had been camping there for weeks. They built walls with bags of frozen snow. She had seen them on the news, the women muffled like her in scarves and shapkas, bringing supplies, cooking vast kettles of soup, swelling the ranks at the rallies.

For decades Ana had heard hardly anything about Ukraine, other than the Orange revolution in 2004, which ultimately failed, and of course her little guidebook to Crimea, and now the country suddenly seemed to be dwarfing her corner of France. What sort of coincidence was that, Ukrainian gentry in the daytime at work, so to speak, then Ukrainian protesters on the news at night? Where was it all going? Who knew—with protest movements, they either fizzled out, or were crushed, violently, or they triumphed.

As for her own Ukrainian heroines, Ana had not read the diary through, so she did not know where they were headed, either. As a rule, she liked to discover a book as she progressed with the translation; it kept her fresh, curious, made her look forward to sitting down to work each day, and this would be no exception, she sensed. But at the same time, she was eager to find out why the diary must be kept confidential, whether there was something more in the text, something remarkable, that might bring her to another level professionally, propel her ever so briefly into the limelight that eluded most translators by definition. She did have a few colleagues who translated Nobel laureates and prizewinning authors; they were interviewed, wrote blogs or books, mingled at conferences as speakers. Their lives seemed to have substance.

She had had enough of being invisible, of slipping inconspicuously behind the more glamorous author whose photograph beckoned from the back cover of a book they had both written. As translator, she mused, she was no more than the lining of the dust jacket. This substance she craved—beyond meaningful texts, beyond creativity—should lead to an identity.

She turned to head home, wind at her back, and looking at the darkening landscape, she knew instinctively that it was not enough to have lived this long in France or to have acquired a French passport to feel French; perhaps it was equally foolish to expect an identity from her profession. Although people often did, and their profession defined them—to others, to society. A sort of representational convenience, when in fact the true self was elsewhere: going for walks at twilight, talking to the cat.

Ana had read somewhere that if you wanted your cat to meow, to converse with you, you had to talk to it. As if it were a furry plant. She had never had a cat before—had adopted Doodle some six months earlier—and she was as disconcerted by the creature's sudden displays of affection as she was by its self-serving indifference. In the end, such unpredictability was proving instructive. In the morning she would turn to the cat and say, Right, Doodle, what sort of day are we in for?, and Doodle's condescending stare would tell her all she needed to know. For twenty years, Ana had lived a life of unquestioning routine and not a little boredom. She had been happiest crafting the very literary translations she favored back then: poetry, memoirs, obscure novels that sold a few hundred copies at best. She had spent her days bent over her typewriter, and then the computer, like some *maître horloger* over his instruments. Mathieu had resented her for it—the hours she spent, the pecuniary pointlessness of it. Now she worked much harder than she ever had, but she was free; she need fear neither routine nor boredom, and she felt a tremendous urge to make up for lost time.

What was most surprising to her, after three years on her own, was how little the absence of a relationship troubled her. In the distant past, before she had met Mathieu, any period of celibacy or recovery from a breakup had been a source of distress and worry; she lived with it, but with a terrible awareness of inadequacy and time passing. Now time was passing faster than ever, yet Ana was poised and cheerfully resigned. She surveyed the rubble of her romantic yearnings with the dispassionate cynicism of the hardened aid worker. She had earned her name in the end. Harding. She didn't think of herself as a hard person, but as a woman gracefully adjusting to the inevitable.

You do what you have to do, her father used to say. Strange, coming from him, the precise, articulate professor of history. She didn't like this catchall phrase, with its negative implication of just making do, the *pis aller*; but she could point to experience, if challenged. Perhaps others had her best interests in mind when they questioned her solitude, but they hadn't lived her life. She always said she was open to new experiences, but maybe she no longer knew how to reach out in this increasingly crowded, competitive world. Or she didn't feel she needed to reach out. Her profession suited her; her reclusion buoyed her.

And her little house was a sanctuary. Rundown but palatial compared to the Paris flat, a disputed legacy belonging to an old family in Thonon-les-Bains. She knew she wouldn't be able to stay there forever, but as she hurried through the door into the warmth, eager for a cheering shot of Calvados, she refused to worry about the future. She tried now, after questioning her furry oracle, to take each unpredictable day as it came—but that didn't exclude the occasional daydream of a perfectible future.

I told myself when I sat down for the first time with this ledger that I would not fill it with regrets. Life has been good to me. I've had opportunities, I have had a good and loving family, but there are one or two things I do regret.

Perhaps to ease my mind, although it will bring a moment's melancholy, I should let my thoughts return to those memories and see if there is still reason for regret.

It was the summer before I left for Petersburg. There was a wealthy family from Moscow staying with their uncle on the neighboring estate. We never had much to do with this uncle, the owner of the estate; just before Papa's death they had argued, and somehow Mama could not bring herself to forgive the man. Still, the family was bored and had children our age, so they sent an invitation. And there was a reconciliation. I began to spend time with Andryusha, the eldest brother, and with hindsight it would be easy to say he was spoiled and arrogant, or that he looked down on us. But I did not feel it at the time, and we went on long walks through the fields, looking for butterflies, and we sat on the hill above the river, and I saw him only as part of that joy of being seventeen, in a landscape of glorious colors. I was with a boy who spoke softly and took my hand and told me about the life he might lead, until he laughed and said, I suppose you are expecting to have suitors and get married?

I must have blushed, but I told him proudly I would be going to Petersburg to attend the Bestuzhev courses and study to be a doctor. He took his hand away from mine and looked at me with amused astonishment: A doctor—what sort of idea is that?

It was my father's wish, and my mother's. They see no reason why a woman cannot be educated and useful.

I could not tell him that I suspected my mother was afraid I might not marry; perhaps I was not yet aware myself of the reasons why. Sitting there with him, watching the fishermen languidly casting their lines into the water, I could believe for a moment that he saw me differently, for who I was and who I wanted to be, since he was holding my hand, and spent these afternoons with me. He was pleasing, and I always felt a certain breathless urgency when Ulyasha or Grigory Petrovich called to me to say that the young man was waiting.

Now he said, Useful? You don't need to be educated to be useful.

He was smiling at me, at the same time playing with a lock of my hair; he had taken it up so gently in his fingers that I hadn't even noticed until then.

Useful, how?

He leaned closer and kissed me chastely on the cheek. I've always wanted, he said, leaning back, to know what a girl's cheek feels like. And now I know.

Before I could say anything, he put his lips on mine. I started to pull away, but he had his hand against my back and he held me and made his kiss more insistent, though still gentle. His other hand had moved up my hair to rest on my shoulder, and he curled my hair round and round with his fingers against my neck and it was as if all of me were being twirled by those soft fingers and lips.

I pushed him away.

He shrugged, raised an eyebrow, and said, You'll have to learn to be more useful than that the day you have to start cutting people open and chopping off their legs, Dr. Lintvaryova.

Andryusha, you're horrid, I said, but my cheeks were burning, and I scrambled to my feet.

He saw me back to the house, kissed my hand in a gentlemanly fashion, his eyes full of irony, and walked away.

In the days to come, every time I thought about that moment, his blue eyes staring into mine, his fingers twirling my hair, I felt a dizziness that left me on my feet but filled me with both shame and surrender. I waited for him. I wanted him to do it again, to blur me into the summer landscape.

He came a few more times but ignored me and went fishing instead with Pasha and Georges, even though they were so much younger. When he saw me, he always called me Doctor and my cheeks went red. Mama looked at me, but I remained stubbornly silent.

I had pushed him away. That is my regret. I don't know if it was instinctive, or my good upbringing, or mistrust. Because even though there were other young men later, in Petersburg or Moscow or even Sumy, and even though there were those I loved who did not kiss me, and those who kissed me whom I did not love, it was never the same. I did not love Andryusha; I don't know what strange luminosity warmed the evening air that summer and stayed with me until I left for Petersburg. Perhaps it was youth, the last days of a certain blissful inexperience, nothing more. The moment above the river reflected it all.

For Andryusha, it had been meaningless—a moment's flirtation, engaged through boredom; the lack of anything better to do, futile but vivid.

Mama told me that he made a wealthy marriage and lives on a huge estate not far from Kharkov.

I suppose I still regret it, yes. Because it won't come again, that I know.

There were other suitors, or should I say real suitors, with nobler intentions; they hardly bear thinking about, but what else do I have to do at this moment? There was the fat one, Konstantin Ignatyevich, with his paunch and his fob watch, like a character out of an English novel; there was Aleksey Sergeyevich, with his spots and his stammer, so servile he made me want to giggle and hit him with my parasol (the rare times when I went about with a parasol—that is Natasha's *manie*). Mama wrung her hands, urged me; Elena dissuaded me. And thankfully so. Could I have continued my work as a doctor? Can marriage provide that satisfaction of good work and generosity? Perhaps with children, but . . . When I see the unhappiness of some of my cousins or friends who have married—they do not know they are unhappy, they delude themselves quite successfully and proudly, but their illnesses and complaints tell a different story—I think I made the wise choice. As did Elena. For Natasha, it is too soon to say. She is immensely happy with her work as a teacher, but she is also a flirt who loves company and laughter and children, and noise and chaos . . .

But am I being truly honest with this page? In the end, is it not a mirror, too, a distorting mirror? There are words that are like faults in the silver behind the glass . . . Of course I could avoid putting down the words that will follow, of course I could be evasive with myself, with the page, but the matter has tormented me—and perhaps Elena and Natasha, too— all my life, and as a doctor who studies the human body and the human soul, I cannot disregard this simple physical fact: We three sisters, without exception, are plain. We do not have beauty to recommend us. Elena is earnest to the point of being stern; Natasha is much more whimsical, but her laughter is perhaps too boyish, even rowdy. Perhaps that is why, early on, all three of us decided to study, and Mama encouraged us. Our Russian boys, like Andryusha, like Pasha and Georges, when

they talk of women—if they talk of women—talk of little
else: appearance. We are prizes in some competition they play
among themselves. For Andryusha, I was an easy prize and a
worthless one. A plain girl, eager and innocent, her affection
easily won, just as easily tossed aside.

If I had placed my hopes in marriage, I might feel bitter.
Instead, I chose a path that brought a sense of usefulness and
hope: Here was something in nature that I could change, where
life's unfairness could be redressed. Knowing that I eased
suffering, even saved lives: those two little girls who had been
caught in a fire in the village, or the infant with the terrible
fever in Baranovka. Every day I think of them.

But even if this journal is my only mirror, I don't wish
to indulge in vanity, however plain it might be. I know, and
my patients know, what was done. Perhaps it was beauty of a
different kind.

I have gotten out of bed—it is the middle of the night—but
I cannot sleep, so I take to scribbling on my writing board. It
calms me to form the words, my sightless scratching against
mortality. I lay in bed for the longest time, listening to the
night through the window, before resolving to get up. The
usual peaceful sounds of the river, and the owls and frogs, and
some dogs far in the distance (and closer, Rosa snuffling in
her sleep), and I thought I could hear someone singing. It's not
impossible, but it was so beautiful, so mysterious, it filled me
with a sudden inexplicable hope: not that I might be cured and
live a normal life after all, but that this short life remaining
to me might be filled with an unexpected happiness of a rare,
special kind—perhaps so rare because of what awaits me (and
that is what is so odd, because it awaits us all, it is just that I
must leave before my time, as they say, and with this suffering

that I bear as best I can)——but now it is as if some strange reward might still come to me, utterly unexpectedly, with a kind of grace, like that faraway singing in the night.

My heart is at rest now; perhaps I can sleep.

The following night

Again insomnia; perhaps it is from the excitement, or an excess of wine, which I know I ought not to drink but, at the same time, I realize how little difference it will make; or perhaps it's the glorious weather, spring rushing up to us with open arms.

I met our guests yesterday——yes, I like to think that they are guests (although they are paying for their room and board) and we are hosts. There is Evgenia Yakovlevna, who must be Mama's age, with dry hands and a timorous voice; then the daughter, Maria Pavlovna, very soft-spoken. According to Natasha, she is not beautiful——if she'd been a man, she says, she'd have been handsome, but she has a calmness about her, and a smooth, sweet face that is most appealing. Natasha went on to describe their conversation at length——the schools, the children, the pedagogy, the problems with the *zemstvo*. I have not yet had a chance to speak with her on my own, any more than an introduction; she is much in demand by her brother and her mother; she has a laugh like a clear, chiming bell, an infectious laugh that makes me want her brother to continually tease her and tell jokes. Which it would seem he does quite frequently already.

This brother, then, is called Anton Pavlovich, and he is the writer. His voice is deep and strong, as befits a man of words; he kissed my hand and held it for a moment, a sensitive touch that did not surprise me when I learned he is also a doctor.

Mama made much of his writing—he has had a play produced
in Moscow, and his stories have been published in *Northern
Herald* and *New Times*—but he seemed to suggest it was almost
accidental, not so much a hobby as a fortuitous source of revenue.
With Elena, the three of us talked briefly about the medical
work here in the environs of Luka, and he offered to assist in any
way he could. Elena was very grateful; she is quite overwhelmed
at the moment. But did he not come here to write or relax? asked
Mama, almost disappointed, and he laughed and said, Oh no,
Madame, to be perfectly honest, I have come here for the fish!
My brother, Misha, told me you have pike and perch and chub
and crayfish and I don't know what else in your river Psyol, and
I'm looking forward to some good sport and excellent food.

Then that you shall have, Mama assured him, if you don't let
my medical daughters drag you off on their house calls! Please
use our rowboats, and when you bring back your catch, Anya is
very good at preparing the fish as you like it, *à la polonaise*—she
is Polish—but also *à la russe*, *à l'ukrainienne* . . .

Natasha interrupted, saying something rather rude in
Ukrainian that our guests did not understand, fortunately;
and Georges grumbled to scold her and apologize for her at the
same time, until Mama suggested he play something for us on
the piano.

I had a moment of sadness, because while Georges was
playing—some Chopin nocturnes, and they always fill me with
melancholy at the best of times—I could hear Anton Pavlovich
murmuring with Elena, and there were words that rose above
the music like the notes of a dissonant melody. His tone was
concerned, the voice of a doctor, yes, but also dispassionate,
one might even say clinical. I may still be a doctor for others,
when my opinion can be of use, but to be my own patient is
impossible, intolerable. So I recognized that professional tone,

and I knew that, for the length of a brief conversation, I was his incurable patient.

This insomnia is torment. Hours lost churning over one's existence, changing nothing, fuming particles of sleep and anger and restlessness. Unless one uses the time to write, as I do now: idle thoughts that might otherwise have washed away, harmless, at dawn.

Although it is said there are writers and poets who find inspiration in sleepless hours, I do not envy them. This dark time belongs to owls and frogs and stray dogs, to foxes and wolves. I do not feel safe until the cock crows. There was a time when candle or lamp could chase away foolish shadows, but now I must do it myself.

THIS BROTHER, THEN, IS *called Anton Pavlovich, and he is the* *writer.*

Ana shook her head, closed her eyes. Surely some ironic coincidence, someone with the same name and patronymic. Perfectly common Russian names.

She took the printout of the text onto her lap and skimmed slowly across the Cyrillic characters until, fifteen pages further along, she found:

Natasha, bold as ever, said to Anton Pavlovich that if we were to *have Pleshcheyev and Tchaikovsky, then we must surely also have* *Chekhov.*

Perhaps they were merely referring to Chekhov, as they had referred to Tolstoy?

Ana set aside the printout and keyed a few words into Google. And found:

In the summers of 1888–1889 Anton Chekhov, with his family, *stayed with the Lintvaryovs on their estate at Luka, near Sumy,* *Kharkovsky Province, Ukraine.*

What a gift this was in her quiet little life! To come upon a completely new, never before published vision of the great man—even if the diarist was blind, it was not his looks that mattered, there was an abundance of photographs to attest to his flair and charm—no, it would be how Zinaida Mikhailovna perceived him, what she told of his days, his words, the thoughts he might share . . . The young man, fresh, spontaneous, and himself, before the brand of fame.

Ana looked around for Doodle, picked her up, squeezed her gently, spoke to her in Russian, *daragaya koshka maya*, and jigged around the room until the cat determined the nonsense had gone on long enough and began to wriggle.

Ana drafted a short message to Katya Kendall, ostensibly to ask advice regarding the diarist's lack of quotation marks, surely a consequence of her blindness—should she insert them?—and confirmed that she would refer to Crimea as *the Crimea*, as was the usage in the past, but should she use *the Ukraine*? She also asked why the journal must be kept confidential and whether the emphasis, when marketing the book, would be placed on *the famous summer guest*, or on the diarist, or on both. After she sent it, she realized it was a ridiculous question; she just wanted to share her enthusiasm with someone other than the cat.

She spent the rest of the morning on the Internet, reading websites, searching, skimming.

Chekhov, she learned, at the time he stayed with the Lintvaryovs, was on the eve of an extraordinary career. His stories had been selling well to various publications in Saint Petersburg; he had made a valuable ally of a publishing magnate, Aleksey Suvorin. He'd had a play produced in Moscow, *Ivanov*, which, although initially not well received, did give him a certain notoriety, and would go on to great success when it opened in Saint Petersburg in January 1889. These were his last weeks of relative anonymity, of normality, before the outside world began to claim him, to celebrate him, in both senses of the term, good and bad. He was twenty-eight years old.

KATYA WAS PEELING POTATOES by the sink, waiting for Peter to come home.

His homecoming, later and later these days. There were excuses—delays on the Underground, the pub with his old friend Jacob, who'd recently been made redundant—but Katya suspected he often just stayed at the office, brooding, drinking.

She was surprised by her strength. She did not confront him; there did not seem to be any point. Some women would worry he had a mistress; if he did, she might be grateful at this point.

She looked through the kitchen window, the familiar landscape of trees, sky, windows with their reassuring glow of a London evening. This had been home for so long. Would they lose it? There were mortgages. Peter had grown up here. They had moved to this house from their tiny flat in North London when his mother died. Katya's mother, back in her dreary flat in the outskirts of Moscow. Tilting in a concrete box against the seismic forces of shoddy construction and dilapidation. They had been shocked the last time they visited. The obscene graffiti, the litter, the mud. The gangs of teenage boys lurking like feral dogs. Katya had wanted to bring her mother to London; the old woman refused. Once you closed the door on the stinking stairway (cabbage, urine, cat piss, stale rain), you entered her world: Everything was there. The small things Katya's grandmother had rescued from before the Revolution: books, photographs, embroidered linens. A clock, still working. Her mother explained that these things could not be moved to an English house; they would be meaningless there, like language.

Katya nicked her finger with the knife. Raised it to her lips: the taste of blood, salty skin, potato starch.

She left the potatoes to soak in water and went to check the computer while waiting for Peter. He could call, at least. But he wouldn't use a mobile. Even Katya's mother had a mobile.

She looked briefly at the news. These demonstrations in Kiev. She worried for them, those young people with a future. But she supposed they thought they had no future; she could see that, too. Their desperation had once been hers.

A message from the translator. Why must the journal be kept confidential? That had been Peter's idea; she did not agree. The world already knew Chekhov had been to Luka in 1888 and 1889. She did not care if word got out; in fact, the more people knew about it, as far as she was concerned, the better. Peter had a plan, he said. A *marketing* plan. The translator had asked about that, too. Katya was not sure what Peter intended to do; they had never been good at marketing, that was part of the problem. He had been so evasive over these last weeks, and not just about the Sumy diary. But then she was being evasive as well.

Let Peter answer the translator. It was out of her hands. From now on she would peel potatoes and look out her kitchen window at the London sky, such as it was. She was not sorry; she had been as active in the press as Peter until only recently; a perverse side of her was grateful to the bankers, to the crisis, for providing her with this excuse to cut down. Peter did not want her at the office, she could tell. He was finding it difficult to speak to her of the practical problems—the falling sales figures, the rising costs, the loans. Letters from the bank, impersonal, mildly condescending. Form letters, but still. He brooded. Clutched at straws, calling tour operators, Russian literature departments, émigré journals in the United States. Anyone who might be interested in their list. Pleaded with Bertrams, with Gardners, with Amazon and

Waterstones for better terms. There were no better terms, he was told; everyone was taking a hit. This was business, after all.

He'd had to let their assistant go, after fifteen loyal years. She moved back to Poland, where the economy was booming. Relatively.

Under communism, Peter's publishing house would not have existed. He never would have known this gnawing fear and loss of pride. Other fears, yes. He would have been a mild-mannered professor of literature somewhere, struggling to convey ideas not through a market but through a screen of ideology. A screen set up to keep an elite in power. Were the banks any different?

She went to the bathroom to put a plaster on her finger. Glanced in the mirror. Still noble, Katya. That aristocratic tilt of her head. Fellow students, their voices lilting with doubtful irony when, even in jest, they called her Comrade. No, she had not been a good comrade, with her personal poems. She had left on Peter's arm in 1986 for the right to say as much. Though soon after, when the Wall came down, it no longer mattered to anyone; thankfully, in her case, love had prevailed. She was grateful for that. It helped now, knowing what they would go through in the months ahead, even if she felt some estrangement at the moment. Her childhood experience of pride, stoicism, and the blurred image of Soviet womanhood she had carried with her would help. Her own mother's example. Who else had kept the country together, fed the children when the men were off fighting wars or nursing at the vodka bottle? She smiled at the cliché—Peter would scold her— but there must be some truth in it.

She heard the key in the lock, sighed, took a deep breath.

Today it rained, briefly, a gentle spring rain that left a
damp fragrance upon the air. Anton Pavlovich and Evgenia
Yakovlevna sat with Mama and me for tea, as did Georges
when he wasn't interrupting or disappearing again. There was
some practical talk between Evgenia Yakovlevna and Mama
regarding Anya and the meals (a gentle complaint that she has
made them the same *polonaise* sauce for three days now) and
between Anton Pavlovich and Georges regarding the fishing—
the pike is best by the old willow, or the roach downstream with
the boat, opposite the church in the distance, and just after dawn
is best for perch, often between the islands. Or something like
that. Then Mama asked Anton Pavlovich what he was working
on, and he gave a gruff little laugh and replied, A Treatise on the
Best Hours for Fishing on the Noble Psyol, and Mama laughed,
we all did, but I could tell she was a little bit put out, she insisted
she was interested in his creative energy, as she calls it, for she
has been reading about electricity and magnetism and so on and
wonders if there are any parallel phenomena to be observed in
the minds and souls of creators. I listened for Anton Pavlovich's
expression in his voice—did he think she was foolish and naive
or merely curious—but he is very polite: He replied, too self-
deprecatingly, I am sure, that inspiration and electricity had
nothing to do with it, that it was merely the size of the pile of
bills to be paid that drove him to his pen and paper. I see, said
Mama, then she laughed and said, At least he is honest and
doesn't put on airs! Did Georges and I remember that dreadful
impostor from Petersburg who claimed to be a poet? He would

sniff the air and wiggle his head as if depositing inspiration for poetry from the scent of our Ukrainian cows. Divine! he would exult. Your countryside is divine! What absolute rubbish, said Georges. He was an insolent bore, I added, half in jest. We all laughed, and Anton Pavlovich concluded, Unfortunately, you do sometimes encounter such individuals in this profession, which is why I avoid Petersburg, where they tend to want to be seen.

There was a moment of silence, then he continued, But your impostor poet was right, it is divine here. Even with the rain; your nature is blessed, unspoiled, abundant—you have found paradise.

He paused until I heard him say in a quiet, intense voice, as if speaking to me alone—he was sitting next to me—This is a place not only for poetry or stories or plays. It is a place for writing novels—on that scale. I should like to write a novel, of course, if only I had the time.

But you will have the time, surely, I ventured.

I'm afraid I'm always in demand, Zinaida Mikhailovna. Today it's the pike and perch, tomorrow my dear friend, and your relation, Ivanenko, will be arriving, and soon after that another dear friend, Aleksey Nikolayevich Pleshcheyev, and in a week or two the rest of my family will descend upon me like a cackling flock of birds, demanding I provide them with entertainment, conversation, vodka, and the company of women—and why not a few short stories, posthaste, while I'm at it, to fill the coffers. Where is the time for novels?

I wanted to say that if he were a member of my family, we would work together, make an effort to ensure he had all the time and space he needed, but naturally, I could not say this, it would reflect badly on Evgenia Yakovlevna, who seems, from the little she has said, or that I have gleaned from Elena's impressions, to be a hardworking and long-suffering woman who lives solely for her family. (Though one might argue that my family is exceptional in enabling women to have lives of their own.) I thought, too, that I idealize my family overmuch, that to others we might seem far too radical, or merely eccentric, or even self-centered in our way.

So I said nothing, and not long after that, they took their leave, as it seemed the sun had come out, but I kept my thought for the next time we would meet and I could ask him what else novel-writing might require.

I have had one of my bad headaches. I don't know how long I have been asleep. Perhaps days, drifting from daylight to darkness, unaware. My body seems to have lost its timepiece; I am not hungry. From time to time I sensed a presence in the room, soft steps, an odor; a hand on my shoulder, or a voice asking something.

In the bed I inhabited a warm, safe place. The sound of my breathing lulled me into memory: childhood. Papa, before. With us still. Outings to the islands on the river. Games in the field. Snowdrifts against the house where we hid. Sleigh rides. The thaw, Easter. The kulich and paskha and brightly colored eggs; the days of feasting and dancing. The priest blessing the house. The visitors, telling us how we'd grown.

There was no difference between sisters and brothers; we were all free, and Luka was our shared kingdom. We invented stories with three wishes, and wise travelers and handsome princes, and the dreaded Baba Yaga if we did not do our schoolwork or preferred some mischief to obedience. We drifted with the islands on the Psyol, gave them different names from year to year. Bali, Java, Borneo; Saint-Pierre and Miquelon and the Île-aux-Chiens. We looked at maps and argued, learned the geography of the real world. Of which Luka was the center, with its willows and poplars and oaks; and the upper field, the lower field, the hayricks like fragile fortresses for endless summer evenings; the slow procession of the women's kerchiefs through the wheat and their voices in song or laughter; the snuffle and rattle of the horses passing, laden with the harvest. That was my childhood, the generosity of it, the sureness of it.

I hear music now. Georges is playing; there is a flute, too. Yes, our cousin Sasha Ivanenko has arrived. The notes are sweet and fresh, they soothe my tired brain and try to make it whole again. It must be evening. I am tired, I'll stay in my bed and listen to the music. There are other doors that open, that restore me. To the present moment. That much I can do; there I can live. A house full of doors, with music in each room.

I've been feeling better. Georges and Sasha took me for a drive into Sumy. To buy writing paper for our eminent summer guest the writer; he must be working on a novel, they whispered conspiratorially.

I waited with Roman in the trap while they went into the stationer's. It was terribly warm, and they seemed to be taking forever. All around me was a dark confusion of crowds and traffic—clatter of harness and carriage, sound of hooves, vendors shouting their wares. Someone singing with an accordion.

I heard my name, a woman's voice calling. I did not recognize her voice, perhaps a former patient or a fellow student or classmate. I realized she was calling insistently because I had not *recognized* her; she must have been on the other side of the street. I poked Roman urgently and discreetly: Did he know the woman calling to me? He did not. Could he describe her? Normal, a round face and blond hair. What was I to do? Why didn't she come to me? Is she alone? I asked Roman. No, mistress, she's with a small boy . . . and a servant, a dusty sort of fellow. She seems to want for you to join her, mistress, she's outside the tearoom, he muttered, she's waving for you to go over there, mistress.

I felt a horrid, shaming moment of panic. I could not shout, in the middle of Sumy marketplace, to a woman I did not *recognize*, and say that I was blind and could she oblige me by crossing the street? Should I send Roman? Ignore her? Clearly she did not know of my affliction; perhaps she had moved away from Sumy and now had come back on a visit. Oh, who was it? If I knew her voice, I could call her name and urge her to cross the street!

At that moment Georges and Sasha returned from the stationer's. I asked them if they saw a woman calling to me from across the street and would they be so good as to go and explain my situation, perhaps accompany her back to the trap so I might talk to her?

Sasha kindly undertook to be my emissary. We waited for a minute or so, and then he returned.

Well. Her name is Ekaterina Kirillovna Smetanina, she said she once stayed at the neighboring estate with her mother and brother. She was quite flustered that you hadn't greeted her, but when I explained why, she went beet-red. She sends her humble regards.

Andryusha's sister, I thought.

And is she staying here? Does she want to call?

She didn't say. I suppose not.

Now I would not have news of him. Perhaps it is just as well.

The market sounds seemed to fade then, and for a moment I feared the onset of a seizure, until I realized it was the violence of a memory obliterating the present moment: I was by the riverbank, with Andryusha, and that irretrievable moment had offered itself to me not as a summoned memory, like the one I have recorded above in these pages, but physically, imperatively. A flush of warmth and pleasure and fear all at the same time.

I almost gasped, and my face must have betrayed me, because Sasha turned to me on the seat and said, Are you all right, Zina? I nodded and the sensation faded, leaving only what I assumed was a puzzled smile on my face.

After stopping to buy a crate of Santurini wine for Anton Pavlovich, we headed back to Luka.

ANA DOUBLE-CHECKED THE SPELLING of *Santurini*. It was not a typo in the Russian; in any event, that was how Chekhov himself spelled it. In her research, she found there had been a large Greek community in Russia in the nineteenth century, many of whom had settled along the shores of the Sea of Azov, to the northeast of the Black Sea. These Greeks had settled, too, in Taganrog, the small coastal town where Chekhov was born. Nostalgia for that island in the Aegean, perhaps, had manifested in the name of the wine they produced or imported; somehow the vowel had changed in its emigration from one alphabet to another.

Ana pulled out an old atlas she had bought at a *brocante* and looked at the map. Still the Soviet Union in this volume. Taganrog was to the very south of Russia, tucked in the curve of the border with Ukraine, not far from Donetsk. Her finger traced westward along the coast from Taganrog, crossing the border, and down around the crooked thumb of Crimea as it curled into the Black Sea; back again eastward and south from Taganrog to Sochi, just before the border with Georgia, and where the Winter Olympics were due to start in a few days. She tapped her finger on Sochi, then traced the border as it went north, curved around to the west, and came to Sumy, north of Kharkov, halfway to the Byelorussian Republic—now Belarus. On the map, distances were deceptively short, but Ana had read that the journey from Taganrog, or Crimea, to Moscow used to take several days even by train, and it must still be an overnight journey, at least.

She decided to splurge and put in an order for several biographies, a few DVDs of the plays, and some fine editions of collected stories in English and in Russian. A good project to speed her through the winter. Her memories of Anton Chekhov were mostly vague, with one exception: *The Seagull*, which had been her first contact with the plays. The old theater in the center of San Francisco. She'd gone with her parents, grudgingly, sullenly, convinced that she was too old to be seen in public with them, convinced that the play would be *boring*. It was one of their last attempts to do something together as a family; now, of course, she looked back and was grateful that her parents had insisted she go with them. Because not long thereafter, their marriage had indeed collapsed. And then there were the play's opening lines:

MEDVEDENKO: Why do you always wear black?
MASHA: I am in mourning for my life. I am unhappy.

Ana had instantly been drawn to this young woman in her habit of melancholy, even though she was not the central, more beautiful, heroine. Masha's words might seem worn and tired to her now, but they still held the warmth and familiarity that had endeared Chekhov to her once and forever. At the time, Ana had already intuited the self-ironic truth to the cliché; nevertheless, she took up Masha's mantra and began to wear black herself. In the 1970s, she was seen as stylish by the other girls at school and then at university; stylish yet vaguely suspect, mistaken more than once for a French exchange student. With hindsight, she could see how Masha's mournfulness might have colored—darkened—her own attitudes during the significant years: She felt misunderstood and prone to inexplicable melancholy of her own. Perhaps it was hormones, or her parents' protracted divorce; perhaps it was all those Leonard Cohen songs she listened to, locked in her room. Until finally, she realized the potentially destructive irony of Masha's stance and her own: While it might be fashionable to wear black, the display of melancholy—as if you were some early nineteenth-century Romantic—had definitely gone out of style. As Ana grew older, she learned to keep it to herself, for momentary lapses of Rachmaninov's *Isle of the Dead* or wistful nostalgia; wine made it worse, as did crowds; long walks in autumn or afternoons skiing through a forest in winter condoned it and told her there was nothing wrong with her, that she was merely in harmony with the seasons.

I am learning to find my way around the house and the garden
on my own. I have been too dependent on the others—their
kindness, their availability—and now that the good weather is
here, I cannot be bound to my bed or my chair. Mama worried
at first and followed me until I finally had to scold her. Grigory
Petrovich has found me a solid stick to help me feel my way. Best
of all, Rosa guides me out of doors; she walks patiently by my
side, and I can hold her by the collar.

I have learned Luka all over again. No longer a place of colors
and shapes; it is measured, surveyed, assessed by my feet, my
stride. By space and an odd awareness of bulk or objects in my
path. I usually go as far as Pasha's cottage or the guesthouse,
but tomorrow I will try to go to the river. This morning I sat
for a short while with Madame Chekhova, Evgenia Yakovlevna.
She is soft-spoken and patient; she talks about her sons with a
mixture of exasperation and pride. Anton Pavlovich is clearly
the good boy, the one who makes sure his parents and sister lack
for nothing; the two older brothers, Aleksandr and Nikolay, are
as gifted as Anton, she says, but ever so troublesome; the two
younger boys, Ivan and Mikhail, are good boys, like her Antosha,
but not as brilliant, still finding their way.

And Maria Pavlovna, her only daughter, is the image of
patience and devotion. Evgenia Yakovlevna sighed and said
she was fortunate to have such a good girl helping with the
upbringing of all those boys. Masha and Antosha are very
close, she said.

Her husband, Pavel Yegorovich, will arrive at the end of June. In time for his name day, she said happily; I told her we should celebrate together, as it is also my brother's name day. It has been agreed, and we drew up a list of zakuski and dishes for Anya to prepare.

We have had a mountain of crayfish for dinner, courtesy of our fishermen guests. They did not join us, however, too tired and smelly, they protested. They ate out in the garden like farmhands.

I went this morning to sit under the willow by the river. I had a restless night, my brain clattering with thoughts about our guests. I was listening to the birds when I heard footsteps. I sat up straight, put on a ready expression, and waited. It was not a step I recognized—in any case, it's difficult to tell on the path, in the house it's something else. It wasn't Pasha or Georges, they would have called to me much sooner. A man's step, I supposed. Solid, no rustle of skirts.

He called my name, tentatively. I answered, Anton Pavlovich? He asked to sit beside me.

Naturally, there were pleasantries, the things you say when you don't know a person very well. He complimented us on the estate, the beauty of Luka, the kindness of the people; I asked him a few polite questions about Moscow, about his medical studies and practice. And all the time I was actually aching to ask him about his writing. He had seemed so self-deprecating the other night when we touched on the subject with the others, but I hoped today he might be more forthcoming with me. So when I thought we had dwelled long enough on pleasantries and I could sense an impatient fiddling of his fingers with the cloth of his suit, I plucked up my courage and said, So, you would like to write a novel.

It was a statement, not a question, but he said, As I told you the other night, where can I find the time, the concentration? I have so many pressing obligations.

Forgive me, this might be rather forward of me, but you must be sure it is what you want and not what others want for you, or what you feel you ought to do, and if you truly want it, then you must be sure you are not using your obligations as an excuse for your fear of beginning. Do you understand my point, Anton Pavlovich?

He was silent. I was afraid I had offended him. So I blundered on: I'm sorry, that's just my point of view, or not view, if you'll forgive the poor humor.

I paused, and as he had still said nothing and I felt a terrible blush coming over me, I tried to apologize: Anton Pavlovich, please forgive me, it's none of my business! It's just that if I had talent— a gift, like yours—I should not want to waste it on trifles—oh dear, that's not what I meant either, I'm sure your stories are wonderful and I'm eager to hear them—

I stopped, and heard his silence and the birds and the terrible echo of my blunt words. It is at times like this, thankfully not frequent, that I am particularly sorry to have lost my sight, for I could not see his expression or understand what effect my words might have had on him. On the other hand, perhaps that is a blessing, for it keeps me honest.

Very briefly and surprisingly, his fingertips grazed my wrist, and he said, Dear Zinaida Mikhailovna, we have just met, but people are rarely as honest with me as you have just been. You are quite right that I must not make excuses to delay what I genuinely want to do—perhaps I am afraid after all. You know, a novel is rather like a marriage, committing oneself to months or years of work, whereas a story is, yes, rather like—

He paused. I finished his sentence: A flirtation, an affair?

He laughed. You don't know me, but you know me well.

Like you, Anton Pavlovich, I am a doctor; perhaps it has nothing to do with art, but one develops a certain ability to diagnose not only the body but also the spirit, don't you think?

Very true, Zinaida Mikhailovna.

We were silent, then he changed the subject, asked about my medical studies and Dr. Chudnovsky, where had I been practicing, when had I stopped?

I've been completely blind for over a year now. It isn't getting better, clearly. Nor will it, I'm afraid.

And did any of the doctors—or you yourself—have any explanation for your illness?

I bent my head as if I could see my hands folded in my lap. No, Anton Pavlovich, alas, there is no explanation; why does lightning strike the oak and not the birch? Some religious person might point to a long-ago sin, but we are not like that in my family. The random cruelty of nature, that is all.

I am sorry.

You needn't be. You're a doctor, you know what life is.

The prognosis? Treatment?

I waved my hand. I am strong, I have always been in good health, I might live for a long time. But there is no treatment. Family. Luka.

Again I waved my hand to include everything I could no longer see.

I must apologize again, Anton Pavlovich, for my bluntness just now, my illness has made me too honest, on occasion to the point of rudeness, although I try not to—

Don't apologize, Zinaida Mikhailovna. You are right. I'm going to give serious thought to starting a novel. I know you will be an ally. But please don't mention it to the others—my sister Masha, or my friends when they arrive. They'll only badger me, in their way.

Rest assured, I'll say nothing.

We sat pleasantly for a while longer, talking of more trivial things. He is very impressed with our porcine menagerie. He has never seen robust pink and brown pigs wandering in and out of a human dwelling. He wanted to know their names so that he could tell his friends. I begged him not to make fun of us and our country ways. What is wrong with treating well-behaved porkers with the same respect you give to the dogs and cats?

He began to laugh uproariously. I should have been annoyed, for Pasha's sake—his prize pigs—but I could not help myself. I saw myself and my family as if we were onstage, seated around the samovar, talking about literature and politics, suddenly visited by our grunting beasts, the dogs running after them, eager to nab them by the ear.

Elena seems to have made quite an impression on Anton Pavlovich today.

They went out on house calls around the countryside, Anton Pavlovich very cheerful and teasing as they departed—how sad I was to be left behind! This was once my daily life, too, in almost any weather. We would take the sleigh in winter, and there was such a light across the fields at dusk, pink and golden on the snow; steam of the horses' breath, blankets across our laps . . .

But this is summer, and they took the small trap with Roman driving, just one horse, a new one that Pasha bought in the spring at the fair. Roman says the horse is the nervous sort, and he's of the opinion that Pasha has wasted his money and there'll be no end of problems with this mare, Agrifina. I remember the fuss at the time. Pasha countered that she'd be an excellent brood mare and would calm down in due time. Why they took her today, I have no idea—perhaps Grusha was lame or overworked—in any event, the mare grew skittish on the road between Luka and Tokari in the typically mysterious way of animals, we don't know why there, more than elsewhere, but Elena suspects there must be a bull in the fields to the north of the road. Agrifina stopped this side of the small bridge over the stream and would not take another step. Roman made some Romanish groans and shouts and was reaching for the whip when Elena jumped down and went to the nervous mare, stood by her with one hand on her neck and the other on her nose, and just talked to her. In a calm, sweet voice, as if speaking to a child, was the way Anton Pavlovich described it, and after a minute of Roman grumbling and Anton Pavlovich offering to help and being told she could manage on her own, Elena took Agrifina by the reins, close to the bit, and led her over the bridge, talking all the while, looking back at the two men *as if we were useless children,* sighed Anton Pavlovich, and then she climbed back up into the trap and took the reins and drove them the rest of the way.

I see her: head held high, back arched, arms ramrod-straight before her, a proud nervousness about her, and something she would share with the animal before stepping aside for the men. I did not say as much to Anton Pavlovich, but clearly, he had never seen a woman so capable with a trace horse, and he even said as much. Then you haven't spent much time in the country, I countered, and he protested that he had spent many summers outside Moscow and had grown up in a fairly provincial sort of town where the countryside was never far away, but the ladies were generally afraid of horses and not about to deal with an animal's fear in addition to their own.

To me, Elena's behavior was not at all unusual; I have seen her react with equal courage and determination on numerous occasions. We have grown up with our beasts, we live with them. I felt a moment of bemused sympathy for Anton Pavlovich, that he was so poorly acquainted with this rich world of country life, or knew it only for tea parties and fishing expeditions. I think he was rather annoyed when I said, It's only normal, it's what we do here. There was a moment's silence, and then he said, Well then, Zinaida Mikhailovna, if I write a novel and it is a success, I shall buy my own country estate and cultivate an understanding with my equine fellows, just as your sister has done.

He went on to tell me he'd met our regular lodger Artyomenko, the one who works at the Kharitonenko factory who is an avid fisherman; they would be going that evening to explore the waters around the islands. A grand fellow, he called him.

Before taking his leave, he asked me about the water bittern. Like many visitors to our region, he is intrigued by the bird's peculiar call and wonders if I know what it looks like, as he would like to see it while he is here. I tell him that it is difficult to get a proper sighting; moreover, if he asks the peasants, each one will describe the most fantastical creature, something like the Firebird, the Zhar-ptitsa, but never two versions alike.

May 20, 1888

Monsieur Pleshcheyev has arrived, and he has brought some scores for Georges! So in addition to poetry, we shall have new works by Tchaikovsky. When Anton Pavlovich learned of Georges's talent and his love of Tchaikovsky, which he says he shares, he wrote ahead and arranged for Monsieur Pleshcheyev to bring the scores.

Georges wants a few days to practice, and then we shall have an evening of words and music. Mama is terribly excited. I believe she feels all of Saint Petersburg—the good side, that is—has come to our drawing room.

Natasha, bold as ever, said to Anton Pavlovich that if we were to have Pleshcheyev and Tchaikovsky, then we must surely also have Chekhov. He gave a short laugh, and there was a moment of silence until he agreed that he would read a story from a collection he had just had published, called *In the Twilight*.

Later she told me he seemed almost annoyed, but flattered in a way as well, that he looked down at his feet before agreeing, as if requesting the consent of his toes.

THE DELIGHT OF SOFT padded envelopes, waiting for her in the crisp February air, in her mailbox. Three biographies, in addition to the volumes of stories (multiple translators) and the major plays, some on DVD with eminent British actors.

For several days of foul weather, Ana stayed in and read about Anton Chekhov. She found the obvious references, which, like Masha in black, had become clichés: the rambling, crumbling estates with their bumbling servants and samovars in the garden; the three sisters. But those familiar elements had to come from somewhere: They were a way of life, his everyday reality. An immense country with an educated, bored middle class; women whose lives were stunted and circumscribed by society and tradition. Zinaida Mikhailovna and her sisters, Elena and Natalya, stood out, anachronisms; they belonged, Ana learned, to the inaugural generation who attended the Bestuzhev Courses in Saint Petersburg, which for the first time in Imperial Russia offered higher education to young ladies of means.

Chekhov, on the other hand, earned his success. He was able to work his way up from relative poverty because he was talented, but also because his childhood had taught him that life was a struggle. As a boy, he and his brothers were thrashed repeatedly by their pious shopkeeper father; later, the whole family fled to Moscow to escape their creditors, leaving the young Antosha alone in Taganrog to finish secondary school. He wrote short, humorous stories, initially to finance his medical studies and help his family. What started as the source of a student's supplemental income evolved into a body of work, turning him, not even ten years after his summers at Luka, into an author and playwright whose stature was almost mythic. Ana studied the photographs, let her mind wander as they told the stories the words could not. He completely looked the part: tall, handsome, youthful, funny—mediagenic, in today's parlance. The props, most of which came long after his summers at Luka, were inimitable: the goatee, the pince-nez, the walking stick, the dachshund—when it wasn't the pet mongoose he brought back from his travels to the Far East. (Apparently, he despised cats.) It would seem that Chekhov hated his celebrity status, the shaking of hands and dealing with gushing admirers on the waterfront at Yalta—even though many of them were women—and going to receptions, being seen in the right places. But for all that, he knew how to enjoy the benefits of his success. He befriended Tolstoy, Gorky, Diaghilev, Rachmaninov; he married late and, on the whole, well—the actress Olga Knipper; he bought villas and dachas and traveled to France and Italy, and he didn't have to go on author tours or give signings or spout witticisms on a social network to keep himself in the public eye.

She learned in an interesting, oddly relevant footnote that Chekhov's paternal grandmother was Ukrainian, and late in life he claimed that as a small child he had been able to speak Ukrainian.

Ana was beginning to feel genuine affection for the blind narrator and her story; that sentiment would show through, surely, in the excellence of her translation. As if it were a book she had written herself. This was her chance. And she felt sure it would lead to other things.

She looked out the window of her attic study. In winter, when the trees were bare, she could see as far as the lake and the mountains beyond. The sky had cleared, and there was a pink wash of sunset on the white peaks. The tree in her neighbor's yard wore a sleeve of ice. She opened the window, let a breath of frost into the room.

For two days Anton Pavlovich has not come. Natasha tells me he is terribly busy with Monsieur Pleshcheyev. She went over to the guesthouse to invite them for this evening—Georges has been practicing and is ready to play for us, and perhaps the gentlemen will share some of their literary work.

Our young cousin Vata is visiting us for a few weeks, so Natasha took her along to meet them, and she tells me Vata was very impressed by the great poet. Naturally, he could be her grandfather, but she is in awe of his stature, his fame . . . Natasha says Vata has grown into a silly, provincial little thing; she hides her hand behind her back to keep from sucking her thumb; we are supposed to be trying to give her some culture, some *finish,* as the English say—now she meets her first poet and goes quite dotty.

And what about Anton Pavlovich? I ask Natasha. He must be more handsome than Pleshcheyev—he's quite young, isn't he?

I think he frightens Vata, said Natasha. She amuses him, so he says teasing, wicked things, practically drives her into Pleshcheyev's arms for refuge. Pleshcheyev pats her on the head and says, There, there.

And with you?

Who, with me?

Anton Pavlovich?

She laughs her short, chiming laugh. With me? He knows I'll only return the compliment, so he's terribly circumspect. For the moment he respects me, which is almost a pity. I rather like that teasing side of his.

After a pause I ask, And he's not engaged to be married?

It seems not. It's odd, no? He's got his mother and sister to look after him, so he's obviously in no hurry, but given his looks, you'd think—

What does he look like?

Tall and lanky, thick dark hair and a little beard, and very nice eyes that don't miss a thing. Rather more like an eternal student than a doctor, a bit like our Pasha without the politics. Or at any rate, whenever we try to pin him down on his politics he evades the issue.

And Monsieur Pleshcheyev?

Elderly, white beard, portly . . . With Anton Pavlovich, they share a certain—how to describe it—gentleness. I cannot decide in the case of Anton Pavlovich whether it is because he is a doctor or a writer. There is something about men who work with words—poets, writers—do you suppose it makes them different?

I knew I was about to make a terribly banal suggestion, but I went ahead with it. Natasha can be so abrasive at times, she doesn't always take the time to understand why people are this way or that, so I said, since she had asked, Well, perhaps they spend more time examining what it is that makes us human in an immaterial way—emotions, language?

Oh, well said, Zinochka. I must read more poetry, then. Improve my soul, in other words.

It wouldn't hurt, I said with a smile.

She reached over and stroked my cheek. After a pause, with a touch of mischief in her voice, she said, But did you know that this same Monsieur Pleshcheyev, who could be anybody's cozy grandfather, was a revolutionary in his youth and was sent to Siberia for ten years? He was in the Petrashevsky Circle with Dostoyevsky. Condemned to hang, then pardoned.

How extraordinary!

Pasha and Tonya can't get enough of him and keep pressing

him to tell them about his youth, but he keeps changing the subject. I'm an old man now, he says, and chuckles, my time for revolutions is past. I've come here to write poetry.

She had lowered her voice in a passable imitation of a contented old man. Then I heard her get to her feet. I grabbed her wrist. Don't go just yet. What else? What other news?

Elena is treating a bad case at the moment, or should I say a very sad case. Do you remember the young woman from Velikaya Chernechina with the tumor on her neck? She's much worse, she's terribly pale and thin, wasting before your eyes, says Elena, who is very upset there's nothing she can do for her. She's asked Anton Pavlovich to have a look at her.

The poor man is supposed to be on holiday, is he not?

And he's meant to be writing. He wasn't joking about that. He supports his family, entertains his friends, agrees to help Elena, writes stories, goes fishing—

Has he caught anything?

Pike and chub, he said, and an old shoe.

I laughed. He needs to have something to throw at you when the time comes.

Georges's recital moved me to tears. My eyes still weep, as if seeing my reduced world through hammers and strings and Tchaikovsky's notes.

Natasha would surely laugh at me again for my emotional apprehension of the world. I was not always this way—we have always tried in our family to be realists, pragmatic and rational—but my illness has shown me the resources of the spirit's more inexplicable manifestations. That music and words (even when they are no longer *legible*) are valuable, potent *spectacles* in their own right; that for all the pleasure I once took in color and dance and visual beauty, there were many things I did not see which now are visible to me. Language, too: So much of it is based on sight that I find it hard to find the words for what I have been *seeing* with this new vision. Perhaps there are no *words;* is Georges's playing, Tchaikovsky's music, not a language of its own?

And Monsieur Pleshcheyev's poetry: I heard him use words in ways that surprise and confuse me. At times I would like for him to repeat what he said, so I could better grasp the sense. I must ask him for a volume of his works so my patient family can read the poems to me again and again.

Anton Pavlovich read from his collection, *In the Twilight,* as promised. A rather bold story about a woman, one Sofya Petrovna, who determines almost on a whim to leave her husband for an admirer. A quite terrible story, really; the woman, according to the narrator, did not really love the man, but she was bored with her husband, with her life; she was made giddy by the admirer's adoration, and above all, she felt an urge stronger than anything, irrepressible and alluring. While admiring his description of her state of mind, I could not help but worry that Mama or even Monsieur Pleshcheyev—or Elena, for that matter—would be shocked by the story. There was a moment of stunned silence at the end when the narrator says, *What drove her on was stronger than shame, reason, or fear,* and we all knew what Monsieur Chekhov was referring to; then Natasha—incorrigible, bold Natasha—began to applaud and laugh somewhat nervously, and we applauded and all began to talk at once.

Anton Pavlovich came over to me later, and I asked him if he believed most women were like Sofya Petrovna, and if he found her behavior commendable or reprehensible.

He laughed and placed his fingers on my forearm. My dear Zinaida Mikhailovna, if all women were like Sofya Petrovna, we would not be here tonight. The world would be an utter shambles.

Then why write about her? What can possibly be edifying or——

But dear lady, I'm not trying to edify or instruct or above
all pass judgment. I'm merely describing a frequent human
dilemma. Not all women act as . . . irresponsibly, or freely,
depending on your point of view, as Sofya Petrovna, but I defy
you to find me a married woman who has not had thoughts of
behaving like that.

And do you really believe we are all so . . . base in our emotions?

Here he paused and answered with a question of his own: You
find her desire base?

It is self-centered, irrational, ungoverned——

And that is base? Are you applying your own opinion or
that of society? Imagine if your own dear sister, Natalya
Mikhailovna, for example, were in such a situation, bored and
unhappy with her husband, and the opportunity presented
itself—in the form of a handsome, devoted man of the law—
to create a new life, full of mystery and discovery. Would you
condemn her, find her base?

I felt my cheeks redden, lifted my fingertips to my face.

He laughed again and said, Forgive me, Zinaida Mikhailovna,
I have spoken quite out of turn. These are delicate matters. I
have witnessed in my own family—my eldest brother, to give
just one example—such instances of desire and the havoc they
bring. Such struggles with nature, as my lawyer in the story calls
them. They are almost always tragic and yet terribly comical
at the same time. When we know what bitter disappointment
comes after so much passion. Such banality. Such emptiness.

He paused, then asked, I assume you've read *Anna Karenina*?

Yes. But there is so much that is tragic and terrible in that book.

My heroines do not go that far. As in life; again, if we all had
Anna's desperate soul, the world would descend into a chaos of
tragedy. That was Tolstoy's vision for the novel, based on a true
incident—so such things do happen. But most often . . . banality.

Which is why I prefer to err on the side of comedy. Otherwise life would be altogether too hard to bear, don't you think? If love always led to train platforms? All this passion tearing people apart, sending decent women out into the night without so much as a bonnet on their head?

He must know that such matters no longer concern me, that, if anything, my life is hardly a comedy and should be too hard to bear, and yet he drew me into his argument, into his vision for the sake of that argument. I smiled. You are quite the magician, Anton Pavlovich, I said.

Ah, yes. I have a special fondness for white rabbits and ladies sawn in half.

He lowered his voice and said very earnestly, I've started, Zinaida Mikhailovna.

Started what?

The novel.

I grasped his wrist; he placed two fingers there in warning.

Don't say a thing or I'll never hear the end of it. Agreed?

Of course! I'm very pleased for you. Do you have a title? No, I'm silly, of course it's too soon—

Too soon for anything: no plot, not a clue where the vehicle is taking me, just a few sketches with a few idle characters standing about waiting for cues. But it intends to be a novel.

And how many pages?

Don't ask, Zinaida Mikhailovna, don't ask! There is only: I'm progressing. Or I'm not progressing. Today I have been progressing.

Good, good. I'm very glad to hear this.

At that moment Monsieur Pleshcheyev called to him, and our conversation ended.

But now, before turning in, I reexamine my long-ago feelings for the shiftless Andryusha. How I would have liked to respect those feelings and honor them, had he been at all honorable. What part my own urging, then, what part nature, and what part society pulling me—or even him—the opposite direction, toward convention and propriety? Andryusha did not pursue me, because I was neither wealthy nor beautiful enough for his image of the way his life should be; but my own nature had left me utterly open and vulnerable for a brief moment. I could picture the girl I once was, setting off into the night without her bonnet on her head.

So these are the things Anton Pavlovich likes to discuss in his stories—or should I say, rather, describe. He does take an interesting point of view, standing back with his arms crossed (I suppose) and throwing the characters together so that he can watch what happens.

THE WIND KEPT ANA housebound. She tried to watch the Winter Olympics, but all the nationalistic fervor left her unable to enjoy the sport for its own sake.

She turned back to the biographies of Chekhov she'd ordered, eager to find the period described by Zinaida Mikhailovna reflected in the printed pages.

Oddly, the biographical material—thus far, at least—had not provided any evidence of a novel written that summer in Luka. Or of any novel, for that matter, unless you counted *The Shooting Party* or *The Duel* or *My Life:* a youthful pastiche, two novellas. Not a hefty Russian novel of the kind people—including Ana— imagined.

Was it as he explained to Zinaida Mikhailovna: lack of time or concentration? Or was it, in the long run, a question of disposition, the appropriate use of his talent?

Unable to find an answer, she turned to writing chatty emails, catching up with friends. Some of them answered, newsy, superficial, and she wondered if the loss of depth in her relationships was proportional to time and distance.

Yves was the only one who wasn't far away, and he suggested the best remedy. *Brave the cold,* he wrote, *and come into Geneva for lunch. Live dangerously. I've got a new brasserie for you to try, my treat. Just get yourself over here. Are you free on Friday? Don't drive, you'll never find parking, but you can read on the bus, or eavesdrop on people on their cell phones and see how many different languages you can collect.*

They had known each other a very long time. Yves worked

primarily as an interpreter but also translated the occasional novel into French from Russian or "American," as the French called it. He liked to joke that, growing up, he couldn't decide whether he wanted to be a cosmonaut or an astronaut. He and Ana had met in Moscow during the summer course for foreigners, but it was only much later that their acquaintance had blossomed into a sudden wild friendship, based on everything Ana had never found with the straight men she had dated, lived with, traveled with, and eventually married (Mathieu had been irrationally jealous of Yves): laughter, irreverence, lightheartedness. Open emotions. Trust.

She envied him. With admiration. His long-term relationship with Yiannis. Their sensible lifestyle: They had separate apartments and saw each other a few times a week. There were adventures on the side from time to time, discreetly, rarely shared with the other partner. Over time, he told her, they had felt less need to go elsewhere, more need for each other. They traveled widely and rekindled. That was how Yves put it, *We went to Copenhagen and rekindled.*

The first time she corrected him: *You need a direct object after a transitive verb.*

Not with you I don't, he said calmly, raising an eyebrow.

Now they were sitting in his brasserie, Les Négociants. The windows were steamed up; waiters glided like a corps de ballet in black aprons and red ties from one side of the room to the other, as if carrying not hot dishes of *suprême de pintade* or *souris d'agneau* but rations of warmth and cheer against the winter chill. Yves described his latest rekindling trip—to the Azores—then asked what she was working on. She cocked her head and said mysteriously, Anton Chekhov.

You're translating Chekhov?

No, the diary of someone who knew Chekhov. (It sounded so reductive that she almost blushed.)

She felt a faint twinge of guilt to be talking about her project despite the Kendalls' injunction—but then she reasoned that they hadn't responded to her email regarding Zinaida Mikhailovna's punctuation and the proper way to refer to Crimea and Ukraine, and above all Chekhov's presence in the diary, and when she'd last checked, she hadn't been paid her advance, either. So she shared this information with Yves, but the more she told him about the actual project, the more enthusiastic they both became, until Yves reached across the table to grab her hand and kiss it.

Here lies Trigorin, he said in Russian. *He was a good writer but inferior to Turgenev.*

You know it by heart! *Seagull*, right?

Act Two, yes. Some of it. It was the way we learned languages back then, wasn't it, by rote. Remember Lyudmila Nikolayevna, with that stick she had to scan the meter? *Tovarishchi! Vnimanye!*

My God! I still know that poem by Pushkin we had to learn. I felt rebellious at the time, but now I'm glad.

Go on, then.

Ana cleared her throat and recited the poem in a hushed voice, while Yves listened thoughtfully and chimed in at one point. When she had finished, he looked at her and said, To get back to my initial misunderstanding—you *should* translate Chekhov.

But there are literally hundreds of translations already. Where's the glory in that?

Ana, you're not doing it for the glory. There's never any glory for any of us, you know that. You would do it for the love of it, no?

I would hope to.

You could find something he wrote during that period, and it could be published along with Zinaida Mikhailovna's diary. Write to the publisher.

That's what I thought, briefly, but they're hopeless. They don't answer my emails.

Don't let that stop you. Try anyway.

There is talk of a novel . . . I mean, Chekhov refers to writing one, starting one, already in what I've translated so far. But I have no idea if it exists.

Yves scraped pensively with a small spoon at what was left of the crème brûlée, then looked up, spoon paused in midair. Imagine, Ana, he said, sighing, if you could translate that novel. It would be perfect.

But Yves, if he did write one, where is it? Chekhov never finished a novel. Published a novel. That we know of.

He paused, licked his spoon. Are you sure?

Well, as sure as anyone else. I haven't finished the journal, so I don't know—

How did the publisher find this thing?

I don't know. I have a file in Word, that's all, typed by someone called Olga Ivanova. I suppose there's a Russian edition planned as well.

Perhaps they also have Chekhov's novel.

Don't be absurd.

Why absurd? Stranger things have happened. Remember the Némirovsky manuscript in the suitcase in the Paris attic? Maybe they found your two manuscripts together, the diary and the novel, in an attic in Saint Petersburg. Or Moscow. Or Kiev. Or Smolensk. Don't you love the sound of it, Smolensk? Sma-*lyensk*.

Ana was briefly and irrationally thrilled by the way he said *your two manuscripts*, but she felt she had to be skeptical. I don't think Chekhov went to Sma-*lyensk*.

On his trip to Sakhalin, then, maybe he left the manuscript in Irkutsk or Krasnoyarsk. Or Blagoveshchensk.

You're making fun, Yves. You didn't know Chekhov never wrote a substantial novel, and yet you remember his itinerary across Siberia?

Idle curiosity and a love of geography. And words. In Chekhov's letters, there's one sent from Blagoveshchensk. That's where he met the Japanese whore who says "ts!" It's priceless. Who could ever forget a Japanese whore who says "ts!"

She said "ts" because she couldn't pronounce Blagoveshchensk.

They laughed quietly, happily, a small rush of complicity, then Yves said, Keep reading, Nastyenka. I'll bet you anything— I'll bet you a live mongoose there's a novel for you in there somewhere.

On the bus home, what Yves had said kept chiming, a silly refrain, but as insistent as an earworm: *I'll bet you a live mongoose there's a novel for you in there somewhere.*

What would I do with a live mongoose? she mused. They're nasty creatures, anyway, what could have possessed Anton Pavlovich to adopt one? The pleasure of proving others wrong? To show them that they are not such nasty creatures after all, that they can form attachments to human beings and make unusual pets?

But if there were a novel, the mongoose would be for Yves. Let him worry about its angry little teeth. Ana would have a novel to translate.

Elena asked Anton Pavlovich and me to go with her to the
village clinic to examine the young woman from Velikaya
Chernechina who has the tumor. Her name is Nadya. According
to Elena, she has lost a great deal of weight and is terribly pale,
in a fair amount of pain. Elena diagnosed a cancer; it would
seem far more virulent than my own at this point. And yet
because there are no visible symptoms other than her weight loss
and discomfort, Nadya retains a terrible hope.

The tumor on her neck, however, can be felt. For a moment I
placed my fingers where Elena's hand led me, as if between the
two of us we hoped a touch might discover a change, something
to grasp at. Her skin was warm; I could hear her quiet breathing.
How she trusted us! I had to lift her long, heavy hair out of the
way; I imagined it a russet color. Her hand grazed mine as she
helped move her hair to one side.

Anton Pavlovich joined us at that moment and placed his
fingers on the spot I had indicated. Our fingertips touched. We
examined Nadya, then sent her into the other room while we
discussed the diagnosis. Elena hoped that Anton Pavlovich might
have a miracle cure to propose, something he had learned at the
university in Moscow, or at least a more favorable prognosis, but
he could only agree with what she had said.

And suddenly, Elena—calm, level, good Elena—was
overcome. She reached out for my arm and grasped it, hard,
and I could tell she must be crying from the trembling in her
voice, and while her words were for Nadya and for her inability
to offer any hope, I knew she must be thinking of me as well,

and letting some of her sadness find its way out under the guise of her concern for Nadya. (We have agreed never to talk of my illness, only to deal with it as needs arise.) Yet it was astonishing that she did this in Anton Pavlovich's presence. As doctors, we learn to separate our human reactions from the task at hand: the understanding of the pathology, the diagnosis, the prognosis, the prescription, the treatment—science, all of it, rational.

Why must she die, cried Elena softly, when I go on living and can't help her! Oh, I'm no good at this, no good at all! God in heaven! Who do I think I am, *Doctor* Lintvaryova!

There was a moment of strained silence, then Anton Pavlovich said gently, You must increase the dose. That's all you can do. Make her comfortable. Do you agree, Zinaida Mikhailovna?

Yes, I murmured, touched that he had consulted me. I squeezed Elena's hand; she withdrew at once.

Later, Anton Pavlovich walked me back to the main house. We were subdued; he told me that he had seen Nadya's family— they were all there waiting outside—father, mother, husband. I thought he was going to say something about how sad it was or what a difficult profession we have sometimes, but instead he took a deep breath and said, Your sister is an excellent physician—an excellent person—but in our profession, it doesn't do well to take things to heart as she does. Don't you agree?

I suppose you're right. She's young still and . . . she cares about people. That is why she became a doctor.

That's all well and good, but she must find a way to detach her emotions from her consulting, or she'll have a miserable time of it. And perhaps not be as effective. Does she often react like that?

Oh, no, I assure you.

This was not true. I remember when I was still practicing, she often came in on an evening after a long day of house calls, and she would sit down and ask Grigory Petrovich to pour her a dram of vodka. Just a small one, mind, she'd say, and then with her elbows on the table and her face in her hands, she would allow her tension to dissipate in the gloom. Once or twice she wept; often she asked me what I would do in her shoes. I was the older sister, the first physician in the family. I must have said things not unlike what Anton Pavlovich had just said: that she must remember her training, must distinguish the person from the body, etc., and yet whenever she concluded with a sigh, But we grew up with these people!, I would find myself unable to offer any other comfort or advice. And we would sit on in the gloom until Pasha or Georges or Natasha roused us from our apathy.

Anton Pavlovich delivered me to my armchair and took his leave with these words for Elena: I would advise her, too, to be less conservative with her prescriptions. Can you tell her that, with all due respect? To obtain maximum effectiveness. Just a thought; it might help. He paused, then added, You yourself seem far more dispassionate, shall we say. It must have been easier—when you practiced, I mean—to keep the demons at bay.

Yes, I generally seemed well suited to the scientific angle, so to speak—why is the body ill? Not why do we, as human beings, tend to react to illness with such terrible anxiety and distress . . . How are we to live, otherwise? I smiled and added, It's just altogether too much if you don't take your distance.

He placed his hand briefly on my forearm and said, Quite so. Good night, Zinaida Mikhailovna.

May 28, 1888

Tonya came to see me today. She is tired of being isolated in their cottage and is terribly worried that Elena and Pasha might be away when her time comes. I reassure her that if worse comes to worst, which it won't, I can deliver the baby with my eyes closed (so to speak) and a bit of help from Mamochka.

She's a lovely girl, Tonya; Pasha has been fortunate to find her. She is hardworking and doesn't mind his politics—in fact, I believe she shares them. She doesn't mind that he dresses like a peasant and works like one, or that he has embraced the Marxist cause. She has taken an interest in his farming methods and helps him a great deal. He has set her up with a loom, and she weaves tablecloths and useful things for us all—rough and full of small mistakes that she apologizes for, pointing them out when you'd never have noticed them otherwise. I used to help her choose the colors. Now I run my fingers over the weave, looking for the irregularities, as if they told a story.

I shall be an aunt soon. It's a strange thought.

I suspect Elena wants children, although she's never actually said as much, at least to me. When your chances of marriage are slim, you don't discuss children. I don't doubt she would have them without a husband if the world allowed it. She doesn't get along with Tonya, and I think it's because she's envious. Or jealous. She's always had a soft spot for Pasha, he is more her little brother than mine, they used to go riding and fishing together as children; and now she's both confused and elated that Pasha is about to become a father. I shouldn't be writing this, I know Elena might read it someday, but perhaps I lack the courage to tell her to her face that she must wish them well, that I'm sure they'll let her spend all the time she likes with the baby, but she mustn't make things awkward for them with her stormy behavior.

If only Pasha had a friend who might take an interest in Elena. Perhaps one of Anton Pavlovich's numerous brothers . . . Who knows, I haven't given up hope for her. It's children she wants, really, more than a husband.

She needs to believe in something being born, growing, prospering. She sees too much of the other, and loses her faith in life.

As for me . . . did I want children? I don't think so. I never loved a man enough to begin to imagine binding with him not just to create a child—that is easy enough even without love—but above all to raise it and love it and bring it to adulthood with an aptitude for life. I loved many children as a doctor, and I am glad I have that to think of.

I'm sitting by the riverbank. Natasha brought me here to my favorite spot, above the willow (where the pike bite), overlooking the bend in the river and the three small islands like heavy rivercraft drifting toward a town where there will be dancing . . . I convert the rays of the sun to images in memory—of course I see nothing but I see everything, because I know it hasn't changed. The smell of warm earth and lilac and the acacia trees, the tang of the Psyol . . . on the far side, the domes of St. Vladimir's reflect the sunlight. There are several small boats in among the islands, I can hear the fishermen calling to each other, can almost tell the distance between them; perhaps Anton Pavlovich is in one of them with his friends. He has adopted a young lad from the village whom he takes with him everywhere. Panas. The boy is very quiet in my presence, and as soon as the two of them go off together, I can hear all the questioning and fascination in his voice as he asks what's wrong with me. My sad eyes, remembering Panas as a small, mischievous boy, always carrying a stray puppy under one arm.

I have the dogs with me for company, Rosa and Pulka; they sit beside me panting in the heat, then run off to explore. It seems quiet, almost lonely, until I hear them scrabbling back up the embankment to splatter me with their doggie happiness and water from the Psyol.

It is so warm! I have opened my parasol and balance it against my shoulder as I write. I should like

Later.

I cannot remember where I left off at that moment; Anton Pavlovich *stopped by*, so to speak, to admire me on my throne above the river. He startled me and apologized; he was alone, stretching his legs before going to join the others. I was not to worry, Natasha had come to find them and would return to me shortly, and in the meantime he would hold my parasol and ward off bandits and highwaymen.

With the parasol? I asked.

With my charm and wit. Bandits are particularly fond of charm, and highwaymen literally go to pieces over a chest full of wit.

I'm in good hands, I see.

He sat down beside me. I sensed he must have been wearing a hat and now was fanning the air with the brim. What a peaceful view, he said simply. I should come here to write, as you do. He paused, then said, My brother Nikolay is a painter. When he comes, I'll bring him here, to this very spot. Perhaps you could sit for him, just as you are, with the parasol and your notebook on your lap. You inhabit your own world, with your notebook.

I blushed and said, It keeps me occupied.

Please don't write anything libelous about my hat. It fell in the river, and I rescued it at great risk to my person and my dignity. I imagine it must smell of water sprites and crocodiles.

I shall write exactly what you just told me.

Do that. And you're not to confuse crocodiles with alligators.

Or water sprites with *rusalki*, or good Ukrainian peasants with amateur fishermen from Moscow.

No risk of that.

There was a moment of comfortable yet searching silence. As if there were much he wanted to say but did not dare. So I went first, boldly: And your novel, Anton Pavlovich? How is it coming along—or have you been using the drafts for bait?

Ah, you're teasing me. I don't answer teasing questions.

I smiled, then said with an excess of indulgence, I don't mean to belittle your work. On the contrary, it's very important, and—

But now you do belittle me.

What do you mean?

Implying it must be important.

But it is!

Medicine is important. Building schools is important—what Natalya Mikhailovna is doing. Writing stories, on the other hand, is negligibly lucrative and entertaining, that's all.

You don't really believe that.

There was a pause, and a scrabbling sound as if he were pulling a handful of grass and tossing it beside him, then he gave a slightly scoffing laugh and said, No.

We need novels somehow, don't we? I asked. And why? We need literature and poetry the way we need music or the view of the Psyol—which I have lost, and which makes literature more important to me than ever. Perhaps I've answered my own question. But *why* literature, Anton Pavlovich? Why words? You must know?

Ah, I suppose it's like anything, Zinaida Mikhailovna, like religion or, as you say, music. Is there really an answer? Do we want an answer? For some mysterious reason, a story—and all the more so a poem—finds an echo in one's spirit, first of all. It can entertain, as I said, then it can console, as you said, and obviously, it helps us to see and understand the world. And it asks questions, helps us to find answers—and beauty. Not to forget beauty. And like any other form of art, I suppose literature can—something your mama would like—literature can be *uplifting*—although I do not like the word, I feel I'm being put in a basket and hoisted on pulleys to some mountain monastery where an unwashed monk will be waiting to take receipt of me along with a side of bacon and some smelly cheese.

Yes, I see what you mean, I laughed. Although I suppose it's not the same for everyone.

Not everyone has access to it—too heavy for the basket, perhaps. Take Anya, for example, with her round bottom. I believe her appreciation of art stops at the difference between *sauce à la polonaise* and *sauce à l'ukrainienne*. She's not been educated beyond that. That is why we need schools, to give everyone the wherewithal to appreciate art. Well, you know what I'm getting at, I'm sure.

Yes. And surely you don't need Anya to read your stories. You have enough appreciative readers.

My voice glowed more than I intended, but I continued: And the novel, then—I mean, your novel?

The novel, the novel . . . Yes, I have started, but what I have thus far amounts to no more than a story without an ending. How am I to find the time and continuity to turn it into a novel, between fishing at dawn, and breakfast, and strolling about with Pleshcheyev and Vata, and soothing Mamasha's grievances, and helping your sister, and meeting my friends at the station—

But if you can find time for the stories, surely for the novel it is just a question of perseverance.

Indeed. So it may be my own fault, not the circumstances. With a story, my character arrives with a flourish, waves his smelly hat at me, says, Here's the dilemma, how do I dry my hat? Get that down on paper. And strides off again. Out of my life, and it's done. But how does one deal with a complicated, irascible, endearing landowner or professor with a flighty wife and five brats and two dogs striding into one's life for a whole year of smelly-hat flourishing?

But you do want to write a novel?

Yes, yes! And there are people who want me to do it. I've no end of encouraging souls, they want me to expand, as it were, get my teeth into the big themes, develop my characters beyond the moment of . . . dilemma, let's say, to see repercussions and conflict and redemption and all that, like Tolstoy, I suppose. Yes, it could be good to write about this very view, and how it looks not just now but in winter, too, or in November with the first snowflakes . . .

Oh, yes! When the leaves have fallen, you can see a little cottage over there behind the trees, and the shack on the island, also hidden behind all that growth. Things come to light. It's very different. Melancholic. You wonder if there will ever be lilac again. It's bleak and yet it's beautiful in its way. There are storms, waves on the river, and the islands seem to move . . .

Yes! I could put all that in a novel, couldn't I? But I could also use just that moment in a story.

You must try, if it's what you want, wherever you go for your inspiration—

Please, none of that! As I said, my inspiration is my bank manager—

Oh, Anton Pavlovich, now you really are making fun of me. Excuse me if I'm presumptuous, but I think your inspiration is this view, and my dogs, and my parasol.

Zinaida Mikhailovna, how can I argue with you? So what should I do? How am I to find the endurance, the continuity, to write this novel? How am I to keep my family and friends and the aroma of Anya's sauces from disrupting my work?

What if . . . what if you were to keep a notebook where you could trace out the trajectory of the story so that you knew exactly where your characters were going, and you would remember where they had been—

But half the time I don't know where they're going! That's the magic of the thing—they are completely unruly, downright intractable. I had no idea Sofya Petrovna would leave her husband.

I fell silent. I didn't know what else to suggest. I supposed that writing a novel was a mixture of determination and concentration, and indeed, external factors—like money or noise or a river full of fish—could be terrible distractions.

Well, Anton Pavlovich, I said finally, if there is any way I can assist you, if an audience for your first drafts could help, could urge you on, like those readers in England waiting for the next installment of *Great Expectations*—

Yes, you can play Queen Victoria, and I'll be the court jester bringing you the daily installment of Adventures and Misadventures on the River Psyol.

How deftly he always stepped away from himself. It was quite intriguing, almost exhausting, to try to get to know a person, only to find the jester constantly stepping in between.

Altogether a rather delightful jester.

As if on cue, Natasha arrived to walk with me back to the house.

Maria Pavlovna has been reading to me, a wicked story by her brother called "The Witch." A narrow-minded, foolish deacon accuses his beautiful young wife of seducing all the strange men she meets, while inducing terrible natural phenomena such as thunderstorms and blizzards. Maria Pavlovna sees the story as an allegory for jealousy, that the husband is using the wrath of nature to explain his own anger against his wife's dangerous beauty. I remind her of the deep superstition of country people, and that any form of envy toward beauty or good fortune can be translated into accusations of witchcraft.

No doubt your brother is aware of this, too, I said.

He is certainly aware of the inexplicable mystery of beauty. He reveres it but is also deeply suspicious of it.

(I love to hear Maria Pavlovna speak, with her intonation so similar to Anton Pavlovich's; she uses the same exclamations, the same rhythm to her sentences. And then there is her laugh, altogether her own.)

He is quite the idiot at the moment, she said. He has been talking incessantly about the miller's daughter. You know the one?

Yes, I remember her, though she was still a child, really, the last time I saw her. Blue eyes and thick long hair in coiled braids, flaxen . . . a pure Ukrainian beauty, straight out of a tale. Have you seen her?

She was silent for a moment then said mysteriously, Antosha cannot reconcile the idea of beauty with his everyday life. He must remain in awe of it. I wonder if that is why he has not married.

This afternoon I took Rosa and made my way to the guesthouse. I forced myself somewhat; I haven't been feeling well, a slight dizziness, possibly signaling a seizure. It is very warm. I sense the sky is deep gray, heavy with storm clouds. Still, I'm not looking for excuses; rather, I need to defy my own traitorous body, tell myself that in the heat and electricity and dizziness, I can still do as I like for as long as possible; I will not be bedridden until I am given no choice. And if my defiance helps to defer that time, so much the better. I do not believe, as Mama does, that some venerable bearded men in night shifts are waiting to usher me into the Grand Drawing Room in the Sky. It is now that I want to live.

So, the guesthouse. We made our way slowly; Rosa is so good, she does not run off, she runs circles round me, whines gently if I am slow, as if to indicate where I must go. We went around the back and into the garden, and I paused and leaned on my stick.

I sensed a presence, but no one greeted me. Was I mistaken? I waited for a moment, again thought I heard a faint sound, as of paper or a chair creaking. Then, just as I called, Is anyone there? there was a simultaneous exclamation, and Anton Pavlovich said, Goodness, Zinaida Mikhailovna, you startled me, you and your dog, what quiet ghosts you are on a warm day!

I smiled and apologized and started toward his voice; his hand was on my elbow instantly, leading me up the steps and to a chair.

He shouted to Anya to bring us some tea, then inquired after my health. Fair enough. The same, I lied. And you? I asked. You're alone here? Where are the others?

They've gone to the river; I'll join them later. I was staying behind to read my correspondence.

A rustling of paper.

Oh, I've disturbed you—

Sit, sit, Zinaida Mikhailovna, these can wait.

When the tea arrived, Anya arranged a small table next to me and poured my glass; rarely has that familiar sound of hot flowing liquid against glass seemed more delicious, despite the heat; I might even venture to say nostalgic. (I'm sure Anton Pavlovich would tell me a sound can be neither delicious nor nostalgic, but my senses are all confused, as are words, with loss of vision.)

I receive so many letters now, he said, it's quite astonishing. Most are from people I know, but quite a few from strangers who hope I'll usher them into writerhood.

And will you?

If I . . . if I think they have talent—then they ought to be encouraged, naturally.

And if they haven't?

Well, it's awkward, isn't it. A bit like a rather hopeless case, medically.

(I heard his smile, he sipped his tea.) You have to tell them something they do not want to hear, that they have no talent.

Precisely, he replied. Or that they have talent but write about uninteresting, dull people, or that no one will understand their fantasy, or that they'll never get past the censor. Speaking of censors—

I interrupted him. But surely you should not be the sole judge of their writing abilities? Just as I was seen by several doctors . . . It is, after all, your opinion; someone else—Monsieur Pleshcheyev or Natasha—might read their writing and find it perfectly acceptable.

Of course, this happens all the time, Zinaida Mikhailovna; but they have asked for my opinion, and I must give it them. I give advice if I think there is any hope, naturally—cut out this scene, make that character less verbose, don't give your opinion on the fish in the Psyol, for no one in Moscow or Saint Petersburg could give a kopeck about that—

I laughed and said, There, you're much mistaken. We have the rising star of the Moscow literary world staying in our guesthouse this summer, and he's quite obsessed with the fish in the Psyol.

There was a pleasant silence.

I confess, Zinaida Mikhailovna, that it is a terrible burden—a responsibility—to have to judge another's literary talent. Who indeed am I to judge? Why don't they write to Tolstoy or Leskov?

I'm sure many of them have. But you are very approachable— they must sense that, in your choice of characters. You don't write about counts and grand dukes. Or Napoleon.

Well then, henceforth I shall. Excellent advice, Zinaida Mikhailovna. *Merci.*

Je vous en prie.

One of these letters—he rustled the paper—is from a young

girl in Novorossiysk. She has sent me a novel she has written, and she tells me it is about the love between a prince from Piter and a young girl from Novorossiysk. I haven't read a line yet, but I dread what I shall find. A novel that my mama would read, with a handkerchief at her side—

Anton Pavlovich, you are hard on us. First of all, you do not know if what this young lady has written will be sentimental rubbish. Even if that is her perfume I smell wafting from the page.

He shook the letter: Damask rose, she doesn't skimp.

And you mustn't have such a prejudice against young girls—it may show up in your writing! What other matter does our fine Mother Russia give a woman to write about? What world do they know other than balls and officers and country estates—if they are well-to-do; or hoping for a decent marriage or, worse still, desperately running off with their lovers, as your characters do? Can she write about going to medical school or becoming privy councillor or traveling to Siberia to inspect the forests? No! Anton Pavlovich, you disappoint me, you lack imagination!

He cleared his throat, continued in a low, uncertain tone I had never heard. Zinaida Mikhailovna, you humble me—yes, I have had a moment of terrible prejudice. What can I say?

Say nothing. Just read the first chapter of her novel. Then you will tell me who is right. You don't know, she may be another Madame Sand—a potential Madame Sand, that is—and if you go into her novel with a determination not to accept it or like it because she perfumes her letters and writes about princes, then you are no better than some of the blind and self-regarding characters in your own stories!

No sooner had I said this than I regretted it. Oh, what a wretched day, with this dazzling blinding light in my brain, and the heat! I immediately apologized; I told Anton Pavlovich that I was feeling odd.

But Zinaida Mikhailovna, you're quite right, I insist. Perhaps I am feeling somewhat odd myself, with this burden of correspondents and family and friends.

Tell me—regarding our young lady from Novorossiysk—what is it in so-called ladies' novels that is so repellent to our male readers? Do you know, Anton Pavlovich? I should like to have your opinion.

He made a sort of nervous sound, not a laugh, exactly, nor quite clearing his throat, then said, I believe, from what I have observed of my own brothers and of men in general . . . that love and relations with women complicate our lives immensely. And we wish it were not so—but we have . . . no control. So if you ask us to read a novel that is about nothing but love—love desired and exalted, as women feel, and often write about when they are writers—then as men, we sense we are not only unworthy of such exalted feelings but also trapped—do you understand, Zinaida Mikhailovna?

I nodded. And added very quietly, For a few pages, you might perceive what our lives are made of.

And a good man will have a guilty conscience—never a pleasant sensation; a bad one will be merely bored. Impatient.

That may be, indeed.

But you have been fortunate in your life, as a woman, no? And please don't think that I judge women as I judge novels by girls from Novorossiysk. I would like to think I've known many women with lives not unlike your own—women who are educated and talented, who are interested in the outside world, participating fully—

My life has been like that, yes. And would have continued in that way.

There was a long silence; we drank our tea.

You are very stoic, Zinaida Mikhailovna. You are an example. More than that. If only—

I raised my head. Anton Pavlovich, what else can I be? Others may weep, but self-pity would only blind me further to the life that remains. Am I stoic? I try to live, to understand this time I have, to share and go on helping others with their lives if I can.

You can. He cleared his throat, then said, How have you learned to live with your illness?

(I was tempted to say something glib, like: It has been a very good teacher. But I decided to try to reach inside and understand how, indeed, I had learned this stoicism. If one can really understand and express such a thing.)

It was very hard at first. Of course it came on so gradually, but once the symptoms were unmistakable, there were some days of tears, and not getting out of bed, and—and almost wishing I could die then, and have done with my suffering, and my family's. But after three or four days, I suppose it was my reason, my will, a determination, though none of those things would ever have been strong enough if I did not love life. It is loving life, yes. I am fortunate to have my family; I want to be with them for as long as I can. That's all.

His hand was suddenly upon mine, very warm, slightly damp with the heat. He left it there for a few seconds, the weight of his palm and fingers. I could not see him, other than through his hand. Then he removed it and laughed gently. It is sticky heat, isn't it?

Yes. Perhaps it's going to rain.

Tell me, Zinaida Mikhailovna, these letters I've received—they're quite roughed up, actually. You have busy censors in Sumy, do you?

Yes. Pasha and Georges keep them entertained. Or rather, don't keep them entertained, they know better than to write anything the tsar's censors might relish. But the censors do keep on hoping, and reading, and I expect now you've caught their fancy as well.

A letter from my publisher in Piter. I've invited him to join us, but it's more likely, knowing his tastes and his lifestyle, that I will go to join him, perhaps in July. He has a villa in the Crimea.

Ah.

A fine man, believe me. Your brothers would not care for his politics, but it is thanks to his generosity as a patron of the arts that I am here at all.

A discerning man, then.

May I walk you back?

The chair creaked; he was on his feet.

I'll be fine. Rosa will take me back.

He took my fingers in his; there was the briefest tickle of his beard and mustache against the back of my hand. I giggled, very untypically for me. It was so hot.

I am quite tired from all this writing. My head is splitting. The house is cool and quiet. I look forward to some sleep.

KATYA WOKE WITH A start and turned to look at the clock on the bedside table. Five-forty-five. Instinctively she stretched out her arm, but the place next to her was empty. Peter had not come back by the time she went to bed, and somehow she had slept all night without realizing he was not there. Usually, she would wake with a start much earlier and lie there sleepless until he came home. Now the empty darkness suited her, all this space to think her gloomy thoughts without worrying that he might notice.

The first shock on awakening: It was always there. The wall they were facing. Sometimes she imagined herself as a little girl, hopping up and down to get a quick glimpse over the wall. What might lie on the other side. But she had been taller and braver as an imaginary little girl; as she had been as a real young woman, to leave the Soviet Union.

Peter had come with a group of students from Britain for summer courses in Russian. She was standing in line to buy ice cream on Pushkin Square, and he was just behind her, and you could tell right away that he wasn't Russian, from his good clothes, then his accent when his turn came to buy his ice cream. She had assumed he was Hungarian or Czech. She was still standing by the ice cream cart, putting her change purse away, and he simply turned and asked her what kind of ice cream she had bought. There were only two kinds, but he wanted to be sure to have one like hers, for some reason. It was vanilla with a chocolate crust; the chocolate always melted too quickly and fell in regrettable flakes onto the pavement. She stood there eating her ice cream and asked him if he liked it. Then, walking a short distance from the ice cream vendor, and seeing that he'd followed, she asked him where he was from. He asked her if she spoke English, and she said, Yes, but let's not talk here. She led him over to a quiet bench.

She was nervous and looked around the park from time to time, fearful of seeing a fellow student who might ask her, Who were you with on Pushkin Square? The young Englishman seemed oblivious to her apprehension, and she had to keep asking him to lower his voice.

They inspected each other with a polite yet avid curiosity. *You are the enemy, Brezhnev always said so. You poor girl, they've brainwashed you, haven't they.* The Cold War had made them mutually exotic, in a way that Katya suspected no longer existed in the world. The fact that she, as a Soviet citizen, was not supposed to be meeting people from the West gave an adulterous spice to their encounter. The political and social transgressiveness of it.

At the time she couldn't imagine that these were the last weeks and months of the nagging, persistent, inbred fear. That only five years later, her country would dissolve into a chaotic openness, for a time, anyway. Nor could she imagine on that warm summer day that she would spend the rest of her life with this pink-cheeked Englishman with his posh accent and slight stutter, who was asking her about her studies and whether it was at all possible for her to travel to England.

She looked at him and laughed. What do they teach you in Russian class in London? Don't you know we're not allowed to travel?

He stuttered an apology, then said, On some of our excursions here, we've been with students who told us they've been to Scotland to study English.

She laughed. Because those are the children of good party members. They've been selected to meet you. I'm just an ordinary student, not a good one. We could get in trouble, you see. The others have permission to meet you. It's called privilege.

They had finished their ice creams, and he asked her name.

For a second she hesitated, then felt the first stirrings of a defiance that would get her all the way to Britain. I'm Katya.

And I'm Peter.

That's a good Russian name, she said. I'm very happy to meet you.

He told her he would skip class if she would meet him the next day. She thought for a moment and said, All right, let's go to the Tretyakov Gallery. Have you been there?

Later, in the early years, he would tell her that he had fallen in love with her over a painting. On a previous visit to the gallery with his group, the Intourist guide had hurried them through the icons and the avant-garde Soviet artists. Now Katya led him to the paintings of Isaak Levitan, whom he did not know. Bucolic, typically Russian landscapes with birch trees and wide expanses, full of stillness and a faint melancholy. Not bold, but unique in their way. There was one in particular where they stood for a long time, oblivious, as crowds of children in their Young Pioneer uniforms and Western tourists with their stern guides swirled around them. It was a river scene, with two churches on the far side, a cluster of towers and onion domes. A road led down to the river and then away from the other side, almost as if a horse and carriage could drive across the river unimpeded. There was a small jetty with some fishing boats, and a larger boat conveying people to the other shore. There was an evening light with clouds, a gentle summer serenity.

Katya turned to Peter and said in Russian, We're in the picture. We are on this side of the river, obviously, and we have to find a way to get to the other side.

He took a moment, probably searching for his words in Russian, then said ungrammatically but eloquently, You don't mind if our English churches don't have onion domes?

She laughed, not sure whether he was joking or whether he had truly read her thoughts. I don't mind, she said.

He took her hand very discreetly, gave it a squeeze, and said, I'll find a way to get us to the other side.

Somewhere she had a reproduction of the painting. It was called *Evening Bells. Vecherni zvon.* Actually, *Bells* was not a correct translation, the Russian word *zvon* stood for the sound the bells made. And it was an onomatopoeia. *Dong.* Not so nice in English. *Evening Dong.* No, definitely not. Ah, the poverty of English. She sat there and said *zvon* aloud several times, as if ringing a bell. She liked the idea that Levitan had given his painting a cross-sensory title. She would look for the reproduction, later.

Now they were standing on another riverbank, without a bridge, and she didn't know who would get them across this time. How wonderful it had been, to have that kind young man literally step into her life. She was not sure that she was still the same young woman he had found eating her ice cream, or that he was the same ferryman. They'd had many good times together, despite the difficulties, and he had given her the best life. Her mother often told her that, in almost every letter, every phone call.

She had not told her mother anything about her current troubles. She did not want to disillusion her or give her added cause for concern.

Later that day, she found the postcard of *Evening Bells* in a shoebox of small, insignificant treasures she had kept from that other life. Other postcards, badges, tickets to the Moscow Art Theatre, the Conservatory. The painting was not altogether as she remembered it; for a moment she wondered if their conversation about crossing the river could really have taken place. On this side, the road seemed more of a footpath for fishermen to reach their boats; on the other side, it brought villagers to enjoy the river.

She propped the postcard against the saltshaker on the kitchen table.

Peter came home in the middle of the afternoon, unshaven and smelling of whisky. He told her he had slept at the office again, which was what she had suspected, although he had not answered her calls.

What's this? he asked when he sat down for tea and saw *Evening Bells*.

Levitan.

The painter? Chekhov's friend?

Yes.

How did you get this?

He flipped it over, saw the inscription in Russian on the back.

I've had it. I kept it. Remember?

Remember what?

The Tretyakov Gallery. The day after the day we met.

We went there the day after the day we met?

Yes, Peter. You told me you fell in love with me over this painting.

It's this one, is it?

Well, it wasn't *Ivan the Terrible and His Son Ivan*.

Why don't I remember it?

She went over to him, put one hand on his head, the other around his shoulder. Because . . . you have a lot on your mind. Because memory is selective. Because you remember Levitan as Chekhov's friend and not as the witness to the moment we fell in love.

You always told me I fell in love first.

You forget I grew up in the Soviet Union. We're very good at rewriting history.

He laughed, shook his head, then looked up at her, his eyes shining. After a moment his smile faded and he said, You won't leave me, will you, Kate, no matter what happens with the business?

She kissed him on the forehead. We'll find a way, she said.

There seems to be a terrific amount of coming and going at the guesthouse. Noise, shouting: Two of Anton Pavlovich's brothers have arrived. Nikolay and Ivan. Nikolay is an artist. According to Natasha, who has been talking to Masha, he is very gifted but leads a regrettably dissolute life, squandering his talents and reputation (she said this with a mixture of irony and admiration) on drinking and women and borrowing money he doesn't pay back. Ivan, on the other hand, is quiet and hardworking and terribly good. He's a teacher, a solid citizen. And he's very good-looking, even more handsome than Anton Pavlovich, she suggests.

How odd. I have not met Anton Pavlovich's brothers, yet I feel a pinch of jealousy. Natasha says they go everywhere with him. Although I've known him scarcely a month, I have grown altogether too dependent on my ability to catch his attention and share some of his precious time—as if I had my own appointed moments in his life. Perhaps I fear, too, the flamboyance of our handsome Russian youth. I hear them shouting, singing, someone is drunk already. It is too tiresome to worry about, but something is pinching at me inside, somewhere between regret and fear.

No doubt because of our shared profession and his, I would say, extraordinary ability to treat me as myself, I do not want to lose the special understanding I have with Anton Pavlovich. It is as if he feels more comfortable with me because I cannot *see* him with my eyes, so he in turn opens a door that the others keep shut: He allows me to go on being normal. That is a great

gift. Even my sisters and Mama tend to fuss over me—and I
let them, at times I have no choice—but to spend even fifteen
minutes talking about this or that with Anton Pavlovich sets
me into the present tense I once took for granted, without the
terrible weight of the future.

June 4, 1888

Perhaps my fears are justified after all—it has been three days
now since I've seen Anton Pavlovich. (I write *seen*, but that is a
convention, language does not accommodate blindness any better
than the rest of nature or society does.)

They have been swimming and fishing, says Natasha.

It is too hot to be outdoors during the day. I spend time on
the veranda, but without company, my inspiration, I am finding
it hard to write. This notebook has been open on my lap for
an inestimable amount of time, my hand closed stiffly around
the pen. The ink dries. Mama, Elena, Pasha, Georges—all are
elsewhere; Natasha is in her social world (she is learning to fish,
but Anton Pavlovich tells her women don't have the patience,
although they have patience for other things, like children. And
men). Only Tonya comes now and again with her heavy body
to sit with me. She is more and more frightened of childbirth
as the day approaches. I reassure her, point to the noisy brood
of Chekhovs to show her how people come into the world to
unshakable sturdiness.

If only I could read. I used to read so much when I was alone,
especially as a girl. Gogol and Dostoyevsky and Turgenev,
of course, but also the foreign authors, Dickens and Balzac
and Madame Sand. And lesser-known authors who wrote of
adventure and travel and discovery. I read of all those foreign

places, all those people whose lives could not be more different from our own, and I would look around Luka and know how fortunate I was. Mama's life has been hard, but she has done her best to create a kingdom for us here. I once had the opportunity to travel to Vienna with Lyudmila Nikolayevna and her mother, but I declined, because it would have meant being away at harvesttime, and I couldn't miss it for anything. The colors, the singing, the festivities—the same renewed each year, but always different. I went briefly to the harvest feast last year and prayed I would find the joy and renewal that had always sustained me, but the colors had faded inexorably—my vision had faded, I should say, was almost gone, and Elena led me here and there, and there were the smells and sounds, the fragrances I had grown up with, more intense than ever, but I missed the kaleidoscope of images.

Now that I live this circumscribed existence, I tend to look back and try to determine what I miss the most, what I deemed necessary for my sustenance—even though now it is no longer *necessary* at all, reduced as I am to idle memories and the tedium of the waiting room.

But let me not think of that.

And how are you doing with the young lady from Novorossiysk? Is she legible?

He gave a hesitant laugh. Edible, is more like it. She's an absolute pudding.

It was my turn to laugh. What do you mean?

She writes well, she has promise, but she doesn't know when to stop. She goes on and on in her descriptions—landscapes, feelings, even the family servants—until the words become as thick as jam.

Then it doesn't seem that she writes well after all.

But she does! All she needs to do is to go back and eliminate the second and third sentence of every paragraph, and she'll have a fine novel!

I believe he expected me to laugh, but when I didn't, he knew that I was not satisfied with his ironic dismissal. And indeed he said, No, of course it's not that simple. She overwrites. Instead of saying Timofey Kazimirovich opened the door with the key, or opened the locked door, she says, Timofey Kazimirovich put the key in the lock, turned it, pressed the handle, and pulled the door open. But I believe she can easily eliminate all the chaff, and she'll have a charming story of unrequited love that will appeal to sensitive young women and their mamas. And perhaps the odd prince.

So the young woman does not get her prince?

Alas, no. She is too provincial, and an heiress from Piter sweeps him off to Baden-Baden.

I could not help but laugh. Oh, Anton Pavlovich, you were right all along, it sounds dreadful!

No, Zinaida Mikhailovna, it's not dreadful—you see, I read it right through, beyond your first chapter; she's established the suspense, and you really do want to find out whether little Tatyana Fyodorovna will succeed in catching her prince. And it's not for lack of trying, poor girl. A clever young heroine, like her author.

Baden-Baden?

Quite. I suspect she's been there, so she's neither entirely poor nor provincial, our author—her descriptions of German matrons are an absolute treasure. I shall tell her as much. Not to cut a word, there, in any case. For all the surplus folds of flesh and swaths of taffeta.

We are by the pond; it is late afternoon, almost evening. The air is cooler; I have had so little time with Anton Pavlovich since his brothers arrived. He is in constant demand, especially from Nikolay. As for his novel, it is, he says, on the top shelf of the wardrobe, at the back, behind three blankets and under a dozen pillowcases.

Tell me what you see, Anton Pavlovich? I ask. Just now, just here, from where we are sitting.

I see, he says, the evening light on the pond . . . the sky is clear, there are two or three clouds over Sumy. There are rushes and reeds on the opposite bank, your sister and Masha are strolling, both wearing long white dresses like summer brides; now Natasha has stopped, she's turning to Masha and waving her hand, as if to make a point, and now Masha is bending at the waist, doubled over in laughter. Vanya and Kolya are farther along, sitting on the bench, slouching, not looking at each other. Vata and her friend Lizaveta Nikolayevna from the town are rowing Monsieur Pleshcheyev around the pond, as they do every evening. They are gazing admiringly at him and are even refraining from giggling, as you can hear. He is like a cat having its whiskers stroked. And here comes Rosa, her tongue hanging out and full of drool, she's been looking for you—

Rosa jumps against my knees. I hold her head, feel her warm ears, her doggie vibrancy.

Perhaps Anton Pavlovich described something more; it doesn't matter. I asked him to tell me what he saw not so much for him to be my eyes but so I could hear his voice. It is a way of seeing him. I did ask him once to describe himself to me—what was he wearing, how had he combed his hair that morning, but he snorted at me in a friendly way and said I would be terrified if I did see him, that he was a cross between a crocodile and a boa constrictor, with a billy goat's beard, and that he had borrowed his brother's tunic, the one with the paint splashes all over it, and some felt boots that Grigory Petrovich had left in the yard, equally smeared with horse manure, and to complete the picture, a pince-nez and a top hat.

But he understood my need to see, to know—and to

laugh—and since that time by the pond, he has spontaneously described the river, the trees, the sky, the figures in white or the young men strolling or Grigory Petrovich and Anya with their loads. There are shadows of light; he has a way of speaking that no laborious efforts of my own can ever reproduce with this sorry pen.

I've been thinking about solitude. Perhaps having company like Anton Pavlovich is making it more difficult for me to be alone. Solitude is something I have discovered only since I became ill. To be sure, I have spent time alone—in Piter as a student; or on the road on a house call to a faraway village; on occasion when traveling to and from Luka. But it was never the sort of deep solitude of unending self-accompaniment, only an interlude, and there was always someone waiting at the other end, or someone who came to interrupt my indulgence in the anatomy textbook.

Now I am surrounded by people, but I am alone, I cannot accompany them in what they are seeing and doing, where their busy steps are taking them. Natasha has quite abandoned me for the Chekhovs, who have swollen in number yet again with the arrival of the eldest, Aleksandr. According to Natasha, he is a tall man with large questioning eyes, as if he's just woken up, although she says his gaze is not so much full of sleep as of vodka.

(With good cause: He has recently lost his wife and has two little boys to bring up alone now; he has left them with an aging aunt in Moscow to come here and literally, it would seem, drown his sorrows.)

So Natasha is there and I am here (with this notebook, among my thoughts), and I am learning—because it is a harsh apprenticeship—how to turn solitude from an enforced exclusion to a welcome introspection. People who are writers, like Anton Pavlovich and Monsieur Pleshcheyev, might be the only people, other than religious hermits and anchorites, who need or seek

solitude. Even if Anton Pavlovich writes in a corner of a crowded
room, he is alone in his head, alone in his thoughts; otherwise,
how could he enter an alternative world to give us a story?
Solitude does this: It is a vast room, emptied of people, where we
must create our own world. Or concentrate upon the world we see
or hear or smell. I have lost my sight but have gained sensitivity
to those other senses that I never suspected could exist. I have
learned not to depend on others but to use my solitude to reflect
deeply on life and not just float on the surface, as I used to,
happy to agree with others or adopt their opinions as my own. I
have learned a greater attentiveness to the world through sound
and smell, and I am somehow closer to an essence of life, to its
significance, than when I was busy as a doctor, always rushing
about and concerned with other things. Thoughts come to me
now that once would have seemed irrelevant or uninteresting,
as if my soul suddenly came out of hiding, no longer ashamed
of its isolation, shouting ideas like those itinerant preachers in
America one hears about. It quite astonishes me at times, and I
will try to reproduce these unexpected visitations on the paper,
as my strength allows. Sadly, I realize that paper is the only
thing that still stands between me and mortality, and the idea
that placing my scrawl—perhaps it is totally illegible by now—
on this page for the generations to follow—Tonya and Pasha's
little one, to start with—is a comfort and a reason to hope. They
may not like what they will read someday, but their eyes will
keep me alive in memory.

ANA LOOKED AROUND AT the snow-covered fields and forest. For a long time she didn't move, until the chill began to penetrate her light jacket. Then she lifted one foot after the other, stomped her skis on the ground in readiness, and set off along the trail.

She had decided to give herself the day off. She hadn't been skiing since she started on Zinaida Mikhailovna's diary; she needed the air, the movement, the silence. The forecast was good—slightly overcast for now but sunshine later on. It had snowed the previous day, and the boughs of pine and fir were heavy with Christmas-card perfection.

For a good quarter of an hour, she simply moved with the progression of the trail—slight inclines, nothing steep that would require too great an effort or instill a fear of speed going downhill. Ana had found a fairly flat trail in the Jura Mountains that she liked coming to; the drive was long, but she listened to music, singing out loud—opera, Irish folk, nineties pop songs, whatever was on her aging cassettes—and once she was here, the trail was worth it, because there weren't many other skiers, especially during the week, and the geography was sublime. None of the drama of the Alps, but old farms tucked in hollows between forests and sloping fields, with the occasional brief sighting of the lake in the distance and, above all, a stillness and serenity that filled her each time with gratitude and wonder. She was alone with the sound of her breath, the smooth swish of her long skis, the occasional crisp reaction of the snow to her passage.

Once she was warmed up and no longer needed to concentrate on the trail and her rhythm, her thoughts began to wander, as they usually did, to the reasons why she loved this simple sport. She might never have tried it, might have followed friends and fellow students to the downhill slopes in a resort near Grenoble, had she not met— just after Moscow and during what was meant to be her only year in Paris—a dark boy with a poetic allure who, almost on a dare, invited her for a weekend of cross-country skiing in the Morvan. Her friends had been teasing him, saying that cross-country was for old people, and where was the excitement, where were the bars and the places for parties—but this boy was unflappable, criticizing them in return for their snobbish bourgeois values, launching into a long tirade about how downhill skiing destroyed the environment and contributed to class warfare. At which point the other students whooped with laughter; only Ana sat there quietly, almost gravely, wondering if he didn't have a point, and concluding that he was certainly brave to express it, and her silent approval earned her the defiant invitation to the Morvan in his battered Deux Chevaux. You can't tip these things over, he said, taking the bends at breakneck speed. You want me to try? Ana was terrified, and euphoric. Before they even passed Fontainebleau, she knew she would go anywhere with this boy. His name was Léo.

Now she paused in the first spray of sunlight, her breath rising in a cloud. Léo had taught her how to ski; she still had that. Mathieu, on the other hand, used to hire a chalet in some high alpine resort, and Ana would have to drive back down the mountain, often in an abortive quest for a well-groomed cross-country trail. They would meet again in the evening, and Ana would listen to Mathieu's long descriptions of his exploits off-piste, the thrill of it, and at least once a year he would say, That damned lover of yours, teaching you cross-country. *Quel con*, what was he thinking? And even now, as Mathieu's remembered taunts resonated in her inner silence, she thought of Léo and wondered if she skied for his sake, as a kind of tribute to their time together.

No, of course not. It had ended badly, he had hurt her, but with the years, in his case, she had learned to separate the good memories from the bad, to be grateful to have had him in her life. To those memories she affixed the label *Love of My Life*, though he would not have approved, not Léo, with his adamantine dislike of emotion. Love was sex; love was skiing on a bright morning through a forest of lace-strewn evergreens, turning every now and again to smile.

She set off again; she could feel her heart working; her left thigh was beginning to ache. I'm becoming too sedentary, she chided herself.

She came out of the forest into a clearing and caught her breath as she slid to a halt. The sky was blue; she could hear the first dripping of melting snow. The clearing was sparkling, blanketed in white, with a ragged fringe of pine trees. The absolute stillness enveloped her in something beyond mere reverence or well-being. Ana, for all her words, could not define it, but she also knew this was why she came here—rarely, but often enough not to forget. She liked to think of these moments as pure distillations of solitude, as a necessary communion with self and nature of the sort that mystics and hermits practiced. There was no loneliness, no longing to be with anyone. She breathed deeply, closed her eyes, flung her head back, and let the sun pour over her.

Once he knew she'd gotten the hang of her skis, Léo had started going far ahead, leaving her behind, instructing her in a skill beyond mere skiing. When, both angry and elated, she eventually caught up with him, she invariably found him smoking in the sun, and he would say something teasing, like, Well, did you find your God?

Now there was no one to catch up with, no one waiting, casually smoking. And that was fine. Yet for a split second Ana thought she would like to see Léo again, or someone like him, with whom to exchange cryptic, teasing remarks.

But then she would lose the silence, just when she had learned how to listen for its message.

There was a dreadful argument over dinner. Mama had made some religious reference, as she is wont to do, something about Our Savior and the afterlife.

Pasha turned to her and said, Mama, you've been listening to the priest again, it's all just superstition, you know that. How can you read your scholarly journals and yet believe that nonsense? Don't you realize the church and the government conspire to enslave the people?

She sputtered a few words of protest: But it's faith, Pashenka, how can you not understand this? You must just let God's goodness—

Goodness, shouted Georges, if God were good, would He have let this happen?

There was a heavy silence in the room, and I sensed he might be pointing at me. Then he cried out, almost in tears, What compassionate God would allow our sister to, to— How can He exist, how can He call himself God if He does exist and yet He sends this terrible disease? It's not as if she were some Petersburg flibbertigibbet, she has been a useful member of society, actually saving lives, not taking them away! What, Mama, what can you say to that?

Elena was trying to break in, her voice soothing, her words unintelligible. Mama was sobbing. I felt quite uncomfortable crushed between Herr Marx and Christ the Lord. Of course Georges is right, and I know from witnessing medical proof of the suffering of others that God is not compassionate, if He even exists—but does that mean He does not exist in Mama's soul? Even if He does not exist in mine or in Georges's?

I held out my hand, waved it, tried to attract their attention. Then I turned to Georges and said, Just because you don't believe, does that mean Mama cannot? Or must not? Your Marx is telling you *not* to believe, and that is no different from the village priest telling Mama *to* believe. Can't truth be relative, or selective, in matters of faith? Does truth even apply to faith? It isn't science . . .

Exactly, shouted Pasha. Which is why it must not be credited. It is superstition, Mama, that is all there is to it. You are afraid of death, so you believe that dying is just going to another place. There is no other place.

Stop it, please, both of you, shouted Natasha, this is cruelty, you are being cruel to Mama, cruel to Zina. Are you so proud that you aren't afraid of death? With your high-minded intellectual proof that God does not exist, you think it makes you immortal? Why can't you see that other people have a right to believe? What difference does it make to you if Mama believes?

Because we love her, shouted Georges, and we want what's best for her. Religion will deceive her, you'll see, Mama, there will be no consolation.

Oh no, my dear boys, said Mama firmly, roused from her tears, I will be saved, and I'll have the satisfaction of knowing my poor daughter is in heaven. And that *she* is saved.

I did not have the heart to contradict Mama openly; I know she wants me to believe in an afterlife, it makes *her* feel better. Georges and Pasha know what I think and that I generally agree with them. But what I feel? As I go toward greater darkness, might I not begin to crave the so-called light of God?

There was a scraping of chairs, and Pasha grumbled that he'd heard enough. He left the room with Georges. We women sat on in silence for a while. Natasha reached over and held my hand. Stupid boys, she muttered, then laughed, more nervously than in amusement.

As I write and think of God and solitude, I find myself sharing my thoughts—too rapid to commit all of them to paper—with an absent Anton Pavlovich. What would he say? What would he make of our discussion? I know he teased Mama gently for reading Schopenhauer; on the other hand, he is friends with that right wing press magnate in Piter, that Suvorin man he mentioned, with his villa in the Crimea, so he cannot wholly defend my brothers' socialist point of view—or can one somehow reconcile such conflicting loyalties?

Perhaps that is the gift of his writing, why he pleases his readers so—to be able to take on all of life's contradictions with equanimity, befriend people of every station and every creed. He is friends with Artyomenko the factory worker; he is friends with Monsieur Suvorin the Petersburg press magnate. He is friends with little Panas and with the venerable Pleshcheyev. Would Anton Pavlovich agree with everything we say or simply refuse to be drawn? He does not share his opinions easily, I have noticed.

June 6, 1888

According to Natasha, Elena seems quite taken with Aleksandr Pavlovich, Anton Pavlovich's widowed brother, even after only a few days' acquaintance. They go for long walks in the evening; they were caught in the thunderstorm last night. Elena came home so drenched, you could hear the water in her clothes and shoes. She didn't seem to mind.

Anton Pavlovich has confirmed to me that his brother drinks but that he has had a very hard life. His parents never approved of the woman who became his wife, and their first child died; now she, too, has died, so recently. He tries to act normally, but I can sense, from the few times I've been in the same room with him, a kind of frenzy, a terrible restlessness trying to hide grief and expiate it at the same time.

What did Aleksandr Pavlovich's wife die of? I asked Elena later that day.

Consumption, she replied. After a pause she continued, The brother has it, too, did you know? Although I'm not sure he knows it.

Which brother?

Nikolay, the artist.

We fell silent. We both knew, we have seen more than our share of the disease. Some sufferers live a long time and are able to fight it; others succumb well before their time, like Aleksandr Pavlovich's wife. I asked Elena her opinion regarding Nikolay; she did not answer. We spoke of other things.

June 8, 1888

Elena came to see me earlier on her way back from a house call. She seemed relieved—a child with scarlet fever who is doing much better—but once she had shared this information, she lapsed into a hesitant silence of sighing and throat clearing. Finally, I said, do you have something on your mind, Lenochka?

(I was beginning to suspect what it might be, as Natasha has made a few comments, but Elena has always found it difficult to speak openly.)

She said, I'm rather confused. I cannot decide whether Aleksandr Pavlovich enjoys my company.

Clearly he does, or he wouldn't be seeking you out—there's no lack of company at the moment.

Oh, but you know, Zina, I'm a doctor, and he needs one. But I'm not sure I'm the right sort. Of doctor.

What do you mean?

Well, he talks endlessly, and he's had the most wretched time of it with his wife dying, and it seems his little boys are very slow in developing, and his life is such chaos. He says so himself. But he seems talented, and intelligent, as they all are. I think he has come to me for consolation, because I listen when others don't. I mean it is a bit much, here his wife died not two weeks ago, and all the others think of is going fishing.

Well, then you, at least, are helping him.

Yes, but you see, I wouldn't like my good nature to lead me astray . . . if you see what I mean.

I paused, then said, Do you mean that you enjoy his company for reasons other than listening to his misfortunes?

Oh, Zina, that's what I don't know! Sometimes the doctor in me is so dominant—the need to care, to heal—that I can't see anything anymore of the person I am, or once was, of my own heart or mind; perhaps the doctor has gone off with them. Perhaps I have become my work.

Bluntly, I said, Would you like to feel something for Aleksandr Pavlovich? Is that the problem?

Oh, it's not a problem! Please, Zina, I've said too much already, but you can see what the situation is: a young widower with two difficult children, and an unmarried doctor with few prospects beyond her work. It's glaring, isn't it?

And the children?

I don't know them! I love children, but I don't know *them*, I hardly know their father! What should I do, Zina? I would hate to let him think something that isn't true.

She reached out and took my hand. Her palm was warm and damp.

I'm not really the right person to ask, I ventured. Have you spoken with Mama?

But she'll only tell me to go after him, as if I were Anton Pavlovich on his way to the river with his fishing pole and basket! She can be such a contradiction—fighting for our education, proud of our achievements, then thrusting us at widowers and bachelors.

I'm not sure she would do that, don't anticipate. I think you needn't do anything, Lena. Give him time. So recently bereaved, he's not seeing things clearly; he's turned to you because you listen. I expect that's all he wants from you at the moment. Don't you think?

She squeezed my hand and put her arms around me and held me for a long time.

Neither of us mentioned the fact that Aleksandr Pavlovich has been drinking vodka almost constantly since arriving at Luka. It would have seemed callous, perhaps, given his recent loss.

June 10

Aleksandr Pavlovich left quite abruptly during the night, said Natasha. It's not very clear why.

Elena does not seem upset, did not even comment on the fact. Perhaps it's all for the best.

June 12, 1888

Monsieur Pleshcheyev departed on the morning train. Mama
sighs, consoles Vata, and they wander around the house like
two restless children. They have come to me on the veranda
no fewer than three times each to say things like, How quiet
it will seem without him (totally untrue, you've never heard
noisier than the Chekhov brothers); or, Just think, this great
man was staying *here* and we rowed him around the pond; or,
I shall reread all of his poetry, and perhaps Georges could set
that sonnet to music. I don't know quite what's overcome them,
they were not so ridiculous when he was here. Perhaps they
worried he might surprise them at any minute. He did have
an odd way of suddenly being there, his voice booming into
the room.

June 14, 1888

I hear the birds; I hear the river, like a whisper reminding me of
other things. Otherwise, Luka is silent. Georges, Natasha, Vata,
and Anton Pavlovich have taken Roman and the carriage and
set off for Sorochintsy, among other places; they will be staying
with the Smagins, who have an estate not far from there. Once
I would have joined them. I could have told them a lot about the
region . . . Never mind, Natasha knows even more, and is not shy,
and will ensure them of a good time.

Maria Pavlovna often comes to join me for tea, as we are quite
alone and dull without Natasha. She is shy with me; she brings
books with her, and when silence weighs on us, she offers to read.
We take advantage of her brother's absence to read more from *In
the Twilight*. When he is here, if he recognizes his own words, he

tries to snatch the book away, tickling Maria Pavlovna, pleading, Stop reading that rubbish.

But we both know that in a deeper place, he is proud of his work; it is the attention he does not like. I can understand that, just from writing these lines. Perhaps he is inventing people and situations, but nevertheless they have come from somewhere inside him, and not just his brain. He has taken close, secret feelings and worked them into a form he can reveal, but he is giving some part of himself to be examined, scrutinized, approved, or condemned . . . It is the same with Georges and the piano: When he first started playing as a little boy, he would chase us all out of the room if he had to practice, and he would say, How can I practice if you are here listening to me? And Elena or Mama would say, How can you want to perform for others someday if you don't let them listen? And he would get red in the face, almost as if he were about to cry, and he would say, You are trying to steal my notes. There won't be any music if you steal my notes. Now go away.

Fortunately for Georges and for us, with time he overcame this fear of attention, though I suppose the notion of performing is a kind of nakedness—soul-nakedness. We are listening, taking words and music into our souls. It is such a dangerous openness, it requires so much trust to give that to another person . . . it's a wonder anyone dares to be so open, and yet thankfully, most of us do open our selves . . . otherwise how would we ever know what is inside another person's soul? What we say when sharing our thoughts is not the same.

For example, Maria Pavlovna talks about her brothers, gives me all sorts of information about them—I have completely muddled up the details of their lives—but what she doesn't say (and that I hear the loudest) is that it is Anton Pavlovich she is closest to; she is very proud of him and protective at the same time. Her Antosha. She is sharing him with my family, but she misses him, and I know she worries—about his future, whether they will be parted, would he be happy with a wife—although she doesn't talk about it. She speaks little of herself, and that, too, is telling.

I believe that she has forfeited a life of her own to devote it to her brothers. Or rather, she has chosen to make them—Anton Pavlovich in particular—her life's work. She is the only girl; her mother is solid yet often overwrought, and Maria Pavlovna knows no selfishness.

June 16, 1888

This afternoon it rained; it grew too dark in the room for Maria Pavlovna to read to me, so she told me of a dreadful — yet comic—incident that occurred last week, shortly before Monsieur Pleshcheyev and Aleksandr Pavlovich left and the others set off for Sorochintsy.

A magician was performing at the summer theater in Sumy that evening, and after dinner Natasha persuaded all the Chekhov siblings, along with Ivanenko and Vata and Elena and Georges, to go to see the show. I could hear their laughter and merriment long after they departed, a kind of echo on the still air. One or two of the brothers were already well into their vodka. I sat with Mama on the veranda—such a night, warm and full of other sounds of insects, and the hoopoe, and the nightingales. She held my hand and reminisced about our childhood; it was sad. I wanted to go to sleep, but I knew she wanted me there with her.

So, the magician. Maria Pavlovna told me the whole story, bemused, half laughing, half annoyed. I will try to reproduce her words, just as she told it.

For one of his tricks, she said, the magician asked for a
volunteer from the audience. My brother Sasha went up:
He began to joke with the magician in his jovial way, and
everyone in the small audience was astonished—he made them
look like utter fools, but the magician himself seemed to be
delighted.

I think, confided Maria Pavlovna almost apologetically, that
Sasha was quite drunk. It was embarrassing. He was shouting
and waving his arms and saying Abracadabra and Boo! and
making faces at the magician. Some people laughed, but Antosha
decided it was time to go up and remove him from the stage, and
Sasha swore and insulted him in front of everyone. By then I'd
seen enough, as had Elena Mikhailovna, and we begged Antosha
to leave with us, and the three of us went for a walk by the river.

Sasha did not return all night—we speculated that the
magician had caused him to vanish. Until we learned from
Georges that Sasha went straight from the theater to the
station and took the first train back to Moscow. At two o'clock
in the morning!

To begin with, your sisters were very worried when they
learned that he had left. They were concerned that he was
somehow displeased with the guesthouse—Sasha is the eldest,
after all—but apparently, he said to Georges—who repeated it
to Natasha, who repeated it to me—*Tell them that the only ones
I'm happy with are you and Ivanenko, but as for the others . . .* It's
dreadful! He didn't even finish his sentence. Goodness knows
what he meant, perhaps the fact that we walked out during
his *performance*? To make things worse, when I mentioned the
incident to Antosha, he conjectured that our brother had spoken
out of drunken spite.

She paused, perhaps for effect, then leaned closer to me. You
see, he wrote a letter to your sister, Elena, asking for her hand in
marriage (here Maria Pavlovna and I could not help but exclaim

and laugh nervously). However, Antosha discovered the letter and tore it up before Sasha had a chance to send it.

What? I exclaimed.

Sasha wasn't serious, concluded Maria Pavlovna softly, he can't have been; he's so confused, he's lonely and he drinks and he thinks of his two small sons whom he must look after, no one understands him at all; he thinks that proposing marriage to your sister is a noble, grand gesture when it is unfounded and hasty and . . . *ridiculous* and makes us all look bad. So I think that's why Antosha tore up the letter.

We sat for a moment in silence. Then she took my hand and gave a quiet, musing, wistful laugh. I sighed. On the surface, it seemed almost a pity; Elena had begun by feeling genuinely fond of Aleksandr Pavlovich, certainly concerned about him and not unaware of the possible consequences. But this behavior at the theater, even related at second hand . . . I felt that for now I could not help but commend Anton Pavlovich's intervention.

I turned to Masha and said, I don't want Elena to learn of this, she takes things far too much to heart. I believe she has been feeling genuinely sorry for Aleksandr Pavlovich. Her pity overwhelms her at times.

Maria Pavlovna mumbled something; I had to ask her to repeat it.

Is she hoping to marry?

I think she doesn't really know. She's torn. She would like a family, but she loves her work. She has been working so hard that she forgets other aspects of life. You've seen her; she treats the entire village like her children, losing sleep if this one sneezes, that one coughs—

Sasha is not a good man for her, said Masha emphatically. Your good peasants need her more than one man with two orphans and too great a fondness for his bottle.

ANA HAD BEEN SLEEPING well, working with ease, losing herself in pages of Ukrainian summer.

When she finished her work, she turned to the BBC website and read about the Ukrainian winter. She watched short videos showing the demonstrations on the Maidan: They had turned violent. The sky was dark with the smoke of burning tires. Already eight protesters had been killed, many others injured.

Young people, despite their broken English, spoke eloquently and passionately to the reporters about their desire for change. *These people died for my future.* In the background, a brightness of flames from the braziers they lit to keep warm. Music, chanting, speeches. Ana had never been part of such a movement. At times she felt a surge of compassion that brought her close to tears, then relief: For all her isolation, she was still part of the human race; she could still feel.

She had never been political; she had left that to Léo. He was the one who went to all the demonstrations, who spent hours in cafés with his friends from university, planning, debating, arguing. Sometimes he would drag her along to the Latin Quarter for a *manif,* to swell the numbers, but she never felt at ease with the French *engouement* for protest. Even when she spoke the language fluently, even when she obtained her French passport—though Léo was long gone by then, anyway. And fluency made no difference to the chanting of simplistic slogans; she could have done as much in Quechua.

Perhaps it was Léo who had inspired her mistrust of political activism. He seemed to think it was part of his education as a Frenchman, a historical duty, a rite of passage, to be on the barricades. Or was it merely macho posturing, or an intellectual trend? Whatever his reasons, there was something not altogether sincere that she could only sense intuitively. He was always going on about unions and workers and the proletariat; he admired the Soviet Union. He envied her for speaking Russian, for having *been there*. Perhaps he was the dreamer and she was merely a realist. Politically, at any rate. But *being involved* was so much a part of who he was, the image he had of himself, the would-be revolutionary with his Guevara haircut (he stopped short at the beard).

When he wasn't plotting the next protest, he wrote novels. Earnest, wooden novels with archetypal peasants and workers and evil bosses. Ana found them difficult to judge: She thought he had a certain way with words, but she could not identify with his characters, their rigid motivation, their lack of emotion. Perhaps if her French had been better back then, she could have read the warning signs. Not one of those novels—she remembered three in the time they were together, written feverishly at night with shots of imported Moskovskaya—ever found a publisher; he used the ancient mimeograph machine at the Marxist student union to print up one of them and joked about capitalist *samizdat*. He would sneer at the paperbacks in English that Ana sometimes read— lusty historical romances that sold in the millions—and tell her she was polluting her brain. But every so often he would calmly, if condescendingly, enumerate the reasons behind those books' commercial success—their accessibility, easy escapism, simplistically sympathetic characters, primacy of page-turning plot—as though he, too, could write such a book if only he cared to.

What had become of him? She had looked for him online more than once, to no avail. She imagined him living in Bolivia or Venezuela or even Cuba, still fighting the fight, cynically, a balding, potbellied bureaucrat, smoking second-rate cigars in the fly-infested offices of a struggling guerrilla movement. Or maybe he was the manager of a Super U or a furniture outlet in Lille or Calais or somewhere dreary like that, driving a Renault through the rain to pick up the kids for a microwaved dinner of Fleury Michon moussaka.

She wasn't sure which would be worse.

She would like to see him on her computer screen, chanting on the Maidan. Handsome, flamboyant Léo. But it wouldn't be him, it would be a young Ukrainian who actually felt what Léo—for all his scorn for emotions—had so desperately wanted to feel all those years ago.

KATYA HANDED PETER HIS umbrella and waved as he went down the path and out the gate. Trees dripping with rain; a swoosh of traffic in the distance. She turned and went back to the kitchen, poured another cup of coffee, switched off the radio with its refrain of road accidents and suicide bombings and child sex abuse. Was it her own perception, or had the world really changed for the worse? Or was it the media, digging up stories that once remained under silence?

She'd grown up in such a vacuum of false good news. Celebratory five-year plans and visits from friendly heads of state or folk-dancing troupes. All the bad things always happened over there, *na zapadye*, in the West. Yet when she'd arrived in the West with Peter, she had seen none of those bad things—she had been dazzled by the novelty of it all, the shelves full of choice, the elegant window displays, the gardens. The gardens above all, justifying and defying the miserable weather, the pervasive damp; rain-soaked villages with their bursts of compensatory color; everywhere you looked, even on the smallest plots of land next to motorways or car parks. Katya was fascinated by plants and flowers, but she had never learned to garden. Peter used to in the early days; they had more time then. They had real weekends. They threw parties in their own little back garden when it was warm. It was a good life. Peter would mow their tiny lawn, then move about on his knees, up to his wrists in soil. Bushes, borders, bursts of color and texture. She never learned the names of the plants. Except the hydrangeas; everyone knew hydrangeas. He prepared the garden for their parties the way she prepared the zakuski. Everyone loved Katya's zakuski. After a while, though, five or ten years, she began to doubt the enthusiasm of those polite English guests or their louder American friends and colleagues: They did not know how to classify her, she was too exotic, she was no hydrangea, so out of awkwardness, they enthused about her zakuski. She used to smile and shrug and say, They're just hors d'oeuvres. But because she was exotic, they tasted better.

Nowadays people just went out and bought expensive sushi.

And those parties: She always went to bed—the dishwasher half loaded, piles of plates and parades of glasses all over the kitchen—with a sense of something lost or never attained. Where were the conversations, the truly enthusiastic and deep philosophic engagement she remembered from parties back in Russia? These people gossiped about authors and actors, or house prices, or where they would send their children to school, or a skiing trip to some French resort whose name she could hardly pronounce (nor could they); they were not stupid, far from it, she just wondered if they did not accept their comfortable lives as glibly as her erstwhile Soviet compatriots had accepted the drivel churned out by *Pravda* and *Izvestia*. She wanted to shake them.

But once, she had sat until sunrise in the garden with a guest. And that time she had felt as if she were back in Russia, philosophizing, questioning life. Do you love your husband? Is it enough to have a job, to travel? What about religion? Death? How do you define freedom? What gives meaning? Where are the limits of the individual?

Andrey Stepanovich. They had paid for his ticket from the newly rebaptized Saint Petersburg. He was a rising young author, and Polyana had published his prizewinning novel. They had spent more on the marketing budget than for any other book in their short history. They had arranged readings and signings and radio appearances for Andrey, which he performed with charm and earnestness. They expected him to become the new Nabokov, the next Kundera.

He seemed to have brought the white nights with him in his pale, vibrant eyes. He made her want to stay awake, not to miss anything, as if he were an ambassador bearing a gift that would dissolve in the morning sunlight. He was not dazzled by the West, because in those early days of transition he believed he could contribute to a new, democratic Russia. The other guests had left, Peter had gone to bed, and Katya sat on with Andrey, wrapped in her shawl, shivering from the chill air, and something else.

Why do you stay here now? he asked her. You could go back to Russia, start a business, teach English, translate literature. Now is the time.

Katya did not remember what she had told him. A flat excuse, *My life is here now,* that sort of thing.

His voice went on into the night, weaving circles around her, entrapping her with a long list of all the reasons why she should go back to Russia. She laughed at some of them — he was such an idealist! But she recalled that by the end of his list, she had an image as vivid and real as if she had turned the clock back to before Peter, before England. Finally, she stopped him and said, This is just nostalgia. I won't find that Russia, because I've changed, too. And what you describe is what you dream of—it's your utopia, it's not real. It's like your book, beautiful but unreal. You have kept all the best things from our childhood, all the eternal Russian values, and added some fantasy of a sort of modernized, enlightened democracy. No such place exists even outside Russia.

He hung his head as if disappointed in her bleak realism or his failure to convince her. Then he turned and looked at her. It is because, he said in English as if for emphasis, it is because when you love, you see everything more beautiful.

She burst out laughing. She thought he was referring to Russia, and she was beginning to find his love of motherland a bit overblown. There was a moment of silence, and then with his voice quiet and even but almost pained, he said in Russian, When I leave tomorrow—I mean tonight—Ekaterina Sergeyevna, will you come with me?

Katya's shivering seemed to grow worse. He stood up and came over to her, put his hands on her elbows, and coaxed her up from her chair. There was a kiss, a very long one. She realized his eyes were the same color as hers. And that he was probably younger than she was. She thought that if she were able to believe a fraction of what he had said, the long poem that had filled her with a homesickness no less potent than this simple desire to kiss and be kissed, she would go with him to Saint Petersburg. But she didn't, couldn't, believe. Her sense of timing had changed. Deep down, she disapproved of his spontaneous declaration.

Andrey had gone back to Saint Petersburg, and Katya and Peter heard nothing more from him. The book did only moderately well. As Katya had found with her poetry, the West was no longer interested in the literature of the former Eastern bloc. There was enough new, democratic material written directly in English. India was hot; Ireland was hot.

Sometimes, in idle moments like this one, she wondered what would have happened if she had gone back to Russia. Left Peter and gone back. There had been those shaky years in their marriage, not unlike now. She would not have gone to Andrey; she would have gone to the evanescent dawn place of her nostalgia, the country they had imagined between them. That something she thought she had lost, or somehow never attained, in her life in England—would she have found it?

No. Because she would have had to define it first; she did not know what she was looking for. It was not geographical, it was personal. Perhaps it was something all exiles looked for: a key, a missing self, a cultural identity.

She thought it was a sad irony that these last months had served to sharpen her understanding more effectively than an entire comfortable adult life in Britain. And then with a rush of something almost like joy, she realized that she had found that key to completion after all—at last, yes, she realized what it was, not that it had been there all along: It had crept into her life unobtrusively, discreetly. Together with Zinaida Mikhailovna.

Laughter, not horsepower, propelled us the entire way, said
Anton Pavlovich. Roman the coachman was so dour and cross
that he made us laugh, and off we'd go, all the faster for his
irritation. Laughter was our fuel!

We stopped off to look at a peasant wedding, and they offered
us vodka so foul, it made your hair and beard stand on end and
induced the most extraordinary belching—Georges and I had
a contest while the ladies went off to comment on the wedding
clothes. We arrived at the Smagins' estate late at night, to an
immediate chorus of dogs barking and geese honking, and
when they came out to greet us, Sergey and Aleksandr Smagin
were half asleep, Sergey tripped and fell over, and Aleksandr
bashed his head, then Vata scraped her neck—but fortunately,
Dr. Chekhov was on duty. Although I was not needed, with
so much restorative laughter: For five days, our convulsions
did not stop. We even roused their sad-eyed sister from her
melancholy beauty to grace us with a touching smile. They live
on a tumbledown estate full of charm, with a sort of poetic ruin
about it, overgrown with plants and wildflowers . . . Do you
know, Zinaida Mikhailovna, after this visit, I am determined
to buy my own farmstead in Ukraine. I want it more than
anything, I want to live the way you do here, I want to practice
medicine, and to hell with Moscow. What do you think, Zinaida
Mikhailovna—I should be able to make a living between a
farm and a medical practice, wouldn't you say? My soul thrives
just on being here—what need would I even have to write, why

invent something? My inventions are for Moscow winters, for Moscow frustrations—you've seen my characters, their *mal de vivre* ... Listen, one morning I heard a small commotion outside my window, and there, just by the sill, was a nest full of chicks: nightingales, performing for me. The miracle of it!

His hand was on my forearm as if to share the smile I could not see, the gleam in his eye; then he continued, And everywhere this endless sky, and the smell of freshly mown hay—like here but stronger, it made you dizzy, by the lungful, and peasants by the roadside when the day was over, playing their violins and waving to us as we passed. Glorious, Zinaida Mikhailovna, just glorious. I wish you could have come along, too. You, and Masha, and Pleshcheyev, and Ivanenko, and Elena Mikhailovna, and Rosa and Pulka and the pigs in their Sunday best—

I felt for his hand. I was laughing, too, but I told him to stop, to spare me, please; his mirth was infectious, and I felt dangerously close to an immense, irrepressible sadness and loss, and I did not want to reach that place, not with him there.

He did stop; he squeezed my hand, let it go, and said, I'm being thoughtless, Zinaida Mikhailovna. It's unfair of me to go on like this, I'm gloating, reveling in the sound of my own voice. Forgive me.

They had been gone barely a week, but I had missed them terribly.

I like to think I missed them as a group, particularly my own Georges and Natasha—the house was so quiet without his piano, her gaiety—but as the days seemed to grow longer, I knew it was above all Anton Pavlovich whom I missed. Just the knowledge of his proximity, that he might stop by to sit on the veranda for tea and a talk.

Now I am heartened by his decision to buy a house in the region. As if something were about to be fulfilled after all, not just for him but for me, for my declining days; as if, with each visit from his farmstead, he would bring the sky and the fresh scent of hay and those waving peasants . . . since I cannot go to them.

St. Pavel's Day, June 1888

So, just now, began Anton Pavlovich, there is a great deal of confusion by the riverbank—Vanya's hat has just blown away, my father is running after it, nearly trips—there, he's caught the hat, but he's bright red in the face and wheezing like an aging opera singer bowing to applause; your brother Pavel Mikhailovich is holding his wife by the arm, she's walking slowly with her hands on her belly and shaking her head; there are waves on the river, Zinaida Mikhailovna, we won't be able to go to the island, it's too rough, and there are dark clouds and in the distance a curtain of rain . . . Now my papasha is waving his arms in the direction of the guesthouse, and my mamasha and your mamochka are nodding like hens and looking around for their chicks, to herd us all to shelter.

There's a peasant in his rowboat, I can see him now on the far side of the island, he's rowing like mad to get to the other shore. The boat rises, he looks around, he finds himself sliding down a wave in a splash of water—he looks surprised and worried, he's rowing, he hasn't got far to go, he's shouting to someone on shore but they can't hear him in this wind, now a wave has washed right into his boat, the poor fellow is drenched.

Natalya Mikhailovna is waving at us; the others have taken the baskets and are heading back up the hill. Come, Zinaida Mikhailovna, we'd better go.

And the man in the rowboat? I asked.

We'll look again from the top of the riverbank—for the moment he's still struggling.

He gave me his arm and led me up the path. From time to time he stopped, turned around, and gave a worried sigh: Not there yet, Zinaida Mikhailovna, the wind wants to push him this way, he's having a devil of a time, after all, and the current is pushing him downstream.

I could feel the wind tearing at my hair, at my skirt, catching in my legs, obliging me to free my arm from Anton Pavlovich's to adjust my skirt so I could walk. Then I waved my hand and his was there again, supporting me.

He paused as we reached the crest of the hill, and he turned to look for the peasant in the rowboat. I don't see him, he said. Perhaps he's gone back to the island to wait. Or they've pulled the boat ashore, but you can't see a thing. I don't know, Zinaida Mikhailovna. We'll ask when next we go fishing.

Last night, I said, I could already feel the storm coming. I could feel the air changing. Natasha said we'd be all right, that she could see the stars, but I told her there was rain on the way.

We reached the house just as the first heavy drops began to fall.

I lie in my bed at night, the window open but securely fastened so it won't bang, and there are sounds of wind in the room and in the garden—things rustling and flying about—leaves, branches; and then in the distance, this roar as of the sea.

Anton Pavlovich has told me he'll be leaving next week to join his publisher friend Suvorin in the Crimea, in Feodosia. How I envy him! I've been only once to the seaside, long ago, as a child. We stood behind a parapet, clinging to our hats in the wind, and far below, the waves were crashing against the rocks as if to break them into a thousand pieces; I thought surely they must, and we would go plummeting into the water. I was exhilarated and frightened at the same time, and I asked Elena—who seemed calmer and more knowledgeable about such things, even though she's the younger one—whether the parapet we were standing on wouldn't be wrecked to pieces and us along with it, and she held my hand and told me not to worry, that the cliff face and the rocks below us were very strong, and it would take the waves centuries to erode them, so we wouldn't be there anymore.

We returned to the parapet a few days later and the water was quite still and gentle, hardly moving, lapping indolently against the rocks. At other times we saw it in the distance as we rode along the shore—vaster than any field of wheat, undulating blue in the sunlight, a few ships here and there like toys.

My picture of the sea is a partial one, transformed by memory and imagination, and the paintings of Aivazovsky, no doubt, among others; now I hear the Psyol in its uncharacteristic fury and wish I could know more of what the sea truly is, yet I know that this is as close as it will come to me, a complete illusion, a freshwater river in a storm. I am landlocked, lifelocked; I will never know what it is to sail.

Why didn't we sail that time we went to the sea? I must ask Mama. Perhaps she suffers from seasickness, perhaps it was too rough or there were no trips available. I don't even know where we were—Yalta or Sevastopol, I suppose, I was too young to notice or care at the time.

I do remember the ice cream.

When next I saw Anton Pavlovich, I asked if he had news of the unlucky fellow in his rowboat. He told me he'd heard the poor man had to spend the night on the island, cold and wet, until the wind and waves subsided and he was able to row back to the other side. I would have done the same, said Anton Pavlovich. I can imagine worse fates than a night with owls and frogs; I might even have seen the water bittern.

There was a long silence; I don't know what came over me, because I asked—thinking perhaps of the man's family, desperate with worry—Are you afraid of death, Anton Pavlovich?

He gave a loud, hesitant sigh, not of annoyance but as if wondering how best to formulate his answer. Finally, he said, We see death all the time, as doctors, you and I. That's both a good thing and a bad thing: We know what to expect, all the clever, malicious ways death uses to lower our vigilance and call us away from life; we know—or try to know—when to continue to fight on behalf of a patient, and when there is nothing more to be done, and I've seen grief that's far worse than death. But as to fear, that's all for other people. My own death? I can't really imagine it; I suppose I'm still too young. My parents are alive and healthy, so I can imagine living to transform this little beard into a long bushy thing like my father's, full of wisdom and thundering ideology. There's a kind of immortality, seen from the age I am now.

I took a deep breath and added, And if you were diagnosed—as I have been—with an untimely illness?

(I must have been mad, asking him things like this—but I have noticed that people are only too pleased to tolerate my madness, and so I say the most untoward things—and I know he enjoys engaging in honest self-examination. Soul dissection, as Mama and I call it.)

And he replied, Then I don't know. I suppose I would fight mentally, imagine all sorts of possible misdiagnoses, or expect a sudden remission . . . which, to answer your first question, is a symptom of fear. Yes. He paused, then said, Zinaida Mikhailovna, I do apologize for this conversation—

No, Anton Pavlovich, I started it. Please don't apologize. It helps me in a way, makes me feel almost normal . . . if I know there are others who share my fear. It helps to talk, now and again, about—

And are you afraid?

(If I'd had my sight at that moment, I am sure I would have found him looking right into my eyes, grave, intent. I could almost see him from the image I have constructed in my imagination.)

At times, yes. Fear of pain, of not knowing what to expect. But the worst is my fear for others' sake—for Mama, for my brothers and sisters—for their pain. I am sorry to cause them this pain.

You haven't caused it! They know that.

As do I, but I feel it nevertheless. It can't be helped. So when I am weak and afraid, I tell myself that at least when I die, their suffering on my behalf will end.

No, it won't, because they will always miss you. He paused, placed his hand on my arm briefly, then continued, We cannot control these things, Zinaida Mikhailovna—what a stupid, obvious thing to say, but it's true! It's an unfortunate, inevitable part of life, the price we must pay to be here in the first place. That is why we must live now, as if . . . We must live well. Every moment.

He paused again, perhaps considering what that might mean for me, because then he added with a hushed excitement in his voice, This, Zinaida Mikhailovna, is living well. Sitting here on the veranda, talking, we are living deeply, with our awareness of each other, our questioning of life. Never let a moment escape that hasn't been turned over in your hands, inspected for honesty and fullness and awareness . . . as I believe you do already. Uncomplainingly.

I did not know what to say. I could have thanked him for his words of wisdom, but I knew it was not something belonging to him that he had given me. It was simply a shared way of apprehending life. I also knew that I did not need to point this out to him. It is why we sit together—on the veranda, in the garden, above the river—and talk.

ANA WAS HAVING DIFFICULTY concentrating on her work. Until now she'd had a quiet, idyllic picture of Ukraine—fields of wheat, slow-moving rivers, and above all, those long conversations by the samovar—but contemporary events were supplanting the sepia scenes, filling the screen and all her attention with people who were real and alive and in danger. And what made the events on the news all the more urgent and charged for her was the connection between the two Ukraines: She could not have felt this draw, this irrepressible need to follow every moment, if the Maidan were located in, say, Belarus or Turkey or Bulgaria. She *knew* them now, those protesters, as if they were all the legitimate descendants of Pavel Mikhailovich Lintvaryov or his brother Georges; she searched the faces of the young women for the features of a Zina, a Natasha, a Lenochka. She wanted to believe in a continuity of emotion as authentic as a genetic heritage, because she was beginning to care for those nineteenth-century Ukrainians who filled her imagination.

The Maidan had become a battlefield. There had been dozens of victims, and even from the artificial front-row seat that technology and modern media offered onto the scene, Ana could sense the feverish waiting, the fear, the imminence of change. She watched as young men in flimsy helmets carried the wounded and the dead; she heard the steady crack of bullets fired by government snipers. It could all so easily spiral out of control, now that blood had been shed. Ana was just old enough to remember the Soviet invasion of Czechoslovakia: her parents glued to the old black-and-white television, their concern, their veiled explanations, not to alarm their little girl. *Don't worry, it's far, far away. The Russians won't come here. Tanks can't cross oceans.* But perhaps now the Russians would send other tanks, would come to the president's help.

Out of solidarity with the victims, a lone female skier from the Ukrainian Olympic team had withdrawn from her competition.

On the Maidan, there were photographs of the victims, votive candles flickering in the night. Ana found a list of their names and murmured to herself. *Serhiy, Volodymyr, Oleksandr.* How old they were; where they were from. Until she came, with a sudden intake of breath, to *Oleksiy Bratushko, shot 20 February by a sniper on Instytutska Street. Aged 39, born in Sumy.*

She closed the computer and went out into the dusk, wrapped warmly against the cold. There was a pastel light from the fading sun that augured the lengthening of the days. Ana gazed at the darkening fields, the flicker of lake, the shadowy peaks on the horizon. She wanted to be present in her life. No matter where her sympathies lay, or how right and commendable they might be, she was not in Sumy or Kiev, she was not from there, and she knew this. She had both the great good fortune and the existential tragedy of having lived all her life in that prosperity and safety and comfort of what she rather ironically referred to as the democratic West. She thought wistfully of Léo and conceded that now she probably would join him on the barricades—if they had been Ukrainian, that is. But looking around, she saw only the dark fields and sleeping villas and a woman in a long coat walking a small fluffy white dog. The woman said good evening as she passed. Ana responded; the dog sniffed the hem of her coat, catching a whiff of Doodle. The woman called to her dog. Ana went on until nightfall, then turned and made her way home. There was a rhythm to her steps, *Oleksiy Bratushko* a faint drumming amid her thoughts, a spontaneous elegy.

Doodle was waiting outside the door and followed her in, rubbed and hopped against her legs, part greeting, part expectation of sustenance. Ana tipped some kibble into the bowl, took off her hat, scarf, coat, then poured herself a small glass of Calvados. The house was cold.

She lit a fire, harnessing her impatience until she had a good burn and a growing circle of warmth. Then she put some Shostakovich preludes on the stereo and opened her laptop again.

There was a message from a small press in Boston, informing her that a translation she had published with them the previous year, *Go Through the Door, Turn Left,* by a young writer, Lydia Guilloux, had been nominated for the Fleur Mailly Foundation French Translation Prize.

In all the time she'd had to struggle to make a living on her own, this was the rare book that she had truly loved; she had read it one weekend just after she moved there from Paris and knew she had to translate it. It was the text of her salvation after her divorce: consolation, challenge, survival. Distraction from negative thoughts. She worked for free, in her spare time, then spent six months sending out pitch letters until she found the small press prepared to take the risk and bring it into the Anglo-Saxon world, and willing to pay her a small advance.

The Fleur Mailly was a rather good prize, with a cash purse that would pay her keep for four and a half months. Which in turn would translate to four and a half months to breathe: freedom up front, a chance to travel, a sort of long-lost irresponsibility of youth, no bills to worry about. Not to mention the recognition: It would be forever on her curriculum vitae, a stamp of approval. At last, after thousands of pages, a few of them had risen above the others; she could almost see them floating against a blue sky, her brilliant white pages.

She read through the rest of the message—benefactors, ceremony, other nominees. Could she afford to fly to New York two months from now? She doubted it.

Ana's author was the only woman on the shortlist of six. There was one other woman translator, she noticed; she recognized the name—Isobel Brookes, for a novel entitled *The Lemon-Rind Still Life*—but had not met her.

Lydia Guilloux's book had not done as well as they'd hoped; so far it had sold a few hundred copies. Ana had sent most of her complimentary copies to friends, some of whom had written to say they loved it; the others were silent or neutral in their congratulations. It didn't matter, it had led to this. She was proud of what she had achieved. Perhaps she might sell a few more copies now.

She thought again of Yves's teasing suggestion that she translate a novel by Chekhov. Which, when Zinaida Mikhailovna last checked, was *on the top shelf of the wardrobe, at the back, behind three blankets and under a dozen pillowcases.* Ana closed her eyes and pictured a Chekhov manuscript she had seen once in a museum in Paris, never imagining she might one day be so close to his life, his reality. Handwriting that was almost fastidiously neat—particularly for a doctor—as if he had copied his words out for someone who had difficulty reading.

Before going to bed, she looked one last time at the news: The reviled Ukrainian president had fled the country. It was a triumph of sorts: The protests had become a revolution.

And this is Kazimir Stanislavovich, but you may call him Kuzma Protapych, says Anton Pavlovich, his voice full of mischief.

A hand takes mine briefly, a palm cold with sweat. There is a mutter, there is laughter, then Anton Pavlovich murmurs in my ear, It's all right. He's gone to speak to Ivan. He's a very shy man. So shy he has no mirrors in his house. Yet somehow he has managed to father six children.

Then his wife must not be shy, I say with a laugh and a blush. He will be in good company with me; I cannot see him. I am free to imagine he looks like . . . Lermontov. Tell him that. A young god, a Lord Byron sort.

Ah, you'd be sorely mistaken. He looks like a struggling writer who collects tickets on Saint Petersburg's trams. His beard straggles, and he collects dandruff on his uniform.

Anton Pavlovich, you are cruel.

But I love him. He's a good writer and a good friend.

Has his wife come?

You idealize, Zinaida Mikhailovna. Who would look after six children? My mamasha has enough with her own six. No, Madame Barantsevich has stayed in her quarters in Petersburg.

Poor woman.

Lucky woman. He's a good fellow. Imagine, he writes at night, when the bambini are asleep.

That's one way, I suppose. But when does he sleep?

In the tram, between two tickets.

Has he published?

A few short stories, but his reputation will grow, I am sure of it. He prefers long novels, of the sort that elude me.

Perhaps you should have six children and write at night.

I don't know if he is smiling at my witticism, but he has placed his fingertips on my forearm, a gesture I have begun to recognize, to expect. For the moment, he murmurs, I'm managing in the daylight, in my wifeless, childless state, to produce a few words. Perhaps a short novel will suffice.

July 6, 1888

The veranda. Evening.

As I told you, said Anton Pavlovich, I must find a small estate. A place like the Smagins'—a big house with lots of rooms or outbuildings, but a bit run-down is all right, so it won't be too expensive, but above all, plenty of rooms, yes, and not only for guests: I want to create a sort of resort or spa, a refuge for writers, fellows like Barantsevich, where they could come to get away from their brats and their tearful wives to write about life and love! And share the companionship of others who know what it's all about and, when the day's work is done, relax at the end of a pier with a line in the water—doesn't it sound like a noble project?

That it does, I replied. When I hear the conditions under which you or Kazimir Stanislavovich have to write—yes, if one doesn't have the wealth to buy the space or tranquillity—

And to be in such soothing surroundings—silence, nature, nothing to trouble one's thoughts. Just a well-scrubbed room with an old table by the window and a comfortable chair. That's all that's needed.

And would you allow women to stay at your refuge?

Of course, why not, if they behave, and are charming, and don't cause us to fall in love and forget why we're there! Love makes a muddle of creativity. Mature, sensible women writers, of course! Yes, it would be splendid. I can think already of a few women like that. And just imagine all the good conversation, and how we could encourage and support one another. But above all, the quiet we could command, yes, that would be an absolute rule, no laughing or singing or loud talking from dawn to dusk—a vow of silence, monastic industriousness—

At that moment a loud cry broke the stillness, the timing so perfect that we burst out laughing, until we heard it again, the dreadful cry of something or someone in extreme pain. I waved my hand. What day are we, Anton Pavlovich?

It must be the sixth of July or thereabouts—

Oh! Tonya! She must be going into labor, it's her time!

Shall we go? Does she need us?

Pasha will send for the midwife in the village, but he knows to fetch us or Elena if there's a problem. Oh, Anton Pavlovich, I'm going to be an aunt!

He chuckled and, hastily kissing my hand, took his leave and promised to send for news before bedtime.

July 8, 1888

I'm an aunt! I went today to see Tonya and Pasha. The baby— they have called her Ksenia—is healthy, and Tonya has recovered quickly, all sighs of delight and little sobs of happiness.

I placed my palms on the infant, her tiny legs and hands, her plump little cheeks—is there anything softer, more tender, on earth? As I stood there, a calm certainty came over me: that she would, in some way, continue my life for me; that I would continue to live, through her. With hindsight, a sort of ridiculous, unrealistic superstition, and I did not share it with Pasha or Tonya or Elena—I did not want to sadden their joyful time—but I could keep it as a secret with myself, something to think of with hopefulness. Mama would agree if I told her. She wanted them to name the baby after me. I told them it wouldn't be fitting and it was far too depressing. Besides, Zinaida is a perfectly ugly name.

Come, Zinaida Mikhailovna, Kuzma does not believe me when I tell him that blindness enhances one's sense of smell.

(Kazimir Stanislavovich protested limply, but Anton Pavlovich had already taken me by the elbow.)

We're going to the kitchen garden. We shall prove to him that you have a superior nose, even though his is twice the size of yours and well adorned with a mixture of peeling sunburned skin and erysipelas; or might it be an overindulgence in vodka?

Again Kazimir Stanislavovich mumbled ineffectively, pointlessly. The gate creaked; we were standing in Grigory Petrovich's little kingdom. My heart was pounding, it was warm, I felt oddly useful and celebrated at the same time.

Right. Both of you, close your eyes. No, I mean, Kuzma, you close your eyes. Zinaida Mikhailovna, please bear with me.

I could not help but laugh. Kuzma continued to protest, a bubbling string of: Antosha, I beg you, my friend, Anton Pavlovich, I beg you.

Don't worry, I murmured to him. If Anton Pavlovich should happen upon the stinging nettles, we'll soon be free of our ordeal.

Now. Here are the rules—you will smell what I have in my hand and whisper your answer to me. No cheating, Kuzma!

After a certain amount of rustling and vegetable snapping and breaking, and a cry of *oy* (the nettles?), the smell of the

air deepened with something sweet and summery: the first
raspberry of the year.

I whispered my answer. Anton Pavlovich turned to Kazimir
Stanislavovich and after a moment he exclaimed, Cherry?

Kazimir Stanislavovich, I beg you, the basics! The absolute
basics! Did your babushka not make jam in the summer?

We were poor, said Kazimir Stanislavovich.

Precisely, said Anton Pavlovich, unforgiving.

Next came a carrot, then a lettuce leaf (which Kazimir
Stanislavovich mistook for cabbage), then a rose (we both
accused Anton Pavlovich of cheating and told him to take
the rose to Anya and tell her to put it in the soup), then
chives (onion) and wild strawberries (oddly enough, Kazimir
Stanislavovich guessed this one), then something terribly faint
and delicate. I hesitated for a long time, then grabbed Anton
Pavlovich's arm and said, Anton Pavlovich, you are definitely
cheating. That is my mama's Earl Grey tea from the English
specialty shop in Sumy.

Poor Kazimir Stanislavovich thought it was pipe tobacco
and pleaded defeat. You have taught me a bitter lesson, Anton
Pavlovich, he said. I'll learn to close my eyes from now on
when smelling.

Take care when crossing the Nevsky Prospekt, however. If the
smell of horse manure is too pungent, you might get run over by
your own tram.

A fist hit cloth, and Anton Pavlovich was pushed against
me; we all laughed, and I cried out for more raspberries. Anton
Pavlovich filled my outstretched palms. I lifted the berries to
my face, felt the soft furry fragrance against my lips and nose,
then the odd cracking of their warm little globes between my
teeth, the release of the juice among the tiny seeds. As a child,
I wouldn't eat raspberries, I was afraid of the seeds, afraid
they would stay in my body and grow into a bush. I told the

story to Anton Pavlovich and Kazimir Stanislavovich, and we remembered other foolish things we'd said or done as children. When we'd had enough of raspberries, we moved to the bench in the shade beneath the oak tree, and Kazimir Stanislavovich began to relax at last. He told us that he lived above a bakery in Piter and that the smell of baking bread sometimes woke him in the night when it was time for him to leave for work, and Anton Pavlovich protested and asked did he not write at night?, and Kazimir Stanislavovich acknowledged that when his writing was going well, he would realize by the smell of baking bread that he'd gone on too long and would have no time to sleep. The worst of it was when they'd spent all his wages and had no money left and had to eat stale bread and dry kasha for three days: Then the warm, comforting smell of fresh bread in the oven was torture. And when he'd been paid and he brought up a fresh loaf, his wife and children would stare at it, no one daring to break the fragrant crust.

But then he would sell a few stories, and they were even able to buy a few pastries. And his ticket for Sumy, where the air smelled not of bread but of the hay and the river and Mama's garden, and something indefinable, a sort of deep warmth from the earth, perhaps the soil itself, baking in a kiln of sunlight.

IF ANA COULD NOT go to New York, perhaps she could at least go to London for a few days. An invitation had come to a cocktail reception at the literary association she belonged to; it would do her good to see people, emerge from her isolation.

She refused to admit to herself that she had an ulterior motive, but Ana nevertheless sent off a quick email to Katya Kendall, saying she would be coming to London the following month, and asking for an appointment. She was eager to know the history of the manuscript—how it had been brought to light, so to speak, and how it had found its way to Polyana Press.

She did not mention Chekhov's novel. She had far too little to go on, only her hopes and Yves's hunch.

Briefly, she imagined the cover, her name in small letters beneath his. Translating Anton Chekhov, just think. Then: No, mustn't get carried away.

Why London? You should go to Ukraine, Yves was saying.

They were in a small café in the old town in Geneva. Yves had to raise his voice above the hiss of the espresso machine.

That's where you'd really like to go, he continued, I can tell. Go to Crimea and visit the places where Chekhov lived, then go to Sumy.

Ana stared at him, half fascinated, half horrified. Haven't you seen the news?

Not lately. Why?

Crimea is crawling with little green men. Russian soldiers—or so everyone says, who else would they be—with no insignia on their green uniforms. They just showed up. Like some virus. The Russians have some of their fleet there, in Sevastopol, in case you'd forgotten. And you say, Go to Crimea, hang out on the waterfront in Yalta and eat ice cream?

Don't worry. Nothing's going to happen.

I beg to differ.

Why?

Because it's not the West, Yves. They're not just going to sit around a table and talk politely and decide the future of the place. Hold a free and fair referendum. Like Scotland or Catalunya or somewhere. Russia has been making noises about Crimea ever since the Maidan uprising started. The Duma has approved military intervention, if need be, for Christ's sake, to, quote, *protect Russian interests.* You don't think nuclear submarines are interesting? Russia wants Crimea.

Well, then, scratch Crimea if you're worried about the green men. Go to Kiev. Go to Sumy.

Ana's heart was pounding. He was daring her. Would you come with me? *Davai.*

I wish I could. I'm on standby to interpret at the World Health. There's an outbreak of the Ebola virus. There's no telling when it will be over.

They looked at each other across the table, troubled.

But you can go on your own to Ukraine, surely. It might even be a good time to go. The enthusiasm of revolution, they'd love to have you there, showing your Western support.

Then he leaned across the table and said, Maybe what you need is a burly Ukrainian poet with a beard down to here, and you will translate his stanzas on the Maidan, and he will take you back to his garret and make mad love to you between shots of vodochka.

Ana laughed, then sighed. Like Isadora Duncan and Sergei Yesenin, you mean? Anyway, I don't speak Ukrainian.

Is not necessary, said Yves in a thick accent, vodochka will translate.

She smiled, fiddling with the unopened square of chocolate that had come with the coffee, then said, I wish I weren't so scared. I don't know what brought it on. I'm sure I haven't always been afraid of the outside world in this way. I used to embrace the unknown, to welcome it. I filled notebooks with descriptions of street scenes in Rome or Athens or Istanbul, small incidents of everyday life that seemed so exotic to me back then, back-packing . . . It was all fascinating, I couldn't wait to get on the road. Then at some point I decided—or realized—the world is not such a welcoming place.

Yves shrugged and echoed, You realized. The same happened to me. A shadow crossed his face, then he said, There's something to be said for naïveté. Up to a point in life, anyway. When did you lose it, do you suppose—was it a person or an event?

A combination of things, I suppose. Naively, yes, seeing that dreams don't come true—or if they do, what you get is disappoint-ing or downright hurtful.

Men, right?

To a degree. But not only. I also blame myself.

He looked at her sympathetically, creasing his brow. You shouldn't, he said eventually, lowering his voice. People can be fucks. Society—it's rigged, corrupt. Even here. He waved his arm to include the well-groomed Swiss shoppers at adjacent tables, then added, You have to protect yourself. You think I ha-ven't been there, too? That disappointing, hurtful place? I had to learn very early to defend myself, even when it meant deceiv-ing, cheating.

You?

Not in a way that would harm others; just self-protection, really. Anyway, look at us now, two well-fed, cynical members of the intelligentsia, with the luxury to debate imaginary trips to Ukraine. Although I hope you will seriously consider it.

Let me see what I find out in London. Maybe if I manage to see the publishers, they will give me some sort of lead, a concrete reason for going there.

Mongoose, he said, wagging a finger at her. Don't forget.

KATYA STARED FOR A long time at the email.

Peter would tell her not to answer the message or to say no. She opted halfheartedly for a middle course. *I might not be here,* she wrote. That would give her time to focus and decide. How much to reveal, if anything. And if she said yes, she would be able to tell right away whether the translator was someone she could trust. Thus far, she was obviously on their side: motivated, interested, eager. But later?

The Chekhov novel.

She and Peter must decide soon.

She did not want to think about it. As long as she didn't think about it, she didn't have to decide or do anything. Everything was urgent, and she wanted to drift.

What Katya feared more than anything was Peter's desperation. She had never, in their years together, seen him so disheartened, so glum. Even in the early nineties, when they had been going through the transition from *samizdat* and avant-garde poets to guidebooks and autobiographies of figure skaters, he had remained upbeat. His inner capitalist, as she teasingly called it, had come alive at last. They enjoyed the new freedom to travel to Russia, to visit Katya's mother without worrying that the neighbors might make her life difficult afterward. Katya had been able to renew her relations with old friends: a poet who now sold pirated CDs in the open-air market; a novelist who had become an English teacher to survive. They were all struggling. Peter counted his blessings, in the end. He was British, after all, heir to an old, stable economic environment.

But now. There was a bleakness about now.

One of her friends in Russia had done very well. Misha the painter turned entrepreneur. He had taken her to a very expensive restaurant—Peter had not joined her on that trip—and spent the evening lecturing her on how to turn her small publishing house into a big business. Katya hated the sound of the word in Russian—*beezness*—and now, even when she heard it in English, she often saw Misha's face, pink with vodka and champagne, his pale eyes promising her an earthly paradise. At the end of the evening he had tried to kiss her; then, disgruntled but still a friend, he'd sent her home in his silver limo with all the appurtenances— bar, stereo, TV. No doubt a stash of handguns, too. Katya had tried to engage the driver in conversation, to rescue the evening somehow, make it human again. Never in her life had she tried harder to be a comrade than on that long ride through Moscow's glittering snowy streets. In vain. It was too late for any of that. The driver was probably a thug at heart. He drove in stony silence, his resentment thundering.

Misha, in the course of their conversation, had offered to help. *Say how much. Just say the word.* It was some years ago, but as far as she knew, he was still prospering. She had seen him in a newspaper photograph, posing with Medvedev. It was always an option; but was she still so kissable? What would she give in return? Above all, how could she handle Peter?

No, it would not come to that. There must be another way. Anton Pavlovich would help them, she felt sure of it. Simply by being who he had always been.

Anton Pavlovich has left for the Crimea.

His two younger brothers are still here, as is Masha; Kazimir Stanislavovich was too shy to stay on without Anton Pavlovich, and our cousin Sasha has left and taken his flute with him. It is very quiet. Ivan Pavlovich brings us fish—he is every bit as eager a fisherman as his brother—but does not have the same gift for conversation. Natasha and Maria Pavlovna spend a lot of time together, plotting something to do with Vata and Ivan Pavlovich. Vata and Vanya, they mutter, dissolving in laughter.

I see them through Anton Pavlovich's words, still echoing in my mind: by the pond in their long white dresses, their gestures of mirth.

Elena sits with me in the evening. She is withdrawn. She won't tell me why, but I wonder if she is thinking about Aleksandr Pavlovich. When the silence grows too heavy, she takes up the volume of Tyutchev. When I ask her why she doesn't read something more contemporary, she says she needs to go to an inaccessible sort of place, one that no longer exists, for it is easier to bury her discontent in the past she hasn't known than to try to struggle with the present. This will pass, Zinaida Mikhailovna, she says, please don't worry about me. Just let us read Tyutchev for a change.

She is right. The past may be inaccessible, but with each reading, the words and music become stronger, more familiar. They burn into you, and with each new reading, you feel something like a joy of rediscovery, so poignant it is almost sorrowful.

I have memorized this one poem by Tyutchev and copy it out here, for my little niece.

> *Pray do not speak, but hide from sight,*
> *Conceal your feelings and your dreams—*
> *To let them rise and set again*
> *As soundlessly in your soul's depths*
> *As stars adrift upon the night—*
> *Admire them—and do not speak.*
>
> *How does one tell the hidden heart?*
> *How might a stranger understand*
> *Whereby you live, and who you are?*
> *A thought, once uttered, is a lie;*
> *To stir the source disturbs its calm—*
> *So drink from it, and do not speak.*
>
> *But live within yourself alone—*
> *For in your soul there is a world*
> *Of secret and enchanted thoughts;*
> *Protect them from the world's great roar,*
> *And shield them from day's blinding light—*
> *Yet heed their song—pray do not speak.*

I've been ill again. A seizure on the veranda at dusk. Poor Grigory Petrovich was passing; he did not know what to do. I heard his voice as if from very far away, Poor miss, what are the devils doing to you, may God have mercy. Then a hand on my forehead, gently stroking, for a long time. I didn't know whose it was, it seemed to belong to a sort of greater entity, not a person. I was in a place where such disembodied hands stroked and comforted, a place of supreme gentleness and love, until Mama's voice reached me at last: And you seemed so much better these last weeks.

She led me to bed and helped me undress. She sat with me for a while and talked to me about the Chekhovs, musing about this brother and that brother, and about the father, and wasn't he an upstanding religious man, but she wasn't sure the sons followed his example, just like her own sons, until finally, I waved my hand and said, Enough, Mama, let me sleep.

I felt her arranging the sheets and the blanket, trying to find a way to keep me closer to her for a moment. My head was throbbing, my hands and feet were icy cold. I drifted in and out, lost all sense of time. I had nightmares: I was able to see Anton Pavlovich, and he had huge wild eyes and was leering at me, and he had a basket full of crayfish in his hands and was shaking them at me and saying, They are good for you! If I had not been so ill and uncomfortable, I might look back and think it was funny—all that was missing was his smelly hat—but there was something so helpless and powerless in the dream. I had regained my sight, but I was so frightened that I could not speak, could not defend myself.

I slept, then had lucid moments when I wondered how much longer I wanted to live—not how much longer I would be allowed to live but whether I would be allowed any control in the matter, any choice. I felt as if I were at the bottom of a great hill, and to go on living, I must decide to climb; but then on each step of the way, I could sense others looking at me, reaching out to me, encouraging me. Their voices filled me with tears and a burning, desperate desire to be with them—Mama, Elena, Natasha, Pasha, Georges, Tonya, and little Ksenia; for their sake, for what I have with them, I could not leave. I felt then as if I had reached the top of that hill and could look around me at a serene, verdant landscape, and even if it was all in my imagination and there was no proof of any of it, no reality, in my half-dazed state, not knowing if it was day or night, it seemed the most important thing, a kind of vivid truth. Was it faith? Or just the ravings of my disturbed brain?

After that I slept, and when I awoke, Natasha was there and said, I've been waiting for you to wake since dawn, it's midmorning, would you like to have some breakfast?

She told me I've been in bed for two days; I haven't eaten, I've only drunk some water. Elena and Natasha watched over me all that time.

Through an open window, I heard his voice in the distance, laughing, scolding. I thought he had come home early, and I waited eagerly, until I asked Mama, and she told me no, it couldn't be Anton Pavlovich, but Ivan's voice was remarkably similar. I could hear the regret in her voice, and she went on to say, Poor Zina, do you feel dull without his conversation?

I assured her I was fine, but my cheeks flushed hot with a wave of disappointment and annoyance at my reaction.

The days are long. I sit on the veranda or above the river with Natasha and Masha, little inclined to speak. I listen gladly to all their conversation, give my opinions and advice, which they accept eagerly. A part of me lives through them—their concerns about teaching, their doubts and hopes regarding marriage or eligible men in the district, their opinions on all our brothers and their lives, which seem infinitely more complicated and passionate than our own. Did Masha have news of Anton Pavlovich? She'd had a few letters; he was traveling, after staying some time at Feodosia with Monsieur Suvorin and his wife. He was on his way to the Caucasus with one of Suvorin's sons. Through places with fairy-tale names: Sukhumi, Novy Afon, Batum, Tiflis, Baku . . . We sighed, thinking of the exotic treasures of the journey, then laughed and agreed we were surely

happier here above the river, and what could be more beautiful
than our own Luka and the river Psyol? Did Anton Pavlovich
need the journey for his writing, or was it merely a luxury, a
gentleman's adventure he could undertake with his wealthier
friends? Natasha seemed to envy him—she is adventurous, after
all—but Masha just sighed and said, I wish he would settle
down, I do worry about him.

July 27, 1888

Maria Pavlovna led me down to the river, with Rosa following
us or trotting ahead, panting in the heat. We found a shady spot
and spread a blanket. I lay down and curled up with my head on
my arms.

You are so fortunate to have such honest, hardworking, and
talented brothers, she said suddenly, almost bitterly.

I sat up again. Whatever do you mean, Maria Pavlovna? Look
at Anton Pavlovich—

Oh, yes, everyone goes on about how good and talented he is,
but the others . . . You've no idea how exhausting it is at times.
Especially with Sasha and Kolya.

Well, at least they stay out of politics—

Yes, but they get up to no end of mischief otherwise. She
leaned closer. I don't know what to do, Zina. Sasha has written to
me twice now, and I'm sure it's because he knows Antosha is in
the Caucasus and can't do a thing.

About what?

He wants to marry your sister. He's insisting, in fact, and he
wants me to speak to her.

Elena?

Of course Elena.

I thought Anton already—

Yes, there was the business of that letter he tore up, but you don't know what they're like, the two of them together. Antosha cannot stand Sasha's . . . bohemianism, the messiness of his life, his women, his drinking, his brats—I'm sorry, but that's what they are, no discipline at all—and it's a constant battle, Sasha provokes him, Antosha replies with long letters, trying to talk sense into him, as if words were vodka and could change Sasha's nature. Now I've been dragged into this. What do you think?

It's dreadful. He has no right to expect this of you.

And he's gone behind Antosha's back.

I'm not sure it's up to Anton Pavlovich, after all. What do your parents say—

My parents! Her tone was one of impatient exasperation. My mother will do nothing but weep, and my father will shout about our lack of religion. They hated poor Anna Ivanovna, may she rest in peace. They would probably love Elena because she would sacrifice everything for their son and make their lives easier. But they won't get involved, they'll only wring their hands or fling them in the air.

There was a moment of silence. I heard little Panas shouting to his friend Mishka down on the fishing pier.

Maria Pavlovna said, Do you think Elena has any feelings for him? Because if she actually does, we must of course take them into account.

If she does, she won't say. Although I don't think she has heard from him since he left, I think we would have known. Where is he now?

In Petersburg. He works at Suvorin's newspaper, perhaps you already knew that. And thank God for Suvorin, he does keep an eye on him, gets a semblance of professional behavior out of him for a few hours a day.

He won't suddenly come here?

I hope not. I hope he won't do anything rash, such as write directly to Elena.

Will you say anything to her?

Of course not. I'll wait until Antosha is back.

We sat in companionable silence for a while. Panas caught something, and Mishka cheered. Then Maria Pavlovna said, What about Georges? Does he intend to marry?

I suppose, but his music comes first for now.

Mmm.

I wonder now what was behind Masha's question about Georges.

August 9, 1888

I sit with my feet on the ottoman, fanning myself. I can hear Grigory Petrovich in the distance, grumbling about the heat. There is nothing to do, Natasha and Mama have gone off somewhere. Tonya promised to come by with the baby later, so I wait patiently, listening to the birds. I feel better, restored, almost buoyant, as if something lovely is about to happen. I just need patience. There will be a visit, or Georges will begin to play.

I was right. I have begun to develop a sixth sense for such things. Like Rosa, who knows when you're coming and races across the field to greet you. I wish I could race across fields—that is how I felt when I sensed he was coming. He didn't come racing, no, I heard his voice with Natasha and Masha when they were still some distance away; I was surprised, I thought he would be gone much longer, there'd been talk of Persia. But there was his voice, not his brother's, here he was, back from the Caucasus.

He kissed my hand—lightly, it is so hot—and sat down beside me. The others went in the house to prepare the tea.

You've returned early, I said.

He sighed, cleared his throat. There's been a tragedy. Diphtheria. Suvorin's third son. We turned back; we had gotten as far as Abkhazia when we received the telegram.

And . . . you didn't want to carry on alone?

He cleared his throat again, as if he were having trouble speaking; if I could have seen him, perhaps he would have shrugged apologetically, at a loss for words. But he murmured, It was best that I return to be with the family. You understand. It would have been insensitive to go on traveling.

Then he slapped his hands against his thighs and said, But I'm very happy to be back at Luka, all the same! Traveling takes a lot out of one, constant demands on the nerves and the senses, everything unfamiliar and exotic and slightly dangerous. I love it, but I confess I've been missing my fishing pole.

We laughed, and then there was a prolonged silence. I would say, if I did not believe otherwise, that it was an awkward silence, that neither of us knew what to say. As if things were not the way they were meant to be; as if he knew he could not joyfully relate his travels to me when Suvorin's son had just died. His thoughts were elsewhere, his feelings, too; and we must seem very provincial to him now.

I sensed he was looking at me. Staring right at me. When you can see, you can look back at someone, absorb or deflect the gaze; but a blind person has no control over another person's gaze, and the sense, the very suspicion, that this gaze is lingering on you—staring, as it were, however sympathetically—makes you feel exposed, quite naked, regardless of your own lack of vision. I felt the heat rise to my cheeks, I did not know which way to turn my head. Finally, he said quietly, And have you been all right, Zinaida Mikhailovna?

I've been fine, everyone has been reading to me, I feel like
a regular library! This rather too hastily, so I added: But I've
missed our conversations, it's true.

And so have I, Zinaida Mikhailovna, so have I. We spoke a
great deal with the Suvorins, of course, but . . . He paused for
a long time, then said, You have a different way of perceiving
things. Through you, I see things differently.

I believe what he might have said, had he been bolder, was
that in my unseeing presence, he could be another, perhaps
truer self; without *my* gaze, he was free in a way that no sighted
presence could ever allow. That is the harsh, uncomfortable truth
about sight that I have discovered only since I've lost it: Others
may use one's blindness to find a place of comfort.

August 16, 1888

This has been a quiet week. The last two days have been
unusually cool, and when I am in the garden, I sense that the
sun is behind a thick cover of cloud. The air seems to breathe in
relief; there are new scents, subtle and fresh, from the flowers.

Anton Pavlovich comes every afternoon now and stays for
an hour or so. Sometimes he is alone, sometimes Masha or Ivan
comes with him. When Masha comes, the conversation is rich
and full of laughter, we hurry over our words to make a point,
we agree and sigh and laugh in dismay over life's foibles. When
Ivan Pavlovich comes, there is a greater distance—which only
I perceive, surely, but it is there nonetheless; they talk about
fishing or marriage: Do Natasha or I know of any suitable
parties for Ivan, who, I am told, blushes and waves his hand
and even shoves his brother on the arm in protest. Natasha and
Elena had been joking about Vata as a suitable party for Ivan

Pavlovich, but lately, I wonder if they are not seriously trying to put our cousin in his path whenever possible. I imagine she must stand before him with her thumb behind her back and her big doggie eyes staring at him expectantly. Personally, I would not mind such a union, for it would bring our two families closer—and it is definitely a more suitable match than Aleksandr Pavlovich and Elena.

When we are alone, Anton Pavlovich turns to me eagerly, as if it is time to tell me the secrets he has kept from his brother and sister.

His voice low and confidential, he says, I am making great strides with the novel. Our guests in May and June—that was all good and enjoyable, but now I can write, such blissful peace and quiet, and the sudden cool weather: all godsends.

I am glad to hear it, Anton Pavlovich. Can you tell me the story? Do you, I don't know, need help with the female point of view?

He exploded with laughter. Dear Zinaida Mikhailovna, I wish I could tell you, but I cannot, that is, I'm quite unwilling; thank you for your offer, but I think I have seen enough of women to manage with the point of view. Although I confess that if I were to need help, I would come to you before anyone else.

You're being polite, Anton Pavlovich. And perhaps a bit presumptuous.

Presumptuous, why? You offered! You see? A perfect example of the woman's point of view!

I must have looked rather displeased, because he laughed gently and said, Forgive me, what I mean is that your sensibility, Zinaida Mikhailovna, is extraordinary. You go beyond the surface straight to the person, to the soul, the spirit. There is something in you—a sixth sense—that removes the barriers that sight imposes in others. Do you understand what I am saying?

I would not tell him that I had already suspected this, at

least where he was concerned. It felt like too great an intimacy, and I was afraid he might withdraw if he knew my suspicions. So I said, But it is nothing I do deliberately, Anton Pavlovich. The barrier—or lack of it—is in you, in your understanding of me. You see me—you may judge or apprehend or accept me based on what you see: a plain, unthreatening woman who will not try to control you or marry you. And because I cannot see you—although I am told you are handsome enough—I cannot judge your physical appearance, it is true, and I accept you as you are, whether you are as handsome as a Greek or as vile as the oldest toad by the river—all that matters little to me. Whereas for Natasha, I imagine it does. Although, to be honest, if your fingers were covered with warts from all those toads you frequent, I should have a hard time when you kiss my hand. But believe me, if you feel there are no barriers in my presence because I cannot see you, you are wrong, and you are being presumptuous. How can you be sure I don't imagine you to be just like that toad? Repulsive!

He laughed, there was a long bemused silence, and then he said, We move differently in the world, there's no escaping the fact. Perhaps, simply, these things are inexplicable. I'm drawn to you for reasons you might deny out of modesty, or perhaps because of a truth I do not see. We don't need to question it, Zinaida Mikhailovna. I am grateful for your presence in my life—that should suffice.

I could have said, returning the compliment, that I was grateful for his presence. But I felt that it might lessen what he was trying to say to me, might sound like mere politeness. I had argued long enough—for the sake of argument—against his extraordinary perception of me.

There was, therefore, another long silence. I could not determine whether it was warm or verging on awkward. A smile in his eyes might have told me. But if he had known I was looking at him, seeing him, his expression might be quite altered, self-conscious. These were presumptions on my part. So I reached out, found his arm with my fingers, a light linen cloth beneath my touch, and his skin warm beneath the cloth.

To change the subject, I said, And your novel? Can you tell me at least whether the main character is a man or a woman?

Both, Zinaida Mikhailovna! There are rivers and woods, and ferryboats, and the railway, and several main characters. A few dogs, and an absolutely vicious cat. That everyone loves, God knows why. And a mill with a lovely miller's daughter—just like the one here. That's all I'll tell you for now.

I could hear the laughter in his words: Of course he was teasing me and would not tell me the truth about his novel. It, too, must remain invisible, behind a barrier of humor.

After that we talked of trivial things, which need no record here, but what was extraordinary was that despite any awkwardness or possible misunderstanding regarding the nature of our ease with each other, that ease seemed to be all the greater. As if the barriers he spoke of were gone, indeed. On my side as well. Was it the warmth in his tone, or the haste with which he repeatedly lowered his voice and touched my arm to make his point?

Why am I even looking for signs? There are other senses to trust than the one that is absent, and there is something beyond sense, perhaps the sixth sense he referred to, but for me it was simply the way we understood each other.

In idle moments, I write down what I remember of Anton Pavlovich's descriptions to me, though I can never recall exactly; there is always something missing.

There's your mama in a pale blue dress, and she's picking flowers, and it's hot and she's forgotten her hat, so she keeps wiping her brow

*with the back of her hand; and Grigory Petrovich is in the shade of
the oak tree, he's whittling something with a knife, he's barefoot and
he's sitting against the trunk of the tree as comfortably as in any
armchair, one leg tucked under him and the other straight out.*

(We can hear him humming.)

*And Rosa is over by the door to the kitchen, half asleep with her
chin on her paws, waiting for scraps; her eyelids flutter, first left,
then right, as she looks imploringly at whoever passes; her coat
trembles now and again as she tries to shake off a fly.*

*Down at the other end of the veranda, your sister and mine are
looking at a book of patterns that came today in the post, the latest
fashion from Paris and Brussels. I teased Masha earlier and said
I didn't know she cared for fashion, but she blushed and said, Oh,
from time to time, and Natasha needs to make a dress.*

*And now Ivan has come out to join them, and he's standing over
them with his hands in his pockets looking bored, which is to be
expected, and Natasha has given him a look that seems to say, Go
away, we are busy, and he cannot imagine that the fashion from
Brussels could be more interesting than his handsome person in
shirtsleeves and waistcoat, his beard freshly trimmed, I believe he's
even washed the river out of his hair.*

But they've ignored him, so he's coming our way.

August 17

There is something that is troubling me, Zinaida Mikhailovna,
and I would like to discuss it in the strictest confidence . . . I
believe I can trust you not to say a word.

Of course, Anton Pavlovich. I am honored by your trust.

It's my brother Aleksandr. You recall that when he was here

briefly in June, he had been recently bereaved, and you recall his extraordinary behavior when he came to visit—let's say you've met him, after a fashion.

Yes, I did speak to him briefly one evening; he struck me as very sharp, but also nervous and unsettled—compared to you or Ivan Pavlovich, obviously.

Precisely. Well, he has this idea that he would like to marry again, as soon as possible, for the children's sake, and he seems to be very taken with your sister, Elena Mikhailovna.

Yes, I know.

You know?

Yes, Maria Pavlovna told us he wrote a letter . . . that you tore up.

(I didn't mention the other letters she had received.)

He was silent for some time, then said, This is dreadful! Whom can I trust? She told you? And who else?

Natasha. Rest assured, Elena knows nothing about it.

He was on his feet, pacing back and forth before me. Then he said almost angrily, although I know he was not angry with me but with the indiscretions of his sister and brother, And does she—your sister—could she love him? Would she give up her intelligent, independent life for my brother, to be his nanny and cook his meals? Could she be that foolish?

Please, Anton Pavlovich, I assure you she would not, unless . . .

Unless?

Unless she loved him deeply.

And does she?

You would have to ask her that, but I don't believe she does. She was flattered by his attention, I know that much, she may even be fond of him, but as to marriage . . .

He sat down again, heavily; the wicker creaked, and then he continued, more calmly: Because however hasty and desperate that letter was, he has not given up. For two months now he's been thinking about it, nagging me, nagging Masha. I must stop this, Zinaida Mikhailovna, he does not love her, this is just a convenience to him.

Forgive me for asking, Anton Pavlovich, but are they not old enough to sort these things out on their own?

(I wanted to say, Must you interfere? but thought better of it.)

My brother is talented, intelligent, charming—and a dangerous, womanizing drunkard. Your sister is talented, intelligent, and far too valuable to the world at large—to those who truly need her—to be wasted on my brother and his two unfortunate orphans. My loyalty should be to my brother, but I know him too well, and I respect your sister too greatly, as a colleague and as a friend. Sasha is rash and does not think. Above all, he feels nothing—of substance—for your sister.

I did not know what to say. I did not want to spoil Elena's chances of marriage, but Anton Pavlovich did seem violently certain of the unsuitability of the match.

Perhaps they could fall in love, given time, I said weakly.

That's it, said Anton Pavlovich. That's the only possibility. He must give it time. He must come and see her again. That's all. He is in such a rush. So eager to sort out his life in a desperate way. As much as I would like to see our two families joined, this is not the way.

August 18, 1888

I waited not far from the small rickety pier by the river. I used to know it well, that pier; I could walk out onto it, absorb the yield and spring of its old planks without fear for my footing or my balance; I would step lightly as a ballerina from its height down into the rowboat. Now I stood in the pleasant dawn chill, listening to their murmuring voices, almost a whisper, not to scare away the fish, they said, not to wake the sleeping world.

It was Ivan Pavlovich's idea. He must return to Moscow in the next day or two, and he suggested to Anton Pavlovich that while he was here to help, they could take me fishing in the boat. It's just getting her into the boat, he said with mischief in his voice—rather like a prize catch, don't you think, Antosha?

So I waited, and when they had loaded their gear, I could hear steps returning along the rickety pier, and then Ivan's strong hand reached out for mine. I felt very trusting, completely without fear. What was there to be afraid of? The river? Their closeness, if we were to fall together into the boat? Here she comes, he murmured, leading me along the wooden pier, and suddenly, he lifted me up into the void and down into another pair of waiting arms. I felt the terrible rocking of the boat until Anton Pavlovich had seated me safely in the middle of the thwart, amid our muted laughter.

How good it felt, the rocking of the boat. I held lightly with my palms to the thwart as Ivan jumped in, then they pushed off, told me sternly once again to be very quiet, and we were out on the river.

The gentle rhythmic jerk of the boat as Ivan rowed; the sense of speed, movement over the water, fluid and hesitant at the same time. The water falling from the oars in a regular flow of sound, lapping, splashing, rushing. My own sense of being suspended between earth and sky, this unstable freedom from land and routine. I had been released from my prison of darkness into a dawn world of gentle movement and quiet voices, a faint breeze on the river. Before long I would feel the first rays of the sun on my arms.

We stopped, and drifted. The men cast their lines into silence. Now and again a hushed excitement, the slight rocking of the boat as they tugged on their expectation only to be disappointed. And again the still, liquid silence, punctuated by birdcalls, and insects buzzing, and the lapping of water against the sides of the boat. Once, in the distance, church bells rang briefly, inexplicably.

They handed me a line, whispered instructions. I feigned annoyance, told them I had gone fishing often enough with Pasha. I sat with the line and my patience and let a sublime peace descend upon me. I felt everything like an embrace—their presence, the water, the sky, the thin line connecting me to the deep water. Once or twice there was a tug, and I waved to my fellow fishermen; every time, the fish got away. It did not matter. I was not there for the fish.

The sun rose, and it was hot. I was grateful for my big hat. I turned my face to the sun, felt a burning brightness—reddish black—behind my dead eyes. An aching of blood vessels strained beyond capacity: I would pay for this beauty, I could feel the headache coming on. I did not care. In that moment I felt as if I had waited all my life to be there, in that silence on the river Psyol. I could feel their heartbeats quicken as they caught their first fish, could hear their whispered excitement; I could picture their smiles, the gleam in their eyes. Have you brought us luck, Zinaida Mikhailovna? asked Anton Pavlovich quietly. Come, feel it, said Ivan, and I reached forward, and he placed the fish's slippery scales just beneath my fingertips. A moment of sorrow for its destiny in Anya's pot. I raised my fingers to my nose and smelled the fresh river smell. And knew that I had last smelled it, without realizing, on Anton Pavlovich's outstretched fingers when he came to greet me at home.

I hope they were not looking at me when the time came to row back to our pier, their basket quivering with the morning's catch. It would have spoiled it for me if they had seen my tears. Fortunately, the brim on my hat was wide, and they were laughing and teasing each other in their bantering way, referring to me as impartial judge, guileless witness.

I was handed safely ashore. Rosa was there, panting with excitement, sniffing the river on my clothes. I thanked them—awkwardly, my throat still seized with emotion—and my dog led me home. The land seemed unsteady, perhaps rocking gently with the recent memory of the river.

Afterward, I lay in my dark room and waited for the headache to pass. I saw Anton and Ivan in the boat as clearly as if my sight were restored. As if somehow the movement of the boat on the river defied the immobility of land and conjured their supple forms to me. Their sleeves rolled up; their bare feet against the wooden planks; the sweat on their brows, their cautious expressions of delight when the catch was confirmed. In retrospect, in my dark cell, I could see it all.

August 20, 1888

I dreamed I went fishing.

It wasn't a dream, Zinaida Mikhailovna. You did come fishing with us.

And then last night I dreamed of it again. Only I was alone in the boat, and I was looking for you and Ivan Pavlovich.

Had we fallen overboard?

No, no, it wasn't that at all, somehow I was alone on the boat and searching for you both. And I could see—that's often the case in my dreams—but you simply weren't there to be seen.

A pause, then I added lightly, I suppose you'd gone back to Moscow.

He sighed and said, Which is true, in Ivan's case.

What a pity. And I didn't say goodbye.

He came last night, but you were already in your room, and your formidable mama would not let him go by.

She protects me . . . I suppose that may have been when I was dreaming.

And did you catch anything in your dream? Despite our absence—or perhaps thanks to it?

No, because I was looking for you and Ivan. And wait, there was something else, you weren't in Moscow, because I could hear your voices, but I couldn't see you. As if you were hiding on the island. But your voices were as loud and clear as if you were in the boat with me.

So your dream was remarkably true, in fact. You could see the river because you have seen it, but in the restored sight of your dream, you were unable to see us because you never have seen us.

I suppose that is why I felt disappointed, why I felt I'd lost you. I wasn't afraid of being alone on the river, but I absolutely had to find you, and I couldn't.

What were our disembodied voices saying?

I don't know . . . nothing important.

As usual. Well, that's all right, then! He paused and said, I don't often remember my dreams. I have such insomnia at times, it seems to chase all possibility of leisurely dreaming from my brain. The dreams I recall are of strangers—warm, benevolent strangers. Strangers who make me feel very safe. Women who love me, men who respect me. Like characters waiting to find their place in one of my stories. It's odd. Perhaps I didn't dream them at all.

Perhaps your characters are like the people in your dreams. Waiting in your imagination or your sleep—could that be the same thing?

So if you dream about me or my handsome brother Ivan, are we the characters in your story?

Of course not. I'm not making up a story, you're very real.

Are you sure? How do you know I'm not in your imagination?

Some of you is, to be sure, but—

How do you know, incontrovertibly, that I exist?

Because you have physical substance, a voice, words—

You know that, but do I? Does Grigory Petrovich?

We laughed; we could hear Grigory Petrovich scolding Georges as if he were still a small boy, for cutting a bouquet of flowers from the border without his permission.

Ah, enough of philosophy, sighed Anton Pavlovich. It's obvious we're alive, God has spoken in the form of your brother's bouquet, which will gladden my sister's heart.

Your sister?

Just imagine that I am winking at you. She is rather taken with Georges. I don't know that it's mutual; Georges seems to have eyes for nothing but his fortepiano.

Poor Masha, the bouquet was not for her. Mama had asked him to choose some flowers for the entrance, as she is expecting visitors later.

Just after Anton Pavlovich had taken his leave and gone to join his family, an exhausted Elena came onto the veranda and flopped into the same wicker chair. She was hot, and perspiring, and breathless.

She updated me on the epidemic of scarlet fever in the village, then asked after my own health. We talked about other things— Georges's application to the conservatory, Tonya's baby: robust and rosy, she tells me. And naturally, the subject of our guests came up, and we speculated whether Natasha might have fallen in love with Anton Pavlovich. Elena tells me she has found her particularly mopey lately; reluctantly, I agreed with her—what else could explain the odd behavior I've noticed? My normally reasonable, cheerful sister, now all sighs and slamming books onto tables and shouting vulgarities at Grigory Petrovich in Ukrainian until he went to Mama and complained politely that at least if she would shout in Russian, it would not hurt his feelings so much, because then he could understand how bad the insult was. We laughed—poor Grigory Petrovich, in all these years since Papa brought him to us from Sevastopol, he has never learned Ukrainian—but in fact he adores Natasha and willingly submits to her tender abuse. Still, none of us has known her to be so nervous and high-strung in months, if not years.

The sad thing, concluded Elena, is that Anton Pavlovich does not seem to be smitten with her to the same degree at all. He laughs with her, enjoys her company. She's clever and not boring, so men do like being around her, and then she mistakes their attention for love.

Surely not. She's more instinctive than that. We all are, Elena, Mama has raised us well.

Are we, Zina? Is it not our instincts that betray us?

What do you mean?

As women, we listen to our feelings, we value them—and you know as well as I do that the study of the body, as perfected by our male colleagues, allows no room for the study of feelings. And the drawing room is no different from the surgery: We women follow our instincts, respect them; they brush them aside, except to flirt and pass the time.

I hesitated for a long time, thought carefully about my recent conversation with Anton Pavlovich. I felt uneasy, as if she had thrown a light on something I did not want to see. My blindness would not leave me impervious to certain truths.

She may feel for Anton Pavlovich, said Elena, but I doubt she can see that it is not mutual, so her instinct has betrayed her.

Does she love him? I asked worriedly.

I don't know—is it that strong? Or just an attraction? A delight in his presence?

I was silent for a moment, then, recalling what Anton Pavlovich had said about his brother, I decided now might be an opportunity to broach the subject with my sister as bluntly as I could, without giving anything away.

How do you define love, Elena?

I don't, dear Zina; other than the love I feel for my family, for my work. This love that we got so worked up over as girls, this thing Anton Pavlovich describes in his stories between men and women—an attraction for biological ends, of course that exists, but some exalted closeness, the need to possess and be possessed—spare me! There are more important things in life, as you know.

And would you ever marry without love in the hope that it might follow as a matter of course?

She reached over and squeezed my arm. Zina, what a thought! I am married to my profession! Just because I have fingers does not mean I must have rings!

You've changed, Elena. I thought you wanted a family, children—

Perhaps I did. Yes. I did. You are right. Her voice softened and she added, I've grown wiser. I've observed my patients, I've observed the wider world. I've seen myself through the eyes of men I might have loved, and I've encountered my own humility, my own reality. We can be blind to it for so long, when society pulls us in the opposite direction with such force. Yes, I would have liked children, but I fear the price I would have to pay. Look at Tonya, poor girl, her youth and beauty fading, already she works so hard—for Pasha, for the baby—and that is her entire life. What thanks does she get!

Pasha loves her, Elena. And she is happy.

Of course he loves her. But there is no one as good as Pasha for me; I know that, I accept it. I must be useful elsewhere. Leave love for Monsieur Pleshcheyev and his sonnets.

She had answered Anton Pavlovich's question but not mine; for only then did I realize I had, indeed, a question of my own.

After that conversation a headache came on, and I was sleeping when Anton Pavlovich came this afternoon. I am better now, but just the thought of my conversation with Elena makes my head throb. She must not read what I have written. Perhaps I should tear up these pages. Or find a hiding place for the diary.

ANA READ KATYA KENDALL'S message: *I might not be here.* She gave an exasperated sigh—really, what nerve, she had not even been paid—but she decided to remain upbeat. *Not to worry,* she replied. *I'll try to get in touch. Either way, it would be wonderful to discuss Zinaida Mikhailovna's diary.*

No reply.

She called the Kendalls when she arrived in London, once she had checked in to her bed-and-breakfast: voicemail. *You have reached the offices of Polyana Press. No one is available to take your call . . .* She left a message and her cell number. If she didn't hear back by ten o'clock the next morning, she would go to Cambridge for some simple tourism and much-needed distraction.

Ana had scarcely left the house for the past three weeks, working steadily on the diary and a few other small but lucrative projects that had come in. Every so often she would feel a pleasant flutter in her belly, thinking about the Fleur Mailly prize, which would be announced in New York in a few weeks' time: The days were passing, and just her presence on the shortlist had led to a small flurry of articles online, of praise for the novel and the translation. She wanted to believe; the competition was not too stiff, she was in with a chance.

For the first hour or so, Ana felt the thrill of iconic strangeness that strikes all visitors when they realize they are actually in London: the double-decker buses, the black cabs, the glimpse of the real Big Ben on the horizon. Gradually, the novelty faded to the simple delight of hearing English all around her, seeing different faces, being on an adventure.

She went to the reception at the writers' organization. An old Victorian terraced house, indistinguishable from the others on the street, but as soon as she stepped through the door, Ana recognized, from her years in Paris, the unsettling false bonhomie of literary gatherings: the assertive male voices; the female laughter; the jostling for position by the wine and the hors d'oeuvres. There was already a good crowd, of the sort that invites a protective hand around a full wineglass when trying to move through the room. Ana suddenly wished she were in one of the cozy living rooms she had glimpsed on her way here, reading by lamplight or talking to a friend, rather than nodding hello to these people she didn't know. As far as she could tell from the name tags and the books on the display table, she was the only translator there. With a mixture of shyness and curiosity, she approached the few people who stood on their own and asked them about their books. They answered her with the pride, the author's glow, that says, *Look what I've done, who I am.* She talked about her work and felt vaguely fraudulent. Not that she was—she had every right to be there, the association was open to translators, and she had paid her dues. She would have liked to be more visible, to make even a faint impression, but these strangers did not seem particularly interested in the work of translation; nor did she want to chatter about herself. She began to question the sound of her own voice— polite, inquisitive, insincere. She thought about Zinaida Mikhailovna and Anton Pavlovich. They were her secret, and she guarded them. Her ambivalence surprised her in the end. She could have conveyed her enthusiasm without giving anything away, without betraying the Kendalls' injunction. *I'm translating this wonderful nineteenth-century Russian journal, full of literary figures . . .* But she felt a sudden kinship with the child Georges Lintvaryov, reluctant to play the piano when others were within earshot.

She spotted a refuge in a corner, an empty folding chair next to an older, tired-looking woman sitting on her own. Ana hesitated: Perhaps the woman was a bore, or perhaps she wanted a lap on which to put her napkin and her plate of little sandwiches. Go for the lap, thought Ana, taking a deep breath as she sat down. The woman greeted Ana as if she had been waiting for her all along; she had a faint Slavic accent and turned out to be of Polish origin, and although she was a writer with a newly published, well-received book, Ana quickly understood from her ironic laughter that she felt as out of place as Ana did. Her English was beyond perfect, in the way that certain foreigners—immigrants—have of inventing a sharper, more colorful idiom, and Ana sensed that the networking nature of the gathering depressed and exhausted her. They exchanged ideas about cultural differences between Europe and the United States, where the Polish woman had lived as well, nodding or shaking their heads with equal enthusiasm; she shared Ana's concern about the crisis in Ukraine, from experience, she said. Ana wished she could keep more of this gentle woman in her life than a business card. (She promised herself she would buy the woman's book: like a postcard or print from a museum shop, a desperate bid to retain, just a little bit longer, the real painting's incomparable light.)

Ana began to make her way through the crowd toward the coat rack. She felt abruptly very tired, weary, sorry she had come all this way for an event that, in the end, did not have much to do with her. She had exhausted her supply of smiles and polite formulas; it was time to go for a proper bite to eat—she'd spotted a sushi place near her B&B—and prepare her strategy for meeting the Kendalls. Or finding them.

She was reaching for her coat when she noticed a young woman pinning a name tag to her jacket. Ana glanced at the tag and flushed when she recognized the name—Isobel Brookes, the other woman shortlisted for the Fleur Mailly literary prize.

Ana took a breath. I was about to leave, and now you're here—finally, another translator!

The young woman (oh, that smooth skin, those bright eyes) looked at her, slightly taken aback, then said, You're a translator?

Ana said her name, and Isobel broke into a smile. Of course, we're both on the shortlist for the Mailly prize, aren't we? The only women, too, if I'm not mistaken. Are you leaving already?

I was about to, but I can stay a bit longer, now that you're here. Ana felt genuinely relieved, as if her presence at the reception had been legitimized at last.

When they were both settled at a table by the window with their glasses of white wine and small plates of smoked salmon, Ana looked around the room and said, I don't know anyone here. I thought there'd be more translators, but they're all authors.

Yes, that's odd. Usually, there are more of us. I know a fair number of people here, but only through my partner.

As if to prove her point, she nodded to a man standing nearby and said, Catch you later.

Ana instantly worried she might be keeping Isobel from the people she had come to meet, and she took too big a sip of wine and sloshed some onto her jacket, leaving a slow-spreading stain. Oh, dear, she said.

Don't worry. When it dries, you won't see it, said Isobel.

Again the clear eyes, the smooth skin, occupying Ana's field of vision like a bright glow.

What are you working on at the moment? said Ana, flustered.

Isobel went into a long explanation about a male French author Ana had never heard of; when she'd finished, Ana said, I get so discouraged that there are not more women getting translated.

Isobel held her wineglass at a jaunty angle and raised her eyebrow, as if surprised by Ana's remark, unaware that she too was about to splash wine on her lap.

Careful, said Ana, pointing, and they both laughed.

Isobel then returned her question, and Ana started to explain, almost reluctantly. A historical document . . . a diary from nineteenth-century Russia—Ukraine, actually . . . I had my doubts to begin with, but now I'm really enjoying it.

She hesitated to go further, but in any case, Isobel said, It's terrible what's been happening in Ukraine.

Yes, said Ana, I'd been hoping to go to Crimea. But suddenly it's all very complicated—putting it mildly.

(As she said this, she realized she was being somewhat disingenuous, that her desire to go there had increased retroactively, with enhanced difficulty and Yves's prodding.)

Isobel nodded politely, looking around the room. Yes, that's right, they voted to be part of Russia again, isn't that it?

Voted, said Ana, that might be a bit of a stretch by Western standards. She gave a curt laugh and added, I even translated a guidebook to Crimea a few years ago! How ironic is that. I don't suppose it will be of use anymore.

Oh, don't say that, you can probably still go to Crimea, though you're right, it will be more complicated. Russian visas, that sort of thing. You'll have to update your guidebook.

Ana nodded and frowned.

Isobel shifted in her chair to look at Ana more closely and said, I can't keep up with the news these days. The world seems to be spinning out of control. I feel like I'm clinging to my family so we don't go hurtling into space. She gave a faint, slightly affected laugh.

Ana shrugged and said, And I'm too well informed. I suppose I spend too much time on my own—I live in a small village—and the world news has become disproportionately important. If I lived in the Balkans or southern Europe, I'd be one of those old women hanging out her window watching the world go by, but in my village, everyone gets in the car and drives off to the shopping mall.

Isobel sat back and held up her wineglass. How sad, she said.

There was an awkward silence. Ana didn't know whether Isobel was referring to her neighbors' lifestyle or her own, so she turned to look more closely at her and said, Do you live in London?

Yes, I'm here with my partner, he's French—I was his translator. Well, I still am. Franck Fabiani, perhaps you've heard of him?

Ana nodded. Of course.

(Heard of him, but not read him; his books were meant to be pseudo-intellectual thrillers with a lot of violence against women and children, counterbalanced by the deep humanity of a gruff, disillusioned male detective. They sold well and had the critics on their side. Well, more power to Isobel, thought Ana, she had a job for life, or at least as long as the relationship lasted.)

Why don't you live in France? Ana asked.

Franck came here when he was writing the first book in the series; they're set in the UK. We met, and he stayed on. We have a two-year-old daughter now.

Ana nodded. The wine stain had dried. Isobel smiled and said hello to a smartly dressed young man with a shadow of a beard.

Isobel laughed and said, Franck is trying to grow a beard, too. It doesn't suit him, he's too old, it makes him look ever so rough, you half expect to see a big piece of cardboard under his arm.

Ana looked at her, puzzled.

You know, like a homeless person. Most of the time he's far too well dressed, but still. Even Chloe seems scared of him. She says, Papa, you're scratchy! Isobel shrugged and smiled.

Ana hooked her bag over her shoulder and stood up. I'd better get going. I'm hoping to go up to Cambridge tomorrow, so I want to make an early start.

How lovely. Pity you can't stay and meet Franck, he'll be here any minute.

Yes, it's too bad, but I'd better go. I'd like to stop in the bookshop before it closes, too.

They shook hands and wished each other luck for the Mailly prize. Ana made her way through the room; when she looked back, someone had already taken her seat at the table with Isobel.

At the front door, she brushed past a man on his way in, a blur of thick gray hair, Burberry, and umbrella. She supposed this was the famous Franck, but by the time she turned back to get a better look, he had vanished inside.

Ana browsed. As if she were rowing on the surface of a lake and all the books were floating just below, illegible, out of reach. Confused, slightly drunk, she could not concentrate, upset by her conversation with Isobel Brookes in a diffuse way she could not clarify.

She came upon Isobel's translation almost immediately, the one nominated for the prize, prominently displayed. Ten copies in a neat, alluring pile. *The Lemon-Rind Still Life.* (*Nature morte aux écorces de citron,* said the copyright page. Ana thought petulantly, *Still Life with Lemon Rind.*) The reproduction of a Flemish still life on the cover; the author photo on the back flap, the young French writer with classic dark good looks, the crisp white shirt; a lovely edition, hardback, with deckle-edged pages.

From there Ana went to the crime section and hunted for Franck Fabiani's novels. She found one, visibly the latest. The usual superlatives, *Spellbinding . . . Best-selling French author . . .* Even one concession to cross-cultural translation: *Franck Fabiani knows the Brits better than we know ourselves. A must-read revelation in every regard.*

She turned the book over and opened it from the back to read the author flap.

At first she thought it must be a mistake, a joke, a cosmic prank. An uncanny resemblance. But even time had no power to alter the shock of hair, now gray, the dimpled half-smile. *French author of the best-selling DCI Hartley series,* said the flap, *Franck Fabiani is translated by his partner, Isobel Brookes. They live in London.*

Léo. Not in La Paz or Lille but right here in London.

Ana liked to think she did not believe in coincidence. It had played no significant role in her life, although she did know of friends who had suffered, mostly in their relationships, from untimely coincidences. Meeting someone—an erstwhile lover—where he had no business being, when you were in the presence of your partner; more happily, missing a plane at an airport halfway around the world only to run into a long-lost friend. No, thought Ana, this was logical: In the small world of literary translators, you were bound to run into your colleagues if you went to professional events.

As for Isobel being his partner, that, too, did not seem implausible. Networks were formed between authors and translators. It was odd that Ana had not seen his picture before now, but it was less common in France, the author mug shot, and she tended not to read crime novels, or watch the literary programs on television or the Internet, where he probably appeared on a regular basis.

But she still felt stunned: targeted, mocked.

She remembered Léo's awful novels. The earnest workers, the long-suffering farmers' wives. So he'd found his niche at last, moving a layer deeper into the dissolution of late-capitalist British society. He had always been something of an Anglophile, Ana remembered; he'd followed the cricket and regularly faulted Ana for her Americanisms. *Gotten. Elevator. Say Tewsday, not Toosday.* It had amused her at the time, the Marxist student who wanted his cream tea at Liberty or Harrods whenever they went over to London for the weekend. He assured her it was only what Engels would have done.

Naturally, he would have chosen to use a nom de plume. He must have broken other hearts besides Ana's, and made not a few political enemies; already when Ana was with him, he was constantly feuding with those who were supposed to be his comrades. He would not want their Gallic scorn, the Marxist turned trendy crime writer. How convenient to vanish, then resurface as the perfect gentleman with Burberry and brolly. And cashmere scarf, of course. *Autres temps, autres mœurs.*

She pushed the book back on the shelf as if it might contaminate her. She tried to recall the blur in the doorway: Yes, there had been a whiff of cologne, too. She had been staring straight ahead, his head was turned, the flash of gray. The raincoat, the scarf. That was it.

Does it matter, thought Ana, am I sorry?

She found herself staring at spines in the Russia section, dear, familiar names dancing before her while her thoughts raced and then tripped over sluggish, unchanged emotions. She no longer felt the love, but she knew it was rooted inside her as historical fact, both to treasure and to regret. Yes, she had been young and naive. Yes, he had been sardonic and far more experienced. Yes, he had diddled her along for two years or more because she was tall and leggy and faintly exotic in those days (*La Californie? C'est trop loin!*), and despite the Americanisms, she improved his English, while her French languished. Yes, she had been devastated when he left her for an older woman who had a farmhouse in the Pyrenees and wove ponchos and bedspreads. It didn't make sense, then or now. After that, his trail had gone cold.

She had thought of him more often since the breakup of her marriage, and not just when she went skiing: wistfully, with a nostalgic curiosity, as if trying to imprint what had been recurring spells of euphoria and physical transport more sharply upon her yielding memory; to imprint them over the failure, ultimately, of her life with Mathieu. True, there were the things she had forfeited in order to be with Léo—she did not go back to California, to the master's program at the Monterey Institute, where she'd been accepted; she had not been there when her mother died; she had lost touch with friends. Yes, Anton Pavlovich, I ran into the night without my bonnet.

And if there had not been Léo, would there have been Mathieu? Did Mathieu not rescue her, in a way, from her disappointment? Did she not trust him where she had been betrayed by Léo, respect him where she had loved Léo? Until he betrayed her in turn?

It was easy, with hindsight, to analyze and condemn, to see one's errors or apportion blame.

But standing there gazing blankly at a volume of Tolstoy's short works, Ana briefly mourned the girl who had lived for her belief in a kindred spirit, in a shared life beyond the mere transports of youth. Léo had sent her back out into the world with that faith damaged; and while she had thought that her belief would be safe in a life with a husband, perhaps it had been hollow from the start.

With a start and a rush of anger, Ana realized Isobel must have known who she was—though that assumed that Franck had told Isobel about his former girlfriends, which he was unlikely to do, let alone tell her their names if even he was hiding behind a pseudonym. Or had Léo been the pseudonym all along—a nod (without the final "n") to a certain revolutionary? He must have seen Ana's name on the prize shortlist, although there, too, he would have kept it to himself. What a dirty little thrill it must give him. What were the odds of such a thing?

As for Isobel's relationship with Franck, she was young, very young; they had a child together; her generation was tougher, women were stronger, more assertive. Or so Ana assumed from hearsay. She did not know those women.

And Franck was older. Perhaps a certain gentleness came with well-aged cynicism.

Ana stared at the books in front of her. *Crime and Punishment. The Brothers Karamazov. The Idiot.* Her eyes filled with tears; she shook her head. In the end, it had not been given to her to meet Franck, because Franck was not her Léo; whoever that Léo was, he existed only in her memory. That was how she must leave it.

She started taking books from the shelf and nearly filled the small basket. A thick new biography of Tolstoy; two novels by Turgenev that she had never read. She was pleased to see that she already had everything on the shelf by Anton Chekhov. She found the Polish woman's book of essays on a neighboring shelf. Back to the Russia shelf, irresistibly: Penelope Fitzgerald's *The Beginning of Spring*—no, she wasn't Russian, but the book was about Russia. Two novels by Andrey Kurkov, misfiled under Russia; he was Ukrainian. But wrote in Russian. About Ukraine. Living proof, if more were needed, of the tangle of historical and cultural ties.

Appeased by the pile in her basket, she went up to the register. I have a question, she said to the young woman. Do you have any copies of a book called *Go Through the Door, Turn Left*, by Lydia Guilloux?

The young woman typed on her computer, then shook her head. It's on order. Would you like us to let you know when it arrives?

No, I'm afraid I don't live here, but thanks for checking.

She left the bookshop with a smile.

KATYA WAS ANNOYED: THE translator was worse than an agent. *Not to worry . . . wonderful to discuss Zinaida Mikhailovna's diary.* They did not owe her anything other than the fee and a cursory appreciation for her work. They did not owe her tea and cakes—that was for authors, and even then.

Or did they? Katya felt irritable, anxious. This wasn't right. Peter had told her he hadn't even paid the woman's advance.

I haven't got it, Katya.

But surely it's only a few hundred pounds, Peter

I haven't got a few hundred pounds. I haven't got it.

This scene, a few days earlier. Over a near-silent dinner of take-away pizza. The cheese, growing cold, congealing. Her nausea. His words like something out of a film. Not a very good film, not one she'd watch, anyway. She had dug deeper, there was more to it, of course, complicated things about returns and distributors and a bookseller who'd gone belly-up. A cash-flow problem.

Katya pleaded common courtesy. Could they not borrow such a small sum, put it on a credit card? What if, she said breathlessly, she refuses to finish the translation or to send it to us?

Peter refused to discuss the matter further. He toyed with the pizza crust, banging it against the edge of the box. He lifted sausage pieces from the remaining slices, chewed on them noisily. Katya closed her eyes.

So if she agreed to meet with this Anastasia Harding, what would she tell her? Where would common courtesy be then? *I'm sorry, I'm telling you politely that we have no money to pay you. Could you do the translation out of your love for Russian literature?*

Katya felt a burst of anger. This diary deserved the best translation possible, the best treatment possible. Nothing halfhearted or hurried or unfinished because the translator had been treated in an offhand manner.

She would find the money; she would agree to see the woman. Not just tea and cakes: full Russian hospitality.

SLEEP WAS RAGGED, UNFORGIVING. Léo strode through her wakefulness, larger than life, both tender and cruel. *What if?*, he shouted, causing a rush of anxiety to her stomach that seemed to shoot through her like caffeine. What if she had gone back to speak to him, to see him? Did Isobel mention their conversation to him? Would he ask about her, veiling his curiosity? Would Isobel say, *Oh, she's much older than I am*, or something vaguely unkind, if he pressed her for a description? How she had spilled the wine? Would he lean over in bed and say, *T'inquiète pas, chérie*, you are by far the better translator, you will win the prize?

In the darkness Ana heard birds singing. It can't be, she thought, maybe it's just a dream, maybe I'll wake up with Doodle at my feet and the sound of birds at dawn where they belong, in an ordered world.

At breakfast she questioned her landlady: Did they have nightingales in their garden? She smiled at Ana indulgently and said, Not as far as I know. Blackbird, perhaps?

Ana was already on her way to King's Cross when she heard a cell phone ringing and realized it was hers.

A woman's voice, unfamiliar, somewhat breathless, her slight accent unmistakably Russian, inviting her to lunch.

Ana turned around and headed back to South Kensington.

She arrived early at the pub and sat back to read the newspaper at the table Katya had reserved, but she could not concentrate.

The pub was Victorian but had been refurbished with a spare, luminous decor that was a nod to modernity and its status as a gastropub. The menu offered odd things such as kidney suet pudding and warm smoked eel with buttermilk chicken; Ana opted cautiously for the almond gnocchi with aubergine caviar.

As people walked in, she watched and wondered if she'd be able to spot Katya. Somehow she could not imagine her. It was as if, should she even try, the woman would turn out to be just the opposite of her imaginings. A tall, elegant woman wearing no jewelry or makeup, with pin-straight brown hair tied back in a ribbon, stopped to ask for her table, then headed Ana's way. Unsmiling, she introduced herself and immediately apologized for not having been in touch, for not having paid the advance, and for having called at the last minute.

Though Ana smiled, she still felt raw. She said, The project itself more than makes up for any . . . practical inconvenience.

Do you think so? I mean, do you like it?

A faint smile, not so much encouraging as worried; to Ana, she seemed absent, as if her thoughts were with the place she had just left.

It's fascinating. And quite beautiful.

Katya's smile broadened.

Where did you find it? asked Ana.

At that moment Katya's cell phone rang. Excuse me, she said. She rummaged around in her handbag—an expensive-looking leather satchel that seemed to overflow with tissues and receipts and small notepads—until she found the phone. She looked at the screen, then tapped it. Just my husband, she said, shrugging. I'll ring him later.

There was an awkward pause, then she said, Are you married, Anastasia? If you don't mind my asking?

Please call me Ana. No, no. I mean, I was, but I no longer have that privilege.

It was a polite, almost ironic formula, but Katya took it quite literally.

You're very lucky. It's not a privilege. You have your freedom, your own name, and none of the associated inconveniences. She dropped her cell phone in her handbag, then gave a heavy sigh as she zipped the bag shut. Let's order, she said. Will you have some wine, Ana?

Yes, that would be nice.

Katya waved to the waitress, and they gave their order. Then Katya turned to look at Ana, scrutinizing her in a direct but not unfriendly way. She asked a few things about France and what other projects Ana had worked on recently. Ana told her about the Guilloux novel and its nomination for the prize. Katya Kendall was warm, effusive, in her congratulations. The waitress returned with the wine; they raised their glasses in a polite toast.

Katya had a poised fierceness that Ana remembered from earlier Russian acquaintances. She could not say how old the woman was, probably in her late forties, but her simple elegance might be misleading.

Without warning, she began to talk about the diary. You asked me in an earlier email how we plan to market the book. Part of our strategy will be a certain element of surprise—we don't want word to get out before publication—which is why we've asked you not to talk about it. Because we are hoping—hoping—to publish the novel Anton Pavlovich was writing at Luka.

Ana looked at Katya and put her wineglass down. Katya was looking not at her but at a point in the middle distance. We are working on it, she continued, more than that I cannot tell you. Obviously, if we cannot publish it, we don't want to be left with egg on our faces. It's a complicated business, legally, you understand, with Russia, and now with the situation . . . it may take some time, but yes, we will try.

She smiled, but this time her smile was strained. When she

turned to Ana, her eyes—gray, luminous—seemed to be almost pleading. There was something else, a personal edginess that Ana suspected had nothing to do with Chekhov or the diary. She noticed Katya was hardly touching her food—she'd ordered a bright pink risotto, which must have been made with beets.

Forgive me for asking, said Katya, are you doing all right— the translation business, you know, with the economic crisis? And without a partner to help pay the rent?

Ana was startled by the change of topic, by its very personal nature. Her thoughts were all on Chekhov, not the practicalities of her profession. She saw him writing by the window in Luka; she saw him handing her a bound book; and for a moment her words escaped her, then seemed too loud, pretentious, false, for the sake of filling a resonant silence.

Well, I don't know, I . . . I've always thought that if the literary translation dried up—it's all right at the moment—I'd specialize in oenology. The rich will always be around, they'll always want French wine. And it's a lovely vocabulary.

She smiled; Katya gave a hearty laugh.

Ah, yes, if only we could bottle our literature and sell it to oligarchs! Art is subversion, though, isn't it. That is, art like literature and music that cannot be made into an object to be sold at Sotheby's or in all these galleries in our fine town of Moscow-on-Thames. Can you imagine the pressure these days on young visual artists to succeed? It must be far worse than for musicians or writers, let alone poets. Do you like poetry? Of course you do, you studied Russian.

Katya poured more wine, raised her glass, then switched to Russian and launched into a surprisingly bitter diatribe against the twenty-first century in general and the United Kingdom in particular. She seemed a different person when she spoke Russian, more self-assured and graceful, yet with a touch of the theatrical. Ana found herself blushing from the effort of speaking. The effect of the wine left her tongue heavy with consonants, her brain fuddled by declensions and lost words. She could not catch everything, the place was so noisy and Katya spoke quickly, telling of the lost opportunities in Eastern Europe, just after the fall of the Berlin Wall, that had led to chaos and confusion under Yeltsin, the consolidation of the mafia with Putin and a new repression, and now the situation in Ukraine . . . Ana nodded in agreement, and all the while she was thinking of what Katya had told her about Chekhov's novel. The room buzzed with it; or was it the wine? Ana tried to read the subtext in Katya's flashing eyes and waving fingers, and when Katya extended her blame to the men in government in general, Ana thought it would be safe to infer that she was blaming her husband, in particular, the unhelpful Peter Kendall of secret marketing plans.

Katya abruptly switched back to English. Have you got a title?

A title?

For the diary. Zinaida Mikhailovna Lintvaryova is such a mouthful for English speakers, no one will buy it. We need something pithy, catchy.

Ana was nonplussed; she had assumed they would use Zinaida Mikhailovna's name.

Diary of a Russian . . . Confidante? My Summers with Anton Chekhov?

Katya shook her head and laughed. Too bland, Ana, come on. Something more in keeping with the spirit, the atmosphere. Oh, I know it's not easy. I suppose we want the word *Russian* in the title, too. Well, think about it. No immediate rush.

After a moment she said, Your name—full name, that is, Anastasia—is it Russian? I mean, is your background Russian?

Ana smiled and said, Only in the most indirect and sentimental sort of way. My mother was very fond of Ingrid Bergman, in particular of a film she made in 1956, a few years before I was born, perhaps you know the one. So I'm named for someone who didn't really exist. For an impostor.

Katya raised her eyebrows in amused commiseration, then said, Still, there was the real Anastasia—the grand duchess Anastasia Nikolayevna—and it's a very beautiful name. It means resurrection, of course. You know that.

Ana nodded, but she didn't know what to say. She couldn't help but think that Grand Duchess Anastasia of the Romanov clan had come to a rather sticky end, however lovely her name. Ana had a soft spot for the Ingrid Bergman character, Anna Anderson, the half-mad woman who had pretended to be Anastasia the miraculous survivor of the Romanov massacre. She had chosen such a plain name for her insane grab at an exalted destiny, because even that was a pseudonym: Anna Anderson's true identity was not Russian but Polish, and her real name was Franziska Schanzkowska.

They sat on, ordered dessert, then coffee. Ana wondered briefly whether she could share her story about Léo/Franck with Katya. All through the meal, she had felt somewhat spacey, at one remove, as if hungover from a surfeit of the past. Finally, she ruled it out as too personal, too intimate. Katya might chuckle, commiserate; or she might merely raise her eyebrows, as if to say, Why are you telling me this, what business is it of mine?

The pub began to empty as people returned to work. Katya seemed to be in no hurry; she did inquire politely whether Ana had to be anywhere. Ana thought wistfully of Cambridge but said nothing. It was too late, and she was reluctant to leave the pub, with its fug of prosperity and cheer, the wine-induced, congenial complicity with this woman, no longer a hostile stranger who did not return emails or pay her translators. She, too, had read the diary; for the time being, Katya was the only person with whom Ana could share her knowledge and understanding of the friendship between Zinaida Mikhailovna and Anton Pavlovich.

They talked about poetry, lapsing into Russian now and again; Katya recited whole poems by Akhmatova and Pasternak in a grave, faintly tremulous voice, her tone like that of a cello. Never hesitating, as if she gave readings regularly. She would reach over, place her hand on Ana's forearm, and her eyes, oddly, seemed to go blue, as if growing brighter with excitement. At one point she raised her voice and looked out at the room. A few diners were staring; one young man had his elbow on the table, chin propped in his palm, and was listening intently, as if he understood the Russian.

But now, a different drama is unfolding:
This time, let me be.

Ana heard the words, and she was back in her brief Russian summer under an open sky full of stars and satellites—perhaps Yves had been there that night, too, she must ask him. There was a guitar, and a campfire, there were songs by Vysotsky, there were blini together with stews and salads, and she saw it all again through the rhythm of the words, the language working on her the way the vodka and the *samogon* had back then, and the wine now, intoxicating, yet reaching somewhere inside where nothing else had ever gone, not in that way, a depth charge of significance and understanding. When Katya fell silent, Ana looked at her and said very softly, Thank you, that was beautiful.

Yes, well. Katya smiled. I don't have many opportunities to share poetry these days. Let alone write it.

You write your own poetry?

I used to. But I think I lost my inspiration when I came to the West. She shrugged, gave Ana an almost apologetic smile, then looked away again, her gaze filled with something like regret or longing. She said, I'm very nostalgic for the nineteenth century, you know. The life that Zinaida Mikhailovna describes. Even that hardship, as a woman. I would be very happy there. Not you?

If my standard of living were at least that of Natasha or Masha Chekhova, I could be happy there, I suppose. I am happy there every morning when I go to work, so to speak.

Again Katya's gaze wandered, and she said, almost as if Ana were not there, I do hope others will feel that way as well. It's so important—for me, for my husband, for the press. So much on Zinaida's frail shoulders.

She smiled and looked at Ana and saw that she understood.

They talked until all the other diners had left and midafternoon drinkers were beginning to take their place. Ana asked what she thought about the situation in Ukraine; Katya replied that although her *English side* agreed it was a violation of Ukraine's sovereignty, her *Russian side* reluctantly and irrationally supported the recent referendum in Crimea and their "decision" (she held up her fingers, indicating quotation marks) to be part of Russia.

I used to go there as a child, I had my first kiss on the waterfront in Yalta! It's a very emotional place for Russians, we never thought of it as a separate country. But now there are these people stirring up trouble, occupying buildings in Kharkov and Donetsk and that region and calling for independence—they are thugs, supported or sent by Moscow, I'm sure. Nothing good will come of their actions. I'm worried. Very worried.

Katya's phone rang again. She pulled it out of her bag, looked at it, gave a sigh of exasperation, and did not answer. My husband, again, she said with a short laugh. He cannot manage on his own sometimes.

Before they left the pub, Katya handed Ana a check, apologizing that it was not the full advance. You'll get the rest when you send us the translation, she said. I promise.

They lingered for a moment outside, and she said, Forgive me while I call my husband, then I can walk with you to the Tube.

Ana looked away while she was on the phone, and she tried not to listen to the conversation, though she could not help but overhear.

And what time? . . . Will you be there? . . . Peter, we can't afford . . . No, I haven't . . . She is . . . Please don't bring that up again . . . Do what you like . . . I have an appointment . . . No, no, I'll be home in time, but can't you at least start the dinner? I see . . . No . . . I can't discuss that now, I told you. Bye . . . Sorry . . . No problem.

Ana followed her through the crowd. When they parted, about to go their separate ways inside the station, Katya hugged her lightly, but for a long time. As she pulled away, Ana thought she saw tears in her eyes. But Katya was smiling. She gave a little wave before she headed down the tunnel to the westbound District line.

I have found a hiding place for the diary, so that no one will come upon my thoughts about this situation with Elena and Aleksandr Pavlovich. One volume is full; I had to ask Georges to fetch me a new one from Sumy.

Will my niece Ksenia read these words someday?

Under the mattress, inside the bed frame, there is a trapdoor hiding a deep square well, just the right size for these notebooks. This was my great-grandmother's bed. She'd had it built when Napoleon's army was advancing, with this well to hide her jewels. (That is something for Ksenia to know, too.) We used to hide our dollies here as children, and other things we didn't want the boys to find. I can leave the trapdoor open to reach my notebook more easily; no one will see it.

Anton Pavlovich has left again for Poltava on his search for a farmstead. I do so hope he succeeds! I told him to be sure of a river (or a lake) and a western exposure—it's best to have the sun at the end of the day. At least in my opinion, for lasting warmth. The rest—views, space, the condition of the estate— won't matter so much if his heart and mind find a place where they can belong.

I did not have time to discuss the issue of his brother and Elena. We were numerous around dinner the night before he left—his mama invited us all—and all I could do in saying goodbye was to whisper that he was quite right where Elena was concerned, and his brother ought not waste his time, unless . . .

There I would have needed to see his expression to ensure that he knew what I meant by *unless.* So much contained in a little word. But he held me back, the time to say good night to Georges, then he whispered, Agreed. Only if his heart so dictates.

You've understood me, I concluded, and we said good night.

Sometimes I suffocate within these pages. The darkness seems to spill out of the ink and engulf them, as if all I am writing is a great swath of black. I cannot describe a smile—Tonya's smile or the proud gleam in Pasha's eyes, or the sunset, or Anton Pavlovich's hand rubbing his beard in thought, or Grigory Petrovich's toothless grin. Although I know these things exist: I have seen them *before,* I have *heard* them.

The voices of the Chekhov brothers as they laugh and prepare their lines for fishing, little suspecting that it is somewhere deep inside me that they cast their lines. They pull me up toward an ever brighter light. I can almost see it glinting on the surface.

Anton Pavlovich once asked me what was the last thing I remember seeing before the light departed. There was a long shadowy period: I could see form and color but not details. I remember the market in Sumy—a blur of movement beneath a sharp blue sky, then a woman in a red dress. A long vivid red dress in the crowd; all the other colors—blues, browns, black, the odd white peasant's shirt—had run together like failed colors on a novice's canvas, but then that surge of red . . .

Long before that, the last sharp detail was Mama's face, I told him. As it should be. I'd just had my first real seizure—when we knew that something was wrong beyond a cold or fatigue—and I was in bed. I awoke when she came in the room, the bright flame of her candle lighting her face, a pale copper glow effacing the lines of worry and the life she'd lived, and restoring the youth to her features; it was as if I were a small child again and my mamochka was there to be sure I was sleeping as I should, that I had not been awakened by some nightmare.

In the morning I could not tell Mama's face from Natasha's or Elena's. They had become shadows against a wall or the sky. I lurched toward them, hoping closeness would restore their features. Over time even their shadows yielded.

You never think, I said to Anton Pavlovich, when you examine a patient, that such a calamity might happen to you. And when it does, there is a moment of shock when you know nothing will ever be as it was, you are wrenched from your dreams, your expectations, above all your illusion of immortality—but then life unexpectedly gives you another birth, another chance. I can't explain it—a different way of apprehending the world. Grandiose words, but . . .

I did not dare tell him that perhaps he, too, was in some way responsible, simply by being there.

He was very quiet for a while, then said something about his brother Nikolay, the artist who is unwell. He wished Kolya had my courage, or philosophy, or something to that effect, and then he said something terrible: Kolya is mourning his life as he lives it. Drinking, carousing, to forget his troubles, and then weeping at dawn when the shock of illness pins him to his bed.

I did not tell him about my dark days when I, too, mourn. They all think I am terribly brave. That in my place . . . They do not know that there are times when their discourse tires me, annoys me, as if they suppose I am already dead. It is in part their apathy toward life and fear of death that I am fighting.

But it is also purely selfish: I love the world, I love life, and

I want as much of it as my darkness will allow. I think grandly of Marco Polo and Vasco da Gama—there are still worlds for me to explore.

I don't explain this to Anton Pavlovich, either; it would sound too far-fetched. And indeed rather grandiose. I must think of a better way to share it with him.

(And do I flatter myself that he might remember me someday in a story, in a novel? Let me be the black ink on the page.)

August 26, 1888

Late-summer storms. For several days now. I have been feeling them, sensing them in my blood. I am nervous, as if I am a cloud charged and ready to burst. The thunder rumbles from far away, then everything begins to fly around in a petulant wind, and the storm is upon us, cracking and booming, hurling the rain. I sit on the veranda with Georges or Natasha or Elena. They watch the lightning—they gasp—and then we all shriek like children when the thunder breaks over our heads.

One morning Anton Pavlovich came to me. He had returned from Poltava, and he described being caught in a storm not once but several times, drenched through, indignant in his person.

The ladies could see how skinny I am, he said, most unflattering—and what to do with a soggy hat?

He was coughing, however, and admitted that he must have caught a cold.

His trip has not yet yielded results. I was hoping he would find a farm right away, so that he would stay in the region; now he must defer his purchase and return to Moscow for

the winter. He has made an offer on a little place near the
Smagins', between the villages of Khomutets and Bakumovka;
he is very happy with the farm and says they need a doctor
there, so it would be the perfect spot, but the owner wants
three hundred rubles more, and Anton Pavlovich won't go
higher, he says.

(If I could give those three hundred rubles, just to be sure he
would be nearby, it would be a happiness cheaply bought. But of
course I can't.)

The others were talking and laughing. He was describing
his stay at the Smagins', and naturally, they wanted news.
Anton Pavlovich was there during harvesttime and was much
impressed by the huge threshing machine, which he described
in minute detail, I think more for the pleasure of refining his
description than to inform us of the intricacies of threshing
machines. We have them here, too, sniffed Natasha. And the
mysterious Smagina sister: There was some muted laughter,
and there must have been some miming or raised eyebrows or
facial expressions that left them all sniggering and sighing until
Natasha burst in: She's unhappy, that's all, I don't blame her.

I could have felt left out, but my heart was still pounding
with hope that the recalcitrant owner of the farm would yield. In
October, said Anton Pavlovich, he would know whether his offer
had been accepted.

We were in the garden after dinner. It had rained earlier and the
evening was fresh, fragrant. There were children by the river,
and their cries and shouts and splashing came to us, mysterious
and thrilling, on the breeze.

I have made good progress with the novel, Zinaida
Mikhailovna, he said. I'm pleased with what I've done, if for
no other reason than I do it without the slightest thought for

anything pecuniary. My characters are truly free men and women, with no thoughts of how to put bread on my table.

And on their own table? Or are they wealthy aristocrats?

Ah, no, Zinaida Mikhailovna, they are simple folk, like you and me.

We burst out laughing.

Let's say, he continued, they are ordinary people, with ordinary human aspirations, and yet . . .

He paused. I encouraged him with a wave of my fingers.

All too often their aspirations are—will be, because I haven't written it yet—destroyed by others or left unfulfilled. Some of them will continue to hope, to fight, while others will give up, become cynical . . . Am I boring you?

No, Anton Pavlovich, please go on, I just hope—

It's the scale of it, you see, to fill a whole novel, you need the trajectory of a life. It's overwhelming at times, I think: Why can't my hero just put his watch in his pocket and walk offstage? End of story? But no, he has to persevere, allow his love or his dreams to take him where they will.

And can he not take *them*? Must he merely submit to life?

He became excited, took my arm. Precisely, Zinaida Mikhailovna—do we forge life, regardless of other people, do we act selfishly at times and thoughtfully at others, but always in accordance with our own will? Or do we wait, attune the senses, allow fate to do the puppeteering work, while we preserve an immense respect for the mysteries—dare I say, the magic of life? Those inexplicable workings that elude the will?

Do you believe, as I do, that there are two sorts of people on earth?

Well, perhaps I do, but tell me what you mean.

Take Natasha. She believes that she can forge her own life, to use your words. Georges, on the other hand, is a dreamer. He waits to see where life will take him, lets people, and love, toss him this way and that.

And you?

Well, me . . . I believe it's obvious, no? Life decided to chew me up and spit me back out; I have had very little to do with it.

And before?

I shrugged. I struggled, more than Georges, less than Natasha, but I was always waiting for something grand to happen.

I paused, then said ruefully, And it did, in a way, but not quite what I expected.

He said softly, You are hard on yourself.

No, Anton Pavlovich, if I cannot laugh at life's ironies, what am I to do? You must bend, bend to the will of circumstances. Just because one is not strong-willed does not mean one necessarily manages *badly;* perhaps one is more sensitive, more attuned to life. Look at you: You did not set out to become a writer, yet you have, almost *malgré vous.* Speak to me of your will, Anton Pavlovich!

Zinaida Mikhailovna, my sympathies do tend to lie with those who leave themselves open and vulnerable to life's vagaries, that's certain. But if they do nothing, do not turn their yearnings into gold, what then is the point of their gifts, their goodness? They must act. As for my own will, I must have a farm and a river full of crayfish, and the rest will follow.

I smiled. The rest?

Ah, you know, love, wife, children, renown as the best doctor for miles around, regular publication in thick learned journals. And a novel that will be read from Edinburgh to Irkutsk.

There was a short silence, and I said, I'm sure it will be.

And if it isn't . . .

He didn't finish his sentence, as if it didn't matter; as if it mattered more than he cared to say.

August 29, 1888

Anton Pavlovich took me aside last night and told me he had
written to Aleksandr Pavlovich regarding Elena.

I felt alarmed, worried that my own part in this episode
might have repercussions beyond what I could have anticipated.
What if I had pleaded *for* Elena, instead of being so vague with
my *unless* that Anton Pavlovich might have misinterpreted?

But I do not know her feelings. Or perhaps I think I do, but I
must not presume to speak for her.

In his letter, Anton Pavlovich informed his brother that there
was absolutely nothing wrong with the idea of his marrying
Elena Mikhailovna, but that he was going about it altogether in
the wrong manner.

I told him, Zinaida Mikhailovna, that he knows your sister no
better than he knows the man in the moon! It's true, you must
agree! You don't propose marriage on such short acquaintance,
in such an anguished and drunken state of mind! He must be
human about it. That is, he must behave as a proper human
being and get to know her—come back here in the winter, for
example—and see what her feelings are. For the time being,
he only wants a nanny and a sick nurse for his loneliness. And
your sister would surely not marry him out of philanthropy or
principles.

Oh, but that is what I fear, Anton Pavlovich, she does so want
to help people and be useful.

Well, it's done, anyway, I think he has gotten the point. I will
have to keep an eye on him, insofar as I can once I leave here,
with me in Moscow and him in Petersburg. You will let me
know if ever he shows up uninvited or unannounced?

He is always welcome, of course, but yes, if he shows up
unannounced, I'll let you know.

We discussed the matter no further.

This morning Natasha came and sat by me on the veranda. I could sense she was restless: The creaking of the wicker told me as much. Finally, she said, They're leaving soon.

I know.

It will be so dull here without them.

I was silent, acquiescing. Then I encouraged her: But you will have your classes soon, the children.

I know, but I shall miss Masha even then—we have so many ideas and stories to share.

I'll listen, you know I will.

She made a small noise between a laugh and a sigh, and said, What do you and Anton Pavlovich talk about all the time?

Oh, life. You know. Do we philosophize? Not exactly, nothing that grand.

(I did not want to talk about his novel; it was our secret.)

About what?

I laughed at her persistence. There is nothing worse than trying to relate an abstract conversation, and besides, I did not want to surrender the thoughts Anton Pavlovich and I had shared in confidence to Natasha's impatient curiosity. So I used a tool, I am ashamed to say, that would cut her short.

About death. About my illness. Why me. That sort of thing.

A short intake of breath, then: But that's terrible! I always see the two of you laughing and whispering as if you're plotting to storm the Winter Palace! She was silent for a moment, then said in what was almost an outburst of pique: He's such an odd man!

In what way?

Masha says he has no end of women throwing themselves at him. He could have the princess of the ball. And yet he does not marry. Does he ever talk about love?

Love? No.

He is so secretive. Masha told me he was briefly engaged to a Jewess two years ago, then just broke it off, no explanation.

I paused, as this was something of a shock to me. Anton Pavlovich has never mentioned it, obviously, since we do not talk about such things. I suppose I have been regarding him as someone who is above the everyday frivolity of romance, despite the fact that Masha has told me of his multiple flirtations. Here he does not flirt. But perhaps I have simply been trying to believe something else about him all along. So I imagine him being rowed around the pond of medicine and literature by friends who speak of earnest worldly things. I did not let my surprise show, or at least I hope not, and reached for what I thought might be rational excuses on Anton Pavlovich's behalf.

Well, Natasha, you know he has a lot of work, not much time for affairs of the heart. And with a mother and sister who are there to take care of things, it's not a wife he needs, not any time soon.

Yes, but love—that's the point! Why doesn't he fall in love? Can he govern that, too?

I suppose. Some people can. They begin to fall in love, then they reason their way back out of it. Men especially.

How would you know?

Natasha, it's common knowledge. As for Anton Pavlovich, perhaps he's been in love, but it wasn't the right time or there were problems.

He hasn't told you anything?

No, Natasha. I'm not his confessor.

After a long pause she said, I do envy him his freedom. The Crimea, the Caucasus, traveling here and there. It must be wonderful.

And yet he wants nothing more than to find a farm *chez nous*!

That is absurd, she said, a hint of awkwardness in her laugh.

Just think, Natasha, if he were our neighbor—along with

Masha and Ivan—we would never find it dull at Luka. At least
not in the summer.

We were quiet for a long time. Then she said, You've been
happy this summer, haven't you, Zina?

I nodded. It relieves the burden on Mama, on you, on Elena.
What burden? No, I say, you've been happy—we all have.
Yes. We all have.

Anton Pavlovich has given me a cloud.

We were sitting by the pond at dusk, and I told him how
I missed seeing clouds. He joked at first, saying clouds all
looked like him and his brothers as hoary old men. Then he
said, Forgive me, Zinaida Mikhailovna, I haven't been paying
attention. It's actually rather extraordinary: There is one fat
little cloud sitting above the pond, gorged with the light of the
departing sun. Everywhere else, night has fallen, but across the
surface of your pond, like the reflection of a path to the moon,
there is an insolent burst of cloudlight.

I am so often alone. I know the change that will come with autumn.
Natasha will return to her school. Our guests will depart. The
veranda will fill with dry leaves, and it will be too chilly to sit here.
Georges will leave for Petersburg and take his music with him.

The days are getting shorter. Warmth recedes from my
skin; birds sing earlier in the evening. The buzz of insects is
fading. Less song on the roads, on the river. Grigory Petrovich
grumbling more. Anton Pavlovich has come twice today,
just briefly to ask something of Mama or Pasha. I sense his
nervousness, his awareness of departure. He apologized that he
could not stay; there was suddenly so much to do.

They came to fetch me for one last ride in the carriage with
Roman and Anton Pavlovich, as far as Olshanka. There was a

good open breeze: I leaned forward on the seat, drank in the air. I've kept my recollection of his description here, too. It might serve again in the future.

The road is leading into the distance, the distance where we are going and which we cannot see; there's a slight rise, toward the horizon of tall grass and a long line of poplar trees. It's deserted, we have the whole world to ourselves; the tall grass is bending to the breeze. The air is the color of candlelight on an icon. The sun has almost reached the horizon. There's not much time, and yet you feel, with so much space around you, that nothing could ever change: not the sun, or the tall grass, or the road into the distance.

September 1, 1888

This is goodbye for now, and we shall meet again in the spring.

Yes, Anton Pavlovich.

I shall—he lowered his voice—come back with my novel. And a play I plan to write.

Do you think you'll manage to finish the novel by springtime?

I don't know. We shall see how much time the demons of Moscow leave me for the things that matter in life.

Demons?

Critics and littérateurs, ladies, my own procrastinating self . . . He let out a sigh that turned to a short laugh.

Embarrassed, I said quickly, And your stories?

Of course I shall continue to write them. Bread on the table, as we said, and the satisfaction of a moment seized on the wing; none of the hand-wringing this novel is giving me. A story is like Luka, small, contained, a world unto itself—the pond, the river, Grigory Petrovich shuffling along with a scratchy tune in his throat, the ladies sipping tea. Whereas the novel . . . Is it from here to Irkutsk or here to Mongolia? I can't see the horizon.

But isn't that the point? To travel into the unseen distance until you *can* see the horizon?

I talked quickly, a bit breathlessly; I did not want to leave time for thoughts of parting to steal my words or seize my throat. I could not see my own horizon. But his was made of words and mine of days.

He did not answer my question but reached over and squeezed my hand. Sometimes, Zinaida Mikhailovna, I am just tired. I would like to throw it all in and sit by the river with my fishing pole for the rest of my days. Can you imagine that?

I nodded.

He could not deceive me; I welcomed his trust. I did not need to encourage him; he came to me for something else.

He continued, And sometimes I feel that fine enthusiasm drain away. I wonder—why do I do it? Then I know why, and it's not that the enthusiasm returns, but there is something that enables me to sit before the page—sheer pigheadedness, perhaps, and then there is a kind of quiet joy, meeting those characters for the first time, throwing them together on a road or in a garden or a drawing room. I suppose it is their life that carries me.

He paused; I nodded, waiting for him to continue.

He laughed gently. I'm boring you, Zinaida Mikhailovna. You've heard it all before. You would surely rather hear about our last expedition with Artyomenko. I told him he must bring you some crayfish from time to time after I've gone. I said, As the Lintvaryovs' appointed purveyor of riverine victuals, I shall be sorely missed, and he asked me to translate.

I smiled. I wanted to say he was right, that he would be missed, but I couldn't speak. So I nodded and hoped he knew what my odd head-bobbing signified. I knew he must leave very soon; already the others were coming from the next room with

Mama and my sisters and brothers. I could hear Mama talking quickly, tripping over her own words, her voice full of tears and recommendations for the journey. Hastily, Anton Pavlovich kissed my hand, and we embraced briefly, and my arms were empty for a long moment until Masha was there, full of emotion, with her light voice carrying the echo of her brother's, and there were promises to write, and to meet Pasha and Georges when they went up to Moscow, and entreaties to keep an eye on the miller's daughter (she must marry only a very handsome Ukrainian fellow, no dreary Russian landowners!). And to look after the water bittern, which we still have never seen, and the pigs, and more entreaties on our side not to forget us in the splendor of the big city, and to keep looking for a farm. Above all, there were the mutual promises of spring: Come back, we'll be back, after the last frost, with the first buds.

Then they were gone, and we all sat quietly, a bit stunned, until their voices had faded and we heard the carriages setting off at last for the station.

Should I be writing more often? Are there rules of journal writing to be obeyed, even when one is blind and full of headaches?

With the autumn chill, my headaches and seizures seem to have gotten worse. There is a tingling, too, in my extremities. Sometimes it is hard to hold the pen. All reasons not to write.

But the greatest reason is dullness. There is little to relate. My greatest joy is little Ksenia; I cannot see how she grows, but Pasha and Tonya let me touch her and hold her, and I can gauge her growing in gurgles and jiggles.

Poor Pasha, he came home so disheartened from Moscow. He has not been admitted to the Agricultural and Forestry Academy. He had such high hopes. But even Mama was shaking her head when he left for the train. It's his wretched politics, she said, he's wasting his time, they'll not want the likes of him.

At least he was able to see Anton Pavlovich and bring us greetings that hadn't been mussed up by the tsar's censors.

Before he left, Anton Pavlovich and I had agreed that he would not write to me, because his message would have to pass through the censorship of my mother or sisters; not that he minded, really, but he wouldn't be able to write what he truly wished to write, knowing that others would read it. And I told him I would be happier if he kept that time for working on his novel. He did something he had never done: He squeezed my chin between his thumb and fingers and bobbed my head in approval.

But Elena has had a letter from Anton Pavlovich. He tells her he has received a very prestigious prize for literature, the

Pushkin Prize, for the collection he read to us this summer, *In the Twilight*. Of course he jokes about it and says, *It must be because I caught crayfish*. I am very happy for him. He says he feels like he's in love. What a satisfaction that must be, to see one's work so justly rewarded. All that grumbling and joking about writing for money, all the modesty and refusal to take himself seriously—well, *he* may not, but clearly, others do!

Will this change him? I wonder. Might he decide to give up medicine and devote himself to his writing—and the novel? Or will this mean a greater obligation to the writing circles of Saint Petersburg and Moscow, giving lectures and going to soirees and being seen with the right people at the Slavyansky Bazaar?

To which he adds that his memories of the summer are fading, as here they fade. The last flowers are dying, leaves are falling, the birds have begun their migration. There is a silence in autumn, a long breath of farewell, still looking back, hoping to keep some part of the summer.

Then Anton Pavlovich describes the Museum of Things His Friends Forgot from the Summer—Barantsevich's breeches, Pleshcheyev's nightshirt—signifying their desire to return? And he adds a long strange farewell, his own and Othello's: *Farewell summer, farewell crayfish, chub, sharp-nosed rowing boats, farewell my languor, farewell little blue suit.*

> *Farewell the tranquil mind! farewell content!*
> *Farewell the plumed troop, and the big wars,*
> *That make ambition virtue! O, farewell!*

I asked Elena to read it three times, and I puzzle over it still. Perhaps it is some private joke between the two of them. Her voice was quite flat and neutral as she read it.

There was no mention of his elder brother in Petersburg.

I have my own Museum of Memories My Friends Have Left

Me With. Less prosaic than nightshirts and breeches, to be sure. And they do not need to come and claim them—only to bring more.

Early December 1888

I tried to write to Anton Pavlovich on my own but gave up. Elena says my writing is becoming illegible, that Anton Pavlovich is too busy to sit down and decipher it. So we wrote the letter together. We had a reply from him not long ago. As I feared, he spends a great deal of time socializing; he says that nevertheless he is writing. But still he wishes he could come to the country and hibernate until spring. Does he really mean it, or is it to make us long for him in some way?

We have had snow. I can sense the stillness when I wake. I remember the brightness and purity. Pasha took me out in the sleigh for a ride. He said the color came back to my cheeks. There was the silence of the countryside, only the sound of the runners and bells and the horses' snorting, their striving in the cold.

Mama keeps my room warm. I sleep a lot; the doctor—Elena—has given me laudanum. It makes things better. Dreamy, hesitant, less painful, as if hope were real.

I am learning to write more slowly, more clearly, so that Ksenia will be able to read this someday. I asked Elena to check; because of the laudanum, I suppose, she says my handwriting looks as if I were drunk. But legible, that's all that matters.

Heavy snow. We were housebound for three days. Pasha chops wood with Grigory Petrovich. Like the rhythm of days, ax on block.

Another letter from Anton Pavlovich. He was in Petersburg. He saw Georges. That we knew; now Anton Pavlovich says he will arrange an introduction with Tchaikovsky for Georges.

The music from the summer: the notes traveling along the corridors of our old house, on out into the garden. They echo even now in my mind. All around me is silence; is it day or night? I hardly know. A sleepless time, that is all.

My little brother, walking down the Nevsky Prospekt, meeting young musicians, meeting Anton Pavlovich and his friends, concerts, dancing, Tchaikovsky. Luka is reduced to snow and walls, to the chopping of firewood, then silence.

Natasha reads to me. An anthology arrived with a story by Anton Pavlovich, "A Nervous Breakdown." At first we laughed, and Natasha is very good at imitating the way he reads, but as she went further, her voice became more somber, until we understood the story's serious import. It left me quite oppressed, and Natasha was in a terrible mood for two whole days.

January 17, 1889

Christmas and the New Year have passed. Quiet festivities; Mama paid special attention to the food, for my sake: kutya, borscht, varenyky. Georges returned briefly from Piter, bringing a bustle of cafés and culture with him. He met Tchaikovsky, who was kind and modest and shared his cigars. Georges's studies are going well, and he has seen old friends. Barantsevich on his tram, no less, quite by chance! For a split second Kazimir Stanislavovich stared at Georges, certain that he knew him, but incapable of remembering where he had last seen him, and when he realized, he laughed and exclaimed so loudly that the passengers turned around to stare. Georges also saw Monsieur

Pleshcheyev, who is doing well, rosy-cheeked in the cold; he took Georges to dinner with Gypsies and caviar. Anton Pavlovich is much in demand since his prize, everyone comes up to him and stops him on the street; half of Petersburg seems to know him already. But Georges said he didn't look all that well— awfully pale, with a dreadful cold, but he confirmed that he'd be returning to Luka at the end of April to continue looking for a farmstead and to go fishing, and Saint Petersburg and Moscow be damned.

Georges brought us some novels. *Germinal* by Zola, and *The Strange Case of Dr. Jekyll and Mr. Hyde* by a Scotsman, Robert Louis Stevenson. You and Elena will appreciate the medical angle in this one, he explained. And he had some new scores of music. Briefly, the house came alive again. I slept better than I have in weeks. The music brought warmth and serenity, each note settling upon me with its weight of comfort until I was blanketed and could not move for the peacefulness of it.

THE
SECOND
SUMMER

Natasha walked with me to the guesthouse.

I am aching all over, and in my heart.

It is hard to write. I must be brief, spare my energy.

Anton Pavlovich has arrived with his mother and Nikolay Pavlovich.

We sat inside, in the guesthouse. Evgenia Yakovlevna fussed over the tea. Anton Pavlovich seemed distracted; Natasha confirmed that he could not sit still. His brother is in bed: Through the wall, we could hear him coughing, like a small relentless animal. I'm here, said Anton Pavlovich, because he is not well. I was invited to Biarritz with Suvorin, but I must stay here. He paused, realized how that must sound to us, then said in a subdued, sad voice, We are so close, he and I—I cannot leave. How could I travel all the way to the Atlantic Ocean and know he is lying here sick while I'm drinking champagne and staring at seagulls? I could never forgive myself if something were to happen while I was away. He needs me here.

On the way back to the main house, Natasha squeezed my hand. Masha will be here in a few weeks, she said. Then things will be like before.

Anton Pavlovich has complained there are no boats for fishing. Mama apologized; there have been other priorities, the boats are upriver in the woods with a forester, she explained.

He looked so disappointed, said Natasha. He just stood

there speechless. Mumbled something about going off to find Artyomenko and Panas.

Mama sighed when he was gone. I should not mind, she said, but I have a feeling it will be a long summer. Long—not in the good sense.

I must congratulate you on your prize, Anton Pavlovich.

My prize for catching crayfish? Or for writing stories with both hands tied behind my back?

Both. I laughed. After a pause: But I am sure it's well deserved. And we feel honored that you have come back to Luka when we know you could have gone to Abbazia or Biarritz. And you know, during the winter, Natasha read all the stories to me again. They improve with each reading.

Zinaida Mikhailovna, you will wear them out with so much reading. They won't survive ten years, believe me. By then everyone will have forgotten about me. Or at best they'll say, Remember that doctor who went and buried himself in Kharkovsky Province, and he thought he was a writer because they gave him a prize? What was his name, Antoine Shponka?

False modesty, Anton Pavlovich! You must enjoy your success, not belittle it. If you won a prize, it was for a reason.

He sighed and said in a more serious tone of voice, It seems like too much good fortune. Should I not be superstitious of it, Zinaida Mikhailovna? Don't you think I'm too young for such an honor?

No, you deserve it, and it will help you to feed your family, as you have often said. Don't forget you have a farmstead to buy.

Yes, this will be the year for finding my farmstead. Then I can retire from writing and be a doctor.

Which would be a fine thing, too, Anton Pavlovich, but I for one should miss your stories. Not to mention your novel.

Yes, please don't mention it.

Will you work on it this summer?

I can't think that far ahead. I've got Nikolay to look after, so until Masha arrives— She sends you her greetings, by the way.

I'm looking forward to seeing her.

She will be glad of some real attention for her own sake. She was getting quite cross in Moscow, being invited here and there merely because she was the writer's sister, as they called her.

Goodness, has your fame spread even to your sister?

But it's ridiculous, Zinaida Mikhailovna! Imagine, people come up to you for all the wrong reasons—for their own sake, for one, to be able to tell others they have met you, and impress their friends; and then for the very things in yourself that you least respect. They don't come to you as one human being to another; they come to you to feel your glorious shadow over their stooped shoulders, and they're not the least bit concerned about your ingrown toenail or your unpaid bill at the stationers', they merely want a piece of your glory, as if it would make them beautiful or immortal or richer than Croesus. You begin to feel like a planet, spinning dizzily from the heat of the sun.

But how are you to get around it, Anton Pavlovich? You deserve recognition for your stories—I suppose it is human nature to admire and be admired—better this than to be admired for your pretty face, with which you had nothing to do.

How do you know I have a pretty face?

I smiled. My sister, your dear Nata-chez-vous, as you call her, told me so.

She's quite mistaken. I believe I told you I look like—

A cross between one of your crocodiles and a boa constrictor?

Precisely.

I do wish I could see you.

You see me, Zinaida Mikhailovna.

Our conversation has given me much hope for the summer. It is true, Anton Pavlovich's fame has spread. Even the peasants line up once again outside our gate to consult the doctor from Moscow.

(He does not charge them a kopeck, either, Elena told me; and he often buys their medication for them.)

I sit in the sun, soak up the warmth and strength. I have headaches nearly all the time: I defy them with the laudanum, and I try to think of other things. I wait for Anton Pavlovich, but he doesn't come. Barantsevich is here; he reads to me from a story he has written. He tells me again about the time he met Georges on the tram. That was more amusing than his story.

Georges will be coming home soon. There will be music; Ivanenko will join us again, and this year he will be bringing his friend Marian Semashko, the cellist.

Anton Pavlovich came this morning with Nikolay. He has spells, he tells me, where he has strength. He needs to get out, it's good for him.

I held Nikolay's hand briefly. It was hot and dry, he must be feverish. I could hear how he struggled against his cough. At the same time he was excited, telling us about an idea he has for a painting. The work he hopes to do this summer. Until suddenly he turned away, walked to the end of the veranda, coughed and coughed, and finally called for Anton Pavlovich: Take me home.

Natasha is beside herself. Aleksey Suvorin is staying at the guesthouse for a week on his way to the famous Biarritz. Don't let that man in our house! she barks. Elena and Pasha support her. Their politics tire me. Anton Pavlovich has always said Aleksey Sergeyevich was not merely his publisher but a friend, a true gentleman who supports the arts, and who has helped his career greatly.

This means that we will not see Anton Pavlovich all week.

———————

Dogs howling in the village keep me awake. Others complain about them; I do not mind. The dogs tell me it is night. They are my eyes, they show me my deep yearning, give it voice. They are berating the moonlight for its false promises.

May 12, 1889

Sometimes I hear voices in the distance. As long as Suvorin is there, I fear Anton Pavlovich will not come. I could go to them, but I feel shy on my own; Natasha and Elena both refuse to meet Suvorin.

We argued again at dinner. Pasha started it; I could hear how he was clenching his teeth. He said, The man is the worst sort of capitalist, the kind who publishes absolute rubbish to oppress the workingman, let alone the innocent peasant. Lies and ignorance.

Have you met him, Pasha dear? said Mama calmly.

I don't need to meet him. I saw the carriage he hired in Sumy to get here. He wants to shame us.

It's pathetic, said Natasha. I cannot believe Anton Pavlovich is friends with such a man.

We know why, Pasha said, laughing. He publishes him, he's making him rich. Ten years from now Anton Pavlovich might be pulling up in that same carriage. If he even condescends to visit us by then.

Shame on you, Pasha, said Mama, he's not like that.

But we don't know, do we, said Elena very calmly. We don't know his politics. He doesn't say anything. None of them does, actually.

Pavel Yegorovich Chekhov is a simple merchant, said Mama somewhat sententiously. His father was a serf, did you know that? Perhaps it takes several generations for our good people to develop their *sens politique.*

Oh, Mamochka, do you hear yourself? Speaking French and all, please, said Natasha, before swearing in Ukrainian.

I waved my hand and broke in, Do they have to profess an opinion? Just because we do?

Well, it makes it awkward when they invite someone like Suvorin to stay. What will Vorontsov say, or Yefimenko, if they find out? said Mama.

Do you care, Mama, really! said Natasha.

It's more complicated than that, said Elena. I work all day to try to better the lot of our *former serfs,* might I insist—and whom did they belong to?—not just to heal them, not just to teach them cleanliness so they don't fall sick. I'm trying to make them take an interest in their world, to possess their world at last, after centuries. What am I to say if they understand that we are hosts to someone like Suvorin, who literally does possess the world with his newspapers and books and fancy carriages? It's hypocrisy! Anton Pavlovich should never have invited him, for my sake!

Hear, hear, said Pasha and Natasha.

He had no choice, I said.

Why are you always defending him, Zina? asked Natasha.

Yes, why? echoed Elena.

It's a terrible choice, isn't it, between politics and art? I said weakly.

Pasha began to howl with laughter.

Zina, you have remained a wonderful idealist, said Natasha. You think it is solely to produce his art that Anton Pavlovich has embraced Suvorin's friendship?

Well, isn't it? He does publish him. And his brother works for him.

They have no choice, said Pasha. Natasha's right. They

don't have the courage of their convictions because they have
no convictions. They have just enough money to live with a
minimum of comfort. Eat, travel, go to the theater. They're like
most middle-class people in our country, and the tsar and the
ruling class are very happy to keep them ignorant and well fed.
And if they join our cause, which some of them do, that's because
it's fashionable.

And what about us? I asked. Aren't you very fashionable,
Pasha, both Marxist *and* Tolstoyan? Look at your *rubashkas,*
made from cloth that you have Tonya weave for you on her
loom, as if she didn't have enough to do already. You're not
displeased with that side of things, are you? Even though you
are helping the peasants and improving their lives at the same
time, so I can't really fault you for that, at least you are *doing*
something.

But Zina, said Natasha, it does sound as if you're taking Anton
Pavlovich's side, why is that? What sort of nonsense has he been
feeding you during your secretive little meetings?

No nonsense at all, I said hotly. He's not here to defend
himself, and I believe he finds politics boring. So, yes, he *has*
chosen art, although if you asked him, I am sure he would not
put such a fine point on it.

No, he'd start talking about the fish in the Psyol or the miller's
daughter, said Natasha.

Ah, yes, sighed Pasha, the miller's daughter.

We all laughed, and the tension lapsed slowly to the ground
like a net lowered over our prejudices.

But for all that, my family refuses to speak to Alexey Suvorin.

It is so hot already. Pasha says they all go swimming. How I
would like to go, too, even just to sit by the river in the shade, but
the heat makes the headaches worse. I stay on the veranda and
pray for a breeze.

Yesterday Natasha walked by and said, What are you writing? The page is blank, poor sister!

It is so hot that the ink dries in the inkwell.

Even my thoughts evaporate. Nothing stays. There is the electricity of storms in the air, but no storms come. Grigory Petrovich grumbles: With no rain, he has to find ways to water the flowers from the well, the river. Even so, they are going brown, he says. The air smells of burning sunlight, parched earth.

Barantsevich is kind. He comes every day with a story. He, too, feels uncomfortable around Suvorin. He's not a bad sort, he says, but clearly, he is used to staying in grand hotels. I think he finds Kharkovsky Province rather backward. He complained to the cook about the soup.

Soup! Why is she making soup in this weather? He has every right to complain.

Well, no, she made cold borscht, and that is what Monsieur Suvorin does not like. He maintains you feel cooler after hot soup.

How is Nikolay Pavlovich?

He keeps to his room. Tatyana from the village brings him fresh milk every day. He talks of getting better, promises to work. He has ideas, plans!

Is it tuberculosis? Already last year Elena suspected—

Anton Pavlovich won't confirm a diagnosis. He said it was typhoid in Moscow; now he calls it a laryngeal infection. Your sister, indeed, just stared at Anton Pavlovich when they were talking about it. Then she shook her head and got up and left. That was before Aleksey Sergeyevich arrived, obviously.

Everyone is so irritable in this heat. I sighed. All winter I longed for summer, and now . . .

When I get too hot, in Petersburg—which isn't often in our wretched northern climate, but sometimes in the tram—I imagine a mountain, in the Alps, say, and pine forests, and a glacial little river. Not that . . . I mean, I've only ever seen such landscapes in paintings.

I laughed. And does it help?

Briefly. Distracts me from all those sweating bodies and the smell of cabbage.

But how am I to distract myself from this oppression? I try to smile, I am patient, I am good. I watch the dose of laudanum, not to overdo it. Elena says it is already too much.

And at night, the air breathes again, toward dawn, while the mosquitoes feast.

May 14, 1889

At last. Suvorin is gone; perhaps the summer can begin. Georges is back, Mama says he has put on weight, and his beard has grown thicker. I wish I could see him.

Last night he played for me—some pieces by Mussorgsky— until he said the keys were sticky, damp from the heat, from his sweating fingers. We talked so long and late, I am exhausted. He helped me to bed, gave me a cool damp cloth for my forehead. I slept well, no dogs barking, and few mosquitoes, or anyway, I did not notice them. I awoke today with a good feeling. We shall have visitors, I am sure.

May 15, 1889

I was sure of visitors yesterday; I was wrong. Only Evgenia Yakovlevna, briefly, to see Mama; she wept. My son, he's

coughing his soul out, she said. Then she remembered about
me, which in all fairness I wish she hadn't, but I was sitting
right there. She said, At least she doesn't cough! Mama did not
know what to say, where to turn—such an awkward silence
in the room. Evgenia Yakovlevna began to apologize clumsily
until I said to her, It doesn't matter, Evgenia Yakovlevna, really,
it doesn't. She hurried away, poor woman, she only came for
comfort, and now she'd made herself feel worse.

May 18, 1889

What do you think, Zinaida Mikhailovna, with your sixth
sense—will there be a harvest this year?

Anton Pavlovich, we have not known it to be this hot and
dry since 1876. The harvest failed that year. It is very likely,
I'm afraid. But perhaps if it rains in the next few days . . . Did
Monsieur Suvorin enjoy his visit?

Very much so, thank you.

I apologize for my family's . . . principles.

You should never apologize for your principles, Zinaida
Mikhailovna, if they are important to you. Otherwise, they are
not principles, just whims, passing fancies.

I smiled. Of course, Anton Pavlovich. What I meant was the
uncustomary lack of hospitality.

You have always shown my family the most generous
hospitality. We'll leave Aleksey Sergeyevich out of it. He has
more than enough hospitality wherever he goes. And now he is
on his way to Biarritz. He is not to be pitied.

There was a long moment of awkwardness that spoke of all
the time elapsed since our last true, warm conversation. Finally,
to say something, I asked, more a statement than a question: I

suppose, with his visit and your brother's illness, you have not
had time to write?

He let out an exasperated sigh. Very little, only intermittently.
Did I tell you I'm also working on a play? Somewhat inspired by
my time here—the setting, that is, not the characters.

Indeed, what a relief. I would not like to find myself in a play.

There was a faint tapping sound, as if he were consulting his
fingertips in hesitation, deliberation. Finally, he said, Zinaida
Mikhailovna, I have a very odd request to make of you.

Yes?

I need to put the novel aside for some time. I cannot
concentrate—my brother is ill, it is hot, there are all these
visits—and yet everyone from my publisher to my friends and
family continues to ask me about it. I put them off, tell them
I'm working on it, tell them it will be ready in November or
in March, give them all sorts of eloquent excuses. Masha has
been begging to read it, she will arrive soon, she . . . In short, I
need a safe place to store the manuscript for a time. It's such a
responsibility, carrying all that paper around, worrying about
nosy family members or journalists from Piter or stagecoach
robbers. Do you have a safe place, may I leave it with you?
Forgive my presumption, but I know you cannot read it, and I
trust you implicitly not to share it with Natalya Mikhailovna—

Anton Pavlovich! Of course you may entrust it to me. I have
a hiding place where I keep my journal. There is room. A niche
designed to withstand Napoleon's armies. Our secrets will
converse *en toute tranquillité.*

That's good, then! Thank you, Zinaida Mikhailovna, thank
you from the bottom of my heart!

I heard a certain unnatural politeness in his voice. He seized
my hand, kissed it briefly. I'll bring it to you in the next day or
two, if you can arrange to be alone.

Come Tuesday. Mama goes in to Sumy on Tuesdays. No one

will be here except Georges, and we can send him on an errand or ask him to play for us.

This morning Anton Pavlovich brought me a heavy box.

You have written a great deal, I whispered as he handed me the box to feel its weight.

Georges was already playing, at our request. I motioned to Anton Pavlovich to follow me from the veranda to my room. He waited by the door while I knelt and struggled to put the manuscript in the hiding place where it would not be in the way of my journals. I could not manage it, so he in turn knelt by the bed and followed my instructions. When the box was safely stowed behind my journals, he got to his feet.

You are dusty, Zinaida Mikhailovna, and so am I. Do you have a cloth, a towel?

The dust would give us away, wouldn't it, I laughed. I groped about for some towels at the washstand.

When I returned, he gently wiped the dust from my sleeves and my skirt. You must scold the housemaid, she's not doing her job properly.

She is a treasure and helps me to wash and to dress, and she does my hair; Ulyasha is irreplaceable. Simply, she's not allowed to dust hiding places and Napoleonic niches. She might be a spy for the *New Times*.

He laughed and thanked me again. We returned to tea, and Georges was none the wiser.

Now at night, I lie awake over his words. I think of last summer—how different it was, how true our complicity was then, not one of childlike conspirators, hiding things, but of gentle friends. Time has taken that away. Anton Pavlovich has given me a great gift of trust, which I cherish, and which is based upon our time last summer; but I regret more bitterly than I can say the change I have perceived in our conversations. He seems distracted, absent, too polite; spontaneity and ease are gone. I know he is preoccupied by his brother's health. Perhaps there are other things I do not know.

Now all those words beneath me, in his handwriting; and here am I—blind, dying Zinaida, who cannot read them. At times it feels a cruel joke. Not on the part of Anton Pavlovich, no, but of life itself.

Although I believe he cannot be unaware of the irony of it.

If I could see, I would be sorely tempted to read the manuscript.

If I were to break his trust, Natasha and I could read it late at night.

But I cannot see, and his trust means everything to me, and I shall not betray it.

ANA LOOKED UP FROM her keyboard and blinked. Here was the confirmation she had been hoping for—the very thing Katya Kendall had hinted at so evasively, the beginning of the long and fascinating story she had refused to tell. What had she said? *We are working on it*, something like that. Which could mean anything: looking for it, following a lead, or perhaps already trying to get permissions for an English-language version.

Ana sent Yves an email: *I am on the lookout for a mongoose.* He immediately wrote back and said, *Don't wear yourself out trying to charm the local zookeepers. A good* andouillette *at the Boeuf Rouge will be ample compensation for the terms of our bet. Look forward to seeing you.*

Ana went through Chekhov's letters for the years 1888 and 1889 and found frequent, steady mention of a novel in progress, particularly in the letters sent from Luka—although there was also obvious confusion, even self-contradiction, as to when he actually started and how much was mere intention, deliberate obfuscation, or wishful thinking.

> January 12, 1888: *In the summer I'll get back to my interrupted novel.*
> February 9, 1888: *If only you knew what sort of subject for a novel is sitting in my head just now!*
> October 9, 1888: *I want to write a novel, I have a marvelous subject.*

Early May 1889: *I just have to get three thousand rubles off the theater management and finish my novel.*

May 4, 1889: *I'm writing a novel that I like better and that is closer to my heart than* The Wood Demon.

May 14, 1889: *I'll go to Piter in November to sell my novel.*

May 31, 1889: *I'm writing a novel [. . .] that I'll finish in 2 to 3 years.*

June 26, 1889: *I've done some work on the novel, but it's more ink-stained fingers than actual writing.*

What happened? Other than events in his life that might have prevented him from continuing? Did something happen to the manuscript at Luka? Discovery, theft, fire? How much had he written? Would it be publishable today, or did it remain a rough, inconclusive draft? Above all, where was it? Since Zinaida's journal had been found, could the novel not be somewhere close by?

Why was Katya Kendall being so secretive! She must have the answers to at least some of these questions, behind her *we are working on it.* If Ana had not drunk so much wine and been so subjugated by poetry that day, she might have dared to press for more information. Who, for example, was the Olga Ivanova who had typed up the diary? Such a common name! To try to find her would be next to impossible.

Ana skimmed Rayfield's authoritative biography; she skimmed later letters. After that fateful summer of 1889 at Luka, Chekhov threw himself into preparation for his trip across Siberia to Sakhalin Island. Ana was beginning to sense—knowing full well she would need to research it exhaustively to have the facts, and even then it would remain conjecture—that Chekhov found he was ill suited to be a writer of novels; he realized his strength lay in short, immediate tableaux: stories and plays. Perhaps he did go back to the Luka novel—or another?—from time to time but did not have the patience or stamina to complete it; perhaps he did finish it but decided not to publish it or was discouraged by Suvorin or another editor; or perhaps he felt no need to expand on his characters' lives, preferred to see them in representative incidents. He painted microcosms, life on the wing.

But this was not to belittle the potential worth of a novel, even unfinished, if it existed.

She knew she must waste no time. She had almost reached the end of the diary. She must write again to Katya Kendall—find out what she meant when she said *we are hoping—hoping—to publish the novel Anton Pavlovich was writing at Luka.* Hoping, a vagueness that confirmed nothing, implied everything; they could have found it and were negotiating rights or other legalities with the Russians, or they didn't have it yet, or they were still searching for the physical manuscript on the basis of the most tenuous of clues.

And did she dare even think it, let alone write it, for fear of jinxing her own shifting hopes, now humble, now grandiose: If Chekhov's novel were in the Kendalls' hands, would they ask her to translate it?

Ana compiled an informal list of Chekhov's translators. She needed to visualize her name on that list, along with so many other unknown translators, most of them men and most of them invisible, with the exception of Michael Redgrave, John Gielgud, and Tom Stoppard. There were literally dozens. But there was one whose name came up again and again: Constance Garnett.

Ana trawled the Internet to supplement what she already knew about Garnett, which wasn't much, other than that she was English and had been one of the first translators of the great Russians in Queen Victoria's time. Ana found a photograph of a prim, bespectacled young woman with big ears, wearing a fussy hat. Ana read that she'd married in that same fateful year of 1889; her husband was an editor for an eminent British publisher; much later, her son would become a member of the Bloomsbury Group and marry Virginia

Woolf's niece. In 1893 Constance Garnett met Tolstoy at Yasnaya Polyana. She began to translate Chekhov only after his death in 1904, and apparently, he was the author she preferred. By the late 1920s, she was half blind; in 1934 *Three Plays by Turgenev* was her last translation; three years later her husband died and she lived in reclusion and obscurity, tending her garden somewhere in Kent, until her own death nine years later.

In her long career, Garnett translated more than seventy works, and no fewer than two hundred of Chekhov's stories. She was a pioneer, venturing into a difficult, unknown, and vastly glorious terrain.

Ana imagined the conversation she might have with her. Mrs. Garnett, she would say respectfully, this novel is something I've been praying for, yet now that I have the proof of its existence, I am losing my nerve. Perhaps I should just finish Zinaida Mikhailovna's diary and let you, please, take over your usual task of translating Chekhov.

But you mustn't be afraid, my dear. After all, it's only words. Look down, read what he's written, look up again, blink, then write it all down in English.

It's not that easy. I want it to be perfect.

There's no such thing as perfect. You know that.

The whole world will be waiting. It's their expectation, their perception, that demands perfection.

Let them wait. Your duty is to the writer.

(Peering at Ana over her wire glasses and pursing her lips.)

But it's Chekhov.

He's not the hardest, my dear, don't worry. Subtle, yes, you must be careful not to miss anything, but he's not tricksy or affected or even complicated. A joy to translate, really.

But it's a whole novel!

You will find it gets easier as it stretches out, you'll become comfortable with his voice, the characters, the words will flow from your pen, my dear. For those reasons a novel is often easier than a short story, let alone a poem! I should know, after *War and Peace.*

I do want his novel to be found, but sometimes the hope that I might translate it . . . it's daunting. Overwhelming. What if the critics say the translation is not good, or that I'm not an academic, so what business have I to do it, or I haven't lived in Russia, or any of these excuses they give when they slam a translation: *stilted, clunky, awkward. Unfaithful.* Or even just ordinary readers on the Internet who say, *I didn't like it, it must be because it was a translation.* It's one thing for a contemporary potboiler, but Chekhov?

But my dear, it is an honor to translate Chekhov, so if the publisher chooses you, it means they must trust you, and you must accept.

Just the thought of it—I've been waking up in the middle of the night with a knot in my stomach, from dreaming about the manuscript—I can actually see his fine, neat script. Not that they would give the actual manuscript to me, of course not, but there's something symbolic about its priceless physical worth in itself, all dust and ink and fraying paper . . . Imagine, it's from the stationer's in Sumy, the paper, the ink . . . What is wrong with me? People translate Chekhov all the time, it seems as though whenever one of his plays is produced, a new translation is commissioned. But you were there first, Mrs. Garnett. And this novel, too, is waiting to be translated for the first time. Thousands, perhaps millions, of people will be waiting to read it for the first time. Please come back and do it for me.

My dear, don't worry, you'll be fine, you'll be invisible. You always are. But that's how you'll know you've done a good job.

KATYA CLOSED HER EYES and tightened her arms around the heavy handbag on her lap. She concentrated on the sounds, all those familiar sounds from decades of living in London and riding the Underground: conversation, laughter, newspapers rustling, the rattle and whoosh of wheels, the voice of the woman announcing the stations, prim and emphatic: Sloane Square, South Kensington, Gloucester Road, the clunk of doors opening and closing. With her eyes closed, her attention focused, it all seemed so different, farther away and yet louder at the same time, as if she were not sitting there on the plush seat but somewhere on her own, listening to a soundtrack through headphones, like so many of her fellow passengers.

Earl's Court. A press of new passengers, and she sensed two people standing by her knees, deep in conversation. A man and a woman. They were talking about a seminar they had attended, *content strategies, trends, digital sharing,* and it was only when the woman said, *Francis landed a major deal for a celebrity cookbook* that she remembered it was mid-April and they must have come from the Book Fair. Katya and Peter had stopped going; they couldn't afford it anymore. They had gone for the last time three years ago, and only because the market focus that year was Russia and they were hopeful. They spent a lot of money on a nice stand in a good location, as if betting their all. They smiled; they handed out catalogs, gave away free books; they had earnest discussions with publishers and agents from Moscow and Saint Petersburg and Kiev and even one from Tbilisi. They made a few small deals, better than nothing, but hardly covered their costs.

There was one young woman, Zhanna something-or-other, from a small literary press in Moscow. After a long discussion at the stand, they had invited her out to dinner. In Zhanna's enthusiasm and love not just of literature but also of the physical book—she would hold up a volume and caress the binding, the paper, the dust jacket, inspect the font and the endpapers—Katya had found something of her younger self from the good years. She had been like Zhanna, traveling all over Europe, not just to Russia and Ukraine but also to France and Italy and Germany: There had been translations, there had been what Peter liked to call the flow, when a single computer file radiated out into the world, sometimes through those translations, and of course through the physical book: the thrill of walking into Daunt Books or Hatchards or Borders, or Fnac, or Feltrinelli, or any of hundreds of smaller bookshops all over Europe, and finding one of their books, sometimes prominently displayed, and knowing they had made this possible. They had never had best sellers—they weren't that sort of press (although they hoped for one now, thought Katya with a melancholy smile)—but the guidebooks had kept them going, steady, reliable sales, rising over the years as more people traveled to the former Soviet Union. There had been the political books, too. Gian Paolo in Rome, always asking her, What have you got for me? Any good dirt on the Cremlino?

Good dirt. If they still had the wherewithal, they could have turned up plenty of dirt. It all started to go downhill with the war in Georgia and then the financial crisis that same year; the Georgia guidebooks sat ominously in a pile in their boxes, unordered or returned. Were it not for their losses now, they would have traveled to Kiev, to Simferopol and Sevastopol, to Moscow; they would have met with authors and journalists, rushed books on the Ukrainian and Crimean crises; and there were plenty of émigrés right here in London with stories to tell. Dirt to dish. But Katya did not have the strength anymore. She couldn't do it on her own, and these days Peter was all secrecy and, she suspected, Scotch.

They hadn't seen it coming. The crisis or the whole digital thing. They weren't financial analysts or geeks. They were artisans, in their way, thought Katya; they stopped short only at printing and binding the books themselves. They belonged to the generation of proofreaders and manual typesetters. Dying, dead professions.

She opened her eyes and looked at the two Book Fair people. Conservatively dressed, much younger than their confident, almost brash voices had implied. The woman was tall, blond, freckled, looked as if she would be the tennis-playing type, with a rough-edged Eastern European name: Sharapova, Azarenka, Wozniacki. Katya dressed her in tennis whites and smiled to herself. She liked watching tennis; it calmed her. The man had the faintest outline of a beard, perhaps the shadow of what was tolerated by a corporate culture. Or perhaps it was in itself a fashion. Katya felt a sudden longing for Peter—his near-white hair, his wrinkles, the tiny ruptured veins on his cheeks—a longing so strong and so physical that she had to look away. These young people seemed to radiate good health and a slight arrogance that, to Katya, evoked power. For a second she felt depleted, replaced, but then she looked at them again and smiled, knowing that she had been there once, in that place of power. She, too, had put books in readers' hands, had helped them find a restaurant in Yalta, or get a same-day ticket for the Bolshoi or the Mariinsky, or make the best borscht. She had even helped deliver a few sacks of dirt, Gian Paolo.

Cremlino. It sounded like ice cream. Zuppa Inglese. Stracciatella. Cremlino. Katya loved Italy. It had been one of their best markets. Perhaps they could go. Forget their troubles for a few days.

There was still Zinaida. It remained to be seen what she might do in translation with her summer companion. Whether they could give Peter a boost, at least.

She imagined the money coming in, the thrill of being not only solvent but also able to turn things around. To defy the recession and geopolitics and the received opinions of the publishing world; to see Peter smiling again, taking her hand and waltzing her around the kitchen, the way he used to when the money came in. Ah, Zinaida, miracles do happen.

Waltzing, whirling around the Piazza del Campo in Siena, laughing when they stumbled and caught each other. They had done that, yes, many years ago. Could do it again. Why not.

Katya laughed out loud. The publishing people looked at her. Do you even know, she thought, you cocksure naive editor-publisher-content provider-literary-MBA types. Do you even know what it really takes to make a book.

Masha is here at last. We have spent nearly the entire day together with Natasha; we went down to the river with parasols and bottles of water. They described it all to me——the small boats in the distance——Anton Pavlovich with Artyomenko, Ivan and Misha, and Georges and Ivanenko, who spent more time falling in the water to cool off than fishing. Natasha went swimming with them, too. She doesn't care about propriety or the fact that her hair was soaking wet. I asked Masha if she would join her; I hope she wasn't offended. In any event, she said kindly that she didn't want to leave me on my own. After a long pause, she added, Antosha would never let me forget it if I were to swim in the river.

I was surprised and was about to answer when she said, almost rebelliously, I'll come back on my own someday, or with Natasha, when there's no one about. It does look so refreshing.

I came so often to the river as a child, swimming with Papa. His strong arms throwing me up in the air, letting me splash back down into the water. Or catching me as I came running from the riverbank. He teased me: Zina, our terror, you're afraid of nothing.

I collected baby frogs and put them in fragile boats made of paper or light wood. I watched them carefully. Only one got away, hopped out of the boat. I can still see that moment, the spring of the creature's legs against the bright water before it vanished. I asked Papa where it went.

Back to the other frogs. It didn't like being away from its family.

But I would have put it back after the boat ride—what if it doesn't find its family?

It will, he reassured me. Don't worry.

When Papa died, I remembered the frog and worried that it hadn't found its way back after all.

Anton Pavlovich came to me with a small bowl of wild strawberries. They're everywhere, he said. I know, I replied, I used to pick them myself.

We talked for a long time, pausing between our words to eat berries. He placed them in my palm; at one point I imagined him feeding them to me, and had to turn away, because I found myself blushing. As if he had truly placed a berry against my lips, the way a parent or an older sibling would with a child. As I closed my lips and teeth, there would be a moment of hesitation, whether I might bite him by mistake, but his thumb and forefinger would slip away in time. And I imagined that, together with the berry, I could taste the salt from his fingers.

May 31

More guests. An actor who has worked with Anton Pavlovich in one of his plays, Pavel Svobodin.

Elena says he has all the signs of the consumptive but hides it with the most extraordinary extravagant behavior. Going fishing in his top hat and tails, for example. Passing himself off as nobility and intimidating all the servants, then bursting with laughter at their gullibility. It might seem cruel if it were not so deliciously defiant.

The days pass, and I write of these insignificant things that are mere hearsay in my life. This is my lackluster defiance, alas.

I cannot strut about in a top hat. So I struggle with drying ink and a trembling hand.

I have strange dreams—the laudanum. Last night, for example: I am in the rowboat with Anton Pavlovich, and I am blind, and the boat is rocking with the waves, and I can hear Rosa barking on shore, I don't know if she is upset at being left behind or is warning me of a storm. We must go back, Anton Pavlovich! I cry, but he doesn't hear me, just hums to himself—dear Lord, it's Grigory Petrovich's hum—then he says, We must catch crayfish for Rosa's dinner, and you'll have a prize, dear Zinaida Mikhailovna.

Then Rosa is swimming toward us, with great difficulty, waves washing over her head—I can't see her, but I know she's swimming—and I'm afraid for her, afraid she will drown, and I wake up.

This made me so upset that I crept out into the corridor and called to her very quietly, and she followed me back to the room, and I lay on the floor with her. I wept and held her warm body until my trembling stopped and I could return to my bed.

June 8

Marian Semashko has arrived with his cello. The concerts we'll have! With Ivanenko on flute and Georges on the piano, our very own Luka Chamber Orchestra.

Our cellist was practicing: mere notes, scales, nothing containing an actual melody, and it was so mournful, that sound, but still the beauty of it surpasses the sadness. And why can sadness be so beautiful?

Fortunately, Anton Pavlovich did not take long to befriend him and fill the room with laughter: He has baptized the cellist

Marmelad Fortepianich Semashechka. Marian Romualdovich takes things in stride; quite spontaneously, he composed a silly song, which he sang very gravely with the deepest and most lugubrious sounds from the cello, about a writer from Moscow called Antonio Konfityurovich Scriblovsky. I think for once Anton Pavlovich was speechless.

June 10, 1889

Poor Marmelad—that's what everyone calls Semashko now. He only made things worse by telling us that, as a boy, he had a ginger cat called Marmelad, so now everyone meows at him. Natasha says he's a splendid-looking fellow, with a mass of curly dark hair and a mustache.

I believe that before Anton Pavlovich had us in stitches, I was wondering about the beauty of sadness. I have had, if not an answer—for I'm not sure such abstract, even emotional queries can have answers—at least an illustration that went some way toward revealing the nature of the sadness.

The flute or the piano on their own can be light and airy—a passage of clouds, a stream, birds, a ladder of sunlight—that is what our modest recitals or Georges's practicing have often evoked to me in the past. And now the cello, this mournfulness. I am grateful to the musicians and the composers—Tchaikovsky, Mussorgsky, Brahms, among others—for bringing spontaneous images of the world to me on their notes. Some might argue that music does not contain images, that Tchaikovsky did not see fields of wheat when he composed his Little Russian Symphony; I only know that is what *I saw* in the music—at times, and in waves or snatches of consciousness—when we went to hear the symphony at the concert hall in Petersburg.

Now Marmelad (I can't help it, it makes me laugh) and Ivanenko and Georges played together last night in our drawing room. All our guests came to listen, including Nikolay Pavlovich. So there were a dozen of us crowded into the room, and Anton Pavlovich took Nikolay Pavlovich and led him out onto the veranda. In case he doesn't feel well, he said, I can see him back to the guesthouse and not disturb you all; we can hear quite well, and will have the added chorus of frogs and owls and mosquitoes, and perhaps, with any luck, the bittern will grace us with a solo performance.

Nikolay Pavlovich tried to laugh, but all that came out was a hacking cough. He gasped for breath and at last fell silent, and we waited for the concert to begin.

Georges played the opening notes. The music was strange, unfamiliar to me. He had told me the name—a Petersburg composer, one of his professors, but I've forgotten it.

I was sitting not far from the French doors that open onto the veranda; I could hear Anton Pavlovich's voice murmuring, gently but firmly, like that of a parent to a child. The tones of the cello deepened and grew louder at that very moment, as if to silence Anton Pavlovich's voice, a sort of desperate reprimand; then again a lull, where the flute tried to restore a bitter gaiety, and from the veranda I could hear, ever so faintly, the sound of sobs, then again Anton Pavlovich's voice, trying to be soothing but failing, his whisper impatient, and again the cello, almost angry, as if trying to drown out the voice from the veranda. Nikolay Pavlovich was coughing again, quite audibly, and after a moment Anton Pavlovich led him away. A lull in the music, and I could hear their steps fading at the end of the veranda, and then three long, sustained notes from the cello, like a sort of final, desolate call.

It was all purely by chance——the choice of the music, and Anton Pavlovich's decision to lead his brother away just when he did, but the sound of those fading footsteps against the sustained notes of the cello was almost more than I could bear. Everything seemed to have gathered into that moment: the sympathy between the music and the injustice of life, and the ephemeral beauty of being there, having my whole life, such as it was now, there in the drawing room and on the veranda, all my loved ones playing or listening to the music. The music seemed to be speaking to me alone, as if it had been written for me, for that moment, when I understood what was waiting for me: what, like Nikolay Pavlovich, I would lose.

The music was scraping me from within, but I needed it more than anything. To prove to myself that I am still alive, to witness the alchemy that turns sadness to a beauty I can still see.

June 13, 1889

Not left my bed for three days. Some sort of fever. Limbs so weak, I can hardly hold the pen.

Outside, beyond, is heat. Elena brings cloths, cold water. No news from our guests, no visits. No music. Laudanum.

I cannot write.

June 14

He took my hands between his own.

I am better, thank you, Anton Pavlovich.

I am glad. A pause, then before I had time to ask, he added: I wish I could say as much for Nikolay Pavlovich.

There's no progress?

He's losing weight. I cannot get him to eat, he only drinks milk, the coughing exhausts him. He won't leave the house now.

His voice was angry; I could not determine whether it was a desperate anger against his brother or against his own inability to change things.

There's a kitten. A tiny gray and white thing. He plays with it, it goes to him, jumps on his hand, he dips his finger in the milk and gives it to the kitten to lick, to suck. For a moment he forgets, loses himself, he stops coughing, he is completely concentrated on the tiny paws and whiskers, on the little animal's curiosity, as if he can somehow learn something. But when I suggest the river or the garden, he shakes his head and coughs again and stares out the window and pushes the kitten away.

I did not know what to say.

I'm thinking of going to the Smagins' again, said Anton Pavlovich, in a day or two. Aleksandr is coming from Moscow with the children and the nanny. I don't want to be around them. It's too much.

I see.

This was quite sudden. We had not heard anything more from Aleksandr Pavlovich since the end of last summer. I was hoping that Elena would have quite forgotten him.

The harvest has failed, did you know that, Zinaida Mikhailovna?

Yes, Pasha told me. It's been a terrible spring, hasn't it?

At least the crayfish have been abundant.

But we can't make bread in the winter with crayfish.

Indeed. How peculiar that would be.

How will we feed the peasants?

You will find a way.

His voice sounded distant, preoccupied, almost as if he didn't care. Although I know he does.

But the moment of tension was there, and carried its weight of silence, until Anton Pavlovich thought of a funny story to tell me about Svobodin, and then Masha arrived to spend some time with me, and he left soon thereafter.

He's overwhelmed, said Masha. She offered no explanation; none was needed.

June 16

They have left. Georges, Svobodin, Anton Pavlovich, and Ivan Pavlovich. I wondered if Natasha was hurt that she wasn't invited to the Smagins' this year; she says she has better things to do, but I believe that is her pride speaking.

She sat down to read to me, and all the restlessness in her heart punctuated her sentences; the characters in the story hesitated, sighed, stared out at the garden, and forgot themselves. Finally, she put the book down in exasperation. Do you mind, Zinochka? It's such a boring book, what do you think?

I disagreed but didn't say so. She pulled her chair closer to mine and took my hand.

There's this woman with Aleksandr Pavlovich, she said. The children's nanny, so they say. She's called Natalya, like me, Natalya Aleksandrovna Golden. They call her Nata-chez-vous, too. I feel almost offended. I thought that was my exclusive nickname.

Is she unpleasant?

No, not at all. I'd say it's Aleksandr Pavlovich who seems unpleasant. Poor woman, it must have been dreadful to travel with him and those children. They're absolute scamps.

We were silent, then she continued: Masha doesn't like being there while Antosha is away. Her brothers argue all the time.

Mikhail Pavlovich has gone off somewhere, and Aleksandr is all alone to look after Nikolay Pavlovich. Evgenia Yakovlevna can't handle Nikolay Pavlovich; she just sits and sobs, and Masha holds her hand. Aleksandr's little boys run around tormenting Anya, she is threatening to leave. They grab her braid and call her Fat Pole.

And this Natalya Aleksandrovna?

She wanders around the garden as if she's come here by mistake. Apparently, the family doesn't like her. They have had to take rooms in the village, Evgenia Yakovlevna won't have them here for some reason. Perhaps because of Aleksandr's behavior last year. I know she's very careful not to offend Mama. Besides, there really isn't room.

I sighed and felt very weary. Not a minute's walk away, there is a man who is gravely ill, and his family continues to squabble and bicker and find reasons to dislike one another and act indignant. Ever since he arrived this year, Anton Pavlovich has made no secret of the fact that he resents his brother's illness, that it keeps him from traveling here and there and beyond with Suvorin. Now he has left Luka not one hour after his other brother arrived, as if to mark his disapproval—or was it simply to leave the burden of caring for Nikolay Pavlovich to his older brother at last?

But perhaps anger is one way to cope with losing someone you love, however selfish it may seem to others. Perhaps it is altogether too much for him, and he feels only an irrational urge to flee that is contrary to all his affection for Nikolay Pavlovich. He cannot bear to see him as he is now.

And Elena? I asked softly. Has she not been to examine Nikolay Pavlovich?

They haven't asked—since Anton Pavlovich was there anyway, until yesterday; I believe she doesn't want to get involved, though of course if they ask her, she will go—but even Mama and Pasha have told her to wait. It seems from what

Masha told me that there is not much they can do except try to keep him comfortable—and make sure Tatyana remembers to bring the milk.

I have not been in Nikolay Pavlovich's company often, and no one has ever described him to me, but I cannot forget how we greeted each other this year when he arrived. The dry, hot hand. The angry, helpless cough. But while I sat talking with Natasha on the veranda, I could see him absolutely clearly: a gaunt, thin young man in his bed, with wild hair and a ragged beard, and a hand feebly lifted, looking around as if he had lost something; calling for a gray and white kitten.

As medical students, we learned, or tried to learn, to overcome our fear and disgust in the presence of death and disease. You had to or you could not be a doctor, it was as simple as that.

Sitting there on our quiet veranda with Natasha, I was almost overwhelmed, and I had to ask her to fetch some poetry. The imagined scene of Nikolay Pavlovich in his bed conveyed to me, far more bitterly than all the patients I saw when I was well, the threshold to one's fragile, too corporeal self. If one crosses that threshold, one is sucked down into a spiral of fear, disgust, and complete loss of hope.

I keep seeing the kitten: I feel its warm fur between my palms, its sharp yet gentle little claws; I hear its frenetic purring, a mixture of love and fear.

June 17

We were having our morning tea. I heard her footsteps, hurried; then a long pause before she knocked.

It was Anya, come to tell us that Nikolay Pavlovich had died at dawn.

The hours that followed—as if I were standing in the middle of a room with people swirling around me, and I could not catch anyone, stop anyone long enough, to find out what had happened, what was happening; like a game of blindman's buff, only it was real, they all hurried by me, eager to escape, all that was missing was laughter.

Elena and Mama have taken charge. At the guesthouse, they are stunned and weeping. The brothers argue, incriminate. Elena has brought Masha and Evgenia Yakovlevna to us for now, while the women from the village prepare the body. There will be a requiem; the coffin and a cross have been ordered. A telegram was sent to Anton Pavlovich. God knows how long it will take him to get back from the Smagins'.

I write these things—practical everyday things, real things that must be done—when neither I nor anyone else is fooled. Insignificant helpless gestures against grief, like this scribbling. Only Masha and her mother, sobbing quietly in a corner of the drawing room, tell the truth. We should all do just that, sit in a corner and weep.

June 18

I slept fitfully. Dreams, sounds in the night. Masha stayed with us. No one spoke. Rosa whimpered by my door. Even the owls, the frogs, seem mournful. Have they always sounded like this?

I am not much use. I do what I can, sit and talk quietly, keep vigil, carry messages. Elena is so good. She has offered to pay for the burial. She takes things in hand. Natasha consoles; her presence soothes, she dares to smile, I am sure, because she is on the side of life, of hope.

We all knew how sick he was—why did Anton Pavlovich believe he could recover? Why these misdiagnoses of laryngeal infection or typhoid when it could only be consumption? You could hear it in the way he coughed!

We are all afraid, that is why: knowing that the disease can strike irrespective of age or rank or talent, that it does not retreat, and it spares no one. Death sitting in our midst, uninvited and implacable. Even as I write this and know my own death sentence, I do not want to accept it, I hope against hope for remission, indulgence. Some miraculous clemency. I go back and forth between my pragmatic medical acceptance of facts and some superstitious clinging to the illusory promise of life. For Nikolay Pavlovich, it was no different.

Midnight.

Elena says Anton Pavlovich has arrived, exhausted. He came by train. The others are following with Roman and the carriage.

The family is keeping vigil around the coffin, with the cantor and the village mourners.

I let Rosa stay in my bedroom with me, fleas be damned. It comforts me to hear her snuffling, her gentle whining as she dreams.

June 19, 1889

Our families joined, but not in the way any of us would have hoped.

Nikolay Pavlovich is buried in our graveyard on the hill.
I am told you can see the cross for miles around.

Many people came from the village for the funeral. I walked
with Tonya and Pasha. Natasha and Elena carried the lid with
Masha; Georges was a pallbearer with the Chekhov brothers and
Ivanenko. Evgenia Yakovlevna has been so terribly distraught,
clinging to the coffin and sobbing endlessly. That is her right;
it is her suffering that pains me, that leaves a tight fist clenched
inside my chest.

Later, when we were sitting for lunch, Natasha confided that
in the midst of all the sobbing, including our own, I would not
have heard Anton Pavlovich. He stayed dry-eyed throughout the
service. No one has seen him weep.

You might think he has no heart; or you might think he
buries sorrow so deep that we ordinary people cannot see his
grief, nor can we share in his rites of mourning.

Either way, we do not know who he is. If we fault him for a
lack of tears, that is our failure to understand, not his failing as
a person.

They have gone to the monastery at Akhtyrka, the entire family.
Luka is suddenly deathly quiet. I use the word consciously,
deliberately. In their need to commune with death, to
contemplate their God and seek consolation, they leave us with
silence and absence.

Natasha broods, reminds me that they visited the
monastery not two weeks ago with Anton Pavlovich and
Svobodin. They made fun of the monks, she said. Anton
Pavlovich introduced himself as Count Wild Boar. What will
he say to them now?

I'm sure the monks have a sense of humor, I replied. They
were glad of the entertainment.

And now?

It's their duty, is it not, to accompany those who grieve, to help them understand their relation with death?

Natasha grunted. They showed us the icons. That helped me understand my relation with life.

In what way?

Art, she said simply, then added, the force of life. The reason not to succumb to despair. We had a long discussion about it afterward. Every work of art—even an anonymous icon commissioned by God, so to speak—is an act of defiance, speaking for the possibility of immortality.

No, Natasha, that is an illusion. Death always wins.

It doesn't! And I know what you're thinking: No matter how I argue that *Dead Souls* is immortal, Gogol has been dead for thirty-seven years.

Well, can you prove that Gogol the person, Nikolay Gogol from Sorochintsy, is still alive?

The fact of the immortality of his work, of his spirit—it's a vast, worthy conspiracy among the living, a consolation and a source of hope and joy—

Precisely: a conspiracy to maintain a vast delusion—

And so it may be, but a delusion that helps people to live, gives meaning to the lowest of lives—

Are you sure? Have you asked Grigory Petrovich or Anya what art does for them?

Art is the conscious knowledge of defiance; religion is unconscious. For them, icons represent the story of Christ, and they find consolation and meaning in religion. Don't you agree?

I paused before answering; I pause now as I write. Once I would have agreed wholeheartedly, believed in the consolation, the brave assertions of art and even of religion. Now my soul is not so permeable. I am well acquainted with unremitting darkness.

Consolation, I said, is this—and I made a circle with my
finger to point at her and include her in my thoughts—this
conversation, this moment, this sharing of life. It's the only way
of knowing for sure, of being absolutely certain of life. For me.
The only immortality we have is in this very second. I speak
on authority, Natasha; I stare down my own mortality every
morning, and I live not for art or icons but for the moments I
might spend with you, and Mama, and Elena, and our brothers,
and everyone else who is dear to me, and even the dog. I do not
believe that when I die, you can go to Akhtyrka and find me
alive there, staring at you from the face of an icon. Nor do I
believe, like Mama, in an afterlife.

But there is memory—others are kept alive through memory.
Why are you writing your journal if not to leave something of
yourself?

Perhaps. I like to think Ksenia will read it someday. But she
will read my words, not me.

And what are words if not the expression of who you are? The
expression of your defiance? Your soul, after all?

I am glad you see it that way, Natasha; perhaps you are right.
I do not like to use the word *despair*, but there are times I believe
my journal is merely an expression of despair. I am like Evgenia
Yakovlevna, clinging to the coffin.

She reached out for my hand. We had come full circle,
resolved nothing, understood little. I felt the warmth in her
hand, my vibrant sister, and that is what mattered more than all
the rest. That mysterious warmth, alone able to calm my heart
and mind.

I remembered what Anton Pavlovich said last summer about
living well, every moment. Yes, it was consolation, and each time
I could realize that crystalline moment, it was like a burst of
pure goodness and serenity. Surely worth living for.

June 20, 1889

I have not seen you in so long, Zinaida Mikhailovna—not seen you, I should say, in our way, where you can see me, too. I expect that, to you, I have been no more than a miserable bit actor this summer, reciting lines by rote, with no heart.

For a moment I wasn't certain what he meant, and then I understood and smiled. He sat down on the wicker chair next to me. The creaking told me he was stretching into the chair, relaxing. I had a sudden hope that he might stay for a while.

He sighed, stammered, as if about to say something, then thinking better of it. I encouraged him, told him I was listening. Then he hummed, sighed again, banged the floor with his heels.

Such boredom, Zinaida Mikhailovna, such restlessness! Do you feel it? Life has—this whole business, Kolya's illness and death—it's not even about grieving, that's normal, you expect it—it's the rest of the time, it's as if all the good passion, the good sap, has gone out of life. As if the terrible heat we have had has dried up every moist, tender, fragile feeling or disposition within me. I'm a husk, Zinaida Mikhailovna, a dry husk, cleaned out, dust.

This will pass, Anton Pavlovich. It is normal, surely, as you say.

Don't say that! That is what they all say—Masha, Vanya. You can do better, I know you can, you must tell me, you are wisdom itself, you are a light when all the others are blinded by convention—

He stopped suddenly, sighed. I'm sorry, he said. I'm not sleeping enough. I shouldn't speak to you like this.

I reached out, searching for his hand, did not find it, sat back again.

Anton Pavlovich. Perhaps what I say will be conventional, too, but it is all I know. Life is mysterious—for now the passion has gone, Nikolay Pavlovich has taken it with him to the grave, and

his death has shown you the vulnerability, the pointlessness, dare
I say the cynicism of life. How can you laugh and go to the theater
and enjoy yourself when your brother is dead? But I say you can
and you will; there will come a time when your spirit will cease
mourning and slowly fill again with that sap, as you call it.

I paused; his silence seemed impatient to me, so I hurried on.

I have died innumerable times since my first headache, my
first dizziness. Each time, with each spell, seizure, degree of
blindness, I have lost a part of life. Each time fear comes in,
showing death to me. You have seen for yourself, from last
summer to this, how life is draining out of me, just as it did
with Nikolay, but more slowly, less dramatically. And each
time I do not die—although I could choose to let go, see the
pointlessness of it all—I do not die because I shake my fist
at fear. This is all there is, yet it is still so much. Even I have
my moments of hope—not for eternity, not even that I might
survive or recover my sight—because I already have survived,
and I have learned to see.

I sat up, tapped my foot on the floor.

What right, Anton Pavlovich, do you have, when you are
fit and healthy, to come to me with your ennui? Boredom will
pass—it is the least you owe your brother! It is *you* who are
blind—open your eyes, look around you!

My head was pounding; a sudden stabbing pain caused me
to gasp and threw me back in my chair. I did not care what he
thought at that moment.

He cleared his throat. Bless you, Zinaida Mikhailovna, I knew
I could count on you to talk sense to me.

It's not sense, I said breathlessly, it's not sense you want. That's
not why you came here. Sense is convention, sense is—

I could not go on, the pain was a vice around my head. I think
I nearly fainted, the floor of the veranda seemed to be tilting up,
and I lay my head back and clung to the armrests to keep from

falling, as if I were on a ship in a storm, as if an earth tremor were shaking the house. Anton Pavlovich was speaking from far away, I could hear him but not understand him, I remember thinking he had his own language, it was music, the sound of his voice, full of sadness but also a bitter humor, and there was a major key in there, too, of hope or understanding. And still the words I recognized were like false notes, dissonances: life, death, soul, weariness, hope, God. Then came long interludes when his words flowed quietly and smoothly, like a lullaby, comforting me as the pain receded.

When I realized he was silent, I lifted my hand from the armrest. Anton Pavlovich, I'm not well, may we talk of this another time?

He must have come to kneel by my chair, because his voice was very close to my ear, and his hand took mine, yet his words seemed to come from far away.

I am a fool, Zinaida Mikhailovna, I have tired you, I am sorry. I am a selfish fool, forgive me.

Something warm against my hand, next to his, it was his cheek, his beard. I do not know how long he stayed like that.

Then he left, and I dozed dreamlessly until Natasha woke me for supper.

I have remembered something: The other day, Anton Pavlovich described his trip to and from the Smagins'.

It was, he said, as if the weather sought to warn him, then to punish him: on the way there, thunderstorms, rain, a gray, lowering sky. He was soaked through, miserable, they all were. During the return trip, he was obliged to wait in Romni for hours for a connecting train. He sat in a garden, and it was dreadfully cold, and in the next building he could hear a troupe of amateur actors rehearsing a melodrama.

He writes his stories, his plays, sets actors to music beneath a

lowering sky. Now life has lifted him helpless into his own sheaf
of papers. He is soaked through; the ink has run.

June 21, 1889

Last night I slept long, my body immersed in recovery, and
I woke again, refreshed, the pain almost gone, just the usual
throbbing that responds to the laudanum, and the residual
tiredness of an excess of sleep; that would pass. I could hear a
gentle rain outside, soothing, washing away the bad thoughts. I
resolved to spend the day usefully, not to dwell on the difficult
conversation with Anton Pavlovich. I begged Mama, who wanted
me to rest, to assign me some useful task—a trip to Sumy, a
visit to the village—so she led me to the laundry, where Anya
was ironing napkins and tablecloths. It would save Anya time
if I helped to fold napkins, that much I could do, feeling the
warm clean edges come together, the wonderful smell of clean
linen—of warmth itself, beneath my fingertips.

At first Anya was quiet, just the heavy banging of the iron,
sizzle of steam. I knew she must find it somewhat awkward for
me to be there, though I could hardly supervise her work, it was
rather she who would supervise mine. But very soon she began to
talk about the Chekhovs, in a surprisingly free, gossipy manner,
which confirmed to me that although she did not find it easy to
be working for them (indirectly, through Mama), they were a
source of endless entertainment. Even their recent tragedy seems
to have been enlightening to her—now she said to me: Master
Nikolay, in the end, mistress, he was the soul of kindness, where
he'd been so difficult before, barking orders at everyone, even
Anton Pavlovich used to call him the General, but then he knew
it was his time, mistress, and it was as if death had told him, I'll

be coming for you tomorrow during the night, so he'd had to say his farewells in a way the others wouldn't notice, and he was ever so kind, at least to me.

And I knew, I did, continued Anya, I felt it, and sure enough . . .

At times her talking got ahead of her and I had to remind her to pass me a napkin.

And wasn't it awful, she continued, the way the others treated that poor woman—the children's maid—who'd come with Master Aleksandr the day before Master Nikolay died. You would've thought Madame Chekhova was the grand duchess herself, and this poor Natalya Aleksandrovna was some scullery maid. And all the brothers arguing, and you could tell it was because she was there, and did she look after those two boys? Not at all, she just sat out in the garden with a sorry face as if she was bored or hurt that no one talked to her. Even Miss Masha ignored her. She had a fan and sat in the gazebo fanning the air, as if it would hurry the long hours. And do you know, mistress, I heard Master Mikhail Chekhov shouting at her, wasn't she a fine one, because before she'd been with Master Aleksandr, she'd—

Anya broke off.

I noticed the scent before I knew he was there—a rich bouquet of flowers, their fragrances familiar yet elusive, mingled together without form or color to identify them. He coughed and asked Anya in a strained voice if he could borrow her mistress, and I wondered if he had overheard what she'd been saying about Aleksandr's nanny. He took my arm and led me to the veranda, and we sat in our usual chairs, and the air was fresh and fine after the warmth of the laundry room.

He reached over and placed the bouquet in my arms. They're from Sumy, he said, from the florist's; all your flowers have succumbed to the heat. So you have exotic blooms that have traveled all this way by train, on ice, from the Crimea, and

Turkey, and Egypt, and the source of the Nile, and distant
Zanzibar. I chose them for their scent.

I smiled and thanked him. I immersed my face in the
bouquet, in the soft petals quivering with raindrops. I saw a
profusion of imaginary varieties, picked in a garden where
flowers were grown only for me.

If Anton Pavlovich were mumbling some sort of apology for
his behavior the day before, I did not hear him.

But when he began to tell me he would be going away for
a few weeks—to meet friends in Odessa, in Yalta—the cloud
of scent seemed to move on. I left the bouquet on my lap and
listened.

I thought of joining Suvorin in Vienna, he said, but this will
be more entertaining. They're theater people, it could be further
inspiration—stimulation, I should say—for my theatrical
endeavors. I need to get away, Zinaida Mikhailovna. I feel like a
leaf in a whirlwind here. I can't get my head straight, even if the
family is beginning to live more normally again.

Of course, Anton Pavlovich, you've had to bear the brunt.

So Vanya and I will head off in a day or two. Masha will
stay here. And Misha. It will be altogether quieter. We've been
turbulent tenants, to say the least. Your mama—

Mama has been only too happy to have you here. She is
genuinely fond of you all, Anton Pavlovich.

I said it somewhat sternly. I could not face more conversations
with apologizing, or sighing, or talk of ennui and death. I picked
up the bouquet again, lifted it to my face. Felt the moisture
against my skin.

Be careful, there are thorns.

Roses, then? That's lovely. I'm not too worried about thorns, I
said with a smile.

I hope when I get back from my trip, in August, to return
to work on the novel. I'll be fresh, inspired, the quiet will be

welcome, not dreary. In the meantime, your dreams can continue to age my manuscript.

Like a fine oak cask?

Precisely.

The chair creaked; he took my hand and said goodbye.

I sat for a long time with the bouquet, thinking I might identify individual scents in addition to the roses, but I couldn't. Elena found me there at dusk.

ONE LAST TIME, ANA thought of flying to New York for the Fleur Mailly awards ceremony—a dinner to be held in the mansion belonging to the foundation that sponsored the prize—but then decided firmly against it. Franck and Isobel would be there. She knew it was cowardly of her, and that she would regret it if she did win, so she tried to convince herself that she couldn't afford it, which was true up to a point—the point where emotions seem unjustified but are so overbearing that a person will grasp at any excuse rather than admit to them.

A polite email had informed her that should she decide not to attend, her publisher would be given advance notice of the results in the course of the day, and naturally, would she keep the information to herself. So, with any luck, taking the time difference into account, she would hear before bedtime.

She spent the morning of the ceremony cleaning and tidying, coaxing out a bohemian chic that she hadn't known her cluttered book-strewn dwelling possessed. She threw the windows open on the spring air, the warmth tentative but the sunshine bright. She dusted, allowed herself to daydream like some urban Cinderella, not of a prince and a ball but of a crowning achievement, a confirmation in her quest for recognition, a nod to her talent. And a cash prize of four and a half months' rent with its interlude of freedom, a real vacation of the kind she had not taken since she lost her flat in Paris. Perhaps she could go on a tour to Russia and then Ukraine, provided things quieted down, and visit the places where Chekhov had lived—Moscow, Melikhovo, Taganrog, Sumy—with the regrettable exception of Crimea. She had not been back to either country since her student years, when both were part of the Soviet Union; this would be her chance. If she won.

She had a bottle of champagne in the fridge. If I don't get the prize, she thought, it'll be the usual Calva.

In the afternoon she went back to work. Anton Pavlovich was about to leave for the Crimea with his brother. She checked the news. The email. Her phone line. All equally quiet.

She looked up Fleur Mailly on the Internet: a French heiress who had married an American banker and used her money to promote French literature in translation. She was no longer alive. What would Madame Mailly think, wondered Ana, of the perceived decline in the status of the French on the world literary scene? But then it seemed the whole world literary scene was in decline.

Ana baked a piece of salmon. The champagne would be nice with it, but it might be bad luck to open the bottle before there was something to celebrate. Besides, she had already decided to keep it for when she finished Zinaida Mikhailovna's diary, if she didn't win the prize.

She had run out of wine; tap water would have to do.

After dinner, Ana eyed the bottle of Calvados. She didn't want to be pessimistic, either. It was nine o'clock—three P.M. in New York—and it was getting dark, but she put on her coat and walked to the end of the village and back. There were stars; Ana decided against superstition and stared at them defiantly.

Still nothing. Not a good sign.

Doodle, wisely, had gone into hiding. Ana picked up one book after another but could not concentrate. She decided to watch *Monty Python and the Holy Grail* for the umpteenth time but couldn't lose herself in the absurdity and switched it off after the knights who said Ni. She resisted running to her laptop every five minutes and trusted her hearing to pick up the chime of incoming mail.

She attacked a pile of ironing. At half past eleven the laptop pinged.

Yves, inquiring if she'd had any news.

Diddly squat, she wrote. *They were supposed to notify me come what may, so what does this mean?*

That you're special and they'll send a singing telegram, replied Yves. *Bearded Ukrainian poet—are you ready with the vodochka?*

She smiled but relented, filled a shot glass, and went to bed. She slept reasonably well, and when she saw in the morning that there were still no messages from the foundation or the publisher, she swore once, then sat down to work.

At three o'clock that afternoon there was a message from the publisher of her translation of Lydia Guilloux's novel. *We're so sorry,* they wrote, *our intern did not realize this should be forwarded to you.*

The prize, she read in the enclosed press release, had been awarded to Isobel Brookes for her translation of *The Lemon-Rind Still Life. There is not a word out of place,* said the judges. *With such agile craftsmen as Isobel Brookes at work we can look forward to discovering a wealth of new literature from France.*

I've been walking around all these days as if I were in love, wrote Anton Pavlovich to Suvorin after he won the Pushkin Prize.

Ana knew love was a gift, not something you could command, but she wondered how much depended on the recipient. There was no answer for such speculation other than to move on to the next moment as if the previous one never existed, and to put herself elsewhere, in a place where, next time, love might find purchase.

Anton and Ivan have left for the south, for their theater troupe, their people from Moscow and Petersburg. Luka is provincial; Luka is a country graveyard where gentlemen bury their brothers and their ennui.

Am I bitter today? Just lucid. It is not a bad way to be, after all. Natasha is angry that she was not invited; Elena is sad and wistful. Masha is sullen and silent. Only Georges is a pleasure to be with, dear Georges, always even-tempered, eager to play for me. He went through all the Mussorgsky pieces again; in a wistful mood myself, I had him play "Une Larme" three times over.

Time no longer measured by the ticking of the clock but by the memory of the metronome. All the hours he spent learning to play, restored to me now, that I might forget time.

Anya has been enjoying her role as chief gossip for the guesthouse. The latest: A ceremony is being planned, the priest has been summoned, a rush of preparations—zakuski and small cakes, bottles of wine and vodka. Try to guess, she says, teasing me. What could it be, scarcely a month after Nikolay Pavlovich's death—not even forty days? she asks insinuatingly.

I give up, Anya.

She draws a breath, pauses for dramatic tension, and says, Master Aleksandr is to wed the children's maid.

A silence, then she adds, As I thought.

What did you think, Anya?

She was never the children's maid, mistress. They just waited for Mr. Anton to get out of the way so's they could get married. I couldn't tell you, the other day when I was ironing, and he came in himself, Mr. Anton that is, but she used to be Mr. Anton's fiancée, she did, some years ago, so Mr. Mikhail said.

I sigh. Please don't gossip, Anya. It's none of our business. Let's just wish them well.

Anya's words have stayed with me, disquieting, along with an image of a faceless Natalya Aleksandrovna Golden standing undecided between the two brothers, one finger to her invisible lips.

A small ceremony at John the Baptist's, I was told, just the family. They went to Nikolay Pavlovich's grave. Not long thereafter, the newlyweds left with the children and returned to Moscow. I should be happy for them—people I hardly know but who are close to us all the same—yet there seems to be something so terribly desperate and sad about their wedding. Why here, in the shadow of his brother's death? The same church, the same priest? And deliberately in Anton Pavlovich's absence?

Perhaps each of them has his own way of reaffirming life, said Natasha later, when we discussed it. Anton and Ivan go off to the Crimea; Aleksandr finally takes his bride, provides a mother for his boys. At least he's not running away.

What do we really know of other people? Who has ever seen my own secret feelings, who might suspect them? How much unspoken love misfires in the dark; how many marry and wait all their lives for a shot that never comes?

I have seen peasants in love, strolling hand in hand by the river at nightfall, their faces flushed and glowing with their amazement at what has befallen them. They ask no questions, life comes to them. Briefly, they embrace each other, they embrace life—the bounty of a season, a full harvest. There is little else, but for the moment, that is all that matters.

Elena has been busy on house calls, but she found a moment to sit with Natasha and me this evening. Eventually, our conversation settled on Aleksandr Pavlovich's recent wedding, as if we had been avoiding it all along yet knew we must speak of it.

Natasha told us she has been talking to Masha. Masha has known all along about her brother and this Natalya Aleksandrovna! she said angrily. She might have told us sooner. They have been living together since last October. She's an old family friend, they've known her for years, along with her sister. Anton Pavlovich was often with her, often stayed with her. For years! One of his regulars! She called him Anto-chez-vous. And she was Nata-chez-vous long before I was. Literally. Nata-chez-lui, more likely.

Do you think that is why we weren't invited? said Elena solemnly.

Fff! I wouldn't have gone if we had been. Imagine, what a woman! First one brother, then the next. Playing the *children's maid* all that time.

We were silent for a moment, then I said, Well, it can't have been easy. Apparently, the parents treat her dreadfully. And what about Aleksandr Pavlovich, then?

What about him, said Natasha crossly.

I wished then that I could have given her a warning glance; I tried to arrange my features and look in her direction, but it didn't seem to help, because she said, What man waits until his brother is out of the way to up and marry his former sweetheart!

After that, I had to say something: Well, it goes to prove that Anton Pavlovich was absolutely right!

Right about what?

I realized I had talked myself into a corner. I would either have to reveal our private conversation about Aleksandr's dubious interest in Elena or find a way to retreat.

He told me his brother was quite desperate after his wife's death.

Well, obviously! barked Natasha. We don't need Anton Pavlovich to tell us that. Anto-chez-vous!

All this time Elena had not said a thing. But now, her voice solemn and resigned, she said, He was a very unhappy man. Men don't cope well with their feelings, don't you think? I suppose she was able to offer him some comfort. I wish them well.

After they had gone, I sat and brooded for some time.

Could I have lied on Elena's behalf, told Anton Pavlovich something that wasn't true but that might *become* true? Could I have seized that chance for her?

Now we shall never know. And I suppose if Aleksandr Pavlovich found it so easy to secure a consoling presence almost the moment he was back in Petersburg, he might not have been a suitable husband for Elena after all.

But only she could have been the final judge of that.

I have been spending a great deal of time with Tonya and little Ksenia. She has just learned to walk and she tries to follow her mama along the lanes. Falls down, says, Oh-oh! in surprise, then her mama snatches her up. Or she clings to my skirt. Often I hold her, carry her on my hip, to feel her warm fresh body, breathe her milky smell. I keep my other hand on Tonya's shoulder as we walk, to steady myself, so I don't trip and drop my precious burden.

I remember one day before he left for Odessa, I asked Anton Pavlovich if he wanted a family. He cleared his throat several times. Then he said, First I would have to want a wife. Then I'll see.

And you do not want a wife?

Perhaps it is, dear Zinaida Mikhailovna, a matter of a wife wanting me.

(I know that in Spain, they fight with bulls, and the bullfighter must be a master of stepping elegantly to one side.)

He continued: I've no doubt there are women who are sensitive to my charms.

There was a pause, as if he were thinking. Then he continued, But they want those charms for themselves, and charms do not make a family. If, somewhere, there is a woman who wants me not for herself but for my sake, our sake, because she knows she will be the best guarantor of my freedom—and her own as well—I expect the day such a woman comes along, then I shall fall in love and have a dozen *bambini* like Count Tolstoy.

Elena told me Anton Pavlovich went with her one day to treat a little girl in the village who had typhus. He had such a good manner with little Katyenka, she said. The child was frightened, her little chin all creased and trembling with sobs, and there was Anton Pavlovich telling her his silly crocodile stories, not to frighten her but to make her laugh and see that even crocodiles can be vanquished.

He will make a fine father someday, Elena added wistfully, as if she wanted him for her own unborn children and knew it was impossible.

July 20, 1889

Ivan Pavlovich has returned from the Crimea already, but on his own. And Masha has had a letter from Anton Pavlovich. He is feted wherever he goes; he eats ice cream and draws ladies to him. I imagine they are actresses who dream of being in a play, or writers who hope some writerly dust will rub off his linen suit onto their delicate ink-stained fingers. We all wonder why Anton Pavlovich wanted to go to such an upstart of a place as Yalta when he could have gone with Suvorin to Abbazia or Biarritz, but he has written to Masha that he misses Luka, that he sits on the waterfront and wishes he were by the river Psyol. He writes that a *pealing sound* reminds him of Natasha's laugh! What does this mean, then, to appreciate a place only when you are far from it? He was so eager to be gone, to put our dry, mournful springtime behind him, to flee toward lights and women and ice cream—and now he claims to miss our Luka?

The more one knows him, the less one understands him.

Or perhaps it is an emotion I cannot understand, as I have always been happiest at Luka and have rarely known what it is to be torn by nostalgia for a place or time. To be dissatisfied in the present moment—what a torment that must be, constantly pursuing one with doubt and disappointment. I don't know whether to pity him or not, he says other very kind things about us in his letter to Masha—says that the murmur of waves reminds him of the *good doctor's* singing. It's true, when Elena is of a mind to sing . . . He also asks where his eldest brother has gone; he will not know yet about Aleksandr's marriage.

The others play cards; it has been raining. I listen and wish I could join them. I used to love our games of vint. I would have played more often had I known. Pointless, wistful regret; now I suffer from other forms of nostalgia. I listen to Natasha's peals of laughter and am glad I am not in Yalta.

July 30, 1889

How long the days seem.

I have said that to Mama, and Elena, and Natasha, and Georges, and now to this page. Perhaps it will break whatever spell is keeping me bound to the slowness of the hours.

Natasha has been reading to me, and Mama has had visits. For once I joined the company, although I usually don't, they fuss over me so.

Nothing seems to help.

It's as if Anton Pavlovich entrusted me with his wretched ennui when he left for the Crimea. I can just hear him: Look after it well! Don't forget, it needs watering three times a day, and the third time add a splash of Grigory Petrovich's poteen.

I'm laughing in spite of myself.

Because I've brought him back for a brief instant.

I suppose I could do that, write him into my life while he is gone, imagine the conversations we have had or might have, and during the time it takes to write them, at least he would be back here with me.

But I fear I've become too eager for his company—how will I manage when he is gone again for the winter? Perhaps for good?

If only I could reread this journal on my own, but that is the cruel irony of my affliction. Although I believe the mere fact of writing it all down does help my memory of it.

Or if I could live long enough to have Ksenia read it to me herself—she will be a smart child, with such clever parents— how old will she need to be? Five? Eight?

I don't think I shall have that long. My headaches are nearly constant now. Only distraction seems to relieve them at times. Good conversation, flowing ink, Georges at the piano.

———

How dark the room seems when I put down my pen.

Words are like spots of light, flickering candles.

August 12, 1889

It is so good to be back at Luka, Zinaida Mikhailovna. I had
to go away to realize what bliss it is to be here. The river, the
crayfish, the clean silence of birds and frogs and lonely dogs.
All that chattering of women, the fashionable set in Yalta—it
distracts you for a day or two, it's exciting and new and flattering,
then it drains you, dissipates you. Here I feel I can work again.
It's as if the season changed during my absence. I know this
is still summer, but it's a different summer, there's a restful
coolness to the morning, and the longer nights are good for
writing: peaceful August.

We were talking on the veranda before dinner. He had
arrived that morning, dusty and hot from the journey, and it was
indeed as if we were starting the summer all over again, as if the
sadness and restlessness of the earlier months had at last been
buried and life could resume. He was full of ideas, there was a
story he wanted to write, and he would go back to work on a play
that had been stalled for months. His energy was returning.

And the novel? I asked, almost embarrassed to bring it up.

He was silent for a moment and said, more a statement of trust
than a question, It is still safely sleeping beneath your person?

It is.

Then let's leave it there for now. When I have a moment
between the story and the play—when I've made real progress
and the intrusion of impatient, neglected characters into my life
no longer fills me with fear and despair—well, yes, perhaps I
shall return to the novel, too.

If you like, you could read to me what you've written so far. It would be a way to reintroduce yourself to your characters.

It came out very suddenly and unexpectedly, my request, or offer, despite the fact that I knew that sharing his work, even finished, was something he disliked doing.

I could hear him scraping the soles of his shoes in semicircles on the wooden floor, could imagine him staring at his feet as they cleared a small space of thought. Then he said, Yes, I like your idea, but only if you promise, dear Zinaida Mikhailovna, to be very good and speak of it to no one, not even your journal. This must be done in the utmost secrecy; you must give me your word.

You have it, Anton Pavlovich.

And so I have agreed, henceforth, not to write another line about Anton Pavlovich's novel.

NOT ANOTHER WORD ABOUT Anton Pavlovich's novel? Ana felt a surge of despair. Zinaida Mikhailovna in such a privileged position, and she agreed to keep the book all to herself, at his almost whimsical request?

Of course this was normal and natural in a friendship, to respect trust, to keep secrets. What was more puzzling to Ana was why Anton Pavlovich was so loath to let anything out into the world about the novel. He spoke quite openly about the story he was writing that summer ("A Boring Story"), or the play (*The Wood Demon*), but he seemed to want to hide everything about the novel.

Perhaps it was too personal or too challenging. Perhaps he was revealing things about himself—in an autobiographical way— that could be found nowhere else in his work, so until he was sure of the novel's viability, he did not want to share it with anyone; or perhaps he was not always pleased with the book, so the less he said about it in general, the less explaining he would have to do if he abandoned the project altogether. Which, historically—until now—seemed to be what he had done.

Zinaida had made the completion of his novel her purpose, something she could reasonably strive for. She wanted to do what she could to encourage and support him, to inspire him.

Ana had seen her offering friendship, trust, consolation, insight. Now she saw that, through gentle urgings, Zinaida hoped to be a muse. Not the ethereal-goddess-on-a-pedestal type of muse, inspiring the artist through beauty and unattainability; no, merely a plain woman who, through her open, giving, and utterly disinterested spirit, could encourage him to continue and find the resources in himself to persevere.

But the excessive secrecy on Anton Pavlovich's part meant that precious information regarding the actual fate of the manuscript would be lost. Supposing it was last seen under Zinaida's mattress, a hundred and twenty-five years ago, supposing he left it with her at the end of the summer? Even if it were still there—even if the estate were standing, and the original furniture existed—how could fragile sheets of paper in a heavy box survive two wars, revolution, foreign occupation, climate, silverfish, mice, damp, and mold, and simply the fading of ink over time?

The same way Zinaida Mikhailovna's journal had survived.

Ana could only hope the manuscript had been found along with Zinaida's notebooks and was being kept in a safe secret place until it was ready for publication.

It was time to write to Katya Kendall for an update. Ana sent suggestions for the title and added casually, Any news about the other novel you mentioned at lunch?

KATYA SAW THE MESSAGE from Anastasia Harding in her inbox. *Update?* said the subject line.

My poor girl, she thought, you do not want an update. Unless you are writing to give me an update, and what will I do with it? I trust you; I know you are reading, translating, living at Luka, and that is all I need to know.

The titles seemed meaningless; as for the other novel . . .

What a pity, thought Katya, that I can't confide in Ana Harding.

We got along well, those few hours. She seems well acquainted with solitude. I have joined her there lately, in trying to understand it myself, given Peter's absence. She seems to have a sort of faith—not a religious faith but an openness, a preparedness, something we share with Zinaida Mikhailovna: a faith that life might come through. Even if it ends up being something we have to look for inside ourselves.

But I keep everything to myself and retreat further. It seems easier this way; easier to keep a handle on Peter, on myself. Soviet womanhood, indeed. Women keeping it together, is all. As usual.

Katya walked into the kitchen, stood at the sink rinsing her coffee mug, and looked out the window at the garden. It was raining, a light spring shower with droplets of sunshine. What in Russian we might call a mushroom rain, she mused, a notion unknown to unimaginative English weather forecasters. A cultural nuance, virtually untranslatable. How will Ana be coping with such nuances, with the relative poverty of the English language? It had been a perpetual and often virulent, although good-natured, debate with Peter from the moment they had met. He would go on and on about Shakespeare and tease her about Pushkin (*Push-kin, Pushkin, what is Pushkin?* like a child's rhyme); he refused to believe that Russian—that any language—could be richer than English. It dismayed her, infuriated her—he had studied Russian, after all, though he never attained complete fluency—and she would call him a retrograde linguistic imperialist, somewhat in jest, but in the end, they both clung to what they knew, to the faith of the tongue they had heard as infants while learning to love the world; they clung to what they believed in. Peter to his country, even though, lately, it had let him down so badly; and Katya to her language, her greatest comfort and pride. Pushkin, Pushkin, what is Pushkin, indeed.

If only they'd had children. That abortion before she knew him; before wanting was possible. The orphanage, too, that dreadful place, the sweet infant with his face smeared with dirt and tears, what was his name, Mitya? Misha? All for nothing, defeated by bureaucracy.

Well, it was too late for children, but perhaps it was not too late for poetry.

She went and sat at the desk in Peter's study. She did not know where he was. Perhaps he really had found a mistress. If so, she would not mind so much, provided he remained considerate. What a strange thought, so unreal. Everything was unreal these days; everything glittered, like the mushroom rain. Yes, she could begin there. She could write these poems for Peter, so he would know. So he would understand that her anger and silence had been to protect him. That she had known of no other way until now. She had tried to drive him away, to make it easier for both of them. Perhaps she had succeeded; he had seen she had no answers for him. Sometimes she said to him, It's only money. We still have each other. Wasn't that what couples said when times were bad? Each other. She was not even sure the notion had currency in this day and age, when a man's identity was so bound to money and success, and a woman's to independence—anything rather than be bound to a man.

She picked up a pen, stared at the blank sheet she had taken from the printer. Imagined Zinaida Mikhailovna, scribbling blindly across her ledger.

Katya began to write.

I often wake early, before the rest of the household. It is the
birds, at first light: I like to hear that day-waking song, jubilation
at dawn, before they subside into their ordinary conversation. I
lie for a long time in bed, listening, and I'm glad I do not have
to hurry to rise. I remember the cold mornings in Piter as a
student, when I had to tear myself from a warm bed, barefoot,
teeth chattering, to dress in the frost for the eight o'clock lecture.
Or not so long ago, rising in the dark to harness the horse and
drive off on a house call, my fingers so cold by the time I arrived
that I would have to thaw them in the horse's warm breath
before going inside to examine my patient.

I wonder if Anton Pavlovich is awake yet. I picture him at the
table in his room, by the window, listening to the same chatter
of birds. But he'll be hearing another chatter, of voices, dictating
his story, his play, or his novel; and he'll hear the silence, too, the
interludes of thought, deliberation, before each image becomes
clear and brings the words to lie upon the page.

These have been fine days. Warm, not hot, with the occasional
short rainstorm to freshen the air. Grigory Petrovich tells me the
garden has recovered somewhat from the drought in June. There
are massive sunflowers, and pumpkins, and the woods are full of
raspberries and mushrooms.

Every day Anton Pavlovich comes for me in the late afternoon.
He reads to me, we discuss what he has read, and then he takes
me for a walk around the pond or to the river. He is my eyes, as
always; he describes the ever familiar, ever changing landscape

as if it were an introduction to a story. In fact, he often teases me, casts me as the heroine of a tale in which the bittern swoops down to abduct me and carry me off to a land of firebirds and boy princes. I could try to retell his stories here for Ksenia, but so much would be lost, I am no storyteller and his odd tales consist in large part of his grave voice rising, falling, now tender, now threatening, then a burst of laughter or a falsetto imitation (of me or Natasha). It is what his words leave me with that must be told: a sense of sight, a puzzled wonder. How does he do this? How does he see the tiny detail that restores sight and, with it, an impression of being somehow closer to my own life—and at the same time, I see everything as if from high above, from the broad back of my bittern-firebird, soaring briefly with exhilaration and delight? He restores a fractured loveliness to my blind world, recalling remembered scenes and suggesting others blurred by time and loss. Or he might give me a shimmering underwater tableau, all clarity on the surface and yet deeper, colors running together in the confusion of waves and currents. He takes my elbow, explains, exhorts; he leads me to touch things on our path: a log, a bush, a wildflower in the shade, a mushroom, and even—poor man!— Grigory Petrovich asleep beneath the cherry tree, his bushy beard moving as he grumbles in his dream.

I know the days are passing. I feel the first chill in the early morning. Grigory Petrovich wakes when I do, and fumbles about, lighting the fire downstairs in the kitchen. I would like to stay longer in the security of these recent summer memories, find a better way to crystallize them, so that I can return to them again and again for sustenance in the weeks and months to come. But I fear I can do no better than what the pen allows; and the moments are transformed irrevocably by memory's hopes and failures. In any event, I cannot read what

I write—although perhaps I shall ask Mamochka in a spare
moment to reread bits of these journals to me; a spare moment
when life is dreary and hibernal and it seems incredible,
impossible, that such days ever existed.

Mama would prefer, no doubt, to take me to church—
chanting, candles, incense, the smells of unwashed bodies, the
shuffling and moaning. No. I can worship right here, without
ever leaving my room.

What do I look like these days, Anton Pavlovich? How do you
see me?

There was a long silence. Then he leaned forward in his
chair, the wicker creaking, and took my hand. Before he spoke, I
blurted, I was never a pretty girl, but now—

Shush, shush. He put a finger on my lips. Then he touched my
brow. You have three lines of worry across your forehead and two
more along either side of your nose—perhaps they were not there
before. But your eyes, Zinaida Mikhailovna . . . your eyes are a
lovely dark blue, full of expression and innocence, like a child's,
as if you see a world all your own, and you worry that you might
not find someone to share it with. Your mouth, too, hesitates—
you have a pretty smile, but too often you keep it to yourself.
You have some freckles, did you know that? Across your nose and
cheeks—here, and here, and here. Your hair is wild and thick—
you shouldn't pull it back so tight, it's too severe, you must scold
Ulyasha, tell her you'll send the Chekhovsky brigade after her for
treating your hair so cruelly.

You are teasing me, as usual, Anton Pavlovich.

But it's true! Don't you know I now have a diploma from the
Yalta Curl and Ringlet Association, that when I was not stuffing
myself with ice cream, I attended classes with the eminent
Professeur Salon de Coiffure, a French aristocrat.

(If only it were true! I had a mad urge to take him completely literally, to remove the pins from my hair and let him brush it.) But I changed the subject and said, Ice cream, how lovely.

The only way, Zinaida Mikhailovna, that I could keep all the aspiring writers and admiring ladies from coming up to me with a million flattering, egotistical remarks was to keep my mouth full. If my mouth was constantly full, I could not dispense any pearls of Shponkian wisdom. But enough nonsense, Zinaida Mikhailovna, we have work to do, and then we'll have some tea.

August 27, 1889

Yesterday we celebrated Natasha's name day.

We went to picnic on the island, something we have not been able to do for a long time because of the frequent thunderstorms at the end of the day. I remember last year, when it was Pasha's name day and we were preparing to row over, how the wind suddenly blew like a gale on the sea, and there was that poor fisherman caught in his boat in waves so violent he could not reach the shore, so he spent the night on the island. And Anton Pavlovich and I, in the early days of our friendship, talking of death as if it were impossibly far away.

Mama settled me on a blanket in the shade. She kept me company for a while, then went off to stroll with some of our guests—Vorontsov was there, and Yefimenko, and others who do not visit as often. I was alone. I suppose it is not something that afflicts only blind people, but it is a terrible thing to be alone when others can see that you are alone. I can sit for hours by myself, peacefully, on my veranda, or by the river or the pond, and even Rosa might abandon me to follow Grigory Petrovich on his rounds, but I am not lonely or self-conscious; on the contrary, Luka belongs to me, and everything around me seems to resonate with that knowledge—not in a material way, no, but in the joy I have in hearing, and smelling, and yes, after a fashion, seeing that world of mine.

But if you take me and put me on a blanket under a tree, and all around I hear laughter and loud conversation, and Rosa barking, and Ksenia crying (oh, why doesn't she come to me! I'd soon comfort her), and there is no one to talk to me or make me laugh, I feel horribly, desperately, visible, as if I were naked.

What have I written! Of course everyone was ignoring me, not deliberately, they'd forgotten about me, that's all. Mama and Evgenia Yakovlevna and Masha were emptying the hampers and preparing the food with Anya and Ulyasha, and Anton and Misha were fishing, and I think Elena and Natasha went with them or with the other guests—I heard voices I did not recognize, and I waited in vain for introductions.

So when Georges brought me a glass of wine, I was more than usually eager to retain his company, and I begged him to sit for a while, although I'm sure he wanted to be with the others by the river, swimming and fishing. I could hear Natasha's shrieks of laughter.

Anton Pavlovich is trying to push her in the water, said Georges.

But he mustn't! She's got a new dress, she'll ruin it!

(Typically for Natasha, she had agonized over the dress, gone into Sumy to the dressmakers' half a dozen times to be sure it would be ready. I had felt the cloth, a lovely summer muslin with a touch of lace—not too much, lace does not suit Natasha. But the matching parasol has lots of lace. She goes around poking Anton Pavlovich with it, I'm told, or opening it suddenly and waving it like a shield as he tries to grab her.)

Georges laughed. Don't worry, Zinochka, he's only doing it as a pretext to hold her, because he knows she likes it. She is bright red, and Anton Pavlovich has the most devilish expression on his face—it's all in fun, I assure you. No harm will come to the dress.

We sat for a while and talked of this and that, and Georges got up to fetch us some more wine, and I felt a sudden darkness, as if he had taken my sight again. And then I realized it was not sight he had taken but, rather, given: something I did not want to see, that had been for some weeks or even months on the periphery of my vision, and why it should irk me I don't know, but it dazzles and throbs, like the effects of the wine, and when Georges came back, he did not sit down, and I knew he wanted to go off with the others, so I said, Find Elena for me, will you?

She came and apologized for leaving me for so long, so I reassured her that Georges had kept me company, but then I took a swallow of wine and said, Lenochka, do you suppose, could there be something between Anton Pavlovich and Natasha?

Her ironic laugh was barely audible above another of Natasha's screams of delight. That depends, dear sister, upon what you mean by *between*. A few layers of linen and muslin, surely, and perhaps a few drops of spilled wine and human perspiration. That much, yes.

Although you could not hear what Natasha and Anton Pavlovich were saying, the tone of voice traveled like their laughter through the air, teasing, inviting, close.

Quite bluntly and not a little bitterly, Elena said, lowering her voice, Natasha is completely infatuated with Anton Pavlovich. I'm surprised you hadn't realized. She has been discreet, and I don't think even Masha is aware of it, although she may be finding out now. Naturally, Natasha didn't want you to know. She both envies and respects your own affection for Anton Pavlovich, which is very different from hers.

And Anton Pavlovich? I said, unable to hide the hesitant catch in my voice.

Elena said nothing for a long time, then sighed—a long, impatient, almost resigned sigh. Finally she said, He finds amusement in her company. It is exactly like what happened just a while ago: He tries to push her in the river, goes as far as he dares, then steps back just in time, holding her to make sure she doesn't fall. She would fall if he asked her to, if he let her, but he'd never get his own feet wet. No, Zina, he does not love her. He enjoys being with her, he trusts her, they are great friends—

She paused, then continued, As he is with you and me, too, in different ways. Natasha flirts with him, so he flirts, too. To her, it means everything; to him, nothing.

I am both dismayed and relieved by what you say, Elena—

As I am. Because we know that if she loves him, she will suffer.

Elena brought me more wine, and meat patties, and chicken, and some blinchiki, and then a glass of vodka, and the air was cooler and a breeze brought a moist tang from the river. There was singing, and someone had a guitar, and I must have lain down and slept, and in all that time Anton Pavlovich did not come to talk to me. Even in my sleep I heard Natasha's laughter, and I could not begrudge her this happiness, especially on her name day, and I knew that if Anton Pavlovich did not return her feelings—and she is smart enough not to be deluded—then in her laughter there would be notes of defiance, courage, and stoicism, and those are things with which I am well acquainted.

Thus reconciled to what I cannot change, I drank too much and was taken home and gently put to bed by Pasha and Tonya.

I slept too long and dreamlessly, and now I have returned to the veranda, with tea and Rosa and a fresh supply of ink.

September 1, 1889

Anton Pavlovich and his family will be leaving soon. He came to see Mama about some preparations for the trip; he came to pay his bill, which Mama refused to even consider. You are our guests, she said repeatedly, you are welcome, we'll expect you next year. She told me he went away shaking his head in bewilderment. I expect Mamochka was not dry-eyed.

We had supper together, the two families, one last time for this year. Georges played, and Natasha sang folk songs she has adapted. Masha read some poetry; I was going to recite Lermontov's "Tamara," but I've been feeling unwell these days and thought it best not to risk it. Anton Pavlovich read from a short story he has been revising, "Volodya"; Elena asked him how he had progressed on his new work, and he was typically evasive and effusive, by turns.

And the farmstead, Anton Pavlovich, I asked later, as no one had mentioned it in weeks, have you found anything?

There is a marvelous shack about two hours' ride from here, on the way to the Smagins', with a dirt floor and a fireplace and a pigsty right next to it, worthy of your own honorable beasts. Just think, Zinaida Mikhailovna, the wonderful roast pig I could prepare! Forget crayfish, pork's the thing! I've made an offer, three rubles for the shack and ten for the pig, when I sell my next story.

What are we to do with you!

Because, he said, sighing, I am disappointed that I have not found anything. The farm I saw last year would have been perfect. But . . . farmerly greed. For a few hundred rubles less, it could have been mine. Lately, I have not had the time or the heart to look. But Sasha Smagin has said he'd continue to look for me, in the Poltava region, at least.

Ah, Zinaida Mikhailovna, I feel . . . I feel I could do such good work if only I had a farmstead. A place where every member of my family could live and work if they wanted to; where I could be useful to the community as a doctor; where I would not have to go out and parade for the Moscow and Petersburg snobs. And the writers' colony, do you remember, Zinaida Mikhailovna? My idea? A creative utopia in a little corner of Ukraine. Natasha would laugh to keep the writers cheerful, and Elena would treat the writers for all sorts of ailments—writer's cramp, writer's block, inflammation of the coccyx, excessive melancholia—and you, Zinaida Mikhailovna, you would listen to the fruit of their endeavors and encourage them with your quiet devotion and expectant smile, and they would call you the Muse of Anton Pavlovich's writers' retreat.

And what if I didn't like what they wrote?

I hope you would tell them that you'd rather listen to the frogs and the owls than to their rubbish.

Then, Anton Pavlovich, may I live long enough to be that muse.

He poured me a small glass of vodka—unusual for us both—and we drank a toast to the elusive farmstead, and to the friendship between writers and muses.

I was on the bench by the pond. A cool day, I could sense the clouds passing as I walked through sun and shade. It had cost me some effort to go that far; I feel a new resistance in my body, a reluctance to comply with the simplest tasks of walking, standing, sitting. My hand, thankfully, still obeys the pen, crawls crablike across the page. There is a solid lump of cold fear inside me—there, I've said it—but beyond that I will not speak.

I heard his footsteps, I knew it was him. Recognized even his way of sitting down—impatiently, abruptly, yet greatly at ease with his surroundings—and a little vocal sigh. Now he said, I am loath to leave Luka, you know that, Zinaida Mikhailovna.

We are sorry to see you go.

It's been a difficult summer, but in a way it has been a lifetime in four months, don't you think?

I nodded. He continued, My time with you and your family has been very special. I cannot emphasize that enough. Natasha and her laughter, and Elena so earnest when we discuss medicine. And with you, Zinaida Mikhailovna, speaking of literature and life. He gave a short, surprised laugh and said, It's as if the three of you were the three faces of nature—you are part of the very soul of the place—

Oh, please, Anton Pavlovich, we're just three very ordinary women. I'm sure you would not even find anything to write about if you looked to us for inspiration.

I don't use my friends in my stories, haven't I already told you that?

But perhaps you will someday, or perhaps you do without being aware of it. How else are you to portray the human race if not through your own observations? Or do you read and borrow a hair from Tolstoy, a sigh from Turgenev, a sinister laugh from Mr. Dickens? Of course you don't!

I leaned back into the bench, unladylike but comfortable, and said, I hope, in any case, that you will be satisfied with the work you have done here these last few weeks. It would be proof that everything you say about Luka is true.

And even if I'm not, even if my play is drivel and my boring story sends all my readers to sleep, and as for my novel—well, you know about my novel—I am certain I have amassed memories and experience for a dozen plays and a hundred stories. And perhaps a handful of novels. And that's as important when one writes as a good table and light and a flowing pen.

We fell silent. I could sense he was looking around him, trying to print the picture—the pond, the ducks, the reeds, the woods—onto his writerly self for future use, and perhaps even on his deeper heart. And the silence gave me a mad, reckless idea: the sort of thing Natasha would ask boldly without thinking, without fear, as a joke, but which came to me so violently that I felt a flush of heat and a nervous trembling that had nothing to do with my illness and everything to do with my older, original self. I sat up and turned to him and said, Anton Pavlovich, I have a very strange request to make of you, if you'll forgive me—

Please, Zinaida Mikhailovna, you must not hesitate. I owe you everything—

You owe me nothing. I am here, that is all. But if you'll indulge a blind woman's fantasy, for a few moments, if you'll let me see you—

I did not know how to put it in words, how to phrase my odd request. I shook my hands in confusion.

He moved on the bench, must have been facing me now.

If you would—if I might touch your face—to understand better—to keep a memory of who you are, a sort of tactile painting—I am so afraid of losing our words—oh, never mind, Anton Pavlovich, what an unseemly thing to ask!

Zinaida Mikhailovna, are we not doctors? What secrets are there for us? I assure you, my nose is in the middle of my face, and when last I checked, my beard was where it should be and not hanging from my left ear.

He seized my hand and placed it on his beard. I was startled by its softness, or by his gesture, I'm not sure which.

Paint your picture, Dr. Lintvaryova.

He took his hand away and left me with my fingertips on his beard.

As if of their own will, while my heart pounded with fear and happiness, my fingers began to move across his face—his chin, cheeks, nose, his wide forehead—where they lingered, paused, feeling warmth and a slight dampness while I wondered at all the thoughts in there, and he stayed unmoving, quietly breathing, until I lifted my fingers away.

I was burning, spinning like a leaf in a storm.

You've missed something, Zinaida Mikhailovna. You make me look like an eyeless Greek statue, I won't have that.

He took my hand again and placed my fingers on his closed eyes, first left, then right, and I touched them ever so gently and felt the faint flutter between his brow and his lashes, felt them with a kind of bewilderment, as if touching the eyes and lashes of a sleeping child.

Then I held his cheek in my palm, feeling the whole side of his face, and it was then that I could begin to see him, a young man of fine looks, not unlike my own brother, Georges, with a firm chin and jaw, an even nose, eyes slightly turned down at the corners—eyes that missed nothing.

Don't forget my hair. I promise you I washed all the eels out this morning.

His voice was deep and slightly strangled.

I ran my fingers over and through his hair—long and thick and waving—right across his brow and down the back of his head to his neck, which was warm, and I could feel the muscles and veins, touched them more boldly with a half-forgotten seeking medical touch, and up to his ears—as they say, the ears are like seashells, and he squirmed and laughed, That tickles, so I drew my hand away regretfully, but embarrassed that I had gone on so long and that he had let me.

Ah, Zinochka, you make a bad sculptor, or even doctor, he scolded, you are still leaving things out.

Again he took my hand and lifted it to his lips, and he ran my thumb along his even, sharp teeth, then immediately afterward along his lower lip, soft and warm, so soft I thought instinctively of little Ksenia, and a powerful yet tender rush went all through me, from my thumb on through my body. His lips closed briefly around my thumb, then his hands closed around my fingers, and he kissed my hand in his gentlemanly way, then for a few moments he sat holding it, the time it took for my senses to mirror the pond once again.

As a doctor, I used to touch.

It was a necessary part of the examination, of diagnosis. Auscultation. To feel for growths, irregularities, fractures. The only way to see what lay below the skin.

I touched newborns, children, men and women, old people with history in their cells.

I had memories of their skin, their muscles, their bones. Touch serves as well as sight, because it tells the greater story.

There were those who died, and I kept the memory of their still-warm, still-pulsing flesh beneath my probing fingertips.

There were those who lived, and I would greet their smiles in the village while my hands quivered with a remembered hope.

I had touched no one in months, only Rosa's warm yielding fur and Ksenia's round little cheeks and limbs.

Now this memory replaces all the others, as if it were the first.

I waited by the poplars at dawn, by the gate.

He had said he would come to say goodbye to me there. The others were loading the carriage by the guesthouse and saying their goodbyes; I had told him, without any explanation, that I would be by the gate.

I took Rosa with me. I felt the night ending around us—a bitter chill, absence of birdsong. We waited for a long time; I didn't mind. I heard bells far in the distance, a lonely, inexplicable pealing; then peasants calling, and some boys already on their way to the river, shrieking insults and impossible challenges to each other, the way we used to. *I'll build a castle so big the tsar himself and all his army can't reach the top.*

I heard his steps, a long way off. Regular and brisk, and he was humming to himself, one of the folk airs Natasha had taught him. Then he called my name. We had not talked since the time by the pond two days ago.

We were silent. I had nothing to say; I had everything to say, but it could not be said. I thought then, ruefully, that if I had my sight, I would be using these moments to memorize his face, to look back and forth over the small territory of his person as if, by knowing it, I might keep it forever; reduced to sound, I could only wait and stare into a familiar void. Until he took my hand in both of his and held it companionably, as he had often done.

Zinaida Mikhailovna, I shall miss our conversations. I know I said the same thing on parting last year, and I know this has been a difficult summer, and we've often been interrupted or distracted—but for that very reason, your presence, our afternoons together, working on the novel—

He broke off, as if at a loss for words. Or perhaps not; he also knew the meaning of silence.

We listened, then he said, Ah, Zina, how I shall miss it here! The sky, the tranquillity, the simplicity, the good people. Now we are headed back to the filth and promiscuity of the city, and the constant interruptions, people always wanting something from me. I shall have to go onstage and masquerade as myself.

Still I did not speak; I nodded and waited for him to go on.

There's no moon tonight, Zinaida Mikhailovna, so you can see the stars brighter than ever, all across the horizon.

I felt a sudden strange distance. I was stretched out on his carpet of stars in the sky, looking down on the tiny points of light that were Luka. I heard the sound of his foot, as if it, too, were far away, moving restlessly in the dirt.

Finally I said, I too shall miss our conversations, Anton Pavlovich. I will think of them often. Perhaps I'll ask Mama to read my journal to me; that way at least I can relive some of our thoughts, and your presence.

I would like that, to know you are continuing our conversations. I'm not sure I'll have that gift—that privilege— where I'm going.

I smiled. Come now, Anton Pavlovich, Moscow is your life, too, it cannot be so dreadful. You have so much to do there. Why you ever even thought of burying yourself in Kharkovsky Province, I cannot imagine—although of course we would be only too happy to have you here—

Realizing I was speaking to a polite formula of the future I would not know, I hastened to add, because now I could hear voices and the clink of the carriage at the top of the lane: Anton Pavlovich, I do not believe we will meet again, even if you come back to Luka next summer, I—I know what awaits me, and I want to say goodbye to you while I am still able. And wish you happiness—

His arms folded around me. I wrapped mine around him. We held each other for a long time. He murmured something that I did not catch, and my name; I felt his warmth and strength and did not want to leave. I saw my father holding me like that as a girl. His beard, too, against my cheek. The memory flared and was gone, and then Anton Pavlovich slowly let me go, steadying me—or was it himself—with one hand, and then the others were there, my family and his, arriving on foot or in the carriage, and they all climbed down to say goodbye, one after the other: Evgenia Yakovlevna, Misha, and Masha. Roman and Natasha would go with them to Sumy station.

I waited by the gate and called goodbye, then listened until I could no longer hear their voices and laughter and the horses' hooves. Then I turned and called for Rosa, and she led me home.

NO ONE KNOWS THE exact color of Anton Pavlovich's eyes.

Ana searched in vain on the Internet and in all the books she had bought.

Vladimir Korolenko, who met Chekhov in 1887, would assert that they were blue.

Aleksandr Kuprin, in his memoir, insisted they were *dark, almost brown,* but not blue—although he said people remembered them as blue. The few oil paintings (Nikolay's, Valentin Serov's, Osip Braz's) are also misleading, as if the artist were undecided or working from a muddy palette.

The morning air through the window chills me. I have asked for the winter quilts.

The hours are long. I walk to the pond with Rosa; I sit on the bench until I am cold or she whimpers to return.

It is getting difficult. My balance: I fell one day, I caught my toe in a root by the path. Rosa knows: She gave a sad yelp when I fell. I told no one, I was not hurt. Still I try.

I gather memories along the path. Lift them like flowers to my face while I sit by the pond. Scatter them like dried leaves as I return to the house.

The page defies me, refuses the past.

I could imagine conversations with him. We might talk about the inevitability of autumn. Or how good it will be when the first snows come and we can harness the sleigh, and Elena and I will take him on our rounds through the village, the way we used to do. Because I like to imagine he has found his farmstead only twelve versts from here. And he comes frequently to dinner, to hear Georges at the piano, to play vint with Mama and Natasha. And to read to me from his novel.

Imagination, dry as leaves.

November 1889

Natasha is in Moscow.

Three weeks, staying with the Chekhovs. She writes short, cheerful letters, you can hear her peals of laughter.

Anton Pavlovich is well and asks after you, says Natasha. He is surrounded by women, I ought to be jealous, but he does not have favorites—it amuses him to have us there. He calls us his harem, and Masha blushes and scolds him.

There followed a list of names, each one longer and stranger than the previous one—indeed, the name Natasha sounds drearily ordinary—Olga, Lika, Glafira, Kleopatra, and an Aleksandra whom for some reason they call Vermicelli (I picture a woman with long, stringy hair).

Natasha must have learned—or will learn now—how to live with the burden of her unrequited feelings. She is never disheartened for long.

Whereas I miss her, miss the summer, our summer guests. Rosa lies at my feet and whimpers. She knows our walks are short and cautious over ice and frozen snow. We go to Pasha's cottage and sit with Tonya and Ksenia. I play peekaboo with Ksenia, then she crawls onto my lap, raises her tiny fingers to my eyes. She knows, although she is so little, that there is something wrong there. She cannot say more than a few words yet, and has no understanding of death or illness, but she knows I cannot see. She brings me her rag doll to touch, leads my fingers to the doll's button eyes. Tonya scolds her because she tries to put her fingers on Rosa's eyes, too, and of course the dog is so patient, but she doesn't like it.

Where will you be when you read this, little Ksenia? Here at Luka? In Kiev? In Petersburg? Have a thought for the woman whose eyes you sought, who wanted so much to see your yellow curls and periwinkle eyes.

December 1

Natasha has returned.

Anton Pavlovich had the premiere of the play he was working
on while he was here, *The Wood Demon*. He forbade Natasha
or any of the family to attend. It did not go well, and he came
home utterly dejected and humiliated. He wanted to see no one.
Natasha left Moscow unable to say goodbye to him.

She was gloomier than I've ever known her to be. He had told
her once, in a joyful mood, that his play was inspired by Luka
and his time here.

Perhaps what we have here is not something that can
be transported to a stage. An actor has to feel it, to know it
instinctively, over time. Perhaps even Anton Pavlovich could not
capture something as elusive as our happiness here, or could not
even believe it exists.

January 1890

He has written to Natasha. He is planning a great trip eastward,
across Siberia to Sakhalin Island. If his plans go well, he will not
be able to come in the summer.

He spoke to me once, after Nikolay Pavlovich's death, of
wishing to do good in some way beyond his role as a doctor. He
thought, as a writer, he could reach thousands of people if he had a
cause. He thought of the prisoners on Sakhalin Island, the terrible
lives they lead there; he wondered if he might help, make their
conditions known, demand improvement from high quarters.

It was an idea; there were many ideas during the summer.
Most of them vanished with the days.

This one, then, has stayed.

He will go to Petersburg for the papers, the authorizations.

February 1890

I grow tired of silence. Elena and Natasha are busy, only Mama and Tonya sometimes find the time to come and read to me. I am bedridden; if I try to get up— No, it's too sad, I won't write about it.

But one day I did get up, just clinging to the bed, and I felt under the mattress into the niche, and I took out Anton Pavlovich's manuscript. I held it against me and thought back to those few weeks in August when we read it together, and every day he brought a few new pages to me. How I wish I could reread them! But he has made me swear not to share it— there is too much of your family, he said—and it's true, I think Mama and Georges and Natasha in particular would recognize themselves and might be hurt by what they see.

Not that he wrote anything unkind or unflattering. But the picture we have of ourselves so rarely corresponds to the picture we give others.

I urged Anton Pavlovich to take the manuscript with him, but he said he cannot concentrate in Moscow, and that it needs time to age, like a good wine or cheese. Now that he has decided to go to Sakhalin Island, when will he work on it? Perhaps I should give it to Masha when she comes in the summer.

Or what if . . . what if I were to take it with me? No one else knows, only Anton Pavlovich. What will happen after I am gone? Will my family read this journal and look for his manuscript? Or will they respect even then his wish for discretion and inform him simply that it is here, waiting?

Or perhaps everything will be forgotten.

I placed the manuscript on the bed and turned the pages slowly, one after the other. I counted 178. I don't think he writes on both sides; he says our paper here in Sumy absorbs the ink too well. But he told me his handwriting is quite fine.

I believe I was playing with fate, hoping Natasha or Mama might come in and discover me turning the pages—and then what would I do?

But I do not hold a manuscript, it is not there for me to see. It is his trust I hold and have promised to preserve. I suppose at a moment like this, out of a certain weariness, I tempt fate. I think Anton Pavlovich could appreciate that and, I hope, forgive me.

Sometimes I lie in bed and remember the story and write my own ending, a different one every time. I'm glad he hasn't finished it yet, that the future can still be written.

March 1890

The winter has weakened me. I can hardly hold the pen.

I asked Mama to read this diary over again to me. We have not read it all, only as far as the end of the first summer. Beyond that, there is a secret to keep. It makes me very happy to hear my words, gives me peace. I cry, Mama stops, I beg her to go on and swear to her I'm happy, not upset. Then she cries, poor Mamochka. And then Anton Pavlovich says something funny, and we're both laughing and crying at the same time.

I am glad I found the strength, while he was here. I did not think there would be so much to tell.

Dear Anton Pavlovich,

I hear, from my sisters, that you are well.

You do not write to me; should I be sorry? But we both know that anything you write to me must be read by others, so it is no longer a letter to me.

Perhaps you received my short missives, wishing you well and good fortune for your trip to Sakhalin Island. But this is not a letter I will send to you. It will stay firmly in the leather-bound pages of my journal. My niece, Ksenia, may read it someday: She will inherit my diaries and be the guardian of my memory.

She may guard memory, but how can she guard the evanescence of emotion? That is what I would wish to preserve, an ethereal monument, after I am gone. That you might remember me and our walks by the pond and the river, and remember not only the ducks and the crayfish or our words about life and work and the uncertain future of our immense unwieldy country; no, that you might recall a glow in my extinguished eyes—who could believe such a thing!—or, failing that, the warmth in your own voice when you argued or laughed with me. Because that warmth, Anton Pavlovich, is part of me now, and it gives me life and strength and hope even when all around is winter, with the silence the snow has brought.

I know that you will be gone for a long time, traveling across Siberia in a bitter springtime, and your summer will be short and harsh, not like the summers you have had with us at Luka.

Perhaps memories of your time here will sustain you, and we will be in your thoughts, as you are in ours. I know, too, that perhaps by the time you return, I will be gone. I cannot leave without hoping that even though we shall not, in all likelihood, meet again, you might at least read this letter someday, through Ksenia's good offices, and know how you brought light and vision to my darkened days.

There, I have said what must be said so that you will know, and Ksenia will know, and I entrust you both with my light, fragile legacy. Look after it well.

May God protect you and give you health and happiness,

Zinaida Mikhailovna

THAT WAS IT, THERE was nothing more.

It was late, it had been raining earlier, and forlorn patches of sunlight were struggling to revive the view toward the mountains. The rest of Zinaida Mikhailovna's story belonged to history, to a footnote in a biography, a few lines in a letter.

Ana sat with her hands in her lap, as if she had no more strength. Gradually, it came to her that she had forgotten the obituary Katya had mentioned and which she had skimmed so carelessly that first day.

She opened the file and read it slowly.

After she had read it, she saved everything and closed her computer. She went for a long walk and thought about the things people rarely share, or talk about, or admit to themselves.

She waited three days before translating the obituary. It was simple, yet so concisely, perfectly worded that she feared it like an imposing presence. In it she could read the gentleness of their friendship, and also a physician's brutal precision. She struggled over one sentence, about Zinaida's fate: Chekhov's Russian would not yield to English, as if Ana's native language were poorly equipped to deal with matters of destiny. Or perhaps it was some failing of her own. In the end she decided to let the sentence keep a strange ring to it, as a nod to other ways of experiencing.

Z. M. LINTVARYOVA
DEATH

On November 24, 1891, in the region of Sumy, Kharkovsky Province, in the presence of her family, Dr. Zinaida Mikhailovna Lintvaryova.

Upon completing her studies, the deceased worked for a short time at the clinic of Professor Yu. G. Chudnovsky. All those who knew her at that time remember her as a gifted, hardworking doctor and good comrade. Unfortunately, what fate had in store for Zinaida Mikhailovna was the bitterest of experiences. Five years ago she lost her sight. A grave illness (visibly, a brain tumor) gradually and relentlessly paralyzed the poor woman's extremities, her tongue, the muscles of her face, and her memory.

For the family, for whom she was a source of pride and brilliant hopes, and for her acquaintances and the persons for whom she worked so ardently, there remains one sad consolation—the rare and remarkable patience with which Zinaida Mikhailovna endured her suffering. At the same time she was surrounded by idle and healthy people who would complain about their own fate, yet this woman— blind, deprived of her freedom of movement, and doomed to die—did not grumble, but consoled and encouraged those very people who were complaining.

(Submitted by Dr. A. P. Chekhov)

IT TOOK ANA TWENTY days to revise the translation.

She would have liked to take longer; would have liked to reread the text in real time, as Zinaida Mikhailovna had written it, over the course of two summers. The slow pace of the first draft had given her something of that illusion—as if she had been present, had overheard their conversations and taken part in them, through the choice of words and tense and the color she could give the scene. Revising was like revisiting memories, and she found herself taking small but warranted liberties with the text to make it come alive in English, to address the reader now, too. She could almost hear Anton Pavlovich saying to her disdainfully, Don't you know we've been speaking English all along? To which Zinaida Mikhailovna might laugh and say, Leave the poor woman alone, Anton Pavlovich, she's done very well unraveling our endless prattling.

Two more read-throughs and it was a clean text, without marks or brackets or question marks or comments; she read it quickly, for flow and effectiveness in English. It worked. It was ready.

She emailed it to Katya Kendall on the day of their deadline.

While waiting for Katya's reply, Ana went back to her ordinary life. She had a sudden and unexpected but welcome workload—a new brochure for one of her regular vineyard clients in Burgundy, and a popular French best seller from a new publisher who had read *Go Through the Door, Turn Left.* The novel infuriated her with what seemed to be a lack of essential truth and simplicity.

Ana knew it would take all her skill to give it the fair treatment it deserved.

She missed Zinaida. In spare moments she reread Chekhov's short stories, looking for her. She found Elena's earnestness, and Natasha's laughter, but Zinaida was not there.

Perhaps she was in his novel. Perhaps Ana would find her there.

Ana lost herself on the Internet in search of Luka, the Lintvaryovs, and their summer guests. There were many articles and references to the two summers (the fishing, Nikolay's death), but apart from what Chekhov wrote in his letters, the Lintvaryov family remained shadowy, far less substantial than in Zinaida Mikhailovna's words.

She discovered there was a small museum-house devoted to Chekhov in Sumy, located in the very guesthouse where he had spent those two summers. She found it on the satellite view of Google maps: ulitsa Chekhova 79, Sumy, Ukraine. Such technology was frightening: She was looking down on the past as if she were a bird perched on a sputnik. A road ran in front of the museum and on to the river. There was a large roof on the other side of the road that might be the big house where Zinaida Mikhailovna had lived; above it, a dark patch that must be the pond. It all looked terribly small.

Ana felt as if she were trespassing.

Two weeks had gone by, and there had been no answer from Polyana Press. She called them half a dozen times.

With a sort of dread fascination, Ana came to realize that she needed to know more.

She opened the bottle of champagne she had bought to celebrate finishing the translation, drank a toast to Zinaida Mikhailovna and Anton Pavlovich, then sat down at her computer.

Elections had been held in Ukraine, and a new president with a name like a child's poem was determined to reunite the country and rid the east of the pro-Russian separatists fighting in the regions of Donetsk and Luhansk. Sumy was much farther north, and Ana prayed that geographical distance from the fighting meant proportionately increased safety. In addition, she had heard reports on the news that Sumy continued to stand behind the Maidan revolution, demonstrating their support amid *a sea of blue and gold flags;* Sumy wanted to remain part of Ukraine.

But it was only forty kilometers from the border with Russia.

The travel advisories from the American and British governments were not good, warning against travel to the east of the country. It's in the north, she whispered to herself, construing her own geography; Sumy is in the north, it's nowhere near Donetsk. There was also a warning against all but essential travel to the neighboring Kharkiv oblast. Essential, essential, thought Ana, Sumy is essential. Kharkovsky Province, it may have been in Chekhov's time, but the map has been redrawn. It's Sumy oblast now. And it's essential.

The French embassy in Kiev had gone even further, posting a map on its website that clearly indicated the dangerous areas of the country. Most of Ukraine was pale yellow for *vigilance renforcée.* Kharkiv, like Crimea, like the whole region around Donetsk and Luhansk, was an ugly orange: *déconseillé sauf raison impérative.* Sumy was pale yellow, like Kiev or Lviv, safely in the west.

Ana gulped down a cold draft of Moët; it burned, made her eyes water.

She remembered how she had spoken to Yves of her fear, and she felt she must overcome it once and for all. Perhaps her invisibility would protect her. Along with her *essential, imperative* reasons for going there.

She almost hoped travel to Ukraine would be impossible for practical reasons, but she quickly learned that, on the contrary, it was completely feasible, despite the alarming news reports. There were regular, reasonably priced direct flights from Geneva to Kiev, then direct trains from Kiev to Sumy.

It was the logical place to start: The museum must know where Zinaida Mikhailovna's journal had been kept all those years and whether the novel had been found with it. They would know how to locate the Lintvaryovs' descendants. They might know who, in Russia or Ukraine, would be publishing the journal or even the novel. In her online efforts to find out more about Chekhov's novel and those summers with the Lintvaryovs, Ana had seen dozens of confusing entries, all wild-goose chases into increasingly obscure websites, multitudes of Ukrainian or Russian brides hovering in the margins with their own, rather more desperate seeking.

She could take the safer route and query the museum by email or over the telephone. But she wanted to go, in defiance of logic or common sense. She could not afford her dream trip to Russia, to all the places Chekhov had lived, and Crimea was out of the question, an orange zone on a French map. But she could afford a few days in Kiev and Sumy. Above all, she wanted to see where Zinaida Mikhailovna had lived, where they had met and sat and strolled.

Ana booked a flight, the train to Sumy and back, hotels, transfers. She took out cancellation insurance, just in case. But it was the right time to go: The weather was balmy. She prepared a list of questions for the museum. She also had Katya Kendall's phone number in her cell phone.

KATYA LAY IN BED. The birds in the garden, obliviously, predictably, calling for the world to wake up. Another day and all that. Yes, all that. Whatever it had come to mean. It was all right for birds, the instinctive simplicity of their lives, a few seeds—that Katya graciously provided—a few twigs, a nest. There were predators, to be sure, plenty of cats in the neighborhood; constant vigilance was required. We have our predators, too, thought Katya. We were not vigilant.

The letter from the bank had come a few days ago. Registered. Peter merely left it out on his desk for her to see. Then he was gone. Not disappeared, exactly; he called to tell her not to worry. He would be at the office, trying to sort things; he might sleep there or at Jacob's. He needed some time on his own, he said, to think things through. He must have sensed her absence; she had tried to show her solidarity, but more and more she, too, needed solitude. She had asked him to read her poems; he had shrugged and told her he could not concentrate.

Oh well.

Her fatalism was serving her well, she thought. She could lie in bed now and it did not matter; let the house burn down for all she cared, although she would not like to be burned alive. She longed for an earthquake, a hurricane, a flood. Ridiculous, of course, London was largely safe from natural disasters, and besides, they had the Thames barrier.

Terrorists, then, yes. There was that worry, remote but ever present. But Katya rarely went out of the neighborhood now that she no longer went to the office. Still, there were other forms of terrorism. Form letters that explode beneath you, taking away a vital limb: a house, a partner.

Let's not exaggerate, Katya, she thought. It has not come to that. A warning; an absent partner who has told you not to worry.

It left her less room to maneuver. She was sticking to her plan, yes, but for the time being, there was little else she could do.

Ana had sent her Zinaida Mikhailovna's diary. It was finished. Katya had read the beginning; it sounded strange, rang a bit hollow at first, but then she let herself go into the English, blocked the Russian from her mind, and it read well. Perhaps it was a bit like all those film adaptations of Russian novels and plays that the British were rather good at. There was a British Russia, and there was a real Russia. She supposed the British Russia was rather like the European version of the American Far West. A sort of mythical place where people were larger than life and violent, passionate, unexpected things happened. Was that something a translator could infuse into a text? They weren't supposed to, but then perhaps it was the language. Just the tortured poetry of Russian names seemed to bleed onto the page for the English reader.

She supposed she should get out of bed, make phone calls—the designer, the printer. The publicist. They should go ahead with it as if nothing had happened. Stick to the plan, yes.

But how would they pay them—the designer, the printer, the publicist? They would want money up front. Especially the publicist; such a rapacious profession. And they still had a bill with the printer. And the translator, of course. Especially if there were a second book. She thought of their lunch together, how nervous Ana had seemed, almost girlish, blushing, laughing, growing wistful as she listened to Katya recite Pasternak.

Again Katya wished she could have confided in Ana. Even now. Ana knew Zinaida Mikhailovna, and they could have talked about her stoicism, her courage. How she did not want people's pity, did not want them to feel sorry and shake their heads. Pity creates a barrier, makes you different, when all you want is to be seen and treated normally. The way Anton Pavlovich treated Zinaida. Would Ana understand that? Katya would have liked such a friend, a confidant. The very person Peter could not be, could no longer be; this thing had come between them, and she did not know if they would be able to repair the estrangement in time.

Katya shifted her head on the pillow, let her mind wander. Imagined herself doing all the things she knew she ought to be doing; imagined the satisfaction of having done them. And didn't move. They could wait.

Later, if she got out of bed, she could write a poem.

It was time to confront Peter, she knew that, too.

She had done so much already. Perhaps today she could just stay in bed. Finish proofing the translation; go back there, to Luka, one last time.

LUKA

AT SOME POINT ANA became aware that she had left the twenty-first century behind. It wasn't in Kiev, where, if anything, she thought she might have landed in the twenty-second century. On the drive from the airport to the train station, she gazed at neighborhoods of massive new apartment blocks, futuristic and frightening in their anonymity, gleaming yet soulless, something Stalin might have built in a place like Dubai. It must have been on the train, then, that the clocks turned back, with every ticking mile of track that led away from the capital. Ana watched dreamily as the train rolled past flat farmland and countless sleepy villages, with rich plots of vegetables growing inexplicably alongside the railway line.

She had gone straight to the train station; she would spend a day in Kiev on the way back, to see the traditional sights as well as the Maidan, still occupied by protesters defending their barricades, consolidating the revolution.

Now she was alone in her compartment; for some reason, it was the only way she had been able to obtain a reservation from abroad. This was both a relief and a disappointment. She thought she might have enjoyed the company of some local people, some small talk that would quickly inflate to a heated political discussion; she might have had difficulty following—even if they were speaking Russian and not Ukrainian—but it would give her a sense of being a witness to something so much larger than her Alp-sheltered existence. The train was a sputnik-era relic, oft-repainted and repaired, although Ana looked in vain for any overt references to the Soviet Union (no stars, no hammers or sickles or *CCCP*s). But from the window, she often saw abandoned factories, their windows smashed, machinery rusting, ironic monuments to some anticipated glory that never came, the ruins of a misguided civilization.

She recalled an endless day on a train from Leningrad to Kiev when she was a student: the flatness, the horizon ever receding and enlarging, the sensation of a country both frozen in time and wrenched brutally from it. And now she could see both the bucolic Tolstoyan landscapes and the Soviet Union that she had known, with its kolkhozes and factories and endless potholed roads and rattling buses.

She sat at the window with her glass of tea in its metal holder and let the memories blur past with the ramshackle villages. How, in Soviet times, they used to herd them, pestilential Westerners, onto buses and on excursions to keep them out of trouble; how the students evaded surveillance whenever they could and sought out the ordinary citizens who had not sold their souls to the system. Earnest bearded Alyosha, bringing Ana pre-Revolution leather-bound editions of Turgenev that she managed to smuggle past the border control; with his parents sleeping in the next room, they used to sit until two in the morning in candlelight, whispering about all the forbidden writers whom somehow he had read: Pasternak, Nabokov, Solzhenitsyn. Where was he now? Was he even alive? Russian men with their dramatic mortality rate, vodka like a plague. They drank too much then, too, and her memories blurred and shone like this view through the train window, streaked with a spring shower.

There was not much to see of Sumy from the taxi on the way to the hotel: a bustling market, traffic, wide streets, plenty of trees, a few shops, a McDonald's. Some gilded onion domes in the distance. At the hotel reception, the young woman was helpful, discreetly curious. They must not get many Western women traveling alone in Sumy, thought Ana, particularly now.

In the room she found a clock on the wall, ticking loudly. She took it down and put it in a drawer.

Tables were set in the courtyard for dinner. Ana ordered a bowl of borscht. The air was warm, pleasantly muggy after an afternoon shower. She looked around: a profusion of trees and shabby, aging apartment buildings. Open spaces were crisscrossed by pathways where children rode bicycles.

The long-forgotten banality of her surroundings stirred more intimations of youth, recklessness, love. Alyosha again; kisses. His father snoring in the next room.

She ordered a second beer, surrendered to nostalgia.

How she had struggled with the language but learned all the while something completely unexpected and equally precious: another way of seeing the world. It was as if material things no longer had any value except as markers of memory; all the familiar concepts of wealth, ambition, power, success, had seemed to fade away, irrelevant. She had been dipped into a rough poetry of everyday life and come out not exactly speaking Russian but versed in an idiom of pleasure in simple things, in sudden friendship, in an almost mystical perception of something deeper and inexplicably vital.

She could still hear the clock ticking in the drawer.

She got up and wrapped it in a towel, but she no longer had an excuse for sleeplessness other than nerves and excitement about what awaited. She had booked a taxi to take her to the museum after lunch. She could have gone first thing in the morning, but she wanted to get her bearings, to explore the town and prepare herself. Practice what she would say, think of her questions.

What did she really expect from the lost novel? Why did the thought of it cause a knot in her stomach, a jolt of sleep-depriving adrenaline? Because it would change her life. It would respond to a yearning, fill a void. Perhaps the thought was naive, but she liked to believe that it might bring out the best in her. She could be someone. Accomplished, respected.

So she lay turning in the bed, daydreaming, projecting. Just let there be Anton Pavlovich's manuscript or news of it. That was all she asked.

After breakfast she went out exploring the town between more warm showers. Pavements full of puddles and potholes; people walking everywhere, carrying shopping bags and briefcases. She entered a church; a stern woman in a kerchief selling candles asked whether she could help, as if they were in a shop. May I just have a look? said Ana, pulling her shawl closer around her head.

This church is not for looking, barked the woman, but for praying.

Excuse me, I am a foreigner, a tourist.

I know that.

Ana walked away but could sense the woman's gaze upon her, a glare so intense that Ana could not even see the icons.

No one, she thought, knows I am here except Yves. I am not registered with any embassy or consulate; I am not connected to a news agency or humanitarian organization or anyone who might look for me if I vanish. And back in France, only the woman at the *chatterie* would fuss and complain and prepare a tirade of abuse if I failed to show up to collect my cat, but I did not tell her where I was going. Poor Doodle, would the woman find her a good home?

Ah yes, I gave her Yves's number.

Ana wandered idly through the market, buying sweets, observing people. They wore their lives on their tired faces so much more openly than the soft people of the West; but in a generation or so—if war spared them, if they *joined the West,* as they hoped to do—they would catch up, they would learn the artifices of consumerism. For the time being, Ana felt as if she were in a small town in the early 1980s in any European backwater, without fancy boutiques or chain stores (save the inescapable McDonald's), without chic bistros or upscale restaurants. Without the ubiquity of smartphones. She noticed a few cafés playing loud rock music, the only customers slick young men, their flash cars parked outside. She hesitated but did not go in, even though she was desperate for a coffee.

She found other churches more welcoming. She stood in the gilded gloom and felt very close to Zinaida Mikhailovna. She recalled how, in the Soviet era, she had visited a few churches that were still operating, and it had always felt subversive: Her Russian acquaintances would wait outside, afraid to go in. Ana had enjoyed an odd privilege back then; now she was the one who was excluded. She did not believe.

ANA FELT DAZED, AS if she had just survived a moment of near-accident, as if she had been promoted to another level of consciousness. The bright sunlight was buzzing with insects, a gardener was working calmly by the house, Chekhov's beloved irises were in bloom. The sound of voices reassured her that all was well. She sat in the shade of a small gazebo and took out her notebook to record the moment.

I've just been on a tour of the house with a group of students from the medical institute. I stole glances at the girls: One was pretty, with heavy eye makeup; two of them were plain and earnest, modern-day Lintvaryova sisters. They listened as the guide led us around the five rooms that are open to visitors, waving her pointer at various photographs and objects while she told the story of Chekhov's summers at Luka. It is all familiar to me, but it resonates oddly in Russian—it is outside my own head, spoken by a short round young woman with wispy auburn hair and a pleasantly bohemian demeanor.

These are the rooms where they lived, conversed, played music, recited poetry. Small, elegant fin de siècle furnishings, plants, items of Ukrainian folklore, embroidered or hand-painted. Before the tour began, I studied the exhibits in the entry hall. A panel of photographs marked "The Lintvaryov Family," but no captions under the portraits. An older woman: That would be Aleksandra Vassilyevna; a young man with fair hair and beard whom I guessed to be Pavel, for the darker one was bound to be Georges—how can I be so sure of this? Then three women: one stern, dark, rather ugly, alas; another with finer features and an almost wistful gaze; finally, a quite lovely, fair young woman with haunted eyes. Could this be Zinaida? Is she not too lovely to fit Zinaida's description of herself?

The guide's stick lingered on the photographs as she told us their names, first Aleksandra Vassilyevna and Pasha, then Georges: I had guessed correctly. The stern, stout sister is Elena, unsmiling, her expression full of glum determination. Natasha is the wistful one—she looks almost too sweet for her raucous laughter. And the lovely one, of course, is Antonida Fyodorovna—Tonya, Pavel's wife, Ksenia's mother.

There was another daughter, said the guide in passing, hurriedly, but we have no photographs of her.

Chekhov's room: modest and simple. A bed hardly bigger than a daybed; a tiny table with his medical instruments; a desk by the window facing the garden, looking out onto roses and irises. To reach any of the other rooms, Anton Pavlovich had to go through Nikolay's room.

On the wall in Anton Pavlovich's room is a tiny photograph of two young people in their teens, probably a sister and brother. Clear, light faces, not yet marked by life. The guide pointed with her stick and told us they were Pavel Mikhailovich Lintvaryov's children, Ksenia and Vsevolod. Of course they would have had more children later. A younger brother.

As the others were leaving the room, I went back for a closer look at Ksenia. An open, sweet face, trusting, with none of the sternness of her aunts. Yes, she takes after her mother. And I can see her as the executor of Zinaida's testament. It all fits.

There is a small kitten in the garden. He has just scampered over to the guide, and she snatches him up with affectionate roughness. He is gray and white and his eyes are infected. He rubs them but otherwise seems healthy and well fed. He makes me think of Nikolay's kitten. This one is purring, biting the guide's arm playfully; she told me his name, Murzik.

Ana was putting away her pen when a woman sat next to her in the gazebo. Sighing and fanning herself with a folded sheet of paper, she glanced at Ana, both shy and curious, then eventually, she said, Where are you visiting from?

France, said Ana, looking more closely at the woman; large brown eyes peered over rimless glasses, as if she didn't really need them but had forgotten to remove them.

Oh, welcome, *bienvenue,* said the woman, suddenly effusive; she held out her hand and said, I'm Larissa Lvovna Petrova, the director of the museum.

Ana's hand lingered in hers almost too long as she took in this information. Had the woman sought her out, or was this merely a lucky coincidence?

How happy I am to meet you, said Ana, happy to be here, really. It's—what's the word—thrilling to see where Chekhov stayed.

(A warm rush of happiness, as if confirming that she was really there.)

Then let me tell you more about it, a few things the guide might have overlooked, said the museum director. You know, after the Revolution, the house was a school library, then was converted in 1960 into a museum for the centenary of Chekhov's birth. You must know we have a local Chekhov circle, and we organize regular concerts and dramatic performances here.

She made a circle with her hands, encompassing the museum and the garden. There's quite a large local intelligentsia, she said proudly, and began to list the titles of performances and names of notables, which all sounded to Ana like so much evocative background noise, until Larissa Lvovna broke off and said, Why have you come all this way—are you doing research, writing a book?

And now they were at the crux of the matter, yet Ana hesitated to divulge her reasons; it was too soon to mention the diary. In the actual presence of *someone who might know,* she found herself at a loss for words. Perhaps it would be better to get to know the director, to find out more about the museum, before she said anything.

I just— I've been reading Chekhov's letters, and I wanted to see this place, where he seemed—where he was happy.

Ah, yes. I agree, I think it was a happy time for him. Would you like to come in for a cup of tea?

Larissa Lvovna led Ana behind a curtain into a sixth room, filled with books, pictures, cupboards, computers, and the wherewithal to make tea. There was something cozily entrenched about the room, as if the daily business of tending the legacy of a great writer had deposited a shambolic warmth, a welcoming layer of clutter that contrasted meaningfully with the museum's order and respectfulness. The guide joined them and was introduced as Galya. The two women seemed disproportionately enthusiastic about the presence of a foreigner in their museum. We don't get many foreigners, particularly now, said Larissa with a meaningful look, before she continued, We used to get the occasional researcher or professor from the West. Now it's mostly schoolchildren, as you saw. We try to interest them in their heritage, but sometimes it's tricky. A Russian writer in Ukraine . . .

They exchanged rueful smiles.

What about—what about the big house where the Lintvaryovs lived, asked Ana, is it still standing? And Nikolay Pavlovich's grave? Is it still there, can we visit either of those places?

We'll be closing soon, said Larissa Lvovna. If you don't mind waiting, I can take you to the house and the cemetery, and then we can walk back into town.

Before leaving the museum, Ana bought a few shiny brochures with photographs, and a small, poorly printed book in Russian, ominously entitled *A. P. Chekhov in the Sumy Region.*

Larissa Lvovna spoke affectionately of the Lintvaryovs' summer guest, Anton Pavlovich. Not Chekhov; that was the distant, professional way to refer to him. It seemed to Ana that there was a mixture of reverence and affection in the polite use of his first name and patronymic, as if he were still among them, had merely gone down to the river for some fishing and would soon come back for a cup of tea.

This little house is not so much a museum as a living stage set, thought Ana, a place to sit and talk and socialize. The river, too, was waiting. She planned to return the next day and go down to the Psyol, perhaps take a picnic.

Larissa Lvovna led her across the street, opened a padlock, and pushed the gate.

This was the big house, she said, where the Lintvaryovs lived. In 1919 it was nationalized and made into a school. It survived until the fall of communism, when it was abandoned.

Ana was surprised to see how close the main house was to the Chekhovs' guesthouse. She had imagined a vast, sprawling estate. Of the house, only crumbling brick walls and part of the roof remained. Empty windows stared onto a yard overgrown with weeds and flowers. On one wall was a faded sign, *Danger, Keep Out.* Collapsed stairways led to gloomy cellars; sunlight filtered through a broken patch of roof into the mezzanine. It was much, much smaller than she had imagined. She thought of all the ghosts: the Lintvaryovs, the Chekhovs, the intelligentsia of Sumy and eastern Ukraine, the visitors from Moscow and Petersburg and Kharkov and Kiev; the Red Army, schoolchildren, Nazis, more schoolchildren. But she saw only what was before her: red brick stippled with remnants of white paint; a profusion of green foliage, sunlight. The ghosts were absent, the walls were silent.

Larissa Lvovna led her to the pond. It used to stretch a kilometer, she said, but now it is so overgrown that it has shrunk in size.

It was no longer a pond for walking around. A thick green scum covered the surface. A plastic bottle floated, a message from the twenty-first century. Are there still fish? Ana asked. Larissa affirmed that there were, but Ana could see only suffocation in the opaque surface. They turned back.

They left the museum behind and headed along the road away from the river, then up the hill to the cemetery. There were many graves, surrounded by iron fences. A majority of headstones; some crosses. Ana said, I never would have found Nikolay Pavlovich's grave on my own, and thanked Larissa, who nodded and pointed out a few eminent citizens on the way. Finally, she stopped by a well-tended grave with a dark stone cross.

It was vandalized a few years ago, she said. It's been restored, but there's still a chip in the cross.

Ana could not see the chip. She read the inscription, Nikolay Pavlovich Chekhov, 1858–1889.

Larissa Lvovna pointed to another grave nearby. There was a young peasant woman, she said, Tatyana Ivchenko, and every day she brought a glass of fresh milk to Nikolay while he lay dying. He would have no one else, only Tatyana could bring him his milk. Shortly before her death in 1953, she asked to be brought from Kharkov, where she was living, back to Luka, so she could be buried near Nikolay Pavlovich. She was a hundred and one years old when she died.

And the Lintvaryovs? Where are their graves?

After the Revolution the family scattered, so the cemetery plots were not maintained.

She looked at Ana, her eyes luminous, and gave a faint, resigned shrug.

It seemed extraordinary to Ana that this crowded cemetery was once their family plot. The Revolution had honored the artist and the milkmaid, but the family of landowners, doctors, teachers, and pianists had been erased even from their eternal resting place.

Come with me for tea with Sergey Ivanovich. He's a member of the Chekhov Literary Circle. He's very knowledgeable, our local Chekhov expert.

They made their way through quiet, leafy streets of nondescript Soviet era apartment blocks and the occasional sturdy brick official building. Ana was pleased by how tidy it all seemed, civilized and industrious, people walking purposefully to the shops or home for dinner; children playing on swings, grandmothers pushing baby carriages, people queueing to buy lemonade or kvas. The air gradually cooled as they drew near the center of Sumy. Larissa Lvovna identified every official or important building—post office, printer, school, technical institute —and nodded now and again to a familiar face. Finally, they left the main road and took an uneven footpath into a cluster of dilapidated apartment blocks, covered with graffiti up to the second floor, where plants bloomed on balconies and colorful washing fluttered. After three flights up a dim stairway (The elevator is not safe, said Larissa Lvovna with a sniff), they rang at a heavy door, which was flung open by a middle-aged man with a beard, thick glasses, and a paunch. Ana was introduced to Sergey Ivanovich Diachenko. Cheerfully, he turned to Ana and said, So! What brings you to the wild East? Are you a reporter?

She offered him the same vague explanation she had given Larissa Lvovna. He nodded vigorously, as if that were a good reason to travel all the way across Europe for anyone who had any sense, particularly when part of the country was at war. Ana was beginning to wonder if she did have any sense, let alone courage: All afternoon she had carried a knot of apprehension in her stomach, hoping Larissa Lvovna might broach the topic of the diary and give Ana an easy way to bring up the question of Chekhov's novel. But Larissa Lvovna had hardly referred to the Lintvaryov family other than in response to Ana's questions. Well, her business was the Chekhovs, after all, particularly Anton and Nikolay.

Just thinking about Chekhov's novel made Ana feel uneasy, as if she might be in possession of something incalculably precious that they could take away from her. She knew she had no right to feel that way; such a novel belonged to the world.

Perhaps, like Zinaida Mikhailovna, she simply felt that these were the last moments of a privileged intimacy; a summer coming to an end.

They drank their tea and talked about the activities of the Chekhov Literary Circle. All the while, Ana felt that Larissa and Sergey were carefully avoiding the topic of the Maidan, as if it might be a source of contention. They asked her about the stage performances and films based on Chekhov's plays and stories produced in the West. They had heard there was a recent film of *The Duel*. His longest story, more of a novella.

Ana saw an opportunity, took a breath. What do you think? she said. What might have become of the novel Anton Pavlovich mentioned so frequently in his letters over the two summers he spent here?

Larissa Lvovna sat blinking in silence, then sighed. Well, this is just my personal theory, but I've always thought of the trilogy he wrote as a novel: *About Love, Gooseberries,* and *The Man in a Case.* Do you agree, Seryozha?

He shrugged, clearly reluctant to contradict her.

Ana said, But those stories were published so much later—what, ten years later? And they still don't represent a substantial work. In length, I mean.

Larissa Lvovna seemed annoyed; Ana felt the heat rise to her own face. She must seem terribly naive. But she'd started now, she had to keep going. She took the leap.

You see, Zinaida Mikhailovna, in her diary, mentions a novel—

Zinaida Mikhailovna? The Lintvaryova daughter?

Yes, said Ana, I've been reading her diary.

There was a silence.

Larissa Lvovna sat back, put her hands in her lap, raised her eyebrows, and looked over her glasses at Sergey Ivanovich. Diary?

Don't you know about it? asked Ana.

It's not in our archive. Although I remember some years ago— many years ago, in fact—when some additional correspondence between Maria Pavlovna and Natalya Lintvaryova was found, there was some speculation that Zinaida Mikhailovna might have left a diary. She had always been a great reader, a great writer of letters, so her sister said. But it has never been found. Where did you hear of it?

It was sent to me by the British publisher. They specialize in translations from Russian. Actually, I'm translating it into English.

Larissa Lvovna looked confused, as if she had misplaced something, her gaze darting around the room. How can this be? Where was it found?

I don't know. I was hoping you might be able to tell me.

Have you heard anything about this, Seryozha?

Again he shrugged, his expression apologetic.

She turned to Ana. Does this diary mention Chekhov?

Of course. It's a diary of her friendship with him, those two summers.

But by that time Zinaida Mikhailovna was blind, epileptic, how could she keep a diary? How extraordinary! Do you have a copy of it?

Ana reached for her bag, where she had a printout of the

Russian. She handed it to Larissa, who took it eagerly and sat reading for a long while, quickly turning the pages, stopping now and again to shake her head or pass a page to Sergey Ivanovich, who continually cleared his throat. She looked up at Ana once or twice, her eyes bright, but didn't say anything. For the museum, this would be a treasure.

Ana took out her cell phone. It was still early; perhaps she could reach Katya Kendall, tell her where she was. She was breaking the confidentiality clause, but she could not imagine it mattered in this case. She dialed the number and got Katya's voicemail, so she left a message, urgently asking her to return the call without specifying why or that she was actually in Ukraine.

Sergey Ivanovich went over to a cabinet and took out a bottle and three small glasses, then disappeared for a few minutes in the kitchen and came back with a plate of small chunks of assorted ham and cheese and some bread.

We must celebrate! he said, beaming.

Larissa put the printout to one side. Sergey Ivanovich poured the vodka, and they raised a toast to the Lintvaryovs.

We must authenticate it, said Larissa Lvovna calmly, but Ana could sense her excitement. You must get the publisher to contact us so we can arrange to see the manuscript.

I've just left a message. I can't believe they haven't been in touch with you.

Yes, it is strange, said Larissa Lvovna, but then we are so far away here. The White Dacha—the museum in Yalta—has had all the attention in recent years. Oh dear. What will happen now in Crimea?

She put her knuckles to her temples briefly, dramatically, then sighed and went back to reading the typescript. Ana talked with Sergey Ivanovich, about general things, her interest in Chekhov, her short summer in Moscow so many years ago. Then she asked him what he knew about the Lintvaryov family after Chekhov's time.

Let's see . . . Natalya Mikhailovna and Georges moved to Kharkov after the October Revolution. All the others died before 1917, or maybe Elena . . . yes, she survived until 1922. Anyway, the only descendant we were in touch with was Ksenia Georgievna, Georges's daughter. She ended up in New York, died some years ago, but she never mentioned any diary, and she would have been the logical person to have it. But her children and grandchildren are spread all over the world—in Russia, in Australia, in the United States. So much time has gone by . . .

Ana turned to Larissa Lvovna and said, At one point the diary was kept in Zinaida Mikhailovna's bed, she had a hiding place there. Supposing the bed was sold recently as an antique—couldn't some unknown person have found the original journal and donated or sold it to a Russian publisher, who then sent it to England?

Larissa Lvovna chuckled, raised an eyebrow. I don't think such a bed would have survived. Firewood was needed on more than one occasion.

But what about your own furniture, in the museum?

It's not original. Most of it was donated, by Maria Pavlovna from the house in Yalta, or from eminent benefactors in Sumy, but not the Lintvaryovs.

She gave an apologetic shrug and went on reading, visibly skimming some of the pages, then slowing down whenever Anton Pavlovich was mentioned. At one point she paused to eat some cheese and ham. They drank another toast, this time to Anton Pavlovich. The vodka made Ana bold. It came out in spite of her, as if everything were at stake now.

That's not everything, you know, she said. You haven't read that far yet, Larissa Lvovna, but you'll see in the journal that Anton

Pavlovich gave Zinaida Mikhailovna a manuscript for safekeeping—a novel he was working on. A heavy box, she calls it. One hundred and seventy-eight pages long. As far as I know, from her diary, she had it in her possession at the time of her death.

Larissa Lvovna sat up very straight and looked at Ana incredulously. Sergey Ivanovich removed his glasses and rubbed his eyes with his fists like a small child.

You must be very careful, you know, said Larissa Lvovna. It's like the art world: There is a traffic in fakes. Everything is possible now. Before, no . . .

No, Ana exclaimed, it's not the same, what would be the point of a fake manuscript? Why would anyone go to so much trouble?

To make money, what else. She gave a fatalistic shrug. What do you think, Seryozha? Larissa Lvovna asked.

Let me call my cousin Yuri, suggested Sergey Ivanovich. He's a publisher. He might know something.

You do that, said Larissa Lvovna. This is too important. If this diary is authentic, it will be a treasure for the museum. We can print special editions, illustrated. The tourists will buy them. As for a novel by Anton Pavlovich . . . if he left it with the Lintvaryovs, Maria Pavlovna could have taken it in the summer of 1890, when she came back on her own; perhaps she kept it for some time, then destroyed it. Or Anton Pavlovich himself destroyed it.

Oh, it can't be, thought Ana. She had read about Maria Pavlovna's visit. It was perfectly plausible that she had taken the novel away with her.

After a moment they heard Sergey Ivanovich's voice booming down the line in the other room, increasingly excited, a chain of exclamations and short, eager questions. Finally, he came back in and began rubbing his hands and looking at Larissa Lvovna almost mischievously.

Lara, he said emphatically, do you recall last year—about this time, yes, late spring, early summer—there was a woman who came to Luka and asked a lot of questions about the Lintvaryovs? And she had a big camera and took a lot of pictures?

Dear Seryozha, we have so many visitors. Or used to, anyway.

I remember her because you asked me to accompany her. She spoke Russian fluently, but clearly, she lived abroad and needed a local guide. She was staying at that nice hotel. A very thin woman, but ever so elegant. She had called ahead, and you asked me to meet her at the hotel and take her to the *marshrutka* and bring her here—

Clearly? Why clearly? You're not being clear at all, Seryozha.

Ana looked away, stared at the rows of books on the wall, the name Чехов dancing volume after volume before her eyes, but she was seeing the gastropub in South Kensington, and Katya Kendall, thin and elegant, with her sky-gray eyes. But it would be normal for Katya to come to Luka, for the same reasons she herself had come, to see where Zinaida Mikhailovna had befriended Anton Pavlovich, to find out more about the elusive novel he was writing.

Don't you remember? said Seryozha. She said she was doing research on prerevolutionary estates. She asked a lot of questions about the Lintvaryovs, but she did not seem very interested in Anton Pavlovich.

Exactly, thought Ana, contradicting what she had concluded not five seconds earlier. She was interested in the Lintvaryov family. Perhaps for publicity purposes, for later. Illustrations for the diary, perhaps.

Larissa Lvovna grunted and gave Sergey Ivanovich an affectionately withering look.

You don't recall, said Sergey Ivanovich. Well, it's not important, because I do, and this lady happened to mention to me that her husband was a publisher. In London, she—

Ana interrupted him: Do you remember the name of the publishing house?

Sergey Ivanovich looked at the ceiling, then shook his head. She did tell me her first name. She asked a lot of questions but was very evasive when I questioned her.

Get to the point, Seryozha! said Larissa Lvovna.

My cousin Yuri—the one I just called—well, he told me that a few months ago, he received a manuscript in the post. It was in Russian but sent from England. With a cover letter in Russian explaining simply that a nineteenth-century journal had been found in London in the home of some Russian émigrés, and would he like to publish it? Yuri said he read the first ten pages or so and it didn't interest him. He sent it back without realizing at the time that it was about Anton Chekhov. What a fool!

How do you know it's the same manuscript? said Larissa Lvovna.

Well, we can't be sure, he said, but it was set in Sumy. Yuri had just published a book about our sugar baron, Kharitonenko. An outstanding capitalist! said Sergey Ivanovich, turning to Ana. Have you seen his new statue in the city center?

Ana nodded. Larissa Lvovna was rolling her eyes and tapping her foot.

Undaunted, Sergey continued: Yuri said he remembers a blind woman, and he thought readers would find it too depressing. Now. He sent it back, but then a colleague of his received it, and read it through, and later told Yuri it was about Chekhov. This colleague said he wanted to buy it, but the British publisher was asking too much. Apparently, the manuscript has been going around Moscow and Petersburg and Kiev ever since, and either the publishers can't afford it or they're afraid it's not authentic.

Is it an old manuscript? An original? Handwritten? asked Larissa Lvovna.

Sergey tutted. Of course not! That would be too valuable, if it were authentic. No, just some computer printout—like this one, he said, pointing to the pages on Larissa Lvovna's lap. Anyway, to continue my story, one woman recently made a small offer and never heard back. Terribly irresponsible. Yuri is very discouraged by the state of the publishing world. He says people will either stop reading altogether or pirate his entire catalog.

Get to the point, Seryozha! insisted Larissa Lvovna.

The point, dear Lara, is the name. I remembered while talking to Yuri—the brain is a wonderful thing. I remembered that the woman I showed around called herself Catherine something-or-other. And Yuri says the woman who signed the cover letter was Ekaterina something-or-other.

But Seryozha, that is a terribly common name! said Larissa. It proves nothing. How are we to authenticate this book!

Sergey Ivanovich, Ana said, was the woman's name Catherine Kendall? Does that ring a bell? From Polyana Press in London? Polyana as in Yasnaya Polyana?

Sergey Ivanovich stabbed the air with his finger. Exactly! I knew there was something to do with Tolstoy!

Larissa Lvovna chuckled and shook her head. What a funny name for a British publisher, she said.

To Ana, it all made sense. It was odd that Katya had not mentioned her trip during their lunch, but there was no reason why she should. Perhaps she had come here, like Ana, on a sort of personal pilgrimage, in addition to taking photographs for the book.

But what does this prove? asked Larissa Lvovna. We still don't know where the diary comes from. What house in London? Who are these émigrés? Oligarchs? Fugitives from the regime? Or from an earlier time?

Ana said, I am sure she will tell me, now that you are interested in the diary for the museum. She just doesn't want anyone else to know for the moment.

Then why is she sending it to publishers? asked Larissa Lvovna. Why hasn't she been in touch with us? It's very odd, but . . . She looked down at her lap again and resumed reading.

Sergey Ivanovich looked at Ana and nodded toward Larissa, placing a finger on his lips. He led Ana over to a bookshelf and began to show her his collection of books about Chekhov. It was impressive: an entire wall, a library in itself, with volumes not only in Russian but also in German, French, Spanish, and English. He explained that he had a passive working knowledge of all four languages. It is very interesting to me, he said, how everyone loves Chekhov. Very different, almost national points of view, down to the way his name is spelled. Look, he said, pointing at the spines, *Tschechow, Tchékhov, Chejov.*

Then he showed her some other volumes at the end of the shelf. My colleagues in other countries send me books as well, look. In Afrikaans it is spelled *Tsjechof.* But in Dutch there is a *v* at the end.

He giggled as he showed Ana the two contrasting volumes. And in Polish, *Czechow,* and in Hungarian, *Csehov,* and best of all, in Catalan, you must see—

Suddenly, Larissa Lvovna exclaimed, What?

They turned and saw her waving her hand, her eyes on the manuscript. What's this? I don't understand, she said, looking over at them. Seryozha, the child—the one born at Luka that first summer, the birth Chekhov mentions in his letter to Pleshcheyev—who was it?

He grew thoughtful, frowned, scratched his beard, and said finally, Of course, the first one was born while Anton Pavlovich was staying with them, July 1888, if I'm not mistaken . . . Yes, a girl it was, Ksenia. She became a doctor. And then a few years later, they had a boy.

Seryozha! Larissa Lvovna exploded. Surely you remember it was the other way around! It was a boy first—Vsevolod. It's right there in Sapukhin's book, on your shelf! She turned to Ana. This seems a terrible discrepancy, she said. I don't know what to think.

Well, there must be a mistake.

Larissa Lvovna shrugged fatalistically. Whose mistake?

Can't we ask the author of that book?

Sapukhin? He died in 1970.

Larissa Lvovna gathered up the pages of the printout, tapped them on her lap, and handed them back to Ana. I've read enough for now, she said, I don't like this mistake.

Sergey Ivanovich protested. It's not a—

I don't like it one bit. It's very odd. When you have the diary authenticated, I'll read the rest.

Ana said, When, then, Larissa Lvovna, was Ksenia Lintvar-yova born, according to this Mr. Sapukhin?

Not until 1894. Three years after Zinaida Mikhailovna died.

They sat in puzzled silence. Ana's heart was hammering in her chest, while her mind lapsed into a vague confused trance close to prayer. Sergey Ivanovich asked her, And what do you think of our new government in Kiev?

Seryozha, please, said Larissa Lvovna.

Well, I'm pleased you got rid of the old one, said Ana, trying to sound cheerful, then instantly wondering if she hadn't put her foot in it.

There was an uncomfortable silence. Larissa Lvovna was shaking her head, and it was impossible to tell whether it was in disagreement or exasperation. Sergey Ivanovich opened his mouth as if about to speak, then thought better of it.

I hope the fighting in the south will be over soon, said Ana, looking at them.

They seemed to agree on that, nodding gravely while withholding whom they hoped would win.

Ana went back to the hotel that night determined, somehow, to prove that Sergey Ivanovich was no absent-minded buffoon, that his version of the Lintvaryov family tree was correct: Ksenia was Pavel Mikhailovich and Antonida Fyodorovna's firstborn child.

She ate a hurried supper—more borscht, not as tasty as the day before—then tried again to call Katya Kendall. She would have no trouble confronting her; all she had to do was ask if Katya had ever been to Sumy, then tell her about the discrepancy and see what she said.

She heard the faraway ringing; there was no answer, not even a voicemail message this time.

The storm-heavy air seemed to reverberate with Ana's apprehension. She went to reception and asked if there was a computer with an Internet connection that she could use, and the young woman led her to a stifling windowless office. If beginning storm, she said in English, please to turn off computer. She pointed meaningfully to the various switches.

Ana wondered why she had not thought of looking on the Internet sooner. Gullibility, a willingness to trust and believe, to give others the benefit of the doubt?

On Amazon she found several books written by Catherine Kendall, all published by Polyana Press: two travel books on Saint Petersburg and a historical novel about Grand Duchess Anastasia, *Anastasia Nikolayevna*. Ana was able to browse a few pages. It was written, as far as she could tell, in diary form. There was no evidence that it was a translation; it appeared to have been written directly in English.

She googled Polyana Press and found a very recent article in *The Bookseller*, published the day before she left for Kiev, reporting that the press had gone into receivership. *This small independent publisher*, confirmed the article, *has been struggling since the financial downturn of 2008. Interest in travel writing has waned dramatically, and lucrative contracts with Russia have also fallen off, due to the economic situation and now the political crisis over Ukraine, according to Peter Kendall, the publisher.*

This went a long way toward explaining their silence and the fact that she hadn't been paid, although that no longer seemed to matter.

She recalled Larissa Lvovna referring to Chekhov's letter to
Pleshcheyev, a letter in which he described the birth of Pavel and
Antonida's child. The letters were available online, so Ana looked
there next, while the thunder got louder and the lights began to
flicker. Storm beginning, must to turn off computer, she thought,
but the receptionist did not come to scold her.

Anton Pavlovich did indeed write a letter to Pleshcheyev on
July 7, 1888, in which he described the imminent birth of Pavel
and Antonida's child.

*I am writing to you, dear Aleksey Nikolayevich, and at this very
moment all of Luka is in a complete uproar, a whirlwind of shouts,
cries, and groans: Antonida Fyodorovna is giving birth. Every now
and then I have to run over to the cottage vis-à-vis, where the newly
minted parents live. The birth is not a difficult one, but it is taking
a while. . .*

Chekhov sent his letter before he knew whether the baby was
a boy or a girl.

Ana skimmed subsequent letters but found nothing. She
switched off the computer and went back up to her room, stopping at the bar to buy a few miniatures of vodka. It had begun to
rain. She opened the window and breathed in the fresh ozone. She
didn't know what to think; the Internet had brought no answer
to her query. It was an old-fashioned query, for rural registry
offices, dusty ledgers, pen and ink. So much could have disappeared during the Revolution, too—and who was this Comrade
Sapukhin to impose his administrative wisdom upon generations
of Chekhov scholars?

She sat down with the vodka, then took out the book she had
bought at the museum and began to leaf through it in the dim
light.

A. P. Chekhov in the Sumy Region, by one P. A. Sapukhin, the
same. She looked more closely, although the quality of the print
was so bad that she began to develop a headache and see spots.

There it was, on page thirty-two, as Larissa Lvovna had said: *1888, born on July 7 and baptized on July 11, VSEVOLOD.* With the names of the parents clearly set out below, *Pavel Lintvaryov son of Mikhail and Antonida daughter of Fyodor.*

Ana did not sleep much that night for brooding. Putting together the possible pieces: Sergey Ivanovich had shown Katya around the museum; she could have gotten her misinformation from him (and had apparently neglected to buy a copy of Sapukhin). But even supposing (as Larissa might) that Katya Kendall had written the diary herself and incorporated Sergey Ivanovich's mistake, why add Chekhov's novel? A straight story about Zinaida Mikhailovna would be believable, even written in the first person, but why add Anton Pavlovich's novel when there was no proof it had ever existed? Wouldn't that raise suspicion?

On the other hand, it would help the sales of Zinaida Mikhailovna's diary if readers thought that every attic and archive from Saint Petersburg to Sevastopol was being turned upside down by literary sleuths—academics, students, publishers, editors, literary agents, theater directors, translators—eager to find Anton Chekhov's lost novel.

But as a prop within a forged diary . . . even supposing Katya had started out writing the journal not as a forgery but as pure fiction: Chekhov himself famously said you don't plant a pistol in Act I if you don't intend to use it.

Ana awoke with a start to distant noises of traffic and two men arguing in the street, swearing drunkenly. They must have been at it all night, she thought; sunlight was streaming through the window. And then she realized with dread that she must look one more time on the Internet. Sapukhin—and Larissa Lvovna—must be disproved.

Authentication, at least as far as Larissa Lvovna was concerned, would start with showing that Ksenia was Pavel and Antonida's firstborn. Without knowing where Katya had obtained the diary, this would be difficult; the émigré attic? Perhaps the next place to look. Ana had an irrational vista of London rooftops stretching for miles, and herself flying over them like some literary Peter Pan.

Why hadn't she pressed Katya, nagged her at lunch, instead of allowing herself to be beguiled by wine and poetry?

Then there were Georges Lintvaryov's descendants: What had Sergey Ivanovich said? Spread all over the world, on three continents. Ana felt a wave of discouragement.

After breakfast—a generous pile of delicious blini but meager consolation—she asked to use the computer again. She mumbled an excuse about having been interrupted by the storm; the receptionist merely smiled graciously. Slowly, Ana keyed in the siblings' names in Cyrillic.

This time she found a document, mostly in Ukrainian, twenty-nine pages long: Родословие Линтварёвых, or Родовід Линтварьових, a sort of genealogical history of the entire Lintvaryov family beginning in 1700, including quotations from Chekhov. She scrolled slowly through it, past names she could reasonably recognize as the family she knew, and finally, on page twenty-four, she came to the brother-and-sister pair she was looking for.

Vsevolod Pavlovich, born July 9, 1888. Baptized July 11, 1888, at St. John the Baptist Church. Godparents: Dr. Basil P. Vorontsov from the city of Saint Petersburg and Elena Mikhailovna Lintvaryova.

Ksenia Pavlovna, born January 24, 1894. Baptized April 20, 1894, at Sumy Church of the Resurrection. Godparents: Georgi Mikhailovich Lintvaryov and Elena Mikhailovna Lintvaryova.

Three years after Zinaida Mikhailovna's death.

Ana stared at the screen, wondering if she had not confused the alphabet. She willed the words to move, to shift places.

She tried in vain to find what authority lay behind this website; it was certainly not the Ukrainian government, only an amateur reproducing—albeit very professionally, as far she could tell—the genealogy of the Lintvaryov family.

Was it incontestable proof? An old document retyped on the Internet? And what about Sapukhin—wasn't he just some stuffy Soviet academic who couldn't have been very interested in children?

But deep down, Ana feared that Larissa Lvovna was right. And she feared for her modest pilgrimage.

She suddenly saw them as vividly as if she were there physically. They were standing on the far shore of the Psyol, waving to her and laughing: Anton Pavlovich, and the three Lintvaryova sisters and their two brothers, and Grigory Petrovich, and Marmelad with his mustache, and Nikolay Pavlovich back from the dead, and Masha and Ivan and Misha and their mother, and finally, Tonya, holding a baby bundled in a pale gray blanket, and it was impossible to tell whether it was a boy or a girl, but they were all laughing and crying out, Girl! Boy! until a silence fell and Anton Pavlovich said in a deep, suspenseful voice, Crocodile!

Ana printed the page, then sat for a long time with her head in her hands. The receptionist tapped gently on the door.

Everything is okay?

Fine, said Ana, I'm just tired, thank you.

She took a taxi back to the museum. She hadn't packed a picnic. All those picnics Zinaida Mikhailovna had described . . . inventions. Katya Kendall's, Ana supposed.

She recognized the affable young man who had driven her to Luka the previous day—how long ago it seemed. He had told her then that he had been to the museum as a schoolboy. Now he looked at Ana in the rearview mirror and winked. So, Anton Pavlovich?

If she'd had more time, she would have told him the whole story. Taxi drivers were confessors by nature. He would have sympathized, found a way to cheer her up. It will all pass, he would have said. But it was only a short drive, so Ana mumbled something about the museum being interesting, and what a pity about the old estate falling to ruin.

The estate belongs to the government. Hah, where is the money? Our ex-president used it for his vintage car collection. Seventy cars he had! One old one worth two million dollars alone! There's your money to restore Luka! Between him and all the other thieves, what do you expect?

Perhaps things will begin to change now, said Ana.

Maybe, said the driver skeptically. Europe will help us now, right? EU, NATO?

Flustered, Ana said, Maybe there's a wealthy Ukrainian emigrant somewhere who'd be glad to rebuild the estate—to flatter his ego, but also for Ukrainian history or culture, no? They could build a writers' colony, for example, a *klimaticheskaya stantsia,* as Chekhov called it?

The driver exploded with laughter. Write Frau Merkel a letter! he said with a crooked smile. She'll send us some German writers!

Larissa Lvovna was waiting. I think you were right, said Ana with a sad smile. She showed Larissa the page from the genealogy that she had printed out.

The director nodded, then said, Sergey Ivanovich means well, he's a good person, but he's not a family man, and details like that mean nothing to him, you see. Come, I'll show you, she said, her expression soft, compassionate.

They went back into the room that had been Chekhov's. On the wall, near the bed, the small photograph of the Lintvaryov siblings.

You see? she said. Vsevolod was older by six years. But he was very ill, he had a wasting disease; he didn't live past twenty. That is what inspired Ksenia Pavlovna to become a doctor.

Ana reflected that there would have been a sad connection there, too, for Katya to have made, between the aunt and the nephew.

Judging from the photograph, the siblings could have been the same age.

Their clear, open faces.

Larissa and Ana walked down to the river. It was a fine day, they could hear splashing sounds, children's cries. Ana felt hungover, though she knew it was from the loss, and a restless night, and had very little to do with a few shots of vodka.

The Psyol, too, had changed. It was not as she had imagined. She recalled the photographs she had seen and Chekhov's own descriptions: The islands seemed to have vanished (how does an island vanish? Soviet engineering?), and Larissa Lvovna told her that the flow had narrowed. As with the pond, the vegetation was thick, encroaching.

Some boys were swinging out over the river on a long rope hanging from a tall tree. Larissa Lvovna told her it was called a *tarzanka*. Ana thought of Zinaida Mikhailovna as a child with her father, then remembered the memory was imaginary. Was it right to feel cheated?

They walked up along a path to a hill overlooking the river. Larissa turned to Ana and said, This is where Maria Pavlovna and Natalya Mikhailovna used to come and paint. Perhaps you saw the photographs and the reproductions in the museum?

Two young women in white dresses on the bank above the river, paint boxes open on their laps, while a gentleman with his hands behind his back looks approvingly over their shoulders.

———

When they were back in the museum office, Larissa Lvovna turned to Ana and said, What will you do? About the diary?

What can I do? It's not my manuscript.

Is it worth publishing as a kind of fiction? Are there other errors, or just the one about Ksenia Pavlovna?

I really don't know, said Ana with a despairing shrug. I would have to compare every detail with every biography, every letter . . .

And it's not your manuscript, repeated Larissa Lvovna. It's not worth it.

No . . . it's really out of my hands now. It belongs to Catherine—Ekaterina—Kendall. It's her book. She wrote a novel about Grand Duchess Anastasia, she added.

Larissa Lvovna could not suppress a laugh, and she patted Ana's hand and offered her some tea.

Ana looked around the office again. It had been Maria Pavlovna's room. On the wall was a reproduction of the famous oil portrait of Anton Pavlovich—the one he hated, she had read, in his pince-nez, looking *like a professor who has eaten horseradish*. Stacks of books. Embroidered hand towels. A glass case full of cups and plates; a dusty samovar. Several reproductions of paintings by Levitan, who once proposed to Masha, not altogether in jest; Anton Pavlovich, predictably, had advised her to turn him down.

Now Larissa Lvovna turned to Ana. Here's the thing, she said. Do you think this . . . diary is faithful to the spirit of Luka? To Anton Pavlovich?

Ana hesitated, then burst out, If I had been told from the start that this diary was a fiction, I probably still would have agreed to translate it—for other reasons, more mercenary ones—but I never would have come all this way, looking for Anton Pavlovich's lost novel.

How far she had fallen. Placing her hopes in a real, as yet undiscovered novel by Chekhov, which she would have been the first to translate. Now not only did Chekhov's novel not exist, neither did Zinaida's diary.

And it was the loss of Zinaida's diary that she felt much more keenly. She was both ashamed and bereft. She realized, not without a touch of surprise, that the loss of Zinaida seemed crueler than anything.

How could the diary not be real? Zinaida had been so alive to her during those early spring days. Could it really only have been Katya Kendall, a frustrated Russian émigré in West London, who had said so much to her, sharing a life that was infinitely rich despite its loss?

She turned to Larissa Lvovna and said, We don't even know what Zinaida looked like! Are you sure you don't have any pictures of her anywhere, even in a crowd?

Larissa shook her head slowly.

Now, in a spurt of anger, Ana thought of how she had been left with a sad, sorry fiction, a scam, a cynical hoax concocted by a lapsed poet who wrote pseudo-diaries of Russian *demoiselles* in her spare time and recited Pasternak in gastropubs to gullible Russophiles like Ana.

In the distant echo I try to catch
What the years ahead may bring.

The famous Zhivago poem, "Hamlet"; Katya speaking, as if in a trance, to a clatter of dishes, a hiss of espresso machine. The young man, rapt, at the next table.

Unless . . . unless Katya's motivation lay elsewhere, thought Ana, not just in Zinaida Mikhailovna's connection with Chekhov. Something deeper and mysterious, known only to herself.

Larissa Lvovna was staring at her, waiting for her to go on. So Ana said, The publisher has gone bankrupt, you know. Perhaps this was their last-ditch effort to save their business. Chekhov wrote to feed his family, did he not?

Larissa Lvovna spluttered, You cannot compare! He was a genius. This is fraud!

Ana sighed and nodded. Yes, it is fraud. Because the Kendalls wanted the world at large to believe not only in the existence of Zinaida's diary but also in Chekhov's lost novel.

The world already knows the lost novel exists, Larissa Lvovna said sarcastically, but perhaps these people planned to write it and publish it, too!

Larissa Lvovna, said Ana, speaking slowly, with a few changes here and there, this journal could work as a novel. It is based on Zinaida Mikhailovna's life, and Anton Pavlovich's two summers here, and the characters are very true to life . . . and . . .

She was not making sense. She was on the verge of tears and couldn't go on. There were no more arguments.

Zinaida Mikhailovna had died. She had vanished. The reality was in the absence of her photograph. Even her grave was gone. There was no trace of her, save in the dried ink of Anton Pavlovich's letters and the obituary he wrote for her.

But then Larissa Lvovna was squeezing her arm. On second thought, she began, it is a terrible but somehow wonderful story— that woman in England, going to all that trouble, writing such a book to try to save her business—I think it is something Anton Pavlovich could appreciate, if it has been done in the right spirit. The lengths to which people are prepared to go in life when they believe in something . . .

Her voice trailed off, as if she were still unsure of the validity of her thought.

How they would laugh, Anton Pavlovich and Zinaida Mikhailovna, thought Ana, if they knew her story! Not in an unkind way, no, but the irony of it! She had placed her hopes in Chekhov's novel for the wrong reasons. To be the translator of Chekhov's novel; to be not so much in his shadow as in his light. Like the very people who would approach him on the street because of his sudden fame after he won the Pushkin Prize:

What is terrible is that they tend to like something in us that we often neither love nor respect in ourselves.

As Ana sat beside Larissa Lvovna in that warm, comfortably cluttered room—the room where Maria Pavlovna had slept in the weeks before embarking on her own career as *the writer's sister*—one small consoling thought came to her.

She saw Katya as she'd been that day in the pub. Quiet, evasive not only about Chekhov's novel but about the diary itself. As if even she had been feeling her own mixture of shame and loss. Perhaps it was only to do with her husband, with the press, as Larissa had suggested. But it seemed to Ana that there was more than that. Mustn't she have cared about Zinaida Mikhailovna, or at least come to care about her? Enough to imagine a whole book about her? To weave that tapestry—every thread so carefully looped into another until the details emerged—Vata rowing Monsieur Pleshcheyev around the pond; Grigory Petrovich asleep under the cherry tree? To conjure Zinaida Mikhailovna's darkness, her mortality, her painfully open heart? It did not *feel* like a book conceived simply to make money. Why, then, choose the doomed Zinaida Mikhailovna as her lens? Why Zinaida and not her more entertaining and expansive sister Natasha or the brooding, poetic Georges? Why, indeed, if not to examine a state of being? Why? *Because Katya Kendall had something more to say.*

Just because the voice was not an authentic one from the past, did the words have any less meaning?

Was that not the beauty of fiction, that it aimed closer at the bitter heart of truth than any biography could, that it could search out the spirit of those who may or may not have lived, and tell their story not as it had unfolded, as a series of objective facts recorded by an indifferent world, but as they had lived it and, above all, felt it? Was there a finer way to honor friendship, and love, and being in the world?

Ana turned to Larissa Lvovna and said clumsily, earnestly, This Katya—she understood the importance of Chekhov's time here; she imagined how precious the friendship of someone like Anton Pavlovich would have been to this woman who was losing everything. She put in all this work—and it's not perfunctory, she brings Zinaida to life, or so it seems to me; she had me fooled, after all! She must have felt a sort of tenderness, affection, for her, for whatever reason, for whatever generous reason—yes—otherwise, why work so hard, why spend so much time, on writing her life?

Larissa nodded, not entirely convinced.

You haven't read the whole book, Ana conceded. Of course, I read it believing a real person wrote it—I mean, a real person did write it, but not the one who lived it. But it's as if she had. That's the power of the imagination, isn't it?

Larissa sat quietly, staring out the window at the garden but seeing something else. Then she turned to face Ana with an earnest brightness in her eyes. Yes, she said, I believe you are right. It's why we read. It's why we need our writers.

ANA RETURNED ALONE TO the abandoned estate. Larissa Lvovna, or maybe the caretaker, had forgotten to lock the gate. She stood in the courtyard and stared at the ruins splashed with late-day sunlight. A single muddy boot she had not noticed the previous day waited, forgotten, by the steps leading to the cellar. A woman on a bicycle rode slowly along a path behind the house, proof that it was pointless to lock the gate. Ana ventured in the direction of the pond and saw the well-worn bicycle trail. It had rained all night, and the path to the pond was muddy and very slippery. She turned back; she would not go looking at the pond's opaque surface for bursts of cloudlight.

Instead, she went once again to stand by the entrance to Zinaida's house. Steps leading up to where there used to be a door. She waited—for a sign, an epiphany. There was only the loud croaking of the frogs in the pond, and birds calling. Children's voices in the distance; a motorbike.

She saw some wild strawberries growing amid the unruly vegetation in the yard. She picked one and ate it slowly, thinking of Zinaida Mikhailovna and Anton Pavlovich. At least she had come to Luka, and they really had been here, 125 summers ago. She had to believe what Katya had dared to write, she had to believe in the truth of the imagination. She was glad she had come, despite what she had learned.

So for a moment she allowed the wild sweetness of the berry to connect her to them, to those moments when they paused in conversation to share some fruit, their words suspended in the still summer air.

AFTER
LUKA

THERE WAS PLENTY OF time to think on the train from Sumy to Kiev.

This strange interlude in her ordinary life. The uprising of her well-planned, obedient days, in defense of the absurd and the sublime, from her near-encounter with Léo in London, to this wild-goose chase to eastern Ukraine.

Now she just wanted to get home, to Doodle, the mountains, tranquillity, her own firm pillow and fluffy duvet. It seemed so far away. For a while she gazed restlessly at the fields, the villages, the abandoned factories. Then she began to read.

She had brought along a slim volume of Chekhov stories—fortunately, as she hadn't seen a single bookstore in Sumy. She read two late stories, "At Christmas Time" and "The Bishop"; they suited her mood of puzzled melancholy. An illiterate peasant and his wife pay a shifty soldier to write a Christmas letter to their daughter, whose brutal husband has neglected to post her own letters to her old parents all along. A bishop senses he may be dying and questions the significance of his life.

The straightforward precision of the language; the lightness of the irony. As if the author were shaking his head or shrugging, with a smile, a nod to the never-ceasing human struggle to give meaning, to put a brave face on mortality and incomprehensible suffering. Our failures to communicate with others, with ourselves. That late in life, sick with tuberculosis, Chekhov would have understood his characters' confusion and helplessness only too well, thought Ana. And yet his lucid, tender portrayals were, in their way, a source of hope, or at least of comfort.

She put the book down and folded her hands over her waist, looking up and out the window at the lush early-summer landscape. How easy it was, amid the superficial pressures—of society, of one's own making—to forget what really mattered. There had been other reasons for her desire to translate Chekhov's lost novel, she saw that now. All reasons that had nothing to do with careers, recognition, or the light a great author casts. She was indebted to Anton Pavlovich for the vision he gave her—that vibrant grasp of life, the next best thing to being in love, without all of love's blindness. If Ana had longed to be his translator, it was so she could take his Russian words and, with each moment of slow, considered re-creation in her own language, enter the prism, where sunlight refracted vision, and know that she was living well.

Ana went to the Maidan, saw the piles of tires, the shields, the tents. Memorials with candles and photographs. A gas mask dangling from a wooden board. People milling about, curious, expectant, some of them ordinary tourists like her, others edgier, rougher regulars, men who hadn't slept, whose blood ran with vodka and outrage. She found the photograph of Oleksiy Bratushko from Sumy at the memorial on Instytutska Street. His smiling, hopeful face. She left a flower and whispered a short, private prayer, as if she had brought it to him from Sumy.

People were friendly and open; they seemed grateful to see her there, just as Yves had said they would be. She wandered through the city and let her mind go blank, the better to absorb the colors and smells and sounds around her. She visited the Pechersk Lavra Monastery of the Caves and was stunned by the contrast between the gilded domes and the sepulchral gloom where the mummies lay; she gazed at the aptly named House of Chimeras; she strolled up and down Andreevskiy Descent and lingered sadly outside Bulgakov's house: The museum had already closed for the day, and she was leaving the next morning.

She had comforting food and cool beer. She sat on a square in the sunshine. War seemed impossible, despite glaring headlines at newspaper kiosks and heated discussions in multiple languages all around her, and as she looked at passing faces she realized it wasn't only about Ukraine—yes, she was here, now, but so was Russia, in her heart, and she was torn, angry, outraged by what seemed, as always, a cynical tragedy scripted by politicians and their propagandists. From all sides, including her own. Because when people heard her accent, they asked where she was from; when she told them, they smiled indulgently, as if they both envied her and knew she must be naive.

Ana could not help her naïveté; she could only show them her sincerity and share her hopes for the best possible outcome to the conflict, and soon, so that people could get on with their lives in the future they had fought for.

In the end, everything she had learned about Zinaida Mikhailovna's diary, about the Lintvaryovs, about Chekhov's novel— these were things she could have learned without leaving her desk in the village. That Ukraine belonged to novels and history books, beneath a layer of dust, behind a scrim of romanticism. But the Ukraine where she was walking now, in the late afternoon sun, smiling at strangers, was a place for which she already felt the nostalgia of imminent departure—a place that did not exist, or did not exist yet, a country that was changing by the hour. She remembered the French map with its polite degrees of warnings. She had reinforced her vigilance, but not in the way the cartographer had intended.

DOODLE MEOWED ALL AFTERNOON upon Ana's return, as if what the cat had to say about six days spent at a *chatterie* was far more interesting than anything Ana could possibly have to tell her. Ana opened her laptop cautiously, as if it might bite her. But there was nothing from the Kendalls.

Yves had written to say he was still waiting for his mongoose. My mongoose now, she thought. She wrote and told him briefly what had happened, but concluded that if they didn't have a *mangouste* at his local pet store, some *langoustines* chez Lipp would suit her just as well.

Lydia Guilloux had written to Ana to congratulate her, somewhat belatedly, on the prize nomination, and to ask her to translate her latest novel, *Rencontre mélancolique*. She hadn't found a British or American publisher yet, but she was optimistic. *After all*, she wrote, *it's full of sex*. Sex was the hardest thing to translate, Ana knew, but she felt up to the challenge.

Not quite three weeks after her return from Ukraine, Ana went out to the mailbox and found a thick business-size envelope with stamps from the UK (Winnie-the-Pooh, how lovely, she thought) and a London postmark. No return address. The envelope was addressed by hand.

Inside were a check and two letters, one wrapped inside the other. She glanced at the check in surprise: It was a personal check in the full amount owed to her for the translation of Zinaida Mikhailovna's journal. She didn't recognize the signatory's name. She began to read the first letter, printed on Polyana Press letterhead.

Dear Ms. Harding,

First of all, my sincere apologies for taking so long to get this to you. I have had to close down the press, at least for the time being. My brother-in-law has been kind enough to advance the money so that you will not have to wait any longer—hence the unfamiliar name on the cheque. You need have no fears for his solvency.

We have been going through a very difficult time lately. The enclosed letter from my wife will explain. She wanted you to know how pleased she was with the translation, and she asked me to send you this to thank you personally. I join her in expressing my gratitude for your good work and patience beyond the call of duty.

Yours faithfully,
Peter Kendall

The second letter was handwritten on plain rough paper. Ana recognized the scrolling Russian handwriting that translates so oddly into Latin script. It was dated ten days before Peter Kendall's note—while she was in Sumy, she realized, trying to call Katya.

Dear Ana,

I have read your translation and I'm very happy with it. I did not trust my English. Besides, I needed to write in the language of my childhood and youth, and to rediscover the reasons why I so loved Chekhov, and still do.

Because, you see, and I'm sorry, as I know this will come as a shock or a disappointment, I am the author of Zinaida

*Mikhailovna's journal. Last year I was diagnosed with a form
of leukemia that sometimes responds to treatment, but in my
case it has not; I have fought, but I have lost. At the time of my
diagnosis I was reading Chekhov's letters: in one of them, Anton
Pavlovich spoke of Zinaida Mikhailovna's incredible courage,
and the obituary of course is authentic. I wanted to understand
that courage, to try to find it in myself, and to make it known to
the world. Just spending time with Anton Pavlovich and Zinaida
Mikhailovna has been good for me, has helped me both in my
struggle against the disease and in learning to accept. I was able
to live normally and hide it from Peter until relatively recently.*

*Our business has not been going well, so when Peter read my
book, he decided to try to find a Russian publisher naive enough
to believe it was the authentic diary of Zinaida Mikhailovna
Lintvaryova; failing that, he would publish it in English himself.
He thought it had potential because of Chekhov's presence. I kept
telling him you cannot fool a Russian where their language
and their great writers are concerned. And yet I suppose we
both hoped I might be wrong, that it would save us. Now, for
my sake, he has agreed to send it out as the novel that it is and
was always meant to be. I have just finished the final touches.
Polyana can no longer publish it, for obvious reasons, but if
Peter is able to find a home for it, you will have full credit as the
translator for the English version. I am sorry we have deceived
you until now.*

*I went to Luka last year to do research on the book. I was
very well received. Do try to go there someday. Sadly, it has
changed since the Lintvaryovs' time. Who knows what will
remain a hundred and twenty-five years from now?*

*But let us hope that people will still be reading Anton
Pavlovich (one sometimes wonders where literature is headed)*

or at least going to see his plays. I think there must be something of Luka in each of them.

He was happy there.

Peter wanted me to write Anton Pavlovich's lost novel, too. I tried, very briefly, but I could not. How could I! How could anyone! I am sorry, too, that when you and I met, I may have led you to believe that such a novel existed. But I went on telling Peter I would do it, to keep his spirits up. And mine, I suppose.

You see, when I was writing the book, I came to imagine Anton Pavlovich's novel as a gift to Zinaida Mikhailovna, just as I imagined he eventually gave up on it—as history would seem to imply—and he left it with her as a token of their friendship. I like to think that is the way it happened, even if we do not know the truth—it is something he <u>could</u> have done.

He gave her a story without an ending.

Heartfelt regards,
Katya

Author's Note

IN MY IMAGINED VERSION of Zinaida Mikhailovna's journal, I have tried to be as faithful as possible to actual dates, events, and details; on occasion there were discrepancies between sources, and in these cases I opted to adhere to what seemed the most logical, appropriate version. The confusion regarding Ksenia Lintvaryova's birth was first accidental, then deliberate. We do not know whether Chekhov actually did entrust a manuscript to Zinaida Mikhailovna; that is pure fictional speculation, as are their many conversations.

All the characters in nineteenth-century Luka are based on historical people. The Lintvaryovs invited many more guests over the summer, as did the Chekhovs, but for the sake of clarity, I have had to leave most of them out.

The characters in twenty-first-century Sumy are fictional but were inspired by people I met during my trip to Ukraine. I hope they will forgive me for the artistic license, as I remain forever in their debt for their help and interest.

The two kittens are real, the coincidence seemed too striking to ignore.

Polyana Press and the Kendalls, on the other hand, are completely fictional, as are the Fleur Mailly literary prize and the authors and translators mentioned in Ana's story.

The primary inspiration for the novel came from Chekhov's

own letters: *Anton Chekhov: A Life in Letters,* edited by Rosamund Bartlett and translated by Rosamund Bartlett and Anthony Phillips. I also referred to the letters in the original Russian and to earlier translations by Constance Garnett. The translations from Chekhov are my own, with the exception of the line from "A Misfortune," which is Constance Garnett's. The poem "Silentium" by Fyodor Tyutchev and the four lines from Boris Pasternak's "Hamlet" are also my translation.

Among the many books I referred to in my efforts to respect the facts within the context of a fiction are Donald Rayfield's *Anton Chekhov: A Life*; P. A. Sapukhin's *A. P. Chekhov na Sumshchinye* (in Russian); Rosamund Bartlett's *Chekhov: Scenes from a Life*; Virgile Tanase's *Tchékhov* (in French); Ivan Bunin's memoir about Chekhov; and the book that launched me on the entire project nearly ten years ago, Janet Malcolm's *Reading Chekhov.*

On contemporary events, Andrey Kurkov's *Journal de Maïdan,* translated by Paul Lequesne, and published in French in 2014.

To Lyudmila Nikolayevna Evdokimchik of the museum-house in Sumy, to her colleague Anya, to her friend Lyudmila Stepanovna Pankratova, and to Irina Danilenko: *serdechnoye spasibo.* Not only did they answer all my questions and inspire a few plot twists and turns, they showed me, once again, the meaning of incomparable Russian and Ukrainian hospitality. Special thanks also to Rosamund Bartlett and Elena Michajlowska of the Yalta Chekhov Campaign, and to Ala Osmond and Larissa Kazachenko at Exeter International: without them this book would not exist.

Warmest thanks, finally, to Dorian Karchmar, for her generous input, patience and persistence; to Courtney Angela Brkic, Maria Belmonte, Javier Fernández de Castro, and Mary Anna, for their early reading and support; to Ivana Bendow and Olga Proctor for their welcome and encouragement; to Aneesa Higgins, and to Steve Goldstein for his ever hospitable ear and some decisive inspiration over lunch at Café de la Presse.

About the Author

ALISON ANDERSON spent many years in California; she now lives in a Swiss village and works as a literary translator. Her translations include *The Elegance of the Hedgehog* and works by Nobel laureate J. M. G. Le Clézio. She has also written two previous novels and is the recipient of a National Endowment for the Arts Literary Translation Fellowship. She has lived in Greece and Croatia, and speaks several European languages, including Russian.

Insights,
Interviews
& More...

Meet Alison Anderson

Francesca Palazzi

Born in New Haven, Connecticut, Alison Anderson worked as an English teacher in Switzerland, France, Greece, and Croatia, before settling down as a consular agent and translator in California. She now lives in a Swiss village and works as a literary translator. Her translations include Europa Editions' *The Elegance of the Hedgehog* by Muriel Barbery, and works by Nobel laureate J. M. G. Le Clézio. She has also written two previous novels, *Hidden Latitudes* and *Darwin's Wink*, and is the recipient of a National Endowment for the Arts Literary Translation Fellowship. She is bilingual in French, and has a working knowledge of six other languages (including Russian). ✥

The Story behind
The Summer Guest
An Essay by the Author

I first read a few of Anton Chekhov's short stories years ago when I was learning Russian. I'd also studied the plays, but although I have always had an enduring affection for *Uncle Vanya*, I had not really explored his innumerable longer stories. But in the early years of the new century I began reading these stories on my way to work, along with Janet Malcolm's wonderful guide, *Reading Chekhov*. In a matter of weeks I was sharing my enthusiasm with a friend at lunch, who suggested I should write a novel about Chekhov.

This was, and still is, a daunting idea, for any number of reasons. I would be poking into the private life of a real person (something I swore I would never do again), and not just any person— a writer who is not only universally revered, but also whose stature borders on the mythical. There would be massive research involved, and I would have to take Russian lessons to revive my dormant knowledge of the language. And above all, how would I approach my subject? Particularly in the context of a novel? It would have to be a tribute; it would have to be light-hearted and respectful at the same time.

Chekhov had a very interesting love life, and so I looked there first for ▶

3

inspiration. There might be room for invention, particularly in the case of one Lika Mizinova, whose rather tragic life was reflected in some of his work. But in the end, I was not sure I wanted to write a traditional love story; I was interested in Chekhov the writer, not Chekhov the elusive lover. (Although he is certainly an elusive writer, as well.)

Ultimately, Chekhov himself gave me the idea for this novel, in a letter he wrote to his publisher Alexey Suvorin on May 30, 1888. He describes a Ukrainian family, the Lintvaryovs, with whom he is spending the summer—a few lines, but enough to go on. After a careful reading of all the letters from 1888 and 1889, and other biographical material, I felt confident that I could tell a story from the point of view of Zinaida, one of the Lintvaryov daughters. Chekhov tells us, in that letter to Suvorin, that Zinaida "has a brain tumor which has left her totally blind, and suffering from epilepsy and headaches. She knows perfectly well what lies in store for her and speaks with extraordinary dispassionate stoicism of her imminent death." Her vision of Chekhov would necessarily be subjective, and limited by her illness and the constraints of society—but her own feelings, as consigned to a private journal, could perhaps reflect some of the admiration and gratitude I have felt toward him myself, as well as his complexities.

I won't say that writing the diary of a blind nineteenth-century Ukrainian woman was easy, but it was certainly easier than coming up with an ending for the story of the beleaguered translator whose job it is to render the diary into English. I went through literally dozens of different versions, none of which were satisfactory. In the end, like Ana, I traveled to Ukraine for an answer—to a very different question.

In 2010 I joined a tour of Crimea that focused on Chekhov's years in Yalta, which was led by a congenial British Chekhov scholar. It attracted an equally congenial mix of people, of all ages and backgrounds, who had one thing in common: a love of Chekhov's work and a curiosity about the world he lived in, some of which, we discovered, is still very much alive in its way. After the tour was over, I journeyed alone by rail overnight across nearly all of Ukraine, from Simferopol in the south due north, to the town of Sumy, where Chekhov spent those two summers with the Lintvaryovs as a young man—the period described in the novel.

Chekhov describes, in his own words, his time there better than anyone else could. As I explored the museum and the estate, my interest was in the Lintvaryov family, and their interaction with their soon-to-be-famous summer guest. From 1919 until 1960, the centennial of Chekhov's birth, the building that had been the summer dacha on their estate had served as a school library. To honor the 1960 anniversary, a small museum was created in the house. The dacha-museum is well-kept and visited regularly, despite the loss of Soviet funding. I was a bit of an oddity there, as a foreigner; nearly all the visitors, I was told, were Ukrainian and Russian. The day I visited I joined the tour with a small group of medical students from Sumy, which seemed appropriate.

Five rooms of the house are open to the public. In the entrance is a display of photographs and historical information, and a few precious artifacts: one of Anton Pavlovich's pince-nez, donated by his sister, and his future wife Olga Knipper's evening bag. The first room to the left is devoted to Chekhov's brother Nikolay, the gifted artist. Behind that room, overlooking the garden at the rear, is the space where Anton Pavlovich stayed. It is now a simple reconstruction of the way that room must have been when he used it, with a writing desk by the window, a daybed in the corner, and a small table covered with medical instruments (which were of great interest to my fellows on the tour). The other room to the right of the entrance was where Chekhov's mother stayed, and directly opposite the entrance was a dining room with a piano where the family entertained.

The place is very much alive, full of the spirit both of the era— thanks to the tasteful arrangement of antiques that either had belonged to the Lintvaryovs or Chekhov's sister, Masha, or that had been donated by well-wishers—and of the writer himself. The women who look after the museum—Lyudmila Nikolayevna, the curator; Anna, the guide; Alla, the caretaker—share an ongoing ▶

love of Chekhov's work and a curiosity about those who come to visit. They refer to the dacha's famous ghost, in fact, as Anton Pavlovich, as though he had merely gone down to the river and they were expecting him back after sunset with a basketful of crayfish. They are also very proud of their literary club, which meets at the museum for recitals, lectures, and performances. This is how we keep the intellectual life of the city alive, said Lyudmila; our local intelligentsia is continuing the tradition begun here so long ago.

They adopted me when they found out how far I had come, and why I was there. I was taken to the back room (which had been Masha's) and plied with tea and cookies and questions, and in return I received more information than my poor head could retain; thankfully there were small guidebooks available and my old film camera cooperated. But for every painstakingly preserved teacup or garden hat or desk lamp in the Chekhov museum, there is an indescribable quantity of elegiac emptiness and absence about the old house across the street, which had once been the Lintvaryov residence. It is a crumbling old brick building where the regulation, waist-high green paint on the walls, visible through the gutted windows, reminds us of its last incarnation as a school. The school was closed in the early 1990s; the building that had survived a revolution, Nazi occupation, the Red Army, and hordes of schoolchildren has not survived twenty-five years of tight-fisted capitalism. Efforts to raise funds privately or interest the government have failed; Lyudmila told me that even an article in the *New York Times* was unable to rouse any wealthy emigrants or other philanthropists from their apathy.

There is still something there, however, evocative of the summers of 1888–1889. The river for fishing, picnics, swimming, and swinging out on "tarzanka" ropes; the bucolic village of Luka, with its country church and jovial priest. The local people of Sumy do not mind that they are so far from the cultural centers of the world; they know what they have to be proud of. Anton Pavlovich wrote, in one of his letters, "Abbazia and the Adriatic are marvelous, but Luka and the Psyol are better." His descriptions are filled with the nostalgia of knowing a privileged moment of youth that is all too evanescent; something of this world lingers not only in his stories and plays, but also in present-day Sumy.

When I visited Ukraine in 2010, no one would ever have dreamed of the Russian annexation of Crimea or of the tragic conflict in the east of the country over recent years. As I was putting the final touches to *The Summer Guest*, I realized I must incorporate contemporary events there, at least insofar as they impacted Ana's journey to Ukraine. Coincidentally (or perhaps not), as I rewrote the final version of the novel I found myself in a small Croatian town a few miles from Abbazia (now Opatija). It seemed fitting to be journeying once more to Luka from that place of longing that Chekhov himself had known. ～

A Playlist Inspired by
The Summer Guest

Pyotr Tchaikovsky

> *The Seasons*, op. 37a
>
> Symphony no. 2 in C Minor, op. 17 *(Little Russian)*

Georges Lintvaryov would have played "The Seasons" on numerous occasions, and Zinaida recalls going to a concert of the Second Symphony when she was younger. This symphony is one of my favorites, particularly the second movement. Ukraine was formerly referred to as "Little Russia," and Tchaikovsky incorporated Ukrainian folk tunes into the symphony.

Modest Mussorgsky

> Works for piano, including *Souvenirs d'Enfance, Impression d'un voyage en Crimée (Une Larme)*, and *Pictures at an Exhibition*

Georges plays *Une Larme* for Zinaida, and would have played other pieces from Mussorgsky's work, including the original piano version of *Pictures at an Exhibition* (later orchestrated by Maurice Ravel).

Anatoly Lyadov

> *From Days of Old*, op. 21
>
> *Eight Russian Folk Songs for Orchestra*, op. 58
>
> *The Enchanted Lake*, op. 62

While Lyadov is not specifically mentioned in the novel, he was a contemporary of Chekhov, and for me his tone poems evoke a certain nostalgic vision of a pastoral, timeless Russia.

Sergey Rachmaninov

"The Isle of the Dead"

Ana Harding listens to "The Isle of the Dead" in her more melancholy, wistful moments. Rachmaninov was inspired by a painting by Swiss symbolist Arnold Böcklin.

Dmitri Shostakovich

Twenty-Four Preludes and Fugues, op. 87

Ana finds comfort and enlightenment in these beautiful pieces by the Soviet-era composer, which were written during the dark years of Stalinist repression in Russia. ໑

Anton Chekhov
A Reading List

Plays

The Seagull, 1896
Uncle Vanya, 1899
The Cherry Orchard, 1904

Short Stories

Mentioned in the Novel:

From *In the Twilight*

"The Witch," 1886
"Misfortune," 1886

Others

"Volodya," 1887
"A Nervous Breakdown," 1889
"A Boring Story," 1889
"The Duel," 1891
"My Life," 1896
"Man in a Case," 1898
"Gooseberries," 1898
"About Love," 1898
"At Christmas Time," 1900
"The Bishop," 1902

A few of Alison Anderson's Personal Favorites

"The Stupid Frenchman," 1886
"The Kiss," 1887
"The Party," 1888
"The Grasshopper," 1892

"Rothschild's Fiddle," 1894
"The Black Monk," 1894
"A Woman's Kingdom," 1894
"The House with the Mezzanine," 1896
"The Schoolmistress (In the Cart)," 1897
"The Lady with the Dog," 1899 ⌇

Discussion Questions
A Reading Group Guide for
The Summer Guest

1. What should be the priorities for a translator of great literature? What are the various challenges of such a task?

2. Consider the three women at the center of the novel: Katya Kendall, Anastasia Harding, and Zinaida Mikhailovna Lintvaryova. In what ways are they similar or different? How is Zinaida valuable to Katya and Ana?

3. For a writer, what is valuable in the three different kinds of writing represented here: fiction, journal writing, and translation?

4. Anton Pavlovich claims a number of times that writing for him is not about "inspiration and electricity" but simply a way to pay bills. What might influence him to say such a thing? Can great art result from practical motivations?

5. What makes each of the Lintvaryova sisters—Zinaida, Elena, and Natasha—unique, complex, and important to the story?

6. What is the complex nature of the relationship between Zinaida and Anton Pavlovich? What does each receive from the other?

7. Of what importance to the story and her character is Zinaida's blindness? In what particular ways might it influence her relationship with Anton Pavlovich?

8. Speaking with Zinaida about how women are portrayed in literature, Natasha criticizes Leo Tolstoy for writing only "of fallen women and ingénues." What is the novelist's responsibility toward such cultural or political issues? In what ways do such representations limit a novel or not?

9. After her divorce, Ana takes on the daunting challenge "to explore her solitude." What might it mean to do such a thing? What are the potential risks and benefits? What does it take to turn solitude, as Zinaida struggles to do, "from an enforced exclusion to a welcome introspection"?

10. Zinaida, a successful physician before her illness, observes that though her married cousins and friends believe themselves to be happy, "their illnesses and complaints tell a different story." What's the relationship between emotional well-being and the health of the body? What is it about traditional marriage that Zinaida believes is problematic?

11. Though Zinaida is "truly honest" in her journal, she acknowledges that it is still "a distorting mirror." What might she mean? What is the potential value of such dedicated journal writing?

12. Zinaida claims that her blindness has caused her to learn greater sensitivity to sound and smell and that this brings her "closer to an essence of life." What might she mean?

13. Despite her training in medicine and a pragmatic and rational family, Zinaida believes her illness has shown her "the resources of the spirit's more inexplicable manifestations." How does this manifest in her thoughts and actions?

14. In one of Zinaida's first journal entries she wishes she "knew the notation of birdsong," that it could later be played by her brother Georges on the piano. Despite the obvious differences, in what ways might music and literature be similar?

15. What is powerful about the landscape of Luka? Of what particular importance is it to Anton Pavlovich?

16. What is added to the novel by the inclusion of the contemporary political unrest of Ukraine? ▶

Discussion Questions *(continued)*

17. Anton Pavlovich claims that instead of inspiring it, "love makes a muddle of creativity." In what ways might this be true or not?

18. How is it appropriate or not that Ana's full name, Anastasia, means resurrection?

19. Zinaida and Anton Pavlovich have a profound conversation about whether one should "forge life," enacting individual will, or "allow fate" and "preserve immense respect for the . . . magic of life." What's a proper balance between these two approaches to living?

20. Natasha argues that art is "the force of life" and triumphs over death. Zinaida counters that art doesn't help the poor and "death always wins." What is the relationship between art and mortality?

21. What has Ana gained from her experience translating the journal, reading about Chekhov, and traveling to the location of his summer visits?